PANCAKES AND POISON

AMI DIANE

Copyright

This is a work of fiction. Names, characters, organization, places, events, and incidents are either products of the author's imagination or are used fictitiously.

To my new kitten Chewie. Thanks for making the editing process take twice as long as it should've and for all of the cute distractions.

CHAPTER 1

FLURRIES OF ANGRY snow beat at the windshield like stars against an inky sky. Ella Barton's grip on her steering wheel tightened as she leaned forward, squinting through the blizzard-like weather.

The snow blurring past the windshield reminded her of various sci-fi films where the spaceships blasted through space at warp speed. Typically, she would've made the accompanying sound effects, but, as it was, most of her brain power was being diverted to keeping the vehicle on the road.

Snow berms spat out by a plow bordered each side of her car like a runway. The back tires on her Jeep fish-tailed, causing Ella to suck a breath in through her teeth. She turned into the slide, fighting to maintain control while the tires searched for friction again. Slowly, the SUV came out of the slide and plodded on like a champ.

Meanwhile, Ella's pulse lowered, and she tried her windshield wipers again for the umpteenth time. They were already on their highest setting, a fact she well knew, but on the off chance the vehicle had somehow magically changed within the last five minutes, she felt it prudent to check again.

It hadn't.

Behind her, Ella's suitcases rattled in protest at the bumpy road. At least she'd be home in an hour.

Her Jeep slid again, and she tapped the brakes, slowing further. *Maybe an hour and a half.*

Thanksgiving with her parents had been more stressful than Portland traffic during rush hour and had resulted in her polishing off the rest of the pumpkin pie. She didn't regret the pie—which was coming back with a vengeance in the form of heartburn—but she did regret not leaving sooner so she could drive while it was still daylight.

Beyond the swirl of snow, tall ponderosa pines blurred into shadows, whipping past. Her eyes skimmed back to the road.

A sudden flash of bright light lit up the snow-ladened forest. It was as if the sun had popped back up and bathed the world with its glow before disappearing again.

Cheese and crackers, what was that?

A bomb? Only, there hadn't been an explosion. Perhaps lightning. She vaguely remembered reading an article about thundersnows, rare thunderstorms with snow instead of rain. That was it. Lightning without thunder during a snowstorm.

Ahead, the road took a sharp right and descended. The storm began to let up, and her grip on the wheel loosened. As she released the tension in her shoulders, the car crested a small rise in the landscape.

The SUV's headlights illuminated packed ice, snowy road, and then nothing. The highway stopped abruptly in a dark shadow of… grass?

Ella's foot let off the gas, and all thoughts of lightning

fled as she leaned forward, squinting. Her brain couldn't make sense of what she saw. The road was gone.

"What the…" The words died on her lips.

She slammed on the brakes, and the steering wheel went limp, the scenery racing sideways as the car hit a patch of ice and spun. A scream climbed her throat but never made it out.

After completing a three-hundred and sixty-degree spin, the Jeep careened to the edge of the road like it had a mind of its own, Herbie the Love Bug style. It climbed the berm which acted as a ramp.

There was a horrifying moment where the car bested gravity, then an even more horrifying moment as gravity ultimately won and the car dropped into the snow drift on the other side.

Ella jerked to a sudden stop against her seatbelt. Her breath came out in ragged gasps, more from shock than anything else.

She leaned back and took stock of her injuries. Other than the stinging in her shoulder where the seatbelt had restrained her and a pulse beating like a jackhammer, she was fine. The airbag hadn't even deployed, which she now wondered if that was a bad thing.

After grabbing a flashlight from the glove compartment, she extricated herself from the Jeep to assess the damage, nearly face planting in the snow. She stumbled to the front of the car then winced as the light splayed across the grill. The right, front bumper had folded into the hood like an accordion.

Ella patted the car, apologized, then realized she was talking to a car while alone—and in the middle of the night no less. Maybe if her car actually was Herbie the Love Bug, she'd feel less crazy.

Swiping loose strands of curly, brown hair away from

her face, she hiked back to the driver-side door and tried the ignition. The engine whined like a toddler needing a nap, refusing to start. Apparently, smooshing a car *wasn't* good on an engine.

Her cell phone had no bars. This part of the mountain pass was notorious for lousy reception—that and Bigfoot. But she'd never really believed the latter.

Think, Ella.

One thing was clear, unless she suddenly grew muscles, she wouldn't be able to get the car out of its snowy tomb without a tow truck. And she couldn't call a tow truck without cell reception.

She could wait for someone to come along the highway, but there were three problems with that plan— well, four if she counted the fact that it was freaking cold.

First, this particular highway wasn't the popular option for traveling over the mountain range, lessening her chances of a passerby.

Second, it was just after midnight. Chances were remote that another vehicle would drive past.

Third, no engine meant no heat, which reminded her of the fourth problem.

With those uplifting thoughts, she slipped her arms into her down jacket before zipping it up. She was going to have to walk for help, Bigfoot or not.

When she'd last had a signal, GPS had shown her twenty miles from the nearest town. However, she knew from previous trips that there were small cabins tucked into the woods along the route. Maybe she'd get lucky.

After shutting the car door, she splayed the flashlight over her surroundings. It was then that she noticed the vehicle had landed a yard away from the strange line of demarcation of snowy road and grass.

Shivering against the cold biting her exposed cheeks,

she crept forward, frowning. The road—snow, pavement, and all—ended in green grass.

The storm had abated over the last few minutes. Small flakes now drifted down lazily, landing on the lush blades of untouched grass where they stuck like freckles.

How was this possible? There were drifts of snow several feet high behind her. And what on earth had happened to the road?

Her face scrunched as she sorted through her memory of the last few hours at her parents' place, trying to recall if she'd had any of her father's spiced rum. Nope, unfortunately, she was definitely sober.

She shook her head against the onslaught of questions and the mental gymnastics her brain was doing to answer them. She had more immediate concerns, like trying to stay warm.

Opening the trunk of her SUV, she grabbed her backpack loaded with the clothes from her Thanksgiving weekend. After shoving her cell phone into her jacket pocket, she tugged a beanie over her ears and prepared to hike through the frigid landscape for help.

The beam from her flashlight swathed over the icy road behind her, then to the now snow-speckled grass ahead. Which way?

Since she couldn't recall having passed any cabins within the last several miles, she decided to plunge ahead into the strange, foreign landscape glittering in the cold. *Because, when in doubt, go* towards *the creepy Twilight Zone landscape.*

As her boots crunched through the snow, Ella's thoughts turned to the mystery, trying to make sense of it. She'd driven this highway dozens of times. How could it just disappear? And be replaced by sod untouched by the storm?

When she stepped onto the frozen grass, it crunched under her boots like soft whispers that shattered the night. The trees fell away on either side, opening to an expansive field of darkness her light couldn't penetrate.

After she'd hiked for a few minutes, a faint, amber light indicative of a town glowed on the horizon. The short burst of elation she felt quickly turned to confusion.

There wasn't supposed to be a town here. Then again, there was supposed to be grass here. Either she'd made a wrong turn or had misjudged how far she'd gone after losing satellite signal.

At some point, the snow had stopped falling. And now the moon glowed behind a cloud. The dusting of snow over the landscape glittered like powdered sugar. Her mouth watered at the thought while her stomach turned in protest, still digesting the pumpkin pie.

The increased ambient light allowed Ella to make out her surroundings for the first time. Gone were the mountains and evergreens, replaced by glittering fields.

Unease gripped her stomach as she plunged ahead. A half-mile later, she passed a dark barn. Large white poles surrounded the structure and winked at her when her beam swept over them. Dozens of them.

Ella walked to the nearest one and tipped her head back, whispering, "Whoa. Definitely made a wrong turn."

Large blades of a wind turbine half the size of her car rotated gently in the night, creaking, blotting and revealing clouds along their circular journey. There were dozens of other similar turbines as far as she could see, blotting the field like a forest of white trees. She was standing in the middle of a large wind farm.

After gawking for another minute, she resumed her trek, her body warming from the exertion. Soon, the glowing haze she'd seen resolved into the porch lights and streetlights of a small town.

Ella paused to take in the beautiful sight, but mostly to catch her breath. That pie really wasn't sitting well.

Before her, a hard, cold ground sloped down and crashed into a small lake—or large pond, she couldn't be sure. When does a pond become a lake?

Antique street lamps and sleeping houses lined the perimeter of the lake-pond.

She ambled to the left, away from what she was now generously calling a lake, towards a street that sliced through the town. Puddles of warm light cast by gas lamps dappled the sidewalk below quaint shops, their windows dark.

An old-fashioned barber pole—still in great condition —hung outside one of the buildings with the words "Sal's Barbershop" painted across the window. The town oozed of days past, of an era untouched by time, and remarkably restored.

Ella's eyes bugged out when she spotted a vintage Mustang, and she wasn't even that into cars—unless it was Herbie, apparently.

As charming as the town seemed, there was something really off about the place, but she couldn't put her finger on it.

A sign posted along the sidewalk caught her eye. It read, "Visitors, turn back. Leave now."

Her brows drew together as she picked over each letter again, sure she'd read it wrong. What kind of town asked visitors to *leave*?

She checked her cell phone again. Oddly, there was still no reception. She would have to use a landline to call a tow truck.

With a sigh, she left the welcoming sign behind in search of a house—any house, but preferably one with lights on. However, the street she was on seemed full of nothing but sleeping shops.

She was just entertaining the idea of trying a side street when she came across her first house—only house wasn't the right word. *Mansion*.

It, along with a double-wide, vintage railcar diner, took up the entire block. The two-story mansion appeared to be from the late 1800s and beautifully restored. English ivy crawled over the rust-colored brick exterior and around the windows. If an English manor had an affair with a Federal-style house from the south, Ella decided, this would be their offspring. It even had two turrets.

The building seemed older than anything she'd come across thus far, stoic as if it had always been and the town had grown around it. More importantly, warm light spilled from the home's windows.

A wrought iron arch over the walkway read, "Keystone Inn." For a brief moment, Ella puzzled over the presence of an inn in a town that didn't want visitors before inwardly shrugging it off.

The gate opened with a soft creak, and she followed the path that bisected a small garden.

Well, if they didn't want visitors, that was too bad. Her feet ached, and she was tired. The inn was going to have one more guest that night.

On the stoop, she fought a chill that crawled over her skin, and she told herself it was due to the temperature and had nothing to do with the strange, old inn.

Her hand hesitated over the large oak door, unsure if she should use the brass knocker or the doorknob. She tried her luck with the knob first, and it turned freely. The door yawned open, creaking in the night.

I'm in a horror movie. And this is the part where I die.

Warmth enveloped Ella like a blanket when she

slipped inside, closing the door behind her. Well, if she was going to die, at least she'd die warm.

An entrance hall opened before her that was roughly the size of two of her living rooms, complete with an ornate crystal chandelier that probably cost as much as her student loans.

Before her, a large staircase wound up and out of sight. Three doors stood open around the perimeter of the room, along with three hallways. Her ears pricked at the crackle of a fireplace and noticed light flickering from beyond one of the thresholds.

She crept forward and poked her head into the room. "Hello?"

The room was empty, the light coming from a dying fire in the hearth. She had never seen a study in person, but that's what the room appeared to be.

Turning back to the entrance hall, Ella approached a large front desk made of cherry wood. An old Tiffany-style banker's lamp sat on top, unlit, over a notebook. It felt like she was in a museum.

The wood plank flooring creaked beneath her, and she realized she'd left wet footprints across the floor, ending at an antique rug.

Ella hurried to the door and kicked off her boots. They landed with a thud next to a coat tree. She was swiping at the small puddles with her socks when the sound of soft steps traveled from one of the hallways near the front door. A light flipped on somewhere inside, and a man stepped out, silhouetted against the bright light.

She froze, mid-swipe of her sock.

His hair was disheveled, and his eyes squeezed shut with a large yawn that displayed the back of his throat. He appeared to be in his mid-forties with a forehead that reached deeply into a receding brown hairline. Despite the hour, his eyes held a keenness that peeled away years.

"Hello." His smile faltered as he took in her face. She brushed her hand over it in case she had something stuck to it. "You don't live here." He spoke with a southern accent. His voice became strained, and his features shifted.

She stepped on the biggest puddle and felt the dampness seep into her sock. "Uh, no. Nope, I don't. Could I have a room for the night, please?"

He studied her. "No, sorry. We're all booked up."

"You're full?" Her eyes wandered to the open doorways and intricately carved staircase. "You don't have *anything* open?"

"No, sorry."

"Is there another hotel around here?"

"No, ma'am. This is a small village. You'd probably have better luck the next town over."

Ella gaped at him. "I can't get to the next town over. My car's stuck in a snowbank—well, more buried, actually—and I'm beat. My phone doesn't work around here.

"All I want is a place to crash, so I can call a tow truck in the morning. I can sleep on a couch or on the floor; I really don't care at this point. I'll be gone first thing in the morning. You won't even know I was here."

The man pursed his lips as if in a tug of war with the empathy filling his eyes. "I'm really sorry, but you shouldn't be here."

She narrowed her eyes in confusion. Shouldn't be here?

"I agree. I should be home. In my warm bed." She stepped closer until she could smell the minty toothpaste on his breath. "I'm hungry and tired. I'm sorry to be difficult, but I'm not leaving. I have nowhere else to go. It's clear this town doesn't like visitors. Message received.

I'll be gone as soon as I get my car tomorrow."

He blinked at her then whispered in words she barely caught, "Keystone."

"What?" She leaned back, wondering how sleep deprived he was.

He cleared his throat. "This town is called Keystone Village."

"Oh. Good to know. Cute name." Ella smoothed out her jacket, unsure of what else to say.

A woman's voice floated in from the hallway. "What is it, Jimmy? Crazy Flo see a ghost again?"

The man Ella assumed was "Jimmy" tensed. "Excuse me a moment," he said to her.

He slipped through the narrow rectangle of light. A moment later, Ella heard frantic, raised whispers that grew to a crescendo before suddenly dying. Jimmy stepped back into the entrance hall, his face red as he gave Ella a tight smile.

Jimmy ducked his head under the counter of the tall desk, and she heard the metallic tinkle of keys before he popped back up.

"Here you go. Room seven. Up the stairs, third door on your right. Breakfast is at seven. If you miss it, Grandma Wink makes a mean scramble at the diner next door." He jerked his head in the direction of the diner.

"Thank you." Relief filled Ella, realizing she'd soon be asleep.

"How much?" She didn't really care about the price. At that moment, she would've paid five hundred dollars for one night.

He waved his hand. "On the house."

"I'm sorry?"

"Don't worry about it. Seems like you're hard up, doll."

10

Heat rose in her cheeks. "Look, I think there's been a misunderstanding. I *insist* on paying for the room."

Jimmy's face was a mask of confusion. Then a light blinked behind his eyes. "Oh, that's right. I didn't mean anything calling you 'doll'. Old habit."

If you're a century old.

"If it makes you feel better, I guess you can pay."

Ella shrugged off her backpack and fished out her wallet. "How much?"

"Eh…" The man's eyes darted to the cherry wood desk as if searching for a number on its rich surface. "Sixty sound okay?"

"What?"

"No? Forty?"

"How much do you typically charge? Whatever the room is that you gave me—" she flipped the key over "—number seven. How much do you usually charge for it?"

He rubbed a hand over his thinning hair, causing it to stand on end. "Sixty." The number hung heavy in the air, full of uncertainty.

Ella opened her mouth to argue but stopped. She hadn't seen the room yet. Maybe it was crap.

He obviously didn't man the desk that often, and she worried that she was taking advantage of his ignorance. She sighed, digging through her wallet; she'd sort it out in the morning.

Slipping out her credit card, she slid it over to him. Jimmy stared at it. "Er, we can't accept that."

Her stomach dropped. "You're cash only?"

He nodded.

Taking a slow breath, she forced a smile and slipped the card back into her wallet. She only had a twenty-dollar bill on her. "Can I pay tomorrow, then?" She'd have to hunt for an ATM.

"Sure thing." He gave her a genuine grin for the first time. "I'm Jimmy Murray."

"Ella Barton." They shook hands, then she threw a strap of her backpack over one shoulder and headed for the stairs.

"Oh, Ella?"

She turned.

"Watch out for Fluffy. If you see him, don't make eye contact. And for God's sake, don't pet him."

CHAPTER 2

ELLA AWOKE TO sunshine pouring through her window. Fractals of light from another Tiffany lamp bathed the floral wallpaper like stained glass. Her backpack lay abandoned nearby. She'd crashed the night before, not even bothering turning on a light.

Now in the light of day, she could see her room properly. It was spacious and tastefully decorated in a "this house is old" sort of way. The furnishings were rich mahogany with a mix of early American and antique English country flare that would've made her mother drool. Whatever the cost of her room, it was certainly worth more than Jimmy was charging.

After throwing off the covers, Ella hissed as the cold air hit her. As beautiful as the old mansion was, it was drafty. She knew there was some sort of unsavory comparison between the manor and an aging lady of the night, but her pre-caffeinated brain couldn't quite pull it from the air.

The grimace from the temperature became a groan as

she pulled a sweatshirt from her bag. Apparently, her body wasn't too fond of landing in a snowbank.

Ella lingered at the window and got her first glimpse of Keystone Village in the daylight—or at least part of it. Snow had fallen during the night and painted a monochromatic world outside.

The lake stretched before her at the base of two tall, steep hills off to the left. An evergreen forest pooled around the hills and flowed all the way to the park on her right.

Ella picked her cell phone up from the nightstand, her mouth turning down at the "no signal" icon in the top right. Maybe her carrier didn't service this area. She just hoped this postage-sized town had a mechanic.

Fortunately, she still had a couple more days of vacation before she had to be back at the local university where she was a TA for Dr. Brown in the linguistics department, so there was no need to worry just yet.

Thinking about her job reminded her that she had procrastinated her thesis work all break and couldn't avoid it any longer. The problem was she'd "accidentally" forgotten her laptop.

Although she loved her research, even she found the comparison of "influence of population density and social networks on phoneme variation" a little dry.

After wadding her curls into a bun, Ella stuffed her phone into her pocket and stepped into the hallway. She descended the stairs, following her nose to breakfast.

Voices and the clattering of dishes floated over the polished wood floor from the back of the inn. She picked the hallway just left of the study and wandered down it, passing a parlor and a couple more doors. She was just about to turn around when rows and rows of books caught her eye.

The hallway ended abruptly in a set of French doors with roses etched into the glass. Ella peeked through a non-frosted pane, spying a robust library full of leather-bound volumes. Trying the handle, she nudged one of the doors inward and poked her head inside.

Something brushed her shin, and Ella jumped, ramming her elbow into the handle on the door. The largest Maine Coon cat she'd ever seen slinked past her and into the room. He turned his beautiful green and hazel flecked eyes on her, purring softly.

Ella rubbed the blooming bruise on her arm and took a step inside. "Hey, buddy." He meowed at her. "You must be Fluffy." He butted his head against her leg in response.

"Now, why would Jimmy warn me about you? You're just a big boy who wants some attention, aren't you?"

He purred in response.

She crouched and stretched out her hand for him to sniff her.

With another mew, his wet nose kissed her fingertips before her hand buried in his soft fur. A deep purr rumbled through him, vibrating her hand. Just as suddenly, he batted her hand—claws retracted—and pounced at an invisible spot on the rug. Then, Fluffy rolled in a patch of sunlight, stretching his back.

"Huh, it seems he likes you," a male voice said behind her.

Ella whirled around to find Jimmy standing in the doorway. Tugging down the part of her sweatshirt that had bunched up, she apologized for being in the room.

"Don't worry about it. That's why we have it here." Waving a hand at the large volumes, he gave her another one of his genial grins. "We want our guests to feel at home." His smile faltered. "Our long-term guests, that is."

She tried not to take the comment personally. Picking

off fur from her clothes, she asked, "Do you have many?"

"Many what?"

"Long-term guests."

His eyes darted over the books as if carefully collecting the right words to say. "We have a couple of boarders, yeah." Opening one of the French doors wider, he said, "Breakfast is the dining room. Come on, I'll show you the way before Edwin eats all the bacon."

At her favorite word, her stomach rumbled. She scratched Fluffy between his ears one last time then followed the innkeeper out of the room.

Jimmy shot a furtive glance back at the cat. Ella heard Fluffy hiss before she rounded the corner.

"I've never seen him like that around another human. When he's not scratching up the furniture or chewing the houseplants, he's attacking the boarders."

Ella chuckled. "Why keep him around?"

"We've tried giving him away, but he just keeps coming back, sauntering in like he owns the place. You know, I kinda think he does."

He led her down a hallway beside the grand staircase and paused outside a large doorway. He excused himself, saying that he'd be in to eat soon, then left her alone.

Inside the dining room, three people sat at a large table. Her eyes were immediately drawn to the plates of bacon and pancakes. The setup reminded her more of a bed-and-breakfast than an inn, but she wasn't about to argue—especially since bacon was involved.

Three sets of eyes shifted to her, and she realized she was still standing in the doorway.

"You must be Ella." A woman who appeared about ten years older than Ella smiled. Her lips were the color of crushed roses, and deep brown eyes stared out from behind dainty, cat-eyed glasses.

She looked like she'd stepped out of a *Leave It to Beaver* episode, with sweeping, strawberry blonde curls, a floral patterned dress that hugged her waist before flaring out, and a Hermès scarf draped around her décolletage. "I'm Mrs. Jimmy Murray, but I'd prefer you to call me Rose."

Ella gaped at her a moment, thrown by the *Mrs. Jimmy* part and her vintage attire. She recovered quickly and returned the smile as she sat down. "Ella Barton. You have a lovely inn."

Rose thanked her and passed her a cup of coffee, followed by toast, fried eggs, ham, steak, and butter. "We only serve meals in the dining room when there's a new guest," she explained.

"Wow." Ella eyed the plates stacking up in front of her. "That's a lot of protein."

After pouring a heavy dose of cream into her coffee, her eyes wandered to the other two people at the table, figuring they were the boarders Jimmy had referred to.

Just then, the innkeeper walked through the door, greeted everyone, then kissed his wife on the cheek.

Rose turned to Ella. "If you're still here around lunchtime, the diner next door is open from eight to eight —unless the winds pick up, and Grandma wink closes shop to go gliding. The soda float is to die for, although my waistline doesn't agree." Her laugh floated over the table like the tinkle of a bell, infectious and warm.

Ella couldn't help but smile.

"They also serve a mean mushroom burger," Jimmy added.

"Horse meat," one of the boarders growled. The woman appeared to be in her sixties and had never gotten the memo that it was the twenty-first century. Her white hair floated up from her head like cotton candy. Ella had only ever seen beehive hairdos in pictures, and seeing one in person was nothing short of spectacular.

Jimmy dropped his fork. "Flo, come off it. They don't serve horse meat there."

Ella remembered hearing Rose's voice the night before, asking if Crazy Flo had seen another ghost. This must've been the woman who she was referring to.

"'Course they do. What else they going to do with that old dappled mare at the mayor's dairy? Hmm? Or that dead cow in his yard?"

Jimmy rolled his eyes. "Bury it?"

"Wasting good meat."

Rose cleared her throat. "I don't think this is an appropriate discussion topic over breakfast, Flo."

Flo lifted one shoulder in a shrug, the beehive shifting dangerously with the movement. "You know it's aliens that did it." She began to smear butter on her eggs and up her thumb.

Rose shifted awkwardly and shot Ella an apologetic smile.

Ella couldn't resist. "Aliens did what?"

"For God's sake, don't encourage her," the other boarder, an elderly gentleman, muttered under his breath.

Flo leaned forward, pushing up a pair of thick glasses that magnified her eyes. "Aliens killed that cow and horse, of course."

Ella bit her tongue at the "horse, of course" comment and to keep from singing the theme song for Mr. Ed. She was really beginning to like Crazy Flo.

"Right. How do you know it wasn't ghosts?" She tried to keep her expression neutral but nearly broke when Jimmy snorted and the other boarder groaned.

Before Flo could respond, however, Rose cleared her throat. "Ella, Jimmy says you got into a car accident?"

"Yeah. Not too far outside of town. Hit some ice then ran into a ditch. Speaking of, is there a mechanic in town I can have the car towed to?"

Jimmy exchanged a weighted glance with Rose. "Probably best to have it towed to the next town."

"Detroit?" Ella calculated the mileage, shaking her head. "That won't work." She tried to keep the desperation out of her voice.

"There's Lou," the other boarder said before Jimmy shot him a look. The old man reminded Ella a lot of her grandfather. Thick gray hair swept back like a wave, surrounding an affable face.

"Not sure that's a good idea, Edwin." Jimmy's grip tightened on his fork. "Lou's slow."

"Only when he's drunk."

"That's always."

"True."

Mulling over her options, Ella took a thick slice of banana bread. It was soft and moist with a flavor that punched her taste buds and practically melted in her mouth.

"Oh, man. This is amazing." She shoved the rest of it in her mouth and grabbed a second slice. A brief concern over calories flitted through her mind but quickly left with the next bite. It was worth it.

Finishing, Ella resisted the urge to lick her plate. She was a guest and didn't want her first impression to be getting to first base with dishware. Also, Rose scared her a bit. Not in a Stepford wife, murderous kind of way, but in a she-runs-the-house-don't-get-on-her-bad-side kind of way.

Ella sat back, sipping her strong coffee and listening to Flo describe the best design of hat to make out of tin foil to keep the aliens from probing one's mind. Steam curled around Ella's face in delicate wisps as she tried to picture what happened to Flo's beehive with said hat.

Her thoughts shifted to her car. Even if this Lou guy was slow, he was her best option. She'd go over to his place as soon as she found the bottom of her cup.

The thought of her crashed car reminded her of the reason for her crash.

"Speaking of snow," Ella began, although they hadn't been talking about weather at all, "I noticed you don't have much here." She thought specifically of the abrupt delineation between the thick blanket and frozen grass.

"Oh, that's not true." Rose busied herself with pouring more coffee from the carafe. "We got a couple of inches during the night. Must have come after you showed up."

Ella grabbed a third slice of banana bread. "That's strange. Just a couple of inches? There were a few feet on the pass."

"The pass?"

Bread stuck to her throat as she swallowed, staring around at the confused expressions. "The mountain pass? You know, the Santiam Pass? For the Cascade Range?"

"Oh, that. Yeah, our weather's a little different here." With delicate hands, Rose cut into her eggs. "The Twin Hills give us a—what do they call that, Jimmy?"

"*Microclimate*'s what the professor calls it," he said. Rose nodded in agreement.

Crazy Flo waved her fork, a chunk of ham hitting Edwin in the face. "When were you born?"

"I'm sorry?" Ella was more thrown by the abrupt shift in conversation topic rather than the question.

"Flo!" Rose pursed her lipstick-slathered mouth into a line, her cheeks flushing.

"What? It's not like I asked her what year it was."

Ella bit back a laugh, turning over the strange

phrasing. Not "How old are you?" but "when were you born?"

"It's fine. I was born in 1985."

"See?" Florence's white hair bounced like an exclamation point on the word. "I bet she's got loads of knowledge up there." The end of her now-naked fork pointed at Ella's head. "Loads. Seems like the educated type. You go to high school, young lady?"

Ella nearly choked on her last bite of bread. "Yes, ma'am. And college. I'm working on my master's degree right now, actually."

"Really?" Edwin's eyes lit up.

"Well, how 'bout that? An educated woman." Flo slurped her coffee. All the while, her beady eyes remaining on Ella.

Ella used her cloth napkin to conceal her half-smile, half-bewildered expression. This had to be the strangest group of people she'd ever met.

After her fourth slice of banana bread and the last drip of coffee from her cup were gone, Ella scooted her chair back and rubbed her snug waistband.

"Thank you for the delicious meal. Is there a computer I can use? I can't seem to get a cell phone signal to pull in my email."

Rose blinked at her. Jimmy rubbed the thinning halo of hair on his crown. "Our phone only makes local calls."

"Oh. And the computer?"

"Sorry, we don't have one," Jimmy said.

"Oh." Ella shrugged. "No worries. I'll try somewhere else."

After getting directions to Lou's shop, Ella ran back to her room and grabbed her wallet, hoping she could find an ATM after she had spoken with the mechanic.

Stepping out of the inn, a winter wonderland opened

before her. The thin blanket of snow had settled over the streets and storefronts like frosting on gingerbread houses.

The park sat on her left, where the town thinned and just before the wind farm she'd walked through. Somewhere behind her was the lake. She made a mental note to check it out later.

Cold air whipped at her face as she kicked white powder up over her boots. Two-story brick buildings rose on either side, complete with old-fashioned, hand-painted signs. It was like stepping into the past.

Following Jimmy's directions, she turned left on L Street. Soon, the sound of metal scraping metal and swearing floated out from a shop. Ella located the source of the noise inside. A man with too little hair on his scalp and too much on his chin wiped at his sweaty face as he stared at the engine of a classic Mercedes-Benz. His belly pulled at the stained fabric of his coveralls.

"Excuse me," Ella said, "are you Lou?" The smell of alcohol and oil hovered heavy in the air.

"That's me." Lou squinted at her as if she was a bright light.

"I'm having car problems, and I was wondering if you could look at it." His eyes squinted to the point that she wondered if he could still see.

He tipped his head, peering past her to the street. "Seems your problem is you don't got one." His face cracked open suddenly, and he barked out a laugh that split her ears.

Ella let out a polite chuckle.

"So, what's the problem?" Lou's belly continued to bounce, still laughing at his own joke.

"It's in a snowbank."

"Why's it there?"

"I thought it'd make a great parking spot?" Ella took a

breath and briefly explained it flying off the highway. "So, can you tow it?"

His laugh lines relaxed, and he rubbed a hand down his stubble, leaving behind streaks of grease. "Where d'you say you left it?"

"Just outside of town."

An emotion flicked across his face so quickly she couldn't be sure she'd seen it.

"How far out?" He turned his back, gathering up tools on his workbench.

"It was dark, but it's just past the field with wind turbines."

His shoulders relaxed. "Yeah, okay. Let's go get it."

"Now?" Ella asked.

"That okay?"

"Yes! That would be great."

He laughed again, his stomach jumping up and down. "I like ya, doll."

Her cheeks heated at being called "doll" for the second time in less than twenty-four hours. However, if he could retrieve her car and get her back on the road, then he could call her whatever he wanted.

CHAPTER 3

GETTING HER CAR out of the ditch proved harder in reality than expected. It didn't help that Lou's easy-going demeanor had shifted suddenly once they'd arrived at the crash site.

He hurried through hooking the vehicle up to his truck. Once the wind farm was in sight, he seemed to revert back to his old self.

Back at his shop, Ella hopped out of his truck. "So, does it look bad?"

Lou dug a chewed toothpick from his front chest pocket and rolled it from one corner of his mouth to the other. "Looks mostly cosmetic, but I won't know till I look under her dress, so to speak."

"Surely, you'll buy her drinks first?" Ella teased. The mechanic's eyes bugged out, and she quickly asked, "Any idea how long that'll take?"

"I'll have a look right now and get back to ya."

She thanked him then said, "I'd give you my cell number, but it doesn't get any reception here."

He picked at his gums with the toothpick then inspected it. "No worries. I know where you're staying."

"You do?"

"Well, sure. Same place anyone passin' through stays. You're at the inn, aren't ya?"

Ella nodded.

"'Kay. I'll just leave word there."

She thanked him, getting a couple of steps before remembering she needed cash to pay for her room. "Hey, is there an ATM nearby?"

Lou's thumb paused over the button for the hydraulic lift on the tow truck. "Eh?"

"Where can I pull some money?"

"I suppose the bank. But you gotta have an account there."

"They don't do shared branching?"

Lou cocked his head as he scratched the mashed toothpick over a hairy fold of skin on his neck. "Dunno. Don't really use money 'round here much." He mashed the button for the lift, slowly lowering her Jeep, and he shouted over the noise, "I should get workin' on this if you're to get outta here today."

Ella's eyebrows pinched together as she turned around, trekking along L Street. What sort of town didn't use money "much"?

Ella paused once she hit Main Street. Keystone Inn was four short blocks to her right, nestled back from the street. Expansive, snow-laden shrubs and ivy obscured part of it from view.

Lou couldn't possibly have her car ready in the next twenty minutes and her muscles were in desperate need of exercise—especially if she was going to burn off those slices of banana bread.

Her mind made up, she turned left with the intention of exploring more of the town. Her boots pressed prints into the fresh snow and made that special squishing noise that sounded like flatulence. *Snow* flatulence.

Ella smiled to herself and drank in the stillness of the world that only a fresh layer of powdered accumulation could bring. She loved that moment after the clouds had sprinkled flakes over the landscape like the earth inhaled its first breath and the exhale wouldn't come until spring.

Soon, cottages and historic houses replaced the storefronts and businesses. Ahead, Main Street continued straight, passing at the base of the left hill of what she was assuming were Twin Hills.

Another road, Lake Drive according to a faded sign, veered off and curved around the lake. Small boats bobbed in the dark water, moored to the docks.

Hunger drew her away from the charming vista, and she glanced at her watch. It was getting late in the afternoon, and her stomach had burned through her eggs, bacon, and banana bread like she'd run a 10k.

Now that she had a better idea of the size of the lake, she decided against trekking around it. Maybe she'd walk it after a late lunch at the diner—unless Lou had her car ready or she could come up with another excuse.

She walked at a brisk pace back to the inn, half out of hunger, half out of the need to thaw her limbs. As she reached the block, a long, lean man stepped out of the dining car next door. His chiseled features were set in a brooding expression that soured his good looks, but Ella's attention was drawn to his choice in attire.

His clothes looked like the wild West and a motorcycle club had a drunken brawl, and he wore the leftovers. A faded gray Stetson hat sat on his dark hair above a sweatshirt, an aged leather vest, brown trousers, and boots with honest-to-goodness spurs. Either a rodeo was in town or he belonged to a theater troop.

He turned down the sidewalk which just happened to be in her direction. His eyes caught hers from beneath the brim of his hat.

Ella nodded by way of greeting before averting her gaze to the words "Belly Buster" advertised in the diner window. Whatever it was, she was having it.

The tall drink of trouble stepped into her path, barring her from fries and the promise of this mysterious *Belly Buster.*

"Well, hullo there, darlin'." Smoke billowed into her face, and she coughed. She hated cigarette smoke.

"Excuse me." Ella attempted to step around him, and his arm shot out.

"What you runnin' for? I ain't gonna hurt you."

Ella clenched her teeth. "Not running. I'm hungry." This man was standing between her and food and was about to get a tongue-lashing if he didn't step aside.

A young woman in a pink gingham waitress uniform stood in the diner window watching them. Her eyes were on the shady man, her expression full of fear and anger. And something else Ella couldn't discern.

He blew out another cloud of smoke. "You're new."

"You're observant."

His lips twitched. "You stranded too?"

Ella frowned. "I don't know about *too*, but yeah, I crashed my car, and I'm stuck here until it gets fixed."

He flicked his cigarette, narrowly missing her ear. "You'd be better off with a horse. They handle weather better than those metal death traps. 'Course if they bring in pretty things like you... maybe they ain't so bad." His eyes glinted under the shadow of his hat. "My advice? Trade it in for a horse and get outta here. Keystone ain't a place you wanna stay."

"Really? It seems like a cute little town full of great people—with a few exceptions." She narrowed her eyes at the last word, hoping he'd pick up on the hint. He didn't.

"Well," he drawled out the word like a sigh, "don't let the sheriff see you. He'll run you outta town faster than the Transcontinental Express." She blinked at him. "No? Well, it's a really fast train. Or at least it was—"

"Er, why? Why would he chase me out of town?"

"You'll see." He winked at her and finally stepped out of the way.

She mumbled a "thanks for the advice" as he tugged on a pair of leather gloves and strolled off, the air jingling with his spurs.

Ella watched his retreating back a moment before she ducked into the diner. A bell over the door tinkled, and the waitress who had been watching the exchange outside told Ella to pick a spot before she whisked into the kitchen.

Hovering over the doormat, Ella blew into her gloved hands while staking out a seat. Since she was eating so late, she had several options. Two other patrons sat separately in booths.

Wandering over the black-and-white checkered floor to the lunch counter, Ella chose a spinning stool and dropped onto it. She rubbed her palms together to get more sensation back into them and swung her legs back and forth. No matter how old she got, she could never resist the urge to spin back and forth in a chair.

The young waitress appeared on the other side of the counter sporting a friendly smile. She had a heart-shaped face with rouged cheeks and long lashes that brushed her penciled eyebrows. Her blonde hair swept back in an elaborate hairdo that would've taken Ella too many hours and a lot of cursing.

The waitress plucked a pencil from above her ear. "Welcome to Grandma's Kitchen. I see you met Six."

"I'm sorry? Six?"

She jerked her head at the window. "The cowboy. Short for Six Shooter—what he prefers everyone calls him. Of course, his real name is Jesse but don't tell him I told you."

The side of Ella's mouth quirked up. "I won't. He's... different."

"He's a menace. Spends more time in the local jail than in the fresh air." She pulled a pad from her apron, and the pencil hovered over it. "What can I get you?"

Ella's eyes darted around. She hadn't looked at a menu yet, but her stomach protested at waiting any longer for food. "How about that Belly Busting thing? The special?" She pointed at the chalkboard easel to her left.

"Good choice. That's Grandma Wink's secret recipe." After taking her order, the young gal walked away.

Finally pulling off her gloves and jacket, Ella draped them onto the stool beside her and took in the quaint diner, from the display of freshly baked glazed donuts and strawberry pie to the homemade banana bread. Her mouth watered, recalling that morning's breakfast. She wondered if Rose had bought the bread from the diner.

The waitress zoomed behind the counter again, grabbing a pot of coffee. With every other step, one of her black kitten heels made a distinct sound as it stuck to the linoleum floor. She held the pot of coffee up in Ella's direction, her brow arched.

Ella nodded. As steam floated from her cup, she said, "Thank you...?"

"Kayline. But everyone just calls me Kay."

"Ella."

"Nice to meet you. Sheriff know you're here?"

Ella shifted on her cushy seat. That was the second time someone had mentioned the sheriff. "Um, no. Should he?"

Kay's pink lips turned down. Her eyes shifted over Ella's shoulder to the person sitting in the booth behind her. "Sorry, gotta run. Your burger and fries will be up soon."

She glided over the floor, floating with the confident grace of a ballerina. Ella tried to focus on the knickknacks and fifties memorabilia covering the walls and not eavesdrop. However, Kay and the patron she approached were sitting right behind Ella, and the lack of competing conversation meant she could hear every word.

"How's the coffee, Will?"

"Same as always. Muddy and perfect," a deep voice replied.

Kay squealed, then paper rustled. "What's that you're working on? Is this your latest project?"

Ella curled a loose strand of hair behind her ear, stealing a glance behind her as she did so. Kay stood over one of the booths, talking to a man closer to Ella's age, with brown hair, deep blue-green eyes, and strong features. He reminded Ella of an old -fashioned movie star: classically handsome.

A large paper sat unfolded in front of him, covering the speckled Formica table and a pile of fries. Complicated lines covered the schematic. His eyes swept up and met Ella's before she quickly turned, face forward again. She caught his reflection in the stainless steel milkshake machine. He was still watching her, a curious expression on his face.

"How's it work?" Kay asked the man.

"It's an outdoor oven, using solar light instead of fire,

gas, or electricity."

"Oh, cool."

"Did you fix my—"

"Yeah, it's right here. It's why I came by. That and the coffee." Ella heard a smile in Will's voice.

She squinted at their reflections. Kay took something small and shiny from Will and stuffed it into her apron.

"And here I thought you wanted to see your ex-girlfriend," Kayline teased.

Ella nearly choked on her coffee. Nothing about the light-hearted tone between the two said they were exes. She couldn't imagine being on such friendly terms with any of her ex-boyfriends, yet not for lack of trying on her part. They all just happened to be jerks.

Above the milkshake machine was a pass-through window with a view into the kitchen. A large hand appeared, setting down an even larger plate of burger and fries. A disembodied voice hollered, "Belly Buster!"

The waitress whisked over and grabbed the plate. As she placed the juicy burger on the lunch counter, Ella caught sight of a red rash covering the waitress's forearms. Kay followed her gaze, and her cheeks reddened.

"Poison oak."

Ella grimaced with sympathy. "I've had that a few times. Isn't it contagious?"

Shrugging, Kay fiddled with the pencil behind her ear. "Not by touch. Only if the oils from the plant are still on my skin or clothes."

After making sure Ella didn't need anything else, she swept over to the cash register, her heels clicking out their arrhythmic beat.

Heat emanated from Ella's plate. Without ceremony, she attacked the mound of thick, salted fries hiding her

Belly Buster—which turned out to be some kind of a hybridization between a cheeseburger, nachos, and a sloppy joe with a third bun thrown in for good measure.

Slowly, she excavated the "burger" from the fries but was then presented with the problem of how to go about eating the gooey mess. Cheese sauce oozed over the sides, mixing with what the chalkboard called, "Grandma's Secret Sauce."

The sauces coalesced and dribbled down her hands. A fork would've been better, but she'd already sacrificed her hands, and her stomach would hear none of this waiting for a utensil business. The flavors of the heart-attack-in-a-bun collided in her mouth, and despite appearances, she deemed it one of the best burgers she'd ever had.

A few feet away, Kay popped up from under the cash register with a wad of napkins. She began to stuff them into a holder when the man with the schematics and blue-green eyes walked up to the counter.

Will slipped a fedora over his chocolate-colored, patent leather hair. "That was great food, but don't tell Grandma Wink I said that. I'm afraid to ask, but what did those pancakes cost me?"

Kay set the napkin holder aside. "The soda fountain's on the fritz. Wink'll want you to fix it."

He whistled. "That's a steep price for one breakfast."

Kay batted her long lashes. "Please, Will. It'll take you two seconds to figure out what's wrong."

Ella tried not to stare. The way Kay looked at Will, how she leaned close when he was near, if those two were still exes by the end of the week, then her name wasn't Ella Barton.

Will chuckled. "Come on, don't give me that look. You know I can't say no to a friend."

Kay leaned back, her face falling a moment before she

recovered. Will didn't seem to notice, but Ella, having been in that position before, recognized the expression.

The man shifted on his feet, leaned over the counter, and dropped his voice. "Listen, I heard something, and before you get all angry at me, just know I ask because I care."

Kay crossed her arms. "Okaay…"

Out of the corner of Ella's eye, she saw Will's head turn in her direction then to the other patron. His voice dropped to a gravelly, unintelligible whisper. Soon, their conversation became heated, sounding like steam releasing from a pressure cooker. Maybe they were more like normal exes than Ella had thought.

Despite the two's attempt at keeping their discussion private, snippets of their argument floated over the sizzle of the fryer coming from the kitchen. Ella swam a fry through a pool of ketchup and hummed to herself to try to give them some privacy. When the phrases "not safe" and "too dangerous" were used in proximity to each other, Ella stopped humming and strained to listen.

Kay was in the middle of whisper-yelling when she stopped abruptly and gasped. Then she shrieked. She stumbled back into a pie stand, sending the covered desserts flying. Crust and glass shattered across the floor.

The waitress's arms flailed through the air like she fought off an invisible attacker as she screamed, "No! Stop! Get away from me!"

Will vaulted over the counter. "Kay! What's wrong?!"

Ella jumped up and rushed over. Kayline's arms stopped flailing, and her hands gripped her stomach. Then she vomited.

"Kay!" Will sidestepped the mess and grabbed the waitress as her body went limp. "Kayline!"

Ella watched the scene in horror.

"Help!" Will shrieked, bringing her out of her shock.

Ella scrambled over the broken glass and smeared pies as they crunched beneath her snow boots. The cook burst through the kitchen door.

"Call 911!" Ella yelled at him and dropped beside Kay.

First aid training from years before kicked in, and she instructed Will to turn the waitress's head so she wouldn't aspirate on the contents spilling out of her mouth.

Will sat on the floor, Kay's head turned in his lap, as he kept calling her name like a song stuck on repeat.

Ella couldn't feel Kay's breath, so her fingers groped the waitress's neck, searching for a pulse while her own raced.

"Kay, please be okay," Will pleaded.

Ella couldn't feel a heartbeat beneath her fingertips, not even faint or arrhythmic like the waitress's heels. Nothing.

The words left Ella's lips long before she realized it was she who had spoken them. "She's dead."

CHAPTER 4

"AND SHE JUST—fell over? Dead?"

"More like collapsed." Mounting frustration crept into Ella's voice.

She was seated in a booth in Grandma's Kitchen, feeling dazed. The tall man questioning her had introduced himself as Sheriff Chapman but looked and dressed an awful lot like Wyatt Earp.

"And again. It wasn't *just*. She waved her arms around, yelling, 'Get away from me!'"

The sheriff's derby hat brushed the ceiling, forcing him to duck as he swept the hat off his head with one hand. With the other, he stroked a long handle-bar mustache, and his eyes narrowed on her. "Did Will put his hands on her?"

"What? No." Ella sucked in a sweeping breath between her teeth. This was her third time recounting the details of the afternoon for the man. She just wanted to go back to her room at the inn. "It was as if she wasn't all there mentally. Like she was hallucinating."

His clear blue eyes watched her from under the brim of his hat for the span of several breaths, making her feel like a specimen under a microscope. "You said she'd been arguing with Will?" his voice drawled, slow but precise.

"I'm sure it was nothing. I wouldn't even call it an argument—"

"And yet, that's what you'd called it." His leathered hand went to his mustache again. "Where you from?"

"Salem. Well, originally, but I'm heading back to Bend."

"Salem...?"

The question threw her, and she blinked at him for a moment before responding slowly, "Salem, Oregon... the capital... of the state..."

"Hmm. Wait here, Miss Barton."

Ella frowned, watching him saunter over to the cook— a short man with thick eyebrows that nearly met. The sheriff's cowboy boots clicked over the linoleum floor and stopped. The cook's hands worried his grease-stained apron, and he stared at the sheriff expectantly.

"Horatio..." Sheriff Chapman addressed him before lowering his voice.

At the far end of the railcar diner, Will sat alone in the corner booth. His fedora rested on the table, forgotten, and his head drooped into his hands, his chocolate locks spilling between his fingers.

Ella's heart went out to him. Some people wanted to be alone in times of crises, and others needed to know they weren't alone. Unsure of which type he was, she shuffled over and sank onto the seat across from him.

"I'm sorry for your loss," she said softly.

Will lifted his head, his features fraught with emotion. His eyes were pools of blue and green that caught the aging afternoon, but at that moment, they also held pain.

"Thank you." He dropped his head back into his hands.

When she realized she was staring, she tore her gaze to the white landscape outside the window. A cold crept through the single-pane glass, causing her to snuggle deeper into her sweatshirt.

Outside, a round woman with a coat a couple of sizes too large crossed the street. A bag was hefted over one shoulder, causing her to walk lopsided under its weight. She swung the door to the diner in with a bang, and the bell rattled instead of jingling merrily as she stumbled inside. Snow dropped from her jacket and boots onto the mat, reminding Ella of a dripping ice cream cone.

Sheriff Chapman nodded in greeting to the newcomer. "Over there, Pauline." His long arm extended towards Kayline's body. Pauline puffed out heavy breaths and lumbered over.

"Coroner?" Ella asked Will in a low voice.

Across from her, Will's head rolled back and forth in his hands in a gesture resembling a nod—well, maybe if she was drunk and squinting, it could be perceived as a nod.

"Town coroner. Doctor. Medic. She's all of them."

Ella was both impressed and thankful that she didn't grow up in a small town. "Huh. A woman of many hats."

"She is not wearing a hat."

"What? No, I meant—never mind."

Across Grandma's Kitchen, Pauline the coroner-doctor-medic plopped her bag down and opened her enormous jacket, revealing dozens of bulging pockets inside and a far less rotund figure underneath.

Soft curses floated from the coroner's mouth and over the heavy air.

Chapman's head turned. "Need help, Pauline?"

"No, no. Just can't find—" Her hand plunged into a different pocket, and she let out a noise of triumph as she pulled out a pair of gloves. "There they are."

Tugging them on, she bent out of sight—the lunch counter mercifully blocking Kay's body.

A few minutes later, Sheriff Chapman told the cook he could leave. Ella watched with envy as Horatio trudged out into the cold, wondering when it would be her turn. She didn't know why the sheriff was keeping her there.

Her mind kept replaying Kay's screams and the way the waitress had stumbled into the pie case. It hurt Ella to think that another human being's final moments had been gripped in such horror. That poor woman.

All Ella wanted to do was get into her car and drive home and try to erase that afternoon from her mind. As charming as Keystone Village had seemed a few hours ago, witnessing the death of a person tarnished that image considerably.

The coroner moved to the other side of Kay and let out a loud sigh, shaking her head. "Someone tell Mayor Bradford, yet?"

"Not yet." The hard lines in Sheriff Chapman's expression deepened. "Not 'till I have more to tell him." He strolled over and hovered above Pauline, recounting a shortened version of what had happened. When he'd finished, he asked, "So, what do you think?"

"About what?"

"The body, Pauline."

"Oh, right. Too soon to say. My first notion is an allergic reaction. See the rash here?"

The sheriff craned his neck to where the coroner indicated. Ella couldn't see clearly but assumed Pauline was showing him Kay's arms.

"That's from poison oak," Ella called out. Both sets of

eyes turned to her and blinked. "Uh, she told me she had it."

"Interesting." Chapman's expression said it was anything but interesting. "You failed to mention that before, Miss Barton."

Ella lifted her tired shoulders in a shrug. "Forgot."

He continued to stare, long after Pauline returned her attention to the body. He seemed to be sizing her up, scrutinizing her. Finally, he looked away, but his expression didn't say if she'd been found wanting.

"If this rash is, in fact, caused by poison oak," Pauline said, "I'm not sure what we're dealing with. I'm not seeing any swelling. And it was too quick to be a virus. With such a sudden onset of symptoms, along with the delirium…" She shook her head. "Won't know more until I can do some blood work. She allergic to anything?"

The sheriff straightened and peered across the diner. "Was Kay allergic to anything, Will?"

Slowly, Will's head rose, and he stared at the sheriff with a blank expression. "Nickel. She couldn't wear the necklace I gave her for our anniversary." He kept his head up, but his eyes dropped to the Formica tabletop and its pocked surface.

Pauline worked her way around to Kay's feet, and her lips pressed into a thin line.

"What is it?" Sheriff Chapman asked.

"Some sticky stuff on her soles. Looks like tree sap." The woman brought her thick shoulders up in a shrug before continuing on to the other side.

The sheriff lowered to a squat beside the coroner—no easy feat given his height and age—then popped back up a moment later, holding a small, metallic object in his hands. "What's this?"

Ella glanced between the device and Will. The color

drained from his face.

"Nothing."

"Don't look like nothing to me, Will." The sheriff pointed to a section on the object. "This gold, here?"

A crevice formed between Will's eyebrows. "Just a coil of it. It's the best conductive wiring I could find. I ran out of copper."

"Is it just a coating?"

"Yes," Will said, drawing out the word. His skin now took on a greenish hue.

"What's the material underneath?"

Will's face morphed into one of horror, his eyes wild. "N-n-nickel. But her skin couldn't have had contact with it."

The sheriff cradled the device in one hand and grabbed his derby hat from off of the lunch counter. "Alright. Come along. Both of you."

Ella tensed and exchanged a glance with Will. "Where?"

"To the office to talk some more."

She relaxed some. An office didn't sound so bad. Then, she noticed the way Will's hands clenched and the fear in his eyes.

"But we didn't do anything," he said.

"That's what I gotta find out. Stand up." The sheriff's face was all hard lines and granite again, leaving no room for discussion.

Ella slid out of the booth, trembling slightly. He was just going to question them further. No need to panic just yet.

The trauma of that afternoon had dulled her mind. As she tugged her jacket over her sweatshirt and slipped on her gloves, it finally hit her.

Unless Kayline had been struck by a sudden brain

aneurysm that caused paranoia and delusions, her death wasn't an accident. And the fact that Sheriff Chapman wanted to question them further meant he suspected that too.

A cold dread swept over Ella. Was this really happening? Was she really a suspect for the murder of someone she'd just met and tried to save?

She sucked in a breath and reassured herself that the sheriff was just doing his job. He'd simply ask her a few questions then release her when he realized she wasn't involved.

After tucking Will's device into his jacket, Sheriff Chapman grabbed each of their elbows in a firm grip and escorted them onto the street. A late afternoon sun shone over the glittering snow like a dying ember trying to warm the air. Ella could feel the cold seeping through her jacket, chilling her bones and creeping into her heart.

CHAPTER 5

THE JAIL DOOR slammed shut on Ella's cell.

"Seriously?!" She gripped the cold metal bars. "You said we were just going to talk some more! You can't lock me up!"

Sheriff Chapman stuck his thumbs in his belt loops. "And this is how I can question you further without fear of you running away. Until Pauline tells me Kayline's death was from natural causes, you're both suspects."

"With what evidence?!" Ella sputtered. "You can't do this! It's illegal!"

She wasn't actually sure it was, but it seemed like the right thing to say. Wasn't there something about being held for up to twenty-four hours then he'd have to either charge her or let her go? She wished she had paid more attention while watching *Law and Order*.

"Is it?" Chapman tipped his head slightly and stroked his mustache like a cartoon villain, only she didn't think he was doing it ironically. "Huh. Well, here in Keystone Village, we do things a little differently."

"Different than the law?" Ella glared at him. The sheriff ignored the question and sauntered over to his desk. She shook the bars and let out a frustrated growl. "This is one crazy, messed up town."

When her breathing had evened and she was confident fire wouldn't come out of her mouth, she took in her surroundings. The six-by-six jail cell was one of two in the small, brick building that housed the sheriff's office. The bars were marred, rusted in places, and the red bricks chipped and faded. The place looked like it was part of a museum exhibit for the American frontier.

In the corner, a cast-iron stove crackled with a fire that made the office toasty and gave off a whiff of smoke reminiscent of a campfire. If she'd been on the other side of the metal bars, she would've found it comforting.

Just thinking about being on the inside of the cell got her worked up again. "Why is there even a sheriff's office in town, anyway?" she hollered over at Chapman despite the fact that he was within spitting distance. "Where's the local police station? Can I talk with one of their officers instead?"

He slipped his hat off and dropped it on his desk. When he spoke, his voice was harsh, like sandpaper over gravel. "I told you, Miss Barton, we do things differently here."

"I noticed." That earned a glare from the stony man.

Satisfied she'd gotten some kind of reaction out of him, Ella plopped onto the lone cot in the cell. It smelled of sweat, tobacco, and vomit.

She coughed and turned her nose up. When that didn't work, she lifted her sweatshirt over her nostrils.

Will sat on his cot in his own cell, facing her. He noticed her breathing into her clothing, and his mouth twitched, his features lifting.

"Whatever you're smelling, I assure you, mine's worse."

She doubted it. She was pretty sure she was going to have to burn her clothes. But he had just lost a friend, so she let him win and gave him a thumbs up.

Taking a deep breath, she pulled the sweatshirt respirator down and said to Chapman, "You know, a coat of paint would do wonders for the aesthetics in here."

"And some curtains," Will added.

"Oh, curtains. Good idea. And maybe, just thinking out loud here, a couple of new cots. You know, ones less fragrant—not that I mind *Eu de Pew*." She smiled at her own joke and looked at Will. "Get it?"

His eyebrows said he didn't.

He looked over at the sheriff. "I can *taste* it. Do you get it? I can *taste* this smell. It tastes like…" He snapped his fingers, searching for the words.

"Tastes like a night gone wrong in Vegas," Ella helped.

"Enough," Chapman growled. His mustache bristled, and he glared at both of them.

Good. Maybe she couldn't do anything at the moment about being stuck behind bars, but she could do her best to make him miserable and regret putting her there.

The idea that someone suspected her of harming another human being burned a fire in her gut, further fueled by the sheriff's handling of the situation.

"So, about those questions…?"

Chapman leaned back in his chair and remained silent.

Ella's head dropped back against the bars. "There weren't any more questions, were there?"

"Nope. Just waiting till I get some answers from our coroner."

Ella's shoulders drooped. Kay's death was strange, sure, but that didn't mean someone had killed her. Did it?

Ella replayed the events leading up to Kayline's death. The more she thought about it, the more she agreed that an allergic reaction didn't fit the symptoms.

Will leaned forward, his cot squealing in protest. "Come now, Sheriff. You don't really think I'd do anything to hurt Kay, do you?"

"Doesn't matter what I think."

"You've known me for—what—eight years? Nine?"

"Doesn't matter, Will. If you're innocent, I'll let you out. Gotta treat you the same as everyone else."

Ella struggled off the flimsy cot. It was so low to the ground, she fell back onto the thin fabric. With a grunt, she rolled off, rather clumsily, but she recovered with a flourish and bounced to her feet. Will cocked an eyebrow.

After smoothing out an invisible wrinkle, she strode to the bars. "What about me? What reason could I possibly have for hurting Kay?"

"Dunno. But you're a stranger here. And I don't like new people in my town."

"Yeah, I noticed the sign posted outside of town." She squeezed her hands into fists then forced the tension out. "News flash, if you don't want people passing through, then maybe you shouldn't live in a town that's right off the highway."

His face flickered with an emotion she couldn't identify before it turned to stone again.

"Come on, Sheriff," Will said. "There's nothing untoward happening here. Miss Barton has nothing to do with what happened. Neither of us do."

Ella spoke out of the side of her mouth. "I appreciate the support, but call me Ella."

"Noted." Will slipped off the cot and climbed to his feet with an agility that made her jealous.

His fingers curled around the bars and framed his face

as he pleaded with Chapman. "We tried to save Kay. What reason would I have to hurt her?"

"Come on, William. It's no secret that you were mad about the breakup."

Will's knuckle's turned white, and his voice dropped. "That was a year ago."

Sheriff Chapman folded his fingers and turned his attention to Ella. "What are you doing in Keystone Village, Miss Barton? We're not on a map, so you ain't—what's it called? Sightseeing."

"My car broke down. Actually, it crashed. Lou's fixing it."

"He say how long it'll take?"

She shook her head. "Not yet. He was supposed to tell me as soon as he had a look." She leaned into the bars and shot him the smile she reserved to get free appetizers at her favorite restaurant. "But maybe if you let me out, I can ask him."

"Nice try," he grunted. Her smile evaporated.

Reaching across his desk, the sheriff snatched up an old rotary phone and spun the dial a few times. "Lou? Sheriff Chapman. There's a lady here claiming you got her car."

Ella clenched her jaw at the word "claiming." Like she would lie about her car needing fixed.

Chapman kept the receiver pressed to his ear and listened to the small, tinny voice on the other end before saying, "Yes. Checks out, then. How long?" His mustache turned down, and a crevice formed between his brows. "That's a problem." After a couple more grunts, he hung up.

"Ol' Lou says about two days. Has to replace the front axle shaft and will have to adapt one he's got on hand."

The prognosis of her vehicle and the fact that she'd be

in Keystone two more days felt like a punch to Ella's gut. "Can't he just order a new part from Bend or Salem?" She'd even pay the extra cost to ship the part overnight if she had to.

"Can't."

Ella frowned. She opened her mouth to ask why not, but the sheriff cut her off.

"Believe me. I'm not happy about it either." His eyes darkened, and he leaned forward in his chair. "Seems your best option is to trade your vehicle in for one of Lou's. And leave tonight."

Ella's first instinct was to tell him to go eat his own mustache. She loved her SUV. But something about the intensiveness in his voice made her churn over his words. "Does that mean you'll release me? You believe me?"

"*Believe* is a strong word. But out of the two of you"— he jerked his head at Will —"he's got more motive for wanting Miss Bradford dead."

Will threw his hands up. "But I didn't—"

"Hobble your lip, Will."

Ella's feelings raced between overwhelming relief and sympathy towards the handsome man in the cell next to her.

The sheriff stretched out of his chair to his full height, jangling a ring of skeleton keys from his desk. Picking a rather large, dark one, he waved it in Ella's face.

"Here's the deal. You trade your car for something that runs and leave town tonight, and I'll let you out."

Ella bit her lower lip. She had sunk a lot of money into her Jeep, even putting new tires on three months prior. However, if it was between trading in her car or being holed up in a jail cell, there was no contest.

Slowly, she nodded. "Yeah, fine. I'll leave."

Chapman jammed the old key into the lock. It clicked,

and he tugged open the door for her. "You're free to go, then. And Miss Barton, I'll be watching to make sure you leave Keystone."

Ella's mouth felt dry as she nodded. While she scurried out of the holding cell, the rotary phone on the sheriff's desk rang loudly, startling her. Chapman scooped up the receiver. Ella scooted towards the front door, unsure if she could just walk out.

"What?!" Chapman's eyes narrowed to slits, and he growled, "That mudsill. Blowhard. Dirty outlaw…" His nostrils flared. "Be right there."

He slammed the phone down and shoved his hat over his gray hair. His boots pounded an angry rhythm, and he marched past Ella and out the door. It banged against the brick before returning to rest in its frame, a degree more ajar than it had been a moment before.

"Uh…" Ella stared at the door and felt the cold air linger. She glanced at Will, still locked up in his cell. "So, I guess I'll just leave, then?"

Some of the sadness had left his eyes, and the corner of his mouth ticked up. "You sure? I was thinking of starting a card game."

"Wow, I'd hate to miss that."

The levity of the moment quickly faded, and a heavy silence filled the room. Ella glanced at the desk drawer that held the jail key.

"Don't do it," he said.

She took a breath and turned away from the temptation. "Look, I know we just met and haven't even been properly introduced, but for what it's worth, I'm sorry for your loss, and I believe you."

He gave her a tired smile. "Thanks." One of his hands threaded through the bars. "William Whitehall."

She gripped the outstretched hand, feeling callouses

brush her palm. "Ella Barton."

"Don't worry about me, Miss Barton—"

"Ella."

"Right. I suggest you leave now, Ella, while you still can." His tone turned heavy with warning.

"Fair enough." She crept towards the front door. "Well, it's been… well, let's not do this again. Good luck, Will."

After one last glance, she slipped out onto the cold street. She sucked in a breath of freedom and tasted the coming snow—the smell much improved over the cot inside.

The sun had dipped behind the two hills, bathing the sky in a dusky, dull yellow. Street lamps flickered on, spilling an amber glow over the snow.

Ella wrapped her arms around herself and trudged through the antique village, reliving the day's events. Lights twinkled over the lake from distant street lamps and cottage windows, but she couldn't fully appreciate the beauty.

Some poor, young woman had lost her life today. Someone's daughter. Someone's friend. Her heart broke for Kay's family, and she began to wonder more about what had killed the waitress. Ella was no expert on death, but the incident had seemed such a strange way to die.

Could the poison oak rash be covering up a rash caused by an allergic reaction? The coroner hadn't seemed to rule out the possibility. Then again, Kayline hadn't shown any other symptoms of anaphylaxis.

And what about the hallucinations? Did that strange device Will had given Kayline have something to do with this? She'd been so quick to dismiss the man as a suspect, but it did seem too coincidental that a few minutes after giving her the small, metallic contraption, the waitress fell dead.

A dark figure jumped out of the alley in front of Ella. She jumped and screamed. The shadow clamped a hand over her mouth.

"Whoa, easy there, darlin'."

Ella caught a whiff of stale tobacco and hay before the figure dragged her into the shadows of the alley. She struggled against the sinewy arms of her captor. The glow from the nearest street lamp pierced the darkness just enough for her to make out a cowboy hat and a sharp, angular jaw.

It was the cowboy she'd bumped into just outside the diner. Ella remembered the name Kay had called him, and when the rough hand moved from her mouth, she yelled, "Jesse! What—"

"Don't call me that. Name's Six Shooter. Six for short."

"Yeah, I'm not calling you that."

"But that's my name."

"Still not saying it."

He gave her a rough spin so she faced him, only he didn't take into account her lack of balance, and she heaved into his chest, hitting her chin hard on his sternum.

"Ow! What d'you do that for, woman?"

Ella rubbed her chin, sure it was going to bruise. "Well, that's what you get for abducting me."

"Who's addicting—"

"Abducting."

"Who's abdicating—"

"Close enough."

"—you?"

"You are."

The confusion in his face melted, and a gleam took root as if she'd given him the greatest idea.

Ella cringed inwardly and took a minuscule step back.

"What do you want, Jesse? I'm having a pretty bad day, and if it's all the same to you, I'd like to go back to the inn now." And burn her clothes before packing. She still smelled the stains from the cot.

He flashed a smile. "You gonna thank me?"

"For…?"

"For savin' you," he said.

Ella lowered her eyebrows in confusion.

He sighed. "It was me that called the sheriff." His voice changed, pitching up and affecting a poorly done accent. "'Someone's been messing with my cattle. They're loose in the orchards.' That was me." His eyes danced with pride.

"Well, thanks. I appreciate the gesture. Topnotch thinking, really. But your timing's off. He'd just let me out of my cell."

While she'd been talking, she'd inched back, putting more air between them, as much for the ability to flee as to stop smelling him. Her olfactory senses had had just about all they could handle.

"Just out of curiosity," she continued, "how did you plan on getting me out of that cell after you lured him away?"

His hand plunged into his sweatshirt. Ella flinched, her legs coiled, ready to run.

Six produced a crude reproduction of a key. "Took the liberty of makin' myself a copy since I spend so much time in there."

"Good Lord, did a toddler carve that out of crayon?" She cleared her throat. "Anyway, makes sense. Of course, you could just stop doing the things you get locked up for, but where's the fun in that, right?"

His expression said he'd missed the sarcasm in her tone.

Slipping past him, she stepped onto the sidewalk, her boots crunching in the snow.

"Night, Jesse." She danced out of reach before he could grab her again.

He remained in the shadows, a silhouette with a voice. "Night, darlin'."

Ella cringed and stared back into the alley. "If you don't want me calling you *Jesse*, then don't call me *darling*."

A light flickered as he lit a match, catching it on a rolled cigarette that hung between his lips. "No promises."

Too tired to deal any more with the cowboy, she shook her head and shuffled towards the inn. It was getting late, and to keep her deal with the sheriff, she would need to visit Lou, trade her car in, pack, and leave—all by tonight.

Fitting in a quick shower wouldn't hurt either, she decided. But first, she wanted to change clothes.

Ella stepped into Keystone Inn, and warm air and soft light welcomed her. She pulled the scent of cinnamon and apple into her lungs and fought the hunger pains in her stomach.

Her to-do list re-prioritized. After she changed, she'd grab a quick snack from the kitchen—if she could locate it in the mansion. Then she would trade her car in.

After throwing her jacket onto the coat tree and kicking off her boots, she whisked into the entrance hall. Rose stood behind the check-in counter, scratching a pencil in a book.

"Oh, Ella! There you are. I was getting worried. You missed dinner."

"Yeah, sorry. I was... busy." She didn't feel like retelling what had happened again for the umpteenth time that day. Her eyes flitted to the cherry wood flooring, and the memories crashed back in. She moved towards the staircase.

"Did you hear about what happened?" Rose's pale skin turned ashen, and she glanced in the direction of the diner next door. "Poor Kay. She was such a sweet thing." Reaching into her dress pocket, she pulled out a handkerchief and dabbed behind her cat-eye glasses. "Oh, Wink's going to be heartbroken."

Ella watched her from the bottom of the stairs, teetering between comforting her and following the sheriff's order to high-tail it out of Dodge. "Did you know her well? Kay, I mean."

"Yes, we were good friends. When she and her father arrived in Keystone a few years back, she felt so alone. She had a hard time adjusting to life here and needed a friend. We'd drifted apart the last couple of years, but Kayline was like a younger sister to me."

Ella abandoned the stairs and draped an arm around Rose's shoulders. "How come you weren't as close recently, if you don't mind me asking?"

Rose's crimson lips quivered. "Oh, I don't know. This was about a year and a half back, so the details are a bit fuzzy, but she withdrew. She seemed to have a great weight on her. But whenever I asked, she wouldn't open up.

"When people stay closed off like that, going through things alone, it eats them up. That's why I was grateful when she started dating Will. Then, they broke up. I just didn't know how to help, anymore."

Ella squeezed her shoulders. "I'm sure she knew you were there if she ever needed you. Sometimes, that comfort alone is all a person needs."

When Rose had composed herself, Ella slipped upstairs to change. As her hand glided up the banister, the innkeeper called up to her.

"Forgot to tell you. Lou called looking for you. Said your car would be ready in a couple days." A smile lit her face. "Looks like you'll be staying here a while."

Ella shot her a wan smile before trudging up the stairs. She would say goodbye after she got back from Lou's.

Edwin passed her at the top of the stairs, and they exchanged quick pleasantries before parting. He seemed in as much of a rush as she was. She briefly wondered where the elderly gentleman was off to in such a hurry at eight o'clock in the evening.

After shutting the door to her room, Ella collapsed on her four-poster bed, telling herself, she'd rest for five minutes then change and head back out. In less than a minute, darkness pulled her down into a deep sleep full of cowboys and dead bodies.

CHAPTER 6

LARGE FLAKES OF snow drifted past Ella's window in a weak, morning light. She yawned and stretched.

The inn was old, and heat seemed to struggle to reach her room, putting her in no hurry to leave the warm cocoon she'd created in the feather comforter.

After snuggling in deeper, the events of the previous day drifted back, ending with the sheriff's deal for her to leave town.

Leave town.

Ella bolted upright and scrambled to disentangle herself from the sheets. She was supposed to be out of town. Last night.

"Crap, crap, crap." She shuddered to think what the sheriff would do when he found out she was still in Keystone.

She tore open her backpack. She had yet to retrieve the rest of her luggage from her car. Most of the clothes peeking out of the bag had already been worn while staying at her parents' place for Thanksgiving, so her selection of clean attire was limited.

She pulled out a fresh t-shirt and tugged on her only other pair of jeans. The ones from the previous day were wadded up on the floor. She kicked them to the corner so she wouldn't forget they were dirty and to pack them last. Her snow boots were down by the front door.

Grabbing her phone, she checked the bars again: still no service.

The scenery outside her second-story window caught her eye. The white blanket sheeting everything had grown fat through the night. Thick flakes continued to fall, reminding Ella of Christmas, fires, and warm cookies.

Her gaze drifted right, in the direction of the park. That part in her brain tickled again that something she was seeing wasn't quite right. Ella shook off the feeling and bolted for the door.

She gripped the banister of the wide staircase, noting the scent of coffee and cinnamon rolls wafting up. She stopped at the bottom of the stairs, torn between seeing Lou and the delicious smell.

She glanced at her watch. Surely it was too early for the crusty mechanic to be up and in his shop? Would the sheriff come bursting into the inn, checking to see if she'd left yet?

Ella chewed her lip. In the end, she decided that his hands had to be full dealing with Kayline's death.

And like a sailor being lured by a siren, Ella followed her nose to the promise of breakfast.

If this ends up being one of those scented candles, I'm going to be really pissed.

She had just rounded the corner in the hallway right before the dining room when she bumped into a plump figure with a mountain of frosted hair reminiscent of the snow-covered hills outside.

"Oh, sorry, Flo. I didn't see you."

Crazy Flo's face scrunched in confusion, creating ripples and divots. "Who're you?"

"Ella. We met at breakfast yesterday."

"No. I don't think you were there."

Ella's lips twitched. "Pretty sure I was. I ate my weight in banana bread. I'm the one born in 1985, remember?"

Flo grunted. "Were you the ghost at the table?"

"Er, no. I'm corporeal."

"Oh, that's unfortunate." And without so much as a goodbye, the older woman marched away.

The dining room table was bare, the naked mahogany reflecting a painting of a boat in a storm. Turning, Ella followed the source of the aroma to another door further down the hallway. It swung inwards, and she found herself in the kitchen.

"Good morning," Rose called from the stove. "Coffee?" She held up a percolator.

"Only while I'm awake." Ella smiled gratefully and accepted the proffered, steaming cup. "You're my new favorite person."

Rose chuckled and returned to the stove. Today, she wore a navy dress with a raised wingtip collar, heels, and her blonde hair coiffed in a victory roll and large curls.

Ella parked herself at the informal dining table and sipped her coffee while surveying the room. The large kitchen was incongruous with the rest of the turn-of-the-century inn.

Rose's seeming obsession with the fifties wasn't just limited to her attire, apparently. The floor was covered in a black-and-white checkered pattern that matched the diner's. The walls were a vibrant yellow, and antique appliances dotted the room.

The table was shoved under a large picture window

that overlooked the lake. The setup was cozy, more intimate compared to the formal dining in the adjacent room.

With some caffeine pumping through her, Ella reached across the maple surface of the table and peeled a gooey roll from the pan sitting in the center. The frosting melted on her tongue, mixing with bits of apple.

"Mmm… Sweet kittens, this is amazing. Is there fruit in this?"

"Yes, chopped up. It's apple cinnamon rolls. One of Grandma Wink's specialties."

"Wow, it's heavenly. I need to meet this Grandma Wink I keep hearing about."

"I'm sure she'd love to meet you, too. She's around. Hard to miss."

Ella became more intrigued. After she swallowed another bite, she asked, "Where's Jimmy?"

"Bathroom." When Rose caught Ella's expression, she added, "The sink in the restroom at the end of the hall is acting up. It gurgles and sounds like Jimmy's stomach after he's had dairy. So, he's seeing what he can do about it."

"Probably not eat dairy."

"The sink, not his digestion issues."

"Sure, sure."

"Of course," Rose continued, "it's no problem if he can't get it. William Whitehall usually comes around once a week to help with repair work."

Ella nearly choked on her last bite of cinnamon roll. "Do you mean Will?"

Rose's perfectly penciled eyebrow arched above her cat-eye glasses, and her spatula paused mid-air. "You know Will?"

"Yeah, we met yesterday. I don't think he'll be around

anytime soon to fix things, though."

Ella sipped at her coffee to try to dislodge the piece of roll. Once her throat was food-free and she'd sputtered a minute for good measure, she told Rose what had happened at the diner the previous day in more detail.

Rose's skin turned ashen. "What on earth is Sheriff Chapman thinking? Will couldn't hurt a fly." Her eyes flitted up to Ella. "How come you didn't tell me this last night?"

"I'm sorry. I wanted to, but I was in a rush." She told the innkeeper about her deal with the sheriff, which only resurfaced her anxiety about needing to hurry out of there.

Rose waved her delicate hand dismissively. "Don't worry about the sheriff. Six occupies most of his time, anyhow. Like cat and mouse, those two are. And now with Kay's unfortunate death, Sheriff Chapman has even less time to worry about you.

"Besides, Lou won't be up for another hour. And if it makes you feel any better, you wouldn't have found him last night, anyway. He likes to nip off early, if you know what I mean." She made a motion of chugging from a bottle.

"Actually, that does make me feel better. It shouldn't. I mean, poor Lou, but we all have our vices, right?" She glanced pointedly at the coffee and apple cinnamon rolls on the table.

A comfortable lull in conversation followed, filled by the popping of bacon grease in the frying pan. Ella took the opportunity to ask a question that had been tumbling around in her mind.

"Did Kay have any health problems that you know about? A heart condition?"

Rose shook her head. Her head pivoted in Ella's

direction, but she gazed out at the drifting snow, her red lips a tight line. "This town. It takes too much, sometimes." The comment hung heavy in the morning air.

"What do you mean?"

Rose's expression was shuttered off, her thoughts deeply inward. "Keystone's a great place. At least it can be. But sometimes, the cost is too high." She blinked, shook her head, and smiled, the light returning to her eyes. "Never mind, dear."

Ella shrugged off the strange comment. The inhabitants of Keystone seemed too quirky to judge through her normal lens.

After Rose's comment about Lou, Ella decided she had enough time to chow down a second apple cinnamon roll. As she bit into the gooey goodness, the kitchen door swung open, and Jimmy strolled in. He kissed his wife on the cheek before greeting Ella.

"Get your car fixed yet?"

"Nope. Lou says it'll be another couple days. I don't understand why he can't just get the part shipped from Salem." When Ella saw the look of dismay on the innkeeper's face, she added, "I'll miss you too."

Rose elbowed her husband.

"Don't get me wrong," he amended. "It's been nice having you, but it'd be best if you left."

"Well, with any luck, I'll be leaving this afternoon." Ella couldn't hide the tinge of anger in her voice. So far, Rose was the only person she met *not* trying to kick her out of town.

Jimmy's face filled with relief.

"Did you get the sink fixed?" Rose asked him.

"Yep. Half-hour ago. I was in the conservatory. Wanted to make sure that seal around the glass wasn't leaking."

"Wait," Ella cut in. "There's a conservatory here?"

Rose's eyes shone. "Yes. In the north wing."

"You get there through the library," Jimmy added. He plucked a bacon strip from the pan, earning a playful smack from his wife.

Ella remembered the library but not a conservatory. Visions of reading a book in a room made of glass, surrounded by plants and snow outside, almost made her wish she didn't have to leave so soon.

After she'd stuffed the last bite of her third apple cinnamon roll into her mouth, Ella decided to grab a quick shower. She gathered her toiletries and a change of clothes, then she stepped into one of the upstairs bathrooms.

"Oh, that won't do."

A clawfoot tub sat next to the wall, sans shower head. It was cute and would be great if she wanted a relaxing soak, but it wouldn't work for a quick wash.

After a word with Rose, Ella discovered to her horror that *none* of the bathrooms had showers. In the end, she settled on a military shower a la wet wipes, dry shampoo, and a spritz of body spray. She set the spray aside, walked towards the door, then changed her mind and added a few more spritzes. Who knew what fresh odors she would encounter today?

As she was girding herself in her winter jacket at the front door, a clicking sound echoed over the hardwood floor behind her. She turned to see Fluffy padding towards her.

"Hey, buddy." Crouching, Ella scratched behind his ears. "I gotta go see a guy about a car."

He batted her hand away and sat on his fluffy haunches. She let out a sigh. He was as temperamental as her last boyfriend.

Outside, the cool air bit her cheeks and hurt her lungs. Two steps later, she heard a meow behind her.

Fluffy was two paws into the snow, crying at her with a look of betrayal. His green and hazel flecked eyes searched the snow. Sniffing it once, he hissed and backtracked.

"Hey, no one told you to follow me. You did that to yourself," she said, tugging her zipper up to her chin. She didn't blame him. She wanted to hiss at the weather too.

After depositing him back inside, she closed the door. He watched her with hard eyes through a pane of glass. She wiggled her fingers, only slightly taunting him, before hopping off the stoop.

Ella made her way gingerly down the icy sidewalk of Main Street, leaning into the wind, and arrived at the mechanic's shop in three minutes.

The garage door was already open, so she stepped into the shelter of the building. It wasn't exactly warmer so much as less cold.

Her voice echoed over the smooth floor and walls as she called, "Hello?"

No answer. She called again, weaving between cars on ramps. Her Jeep was in the back, elevated in the air on a hydraulic car lift.

Something about the scene jarred her, like stepping into an operating room with a patient's innards laid bare.

She turned away from the vehicle and spent the next several minutes searching the building in case she'd overlooked an office or a back room hiding the mechanic.

Grease and the smell of stale beer permeated the air. It had been a good call to douse herself in perfume before leaving.

When she could no longer feel her fingers, Ella gave up and drifted back to Main Street. At least she had a good excuse if she ran into the sheriff. And as anxious as she was to get home and put Kay's death behind her, she wasn't looking forward to parting with her SUV.

When she reached Keystone Inn, she glanced at the railcar diner beside it. The windows of Grandma's Kitchen were like dark, lifeless eyes staring back at her.

Hopefully, the diner wouldn't have to remain closed much longer. It seemed a shame to deprive the public of the pleasure of a Belly Buster.

Thinking of the diner made her think of Will. The poor guy was probably still stuck in that musty cell. She didn't think he had anything to do with Kay's death, but if there was one thing she'd learned over the years, it was that people were complicated and full of secrets.

Inside the mansion, the apple cinnamon aroma still clung to the air. She smiled as a thought occurred to her. It wasn't much—just a small gesture—but it would be something, and small somethings could mean the world to another person.

After trekking to the kitchen, she grabbed a couple more apple cinnamon rolls and wrapped them in a cloth napkin. She stuffed them inside her jacket and retraced her steps through the front garden. Her breath puffed out in small clouds in front of her as she turned right on Main Street and marched until she could see the sheriff's office a block away.

She was just passing the library next door when she caught movement behind the sheriff's glass and the silhouette of a tall man with a derby hat.

Ella about-faced faster than a sneeze and ducked into an alley—the same alley Six had pulled her into the night before. She could almost smell his hay and tobacco scent now.

She peered around the edge of the brick building,

momentarily distracted by the rows of books in the library window, and studied the sheriff's office. If Sheriff Chapman was inside, she didn't want to waltz in there without having worked out a deal with Lou yet.

Outside, an Appaloosa horse stood reined to an honest-to-goodness hitching post. The beautiful beast's doleful eyes blinked her way, its tail swishing. Ella quickly got over her shock at seeing the equine transportation and stamped her feet for warmth as she waited.

Several minutes later, when she could no longer feel her toes, it was clear the sheriff was in no rush to leave.

Another idea began to form. It wasn't a great one—probably in her top ten worst, right behind perming her bangs, but it would get Chapman out of the office.

Ella stole up the sidewalk and sidled up to the horse, putting it between her and the window. It eyed her warily.

She patted the horse blanket over its back in what she hoped was a comforting gesture. Her experience with horses didn't extend beyond a couple pony rides growing up.

After slipping off her gloves, she worked the knot out of the reins. What should've been an easy task was made far too difficult with popsicle fingers.

Finally, the leather ends fell away. Ella rested them on the saddle horn and patted near the horse's backside.

It didn't move.

She checked to see if the sheriff was still at his desk then stood back, staring at the horse while scratching her own chin.

"Go. Shoo." She nudged the horse. A back hoof stamped the ground in annoyance.

Ella searched her memory, recalling old western movies. She shook the reins and gave a good tap to the horse's side. It neighed in protest and took off at a trot.

She paused in admiration at the picture of the animal prancing down a snow-covered street of old shops and street lamps before she hightailed it back to the alley.

She had just reached cover when she heard the sound of a door being thrown open. Sheriff Chapman stomped through the snow in a series of growls and obscenities as he ran after the horse.

She waited a few breaths then poked her head out. Several blocks away, the Appaloosa slipped through the yard of a white church. Chapman jogged towards it, slipping and sliding in the snow, calling and cursing it in the same sentence. Both horse and sheriff disappeared around the side of the building.

Ella slipped out of her hiding spot and stole towards the still open office door. Her conscious threatened to surface, but she figured both horse and owner could use the exercise.

She flew into the office and shut the door. Snow fell from her boots and spilled onto the mat as she rubbed her arms in an attempt to return sensation to her extremities.

In the farthest cell, a mound of blankets that was Will lay on the cot, his back to her. Ella tapped on the bars and called his name.

He rolled over, peeling an eye open. When it focused on her, he shot up. "Ella?"

Maybe it was just the heat finally making its way into her skin, but her cheeks and ears began to burn. Why was she risking the wrath of the sheriff for a stranger?

"I see you decided to stay another day," she teased.

"Well, with comforts such as these, who can say no?" He gestured from the moth-eaten blankets to a plate topped with unidentifiable food that reminded her of something she'd once pulled from a clogged drain.

"Oh, so you probably wouldn't want this?" She dug

into her jacket pocket and unwrapped the apple cinnamon rolls. She shrugged. "More for me."

Will flew from the cot and snatched the treat from her hand so quickly she could swear it broke the laws of physics.

Her eyebrows rose. "Er, it was soft and warm when I left the inn, but I had to wait for Chapman to leave, sorry."

As he shoved the frosted pastry into his mouth, his eyes grew to the size of plates. "Are these Grandma Wink's cinnamon rolls?"

"Apparently." She watched him tear off another large chunk and stuff it into his mouth, his eyes closing.

"Ah, you're a peach," he said.

"A peach? Okay, grandpa."

His eyes widened. "Don't they say that where you're from?"

"Nope." She laughed when she noticed his ears turning pink. Then his expression suddenly turned serious.

"What are you still doing here? If the sheriff finds out you haven't left yet—"

"I'm working on it. It's not like I can get an Uber here."

His mouth turned down slightly at the corners.

"Any more on…" Ella paused, unsure of how to phrase the delicate question. "Do they know what happened to Kayline yet?"

Will's expression fell as he sank to the cot. "The coroner called a few minutes ago. From this end of the conversation, it sounds like Kay's death wasn't an accident. That's where Chapman was heading when he left here. To hear what else Pauline had to say."

Ella rested her forehead against the bars, noting the whispers of dark circles under his eyes. "I'm so sorry, Will. That's terrible. Do you know—wait." She pulled her head away. "Did you say the sheriff was leaving? As in, he was already walking out the door?"

"Already?"

She inwardly groaned. The whole debacle of untying the horse for a diversion had been unnecessary. "Never mind. So, why did Pauline think Kay's death wasn't an accident? Does that mean she's ruled out an allergic reaction?"

"I don't know. Maybe it was, but Pauline has reason to think it was intentionally caused. And with me giving Kay a present right before her passing..." his voice trailed off, and he and chewed quietly, lost in thought.

"I had a thought," she said softly, unsure if he was listening. "I'm not a doctor, but I'm pretty sure when someone goes into anaphylactic shock, there's more swelling, choking, or something."

Without looking up, he said, "Hmm, but she did have a rash, and she vomited."

"But she had the rash *before* you gave her the device."

"How do you know that?"

"I saw it."

He finally looked up and met her gaze. His features arranged into—not hope, but hope adjacent.

Ella couldn't explain all the symptoms yet, but the more she mulled it over, the more it didn't make sense. The vomiting. The delirium.

One word surfaced as an answer, but first, she wanted to rule out the possibility Kay's symptoms didn't align with that of an allergic reaction.

Will folded the inn's cloth napkin up, eyes squinting, and she could almost see the gears turning behind his bright blue-green eyes. "Maybe she was exposed to the allergen before today." As he slid the napkin between the bars, his fingers brushed hers. "That would make sense."

Ella still wasn't sure Kay's death was the result of anaphylaxis, but instead said, "So, how does one even go about finding that out?"

"Blood work would probably confirm that. Elevated histamine levels and such. That's probably what Pauline told Chapman over the phone. Look—" his eyes darted to the front door "—I appreciate you coming by, but you need to get out of here before he comes back." A rare smile graced his face. "Thanks for breakfast. And the visit."

"Yeah, sure. I'm a great conversationalist."

"Well, I wouldn't take you to a party or anything."

She let out a hollow laugh. "Stay out of trouble. Oh... wait." She rapped the bars with her knuckles. He laughed.

She lingered a moment, wondering why she felt so invested in a stranger, then turned to leave. When her hand closed around the brass doorknob, he called her name. She turned to see his eyes fixed on her.

"Ella, promise me, if you get a chance to leave, you'll take it. Leave Keystone and don't turn back."

His words were so similar to Jimmy's but lacked the tone of dismay. He was warning her, and it sent a chill up her spine.

Maybe she'd misunderstood Jimmy too. Had he also been warning her? But why? What was so dangerous about Keystone that she needed to leave as soon as possible?

Ella dipped her chin in a small nod then tugged the door open and stepped out into the cold.

CHAPTER 7

THE SNOW HAD stopped falling, leaving a gray sky over a white world. Ella checked Lou's shop, but he still wasn't there.

After her conversation with Will, she needed to clear her head. She wanted to make the loop around the lake but wasn't sure where the sheriff and his steed had wandered off to, so she ambled south of town towards the park, stopping at the inn long enough to make a ham and cheese sandwich, wrap it in wax, and stuff it into her pocket.

Her head down to stave off the icy wind, she turned left towards the diner and park. Ella passed a horse tethered to a hitching post outside Grandma's Kitchen, a post she'd failed to notice the day before.

She stopped.

She backtracked and looked up into the same beautiful brown eyes of the sheriff's Appaloosa. It blinked at her with indignation and took wariness.

Ella bent, ready to speed walk away, but a deep voice

stopped her.

"I thought I told you to leave Keystone."

Her heart dropped, and she whirled around. She hadn't even heard the diner door open.

Sheriff Chapman's eyes bored holes into hers, and his mustache turned down at a such an angle it was in danger of becoming a goatee. She didn't have to know him well or long to know he wasn't happy with her.

"I was. I tried. I stopped by Lou's shop, but he wasn't there."

His eyes narrowed, but his mustache was looking less like a goatee. "Hmm. Probably not awake yet."

Ella frowned and glanced at her watch, noting that it was nearing noon. Her job as a T.A. was becoming less appealing, and she began to consider a hungover mechanic as a promising career.

The sheriff strode past her and untied the horse's reins. She made note of how he did it in case she ever needed another diversion.

With a grace belying his age, he hoisted himself up and over the black and white spotted horse then adjusted the reins.

"Just like Clint Eastwood," she muttered.

"Pardon?"

"Nothing."

"Look, Miss Barton, my plate's full right now, but if you don't see that roostered mechanic by one-thirty, come find me. I'll go to his slop of a house if I have to and wake him."

She nodded and shifted her weight from one boot to the other, deciding that it couldn't hurt to pry him for information. "Do you know what killed Kay, yet?"

His head tilted low, shielding his eyes from her with the brim of his derby hat. "Got some theories. But that's not something I aim to share with a suspect."

Ella's throat constricted. She was still a suspect?

She wasn't sure, but she could swear she saw his cheek twitch with a smile. He tugged the brim of his hat in farewell then trotted off.

"Hey!" she called after him, "Can you say, 'Go ahead, make my day'?"

He ignored her.

Yeah, definitely Clint Eastwood.

The horse's hooves left deep, horseshoe-shaped prints in the snow. The cold began to permeate her jacket, forcing her to move for warmth.

Ella continued her brisk walk to the park and turned the events of the last couple of days over and over in her mind while she nibbled on half of her sandwich. The way Kay had hallucinated. Her vomiting. The device.

What was it that Will had given her? She made a mental note to ask him—if she saw him again before she left town.

And that rash. Kay had mentioned it was from poison oak. But what if it wasn't?

Ella brushed crumbs off the front of her jacket and reminded herself that this wasn't her job. The sheriff would get to the bottom of what had happened. Sure, she was involved in that she'd been there when Kay had died, but this wasn't her profession.

And if anything was best left to professionals, it was death. Or murder.

Also, probably haircuts.

She winced remembering an incident that involved wine, scissors, and a couple of friends who thought she'd look great with short hair and wouldn't it be cute if there were also layers? It wasn't.

As she picked up her pace, her thighs began to burn

from disuse. It was only the beginning of winter in the Pacific Northwest, and, already, she looked forward to spring when she could go on long, *dry* walks.

Winters in the valley were a nearly endless succession of dark, dreary days full of rain. It was normal to go months without seeing the sun—great for catching up on reading. Bad for getting a tan. It led to a well-read, vitamin D deficient populace.

When the buildings on Main Street stopped, the street continued straight, but the sidewalk bent towards the lake. Ella's boots crunched over the sidewalk, and she was careful not to slip on any patches of ice. She was so focused on the ground, she didn't realize she'd reached the heart of the park.

Her breath came out in wisps like a dragon as she paused to admire the sweeping vista. Her jacket proved too efficient, and the heat trapped inside from her exertion felt like a furnace.

She found a picnic table a few yards away. Swiping four inches of snow off with her gloves, she sat on her jacket and pulled out the other half of her sandwich. The cold quickly sapped away the heat, but she didn't plan on staying too long.

Her eyes drifted from the water to the trees then to the fields behind her. She gasped. The trees. *That's* what had been bugging her.

She gaped at a nearby maple. Snow clung to its branches and *leaves*. It was the last week in November, and there were still leaves on the trees.

Ella swiveled around, her sandwich forgotten. Oak trees. Maple trees. Even a big Willow. All of them still had their foliage. How was that possible? Had Fall skipped Keystone Village?

From her right, a blur of gray fur and polka dots shot

past her face so close a breeze fluttered her cheek. The blur snatched her sandwich from her hand.

"What the—"

"Chester!" A woman with bright blue hair cut into a short bob and wearing a hot pink tracksuit ran across the snow. "Chester, no! Bad squirrel!"

Ella stared at the woman chasing a squirrel in a black-and-white polka-dot dress, her sandwich clutched between its two paws. The gray-furred rodent stopped at the edge of the water and tore into the rest of her meal. Its cheeks bulged with each bite, crumbs scattering over ripples of ruffles and lace.

After the shock wore off, Ella sprang up from her bench and sprinted towards what remained of her meal. Chester froze mid-chew and turned a beady eye on her, crust dangling from its grip.

Ella slowed and crept sideways, flanking it. It turned sharply and chittered at her. She rolled her shoulders back.

"Are you scolding me?" She turned to the blue-haired woman. "Is it scolding me?"

"Bad boy!" The woman stopped a couple of yards from Ella and bent over her knees, gasping for air.

Boy?

Ella's gaze roamed over the frilly dress, noticing it had bows, and shrugged.

The rodent let out a long string of noises. She didn't speak squirrel but interpreted them as obscenities and something about her mother.

"Oh yeah? Well, your mother lives in a tree!" Ella whispered out of the side of her mouth at the woman. "Right? Squirrels live in trees?"

Chester turned his back on them and flicked his tail, which Ella assumed was the squirrel equivalent of the middle finger.

The woman straightened, no longer sounding like a bad muffler and in danger of passing out. Up close, she was at least thirty years older than Ella had pegged her for. And despite her puffing for air, she appeared in relatively decent shape.

"I'm sorry about that. Chester's been in a foul mood. Lady problems."

"Sure, sure." Ella scratched her chin and nodded as if a squirrel's love life was a topic she was familiar with. "The dress might have something to do with it."

She looked back and forth between the two, not sure what to make of the pair. "I wasn't that hungry, anyway, and was just thinking I'd like to give the rest of my sandwich to a squirrel in a dress."

The woman's eyes twinkled. "Problem solved, then."

Chester eyed Ella, the last of the crust disappearing into his mouth.

"He's taunting me, isn't he?"

"Yes, I believe so."

Ella flipped him the bird. "I got to ask, what's with the dress?"

She shrugged. "I let him pick out his outfit today."

"Fair enough."

"I sewed it myself." A hint of pride touched her voice.

"It's very… pretty." Ruffles and lace weren't Ella's thing, but she could admire the work put into making such an outfit.

The woman cocked her blue head to the side. "You're new here."

Ella came to the conclusion that either she had a sign over her head letting everyone know she was from out of town or that the population of Keystone was small enough she stood out. She glanced overhead to be sure it was the latter.

She stuck out her hand and shook it with the elder woman. "Ella Barton."

"Pearl Winkel. But everyone calls me Grandma Wink or just Wink."

"Ah, so you're Grandma Wink."

"Heard of me already, have you? My name gets around more than I do." She laughed when she caught Ella's expression. "I'm kidding."

"And here I thought it was your name because you had some kind of twitch and winked a lot." After a moment, Ella patted her stomach. "I'll have you know, you're the reason I need to walk off all of these extra calories."

Grandma Wink smiled. "You only live once, my dear."

The conversation shifted as she asked the usual questions, and Ella explained how she became stranded a couple days before and would be trading her car in for one of Lou's if she could ever find him.

Wink's eyebrows pinched together, and she seemed to rummage through her memory. "Ella... Ella... You were in my diner yesterday, weren't you?"

Ella's gaze fell to her scuffed boots. "Yes, it was terrible. I tried to help, but I couldn't. It was too late—" Her hand flew to her forehead. "Oh my gosh! I forgot to pay for my meal."

Wink flipped her hand through the air. "Don't worry about it. Please. I'm just grateful you did what you could to save Kay." Her voice broke, and her eyes glistened.

Ella realized her oversight and felt like an even bigger jerk than someone who'd skipped out on their bill. Kay had been Wink's employee. "I'm so sorry for your loss."

Grandma Wink watched Chester and blinked away the moisture. "Kayline was a good person. So full of potential.

So full of fear." Her voice broke slightly.

"Fear? What was she afraid of?"

Wink's eyes darkened, and she whispered, "A life she couldn't escape." She sighed and shook her head. "That's the most important lesson life can teach you, Ella: live without fear. No matter where you go, what you do, do it despite fear. Live fearlessly. Love recklessly, because it can all be gone in a moment.

"Kay's was a life snuffed out too soon. A story that was yet to be written. Gone forever." A tear escaped and slid down her face.

For the second time in as many days, Ella reached out and comforted a stranger. After they had stood quietly for a while in the cold, she asked gently, "Do you know when you'll be able to open the diner up again?"

"Oh, I don't know. To be honest, I'm happy for the break. Gives me more time for my hobbies." She pointed towards Twin Hills. "See that left hill? My house is near the top. I hang glide when the weather's right."

Ella searched the hill, spotting two dots near the crest. "Which one's yours?"

"The one on the left. The house on the right is the professor's."

"Hang gliding, huh?" Ella pictured flying over the beautiful town, the wind blowing through her hair, the ground so far beneath her. So very far. Too far. She shifted in her boots, smashing the snow underneath, and suddenly felt an affinity for the ground.

"I took it up to conquer my fear of heights. Live fearlessly, remember?" She smiled at Ella.

"I don't know. If I jumped off one of those small mountains strapped to nothing but steel and fabric, I'd have to wear a diaper."

"I wear diapers."

Ella sucked in a breath. "I'm sorry—"

Wink burst out laughing. "I'm just pulling your leg."

Ella laughed, growing fonder of her new, blue-haired friend by the minute.

"Lou?"

The scent of stale liquor stung Ella's nostrils, making her grateful the shop door was open despite the frigid temperature. From somewhere in the bowels of the shop, there was a loud bang followed by an even louder string of profanities.

Ella picked her way towards the noise, finding stout legs and a wide belly sticking out from under an antique car that looked like it belonged to a gangster in a black and white movie.

"Lou," she repeated, afraid she'd scare the mechanic.

"Huh? Who's there?" Lou wheeled across the floor. His eyes were bloodshot, and his coveralls reeked like they'd been marinating in a keg of beer.

"It's me. Ella." He struggled to focus on her, so she bent closer and tried not to breathe. She repeated her name, slowly, as if speaking to a toddler. "Remember me?"

"Didn't you get my message? Your car won't be ready for another day, at least." Gone was the toothy smile. She wondered if it was the hangover or if he was just having a bad day.

"Yeah, sorry. I got your message, but the sheriff wants me gone sooner."

He waved a socket wrench in the air. "Look, I can't work miracles."

Ella bit back a sharp response and instead asked, "Everything okay?"

"Fine." He disappeared under the car again. "Just

don't get your panties in a twist, alright? I got the sheriff breathin' down my neck enough as it is."

So that was what was bothering him. The sheriff had obviously stopped by.

"If it makes you feel better, he's breathing down my neck, too." She fidgeted with the hem of her jacket and took a deep breath. "Do you know anyone who'd be willing to make a trade for my car?"

She heard his wrench stop, and he slowly slid back out. "Really?"

She didn't like the way his eyes glinted. "I don't *want* to, but I don't have much of a choice."

Lou's lips curled up. "Well, why didn't you say so." He rolled over onto his knees and staggered to his feet. Ella's hand shot out in case he needed it for balance.

Waddling out of the garage, he gestured for her to follow. They walked around the shop to a large, fenced-in lot full of used cars in various states of disrepair. She eyed the chipped paint and rusted hubcaps of the nearest one. "Do any of these run?"

He puffed out his chest. "Lady, you insult me. I've fixed up all these here myself. They have the Lou guarantee." He hiccuped.

Ella narrowed her eyes and murmured, "Uh-huh."

With a loud sigh, she trudged to the nearest one. As she touched the side-view mirror to brush off snow, it fell to the ground.

Lou scratched the deep shadow of scruff along his jaw. "This shift in weather's been hard on the cars."

"Uh-huh," she repeated. The car was as dubious as the mechanic. Her eyes lit up. "Hey, you wouldn't happen to have a light colored Volkswagen Beetle, would you? Maybe with some racing stripes and the number fifty-three painted on it?"

He blinked at her. "Huh?"

"You know, Herbie the Love Bug? Beloved sentient car?"

"What are you on about?"

"Nothing. It's not important." She stared at the bland, non-anthropomorphic car in front of her, trying to hide her disappointment. "Do you have anything newer than this?"

"No, ma'am." He teetered forward and clung to the fence for support, a belch rumbling his chest.

Ella cursed under her breath and turned her nose from the onslaught. "Can I at least get one with both mirrors?"

"Probably."

She caught her lip between her teeth, not liking the non-committal response. "I'll have to think about it some more."

"Sure thing. Just don't let the sheriff see you still here."

Ella slid her eyes over the lot, her heart sinking. There wasn't much to think over, she knew. This was her only option, but she clung to a sliver of hope Lou could work miracles and her Jeep would be ready.

The mechanic toppled over, sending clouds of snow into the air. Another belch broke from the ground.

CHAPTER 8

ELLA LEFT THE shop in low spirits, the drifting thick snowflakes matching her mood. Her thoughts tumbled over each other, trying to come up with some other solution.

A cab. She would just use the inn's phone, call a cab, and eat the cost. Once her car was fixed, she'd have a friend drive her back to Keystone to pick it up. Her heart lifted a little with this new plan.

As she turned onto Main Street, she paused. A few souls had braved the weather, darting in and out of storefronts. Down the street on her left, shadows moved inside the sheriff's office. She averted her gaze, afraid that just staring at the building would somehow summon Sheriff Chapman.

Next-door to the station, someone stepped out of the Keystone Library. Ella straightened, her thoughts turning from the sheriff and calling a cab. It occurred to her that she could get some of her questions answered about Kayline's symptoms from a book since her cell phone was still out of commission.

Ella waited for a car to pass then tromped across the street and entered the two-story brick building.

Rows and rows of leather-bound volumes and hardback books stretched the length of the building, pulling her in with their scent. She'd never seen heaven before, but she was pretty sure this was it.

Her fingertips danced over the spines as she walked the aisles. By the third row, she realized that the library's collection was outdated by several decades, which surprised her since most of the books seemed to be in great condition.

Ella scanned the section signs, hoping they'd give her a hint as to where she'd find the book she needed. After searching for several minutes, she caved and wandered over to the reference desk. A stout woman with horned-rim glasses looked up from her Steinbeck novel.

"Can I help you?"

"Um, yes." Ella tugged off her gloves. "I was wondering where your medical books were?"

The librarian arched an eyebrow. "Like first aid or survival?"

"Er, no. Something more along the lines of allergies." As an afterthought, she added, "Maybe something that lists side effects of specific medications or interactions."

The woman's lips tightened into a thin line. "You must be new here."

Ella's stomach dropped to her boots. This was a small town. If word got back to Sheriff Chapman that she'd been asking for books about allergic reactions and drug interactions, it would be perceived as suspicious. He'd probably throw her right back in that stinky jail cell.

Her brain scrambled to come up with a plausible explanation. "It's just, I'm a grad student, researching adverse medical reactions and negligence in the medical community." Ella bit her bottom lip to stop the lie from sounding worse.

"Grad student, huh?" The woman peered down her nose at Ella, inspecting her. "Then I was right. You are a visitor."

"Yes." Ella clenched her jaw. Why was everyone so hung up on that?

"Well, we have books on medication administration and pharmacology. Aisle six."

Ella thanked her and wandered until she found the correct section. The pharmacology books were lumped together with the medical administration ones, near the biology section.

First, she slid out *The Merck Manual*, the edition so old her grandmother had probably used a similar one in her nursing days. Next, she grabbed all of the pharmacology ones she could—a total of three—and grabbed a few of the medical administration ones for good measure.

Her biceps ached by the time she found an empty table. Plopping down her stack of books, she settled into a chair and cracked open the medical information book. The scent of aged paper and dust rose from the pages. Ella pulled the banker's lamp on the table closer and searched the index for "allergy" or "allergic reactions," as well as "anaphylactic reactions."

As she suspected, the only symptom that aligned with high histamine levels was the rash. Kay had shown no accompanying swelling, a struggle for breath, or even seizures in the case of an anaphylactic reaction. Nothing to explain the vomiting or the appearance of delirium.

On a whim, Ella searched out the section on poison oak and found an accompanying picture of a rash. Best she could tell from the black-and-white photo, it appeared similar to the waitress's rash.

With a sigh, she rubbed her forehead then pored over one of the pharmacology books—also outdated by several decades. After reading through all the statins, beta-blockers, and ace inhibitors in the first book, she pushed it aside and began reading through the next book. Again and again. None of them had the side effects Kay had exhibited.

Ella's eyelids drooped, and her attention wandered as the light waned through the windows, growing the shadows on the hardwood floor. Without knowing more about Kay—if she was even taking medication for anything—it was pointless to search through mounds of books, guessing what could've caused her death.

She closed the book in front of her and gathered the others. What was she doing? She should let the professionals handle this, and she should be working on either getting out of town or on her thesis.

Yet, a knot in her gut formed and remained. The sheriff seemed fixated on Will being guilty, and she didn't know anyone else trying to help him.

Hunger gnawed at her, and she glanced at her watch. It was nearly dinner time. As Ella jumped to her feet, her chair fell back. The librarian shot her a look.

Ella mumbled her apologies as she relocated the chair to its position behind the table. After replacing the stack of books, she thanked the surly librarian and headed back to the inn.

The temperature jumped as she stepped into the mansion. After shaking the snow off her coat, she hung it on the coat tree just inside the door then kicked off her wet boots.

"Lucy, I'm home," she called to the empty entrance hall.

Firelight flickered on the parlor door. She longed to warm up by the flames, but the smell of food and laughter from the kitchen tugged her down a different hallway.

As she swung the kitchen door inward, there was a loud crash. Ella started, frantically searching for the source of the noise.

"Get that varmint out of here!" Jimmy stood in the middle of the kitchen, his feet wide and his hands curled into tight fists.

Chester sat on top of the cabinets, near the ceiling, his bushy tail twitching behind an elegant tuxedo complete with bow tie. Apparently, he'd had a change of heart about the dress.

"It was an accident!" Grandma Wink snatched a dishrag from the sink and scooped up bits of a pecan pie from the floor.

"It's okay, Wink. I'll get a mop." Rose gave Chester a wide berth and squeezed past Ella through the doorway.

From somewhere near Ella's feet came a loud hissing sound. She jumped back, jamming her elbow into a cabinet. Pain shot up her arm as Fluffy bounded forward, spewing at Chester high above.

Ella dropped beside Wink and helped collect bits of pie. "Well, from what I can tell—" she held up a chunk of filling "—it looked delicious."

"Thanks, dear. It was."

"Would it be gross if I still tried a bite?" She dropped the bit of pie after catching Wink's mortified expression. "Yeah, no, it'd be gross. I know."

Wink looked at her sideways.

"But would you judge me?"

Wink grabbed the garbage can.

"Yeah, me too," Ella continued.

When Grandma Wink turned her back, Ella picked up

a bit of pie crust, mushy side up, and began to bring it to her mouth just as Rose came sweeping back in.

"Ella, no!"

Wink turned. "Oh for heaven's sake. I'll make you one if you're that hungry."

Ella let out a hollow laugh. "Seriously, I was kidding."

Wink shot her a stern expression, pointing at the bin. Ella dropped her head and reluctantly deposited the dessert into the can before continuing to clean. She, Wink, and Jimmy gathered the largest pieces while Rose worked the mop, Grandma Wink's eyes on a constant swivel in Ella's direction the entire time.

After the floor had a nice, glossy sheen to it, Wink tried to coax Chester from his perch.

Jimmy resumed his rampage, his face a violent purple. "I told you not to bring that critter around here, Wink."

"I can't leave him at home by himself. He gets lonely."

"Lonely? Squirrels don't get lonely! And what on earth is he wearing?"

Grandma Wink brushed a lock of blue hair away from her face. "I think he looks dashing."

"He looks like an undertaker," came a creaking voice from the table. Ella jumped and turned to see Crazy Flo by the window.

"What the—how long have you been there?"

"Long enough to see you try to eat pie from the floor."

"Did not." Ella stuck out her chin but didn't meet Flo's gaze.

Putting her hands on her bony hips, Wink said, "He does not look like an undertaker. He dresses better than any of your ex-husbands ever did."

Flo raised a glass of what looked like iced tea, but from the smell wafting Ella's way told her a generous helping of something alcoholic had been added. "Can't argue with that. That includes the one who was an undertaker."

Wink's brows rose. "Oh, I forgot about him."

"Good Lord," Ella said, "how many times has she been married?"

Before either could answer, Rose interjected, "Look, the mess is all cleaned up. No harm done."

"Yeah, no harm," Jimmy muttered, his eyes resting on the garbage can, full of disappointment. Ella realized he wasn't mad about the commotion or sticky floor so much as the demolished pie.

Wink gave up on getting Chester down from the cabinets. "Why don't I just pop into the diner and grab another pie? They're going to waste in there, anyhow, since I'm still closed." Turning to leave, she caught Ella's eye. "And everyone keep Ella from eating off the floor, please," she hollered before slipping out.

Rose gathered the mop and bucket, her chiffon dress whipping around the room like a cloud.

"I don't want to intrude on your dinner," Ella said, feeling it the pertinent thing to say. The truth was, she did want to. These people were fun and warm, and she was starving. "I'll just grab something from the fridge—"

"Nonsense!" Rose sloshed the pie-water from the bucket down the sink. "There's plenty here."

"Less than there was before," Jimmy mumbled. As he sank into a chair, he shot a death glare at Chester who stared back, still high above on the cabinets. Fluffy had inched closer, tail swishing, eyes locked on his target.

Scraping a chair across the floor, Ella sat between Jimmy and Flo. Wink whisked back into the room, carrying another pie. She glanced at Chester, her face falling with relief as if she'd expected him to cause more trouble in her short absence.

Ella poured tea from the pitcher on the table into her

glass and sniffed it. "How come we aren't using the dining room?"

"Dining room's too formal," Grandma Wink responded. "This is a family meal."

Ella glanced around the table. "Should I get the other boarder? Edwin was it?"

Wink sat across from her and unfolded her napkin. "Oh, he usually doesn't join us for meals. If you hadn't noticed, he's the shy type." She cleared her throat and peered over her shoulder at the counter. "Where's this mold I've been hearing so much about, Rose?"

Rose, who had just set the bucket by the door, called from the open refrigerator door, "It's coming."

Ella's eyebrows pinched together, and she glanced sideways at Jimmy and mouthed the word, *mold?*

He leaned closer and dropped his voice. "They take turns. One does the meal, while the other does the dessert." His voice hitched higher when he glanced towards the fridge. "Tonight was my wife's turn for the main course."

He shuddered and gave a subtle shake of his head in warning about what was coming next. Ella gave him a weak smile, leaned forward, and grabbed her fork.

She was so hungry, she'd eat anything. Although, the word "mold" made her hesitate. Could it mean cheese? Had Rose prepared a cheese platter of some kind?

"Alright," Rose called in a sweet, sing-song voice, "ta-da!"

She laid a large tray in the center of the table. A massive, green blob wriggled on the platter like Slimer from the Ghostbusters.

Ella froze, Jimmy recoiled, and Flo swore loudly.

Ella couldn't make sense of the undulating mass in front of her. The green tower stilled, and she realized she was staring at gelatin.

Memories of grade school and snacks and bold flavors came to mind, followed by hospital food, then an unfortunate incident involving food poisoning. What was disconcerting were the chunks of *something* inside of Slimer.

The table had fallen completely silent.

Finally, Grandma Wink broke the spell, clapping her hands and saying, "I'm always game for a good gelatin mold." But Ella noticed the pallor of her skin. "What flavor?"

"Lemon-lime trout." Rose's ruby lips smiled with pride.

Ella's stomach lurched, and all appetite vanished.

Flo jabbed a fork at the mound. It wiggled to life again, and Jimmy flinched. "I thought we agreed. No more molds."

Grandma Wink shot her a look. "Well, I'm game." She handed her plate to Rose, who smiled like she'd won a prize.

Rose plopped a large glob onto the plate. As it passed by Ella, she caught a whiff of the trout mixed inside and quickly turned away, pretending to stare out the dark window.

"Ella?" Rose stared at her expectantly.

A wheezy noise escaped Ella's mouth as she held up her plate. Rose clasped onto the edge, but Ella couldn't quite let go of the other. They played tug-of-plate over the middle of the table.

"Ella, if you just—that's it." Rose came away with the plate, plopped a blob of green on top, and handed it back.

"Oh God," Ella breathed, watching it dance on her plate.

"Hey, you're spiritual too?" Flo elbowed her in the

ribs. "Rose and Jimmy go to church every Sunday."

"Do they now," Ella said absently. She poked at her food. "Is it alive?"

"Of course not," Rose scolded. "Don't be silly."

Ella poked again. "Right. Gotcha. But is it alive?"

Rose let out an exasperated sigh. "No. It's not alive."

Ella frowned picked at it with her fork, trying to separate the meat from the sweet treat. She liked trout. She liked gelatin. But like oil and water, they didn't combine well.

"I'm happy you're here, Ella," Rose said once everyone had been served up. "The table would've felt empty tonight." She glanced at Ella's spot, a sadness filling her eyes behind her glasses.

"How do you mean? Who else is usually here?" The instant the sentence left her mouth, she regretted it. Kay. She was who was missing. "I'm sorry. I didn't mean—"

"It's okay, dear," Grandma Wink said, holding up a hand. A glob of jello rolled off of her fork and splatted onto the table. "We weren't sure if we would have our usual get-together, but we figured we'd do this in Kayline's honor. And Will's, since he's unable to join us."

Jimmy lifted his glass of iced tea. "To Kayline."

All around the table, the sentiment was echoed, and the kitchen was filled with the clinking of glasses.

Grandma Wink dabbed a napkin over her mouth. "William will be back soon enough."

Jimmy moved a pile of green covered trout around his plate, trying to pick off the gelatin. "Hope so. Chapman's got him in his sights, though."

Ella took a long swig of tea, hoping it would dilute the flavor of lime trout. It didn't. She wondered if Flo could spike the drink for her. "Won't the sheriff release him when he doesn't have enough evidence?"

Jimmy sighed. "It doesn't quite work that way here. We don't have that luxury."

Ella was about to ask him what he meant when he asked her about her car. Now it was her turn to sigh.

"Lou says another day. Chapman wants me out of here yesterday. So, I'm going to call a cab once I've finished eating."

Jimmy dropped his fork and fumbled to retrieve it. "Sorry, our phones only make local calls."

"I'm sorry? What about at the diner?" She looked at Wink.

Wink picked at the green mush on her plate.

Jimmy answered for her. "Diner too. All Keystone Village phones."

Ella's mouth worked back and forth like a fish. "But how-what?"

"Best if you just traded your car in."

Ella was still reeling over the fact that none of the phones in the village made outside calls. She understood wanting to be off the grid, but that was taking it a bit far. And now, she'd have to trade her SUV in for one of Lou's lemons.

"What's the rush? Sheriff won't notice her." Flo took a long swig from her iced tea, unaware of the weighted stares around the table leveled at her. "He's too busy with Six." She finally looked up. "What?"

A pregnant silence followed. Ella leaned in, her gaze traveling the table. She wasn't being paranoid. They were hiding something.

Ella shifted the topic back to Kayline. "Even if he hadn't demanded it, I want to get out of here fast because Sheriff Chapman suspects I might have something to do with Kayline's death."

"Poppycock," Flo growled. The others bobbed their

heads in agreement, and some of the tension broke.

"Well, something killed her." Ella waited a breath then asked casually, "Do any of you know if she was taking medication for anything?"

Rose brought her tea to her mouth. "Not that I know of. Wink?"

Grandma Wink's blue hair whipped back and forth as she shook her head. Then, she reached into the breast pocket of her button-up shirt and pulled out a handful of peanuts.

Without a word, she held out her hand. Chester leaped from the top of the cabinets to the island and then to the outstretched nuts.

Fluffy dashed across the floor, his furry paws sliding across the smooth surface despite his claws. He froze under Wink's chair, his large green and hazel eyes fixed on the squirrel.

"Wink, please. That's so unsanitary." Rose got up from the table and gathered their empty plates. When she picked up Ella's, she said, "Ella, you hardly touched your food. Didn't you like it?"

"It was delicious, thank you. I'm just not that hungry." She hid behind her glass of iced tea, hoping the innkeeper wouldn't notice the flush in her face.

When Rose turned her back to drop the plates in the sink, Jimmy said in a low voice, "There's salami in the ice box."

She smiled gratefully at him.

"Save some for me," Flo grunted.

CHAPTER 9

ELLA SLIPPED HER beanie over her curly hair, the hat still damp from her previous outing. Every move she made was slow—sluggish with dread. Outside, her boots crunched over the snow and through puddles of light cast by the antique street lamps. Shadows diverged into the dark alleys and side streets, and she wondered if Six lurked in the darkness somewhere nearby.

She arrived at Lou's just as he was closing up his shop.

The words whooshed out of her before she could take them back. "Alright. I'll do it."

His beady eyes trained on her. "Stella?"

"Ella."

"Close enough." An unctuous smile she'd only ever seen on used car salesmen spread over his face. "Wise choice. Trust me, she may not be much to look at, but this car's a beast under the hood."

She didn't care about that. She just needed it to run and take her home, far from the eccentric, beautiful town full of death, shady cowboys, and thieving squirrels in dresses.

Lou's hand scratched at several days worth of stubble before moving to his belly. Then he snatched a rusty key from the collection on the wall and led her around back. With his sleeve, he swiped the driver-side door until he located the handle.

After several unsuccessful tugs, he mumbled, "Frozen shut."

Ella's mouth pinched into a thin line, and she eyed the surrounding cars, wondering if this really was the best option on the lot.

With one last pull, the door swung open with a groan that rent the quiet evening. He dangled the keys in front of her face. "Might want to let 'er run for a few minutes first. I'll pull the gate open for ya."

After a deep breath, she thanked him, albeit with a tinge of sarcasm.

As he waddled away, she slid into the seat. The scent of stale tobacco and curdled milk punched her in the face. Gritting her teeth, she turned the key, surprised when the engine roared to life. Maybe she was being too hard on the mechanic.

While the engine warmed, she ran inside and grabbed the luggage she'd left in her Jeep, giving her car a final tap on the hood.

Back outside, she brushed and scraped the windows of her new-old car with an ice scraper she'd found on the passenger seat. The scraper looked like it had seen better days and scraped almost as much glass as it did ice, but it de-iced enough for her to be able to navigate the snowy roads.

The circle around the vehicle complete, she checked the tires, and some of her determination faded. Snow tires they were not. Crude snow chains hugged them and looked like they'd been put on recently, which suggested Lou had been confident she'd return for the piece of junk.

Back in the car, Ella rubbed her gloved hands together to gather some friction then placed them in front of the vents spewing out lukewarm air. Her breath came out in small clouds, and for some reason, the sight made her shiver even more.

Ella searched for the positive. The engine hummed, even if there was a sputtering with it, and the seatbelt worked. So, there was that.

She put the car into drive and nosed the vehicle forward. First, she would stop at the inn to gather her things and say goodbye. Also, she needed to settle the bill for her room. Since she couldn't use an ATM—not that she'd seen any—a check would have to suffice. At least she happened to have a few left in her purse.

The two-door sedan crept over the snow. Her trust in the vehicle climbed with each passing yard.

As she slipped through the gate, Lou waved. Ella nodded back, not wanting to take her tight grip off of the steering wheel. The car chugged along, vibrating her whole seat like she was on a tractor. Or a massage chair. She added that to the column of positives.

When she turned onto Main Street, the engine sputtered like it had tuberculosis. Her grip on the wheel tightened, her fingers tingling.

Ella pleaded with the car. "No, don't do this to me." She should have named it. Vehicles usually treated her better once she named them.

Keeping one foot on the brake, she fed it gas. It roared to life, but as soon as she let off the gas, it chugged and the whole car shuddered.

Just got to keep moving.

She bounced along, clipping past other cars slower

than she would've liked considering they were parked. Most of them appeared to be classics, and most of them appeared to be drivable.

Ella's teeth chattered, half from the temperature, half from the tension. Ahead, Keystone Inn shined like a beacon. The warm glow from the windows spilled onto the garden, beckoning her on like the end of a finish line.

It occurred to her she'd have to park the car in order to gather her things, thus taking a chance it would die. She briefly toyed with the idea of letting it continue on at a snail's pace, run in and grab her stuff, then catch up to it, before dismissing the idea. Then she thought about it again as the car sputtered.

Just as she passed Sal's Barbershop, the engine coughed a final time then died.

"No, no, no." Ella rotated the key several times, but the engine never turned again. Apparently, the drive down L Street had been its swan song.

Her forehead hit the wheel in frustration and stayed there. Everyone had been pushing her to leave, wanted her out of Keystone Village, but it seemed no matter how hard she tried, the town just wouldn't let go of her.

"Stupid Lou. Stupid lemon." There would be no making lemonade out of this jalopy.

The mention of the mechanic's name brought Ella's emotions to the surface. Her frustration turned to anger— a rare emotion for her. She was always the level-headed, positive person in her circle of friends and family. But that greasy mechanic became her breaking point. Lou had traded her a piece of junk that hadn't gone more than three blocks.

Ella kicked the door open and didn't bother closing it. Her boots stomped through the snow as she retraced the defunct car's tracks.

He was about to get the mother of all tongue lashings. Maybe she'd throw in a few finger wags for good measure. She wasn't sure. She'd wing it.

But one way or another, Ella would leave Keystone with a working vehicle, even if she had to steal Lou's tow truck.

Her hands curled into tight fists as she made a bee-line for his shop. She was so focused on her destination, she missed seeing the figure sprinting towards her in the dark.

"Ella!"

She whirled around, fearing Six was chasing her. Will's tall silhouette jogged towards her.

Ella stopped short, and some of her frustration dissipated. "Will? How did you…"

"Get out of jail?"

A nearby lamp caught an infectious smile from under his fedora as he came up alongside her. They stood in the middle of the street as miniature flakes fell around them.

"Chapman let me out. Pauline suspects some kind of accidental medication interaction, but she's sure it wasn't my device. And since the sheriff doesn't have any evidence…" He trailed off and shrugged.

"That's great! I mean, that he let you go, not about the whole medication interaction." Her smile faded. So, the coroner had come to the same suspicion. "Was Kayline on any medications?"

"Not that I know of. But we'd grown apart, and I knew she was dealing with depression. Pauline, who's also the town's physician, remember, wanted to try giving her medication for it but that was right before we broke up, so I'm not sure what ever came of it."

"Well, congratulations on being released. Wait, is that what you're supposed to say when someone gets out of jail?" She clicked her tongue against her teeth, remembering how she had felt when Chapman released her. She would've appreciated a congratulation. She nodded, satisfied. "Yeah, congrats."

He chuckled. "Thanks. And I'm not off the hook yet. Sheriff Chapman still thinks I had a motive to kill her, but he can't hold me on his suspicions."

"So, he still thinks it wasn't an accident?"

He shifted his weight on his feet. "The medication interaction is just one theory. Pauline hasn't ruled out poison yet."

Ella's brain began turning. Poison usually meant intention. Poison usually meant murder.

Will's gaze drifted over her head. "Did I interrupt you from something? You seemed like you were in a hurry."

His question drew her back to her current predicament, and her anger towards Lou returned with vigor. By way of explanation, she waved a wild hand at the broken down sedan sitting in the road.

"Yes. I was just on my way to make that slimy mechanic pay. Excuse me." She resumed her march.

Will caught up easily, matching her pace with his long strides. "He sold you *that* thing?"

"Not sold. Traded. And I definitely got the raw end of the deal. I made it a whole three blocks."

Will's snort quickly turned into a cough when she shot him an icy glare. The shop was dark, and all the doors were closed.

Ella banged on the entrance. "Lou, get out here! I know you're in there!"

When nothing happened, she yelled for him again and pressed her eyes to the glass window. Dust and cobwebs obstructed most of the view, but the shop appeared empty.

"Ella," Will called from the sidewalk. "He's not there."

"I *just* left here."

"He probably high-tailed it out as soon as you drove off."

"Where does he live?"

She could barely see his face in the dark, but it was hard to miss the surprise in Will's voice. "You want to visit him at his house?"

"Yes. If I don't leave town tonight, the sheriff will be furious, probably put me back in that cell. Although, I don't see how, seeing as how that's not legal. But then, he doesn't really seem to care about the law."

Will considered this a moment. "No, he cares about the law. He's just got a loose interpretation of it. Come on. I'll help you push your car out of the street."

"That *thing* is not my car," she muttered. Then, she realized how she sounded and closed her mouth.

Inside the sedan, fresh flakes coated the seat through the open door. After putting it in neutral, Will pushed it from behind while she walked alongside, pushing and reaching in through the window to steer.

Slowly, the vehicle ambled forward, and she aimed it for an empty spot along the road several yards ahead.

The quiet street was filled with the sounds of the chains on the tires crunching through snow. Ella searched for a topic of conversation.

"So, Mr. Whitehall," she said his name with an air of faux formality, "what is it that you do? I heard Jimmy and Rose talk about you fixing things around the inn. Are you the town handyman?"

"Most of the time, Miss Barton," he said, mimicking her tone. "But I was—*am* an inventor. I used to travel door-to-door selling my inventions and gadgets."

"A door-to-door salesman? Don't really see many of those anymore."

"No?"

She pulled the wheel counter-clockwise, guiding the car into the large, empty spot.

"Do you have an occupation?" He eased off the back of the sedan.

She chuckled. "Of course. A woman's got to eat, doesn't she? I'm a teaching assistant at the university. Doesn't pay much, but it helps offset my graduate expenses. I'm getting my masters in linguistics." She put the car in park, rolled the window back up, then closed the door.

"Fascinating."

She searched his expression for sarcasm, but his eyebrows were up in genuine interest. Usually, when she told people her profession, their eyes glazed over.

"And what can you do with that?" he asked.

"A few things, but English as a foreign language teacher is my goal. I love languages—love studying them and learning them. So, this just seemed the best fit. Plus, it would open doors for me to work overseas."

"Do you speak many languages?"

Ella opened her mouth to respond then froze. All around them, the sky was beginning to glow, like a reverse sunset, and getting brighter by the second.

Will whipped his head back. "Oh, no! Run!"

Ella stood rooted to the spot, trying to make sense of what she was seeing. Will pushed her and yelled at her again to run. He didn't let up until she was sprinting.

"What's going on?" she cried as they raced down Main Street. She slipped in the snow but managed to maintain her balance. "Where are we going?"

"You have to leave town *now*!" His hands pushed the small of her back, prodding her to run faster.

"What? Why?!"

Panic filled Ella. What was happening? Had there been

some kind of nuclear bomb? She hadn't heard an explosion.

Her thoughts raced out of focus like a bad camera lens. What about her stuff? And she still didn't have a vehicle. Where was she supposed to go on foot?

The sky now blazed like the day. Blue and purple electricity swirled and arced constantly, so close together, they covered the town like a dome.

Ella went from a fear she was going to die to a surety she was going to die to praying to every deity she could think of.

"Will! I don't understand. What's happening?" Her lungs burned, and her thighs ached.

"Hurry! Don't slow down!"

The last of the town buildings swept past, and still, they continued sprinting, heading in the direction from which she entered Keystone Village.

The bluish-purple electric wall bisected the whole horizon in front of her. A new surge of fear filled her when she realized that was where they were headed. Will wanted them to run *towards* the scary electric field.

A new sensation crawled over her skin. A tingling traced from her fingertips and toes, up her arms and legs. Every part of her wanted to turn and run the opposite direction, but she had to trust the fear in Will's voice, the strain on his face.

Ella felt like her lungs would burst, and her calves began to seize. She pushed through the pain, digging her boots hard into the snow. They were nearly at the edge of the flashing wall.

The electrical field built, turning white hot. The lines pulsed, grew, and coalesced, climaxing with a brilliant, blinding flash.

Ella let out a startled yell, her retinas blazing. She

squeezed her eyes shut, but the light still bled through her lids. She had never seen anything brighter, and all she could fixate on was that it was the end of the world and any minute she would die.

Ella braced for the impact from the shock wave, but it never came.

"You're too late," Will rasped behind her, his voice broken. "I'm so sorry, Ella."

Her eyes were still closed, but she could see the light fading. She peeled open one lid, then the other, and looked around. It was no longer night in Keystone Village. Waves of heat rushed towards her like an oven.

A hot sun crested the horizon, creating a fiery sunset. Or sunrise. Since it was in the wrong spot in the sky, she couldn't be sure if it was east or west. She couldn't be sure of anything.

Ella turned slowly, taking in a new landscape. All words left her. The dome of electricity was gone, replaced with an abrupt edge of snow and asphalt. The berm she'd crashed her car into had been replaced by a crest of sand.

She blinked. The highway, the forest, the mountains, all were gone. Large sand dunes stretched before her as far as she could see.

But they weren't just south. The tan slopes wrapped around the park, the large forest, and the base of Twin Hills. The hills blocked most of the northeast view, but she was sure the dunes continued on behind them.

Ella closed her eyes, counted to ten, then opened them again. When nothing changed, she pinched her arm, but that did nothing more than shoot pain over her skin.

She stood at the edge of a snowy town in the middle of a desert, and the wintery night had been replaced by a fiery sunset dipping behind the dunes.

"Will, what just happened?"

CHAPTER 10

"WHAT WAS THAT?" Ella tore her eyes away from the miles of sand and searched his face. "Am I having a nervous breakdown? This feels like one. Or some kind of delusion. Oh no. This is what happened to Kayline, isn't it?" Her breathing quickened.

"No, it's not a breakdown or delusion." The inventor's chest deflated. He searched the sky as if searching for words.

It took her asking him a third time before he answered her questions, and even then, the answers came slowly.

"You're trapped here. Just like the rest of us." His gaze slid from the melting snow at their feet and met hers. They were full of sadness and regret. "I'm so sorry, Ella."

"Trapped where?"

"In Keystone."

Ella looked from him to the dunes to the town behind him. "I'm sorry. I'm trapped?"

"Yes. In Keystone."

"Who is?"

"You are."

"Me? Trapped?"

"Yes."

"No."

"Yes."

"Huh."

Ella ran a hand through her hair, realized her hat was still on and pulled it off. She searched the sand behind her again.

"I have another question for you. Bit silly, really. But, um, where did the forest go? And the mountains? And the stars?" She pointed up in case it wasn't already clear which stars she meant.

His cheeks puffed out as he let out a slow breath. "It's kind of hard to explain."

"Sure, sure. But you should probably try. I'm keen on the answer and a very good listener, especially when I'm on the verge of losing it." Ella tried to keep her voice calm, tried to keep the rising panic from overtaking her.

What did he mean by *trapped*?

Will rubbed the back of his neck and turned around. Ella shuffled beside him, and they ambled towards the town.

The temperature was dropping as the sky grew darker, but it was at least thirty degrees warmer than it had been a few minutes before, causing a good breeze to blow. All around them, the snow shimmered like crystals as it began to melt.

"It began about ten years ago. No one knows for sure *why* it started, only that they know *when* it started. It was the middle of the day in a rural town in Colorado in 1951. A blinding flash of light—much like what you just witnessed—transported Keystone Village to 1932, a few miles outside of Boston.

"About four days later, I was traveling the road with one of my inventions and wandered into town. I thought I'd stay the night at the inn then get an early start the next day. Jimmy tried to get me to leave, but I wouldn't listen."

He shook his head. "I was a fool. When I awoke the next day, the town had *jumped*, or *flashed*, if you will, for the second time, and it was too late."

Ella's expression pinched with an onslaught of questions. "Are you telling me the town travels through time?"

"And space, yes."

"And you're from the 1930s?"

"Yes."

"No."

"Yes."

"N—"

"Ella." His tone brought her to a halt.

Running her fingers through her hair again, Ella didn't speak, trying to absorb everything. "This isn't possible. Towns don't just time travel. People don't time travel."

"Believe me, I know. It shouldn't be possible. I studied theoretical physics. I'm a scientist, and this doesn't make sense. I've pored over books and researched it for the past ten years, trying to understand. And I'm not the only one. Others are working the problem, too. But the bottom line is we are stuck."

While he'd been speaking, they had arrived back in town.

"Can't people just leave?"

"They can. But they're trapped in whatever location and whatever time we are currently in. Still, we've had many villagers choose to do this."

Ella felt dizzy. The ground swayed beneath her feet. She sank to the sidewalk, not caring about the snow wetting her pants. Will settled in beside her.

"So… my friends, my family, my job…"

"Gone."

That one word sent a sharp pain through her chest. Gone. She thought of many other things: her best friend, her home, the stray cat she'd been trying to adopt. All were lost, ripped from her life.

Her breath quickened, and she wrapped her arms around her knees then rested her forehead on them, shutting out the strange world around her. It was all she could do to keep the bile at the back of her throat from coming out.

Will draped his arm around her shoulders. They sat in silence for several minutes while Ella replayed the last half hour over and over again in her mind. If she had done things a little differently, if she had just listened to everyone and traded her car in the first day, she'd be home by now.

Her eyes stung, and she blinked, trying to keep it together. A numbness took over. Later, when she was alone, she knew it would hit her full force. The pain would well up from the depths, and she would sob until she had no tears left.

But she would hold it in until then.

Ella lifted her head, her voice raspy. "Does the town ever jump back to the same place or time?"

"Sure, it's possible, but the probability is remote. It hasn't happened yet, no. A couple of people who have gotten stuck here get lucky and leave when the town is within a few years of their original time. They cross the border—" he nodded at the demarcation between melting snow and sand in the great distance "—traveling back to their homes by car or horse or whatever."

Ella shook her head, blinking back hot tears and sat

up. "I can't just be trapped here. I can't just have my whole life gone, like that." She snapped her fingers and searched his face.

His eyes were warm pools of ocean. They shimmered, feeling her pain, but there was no mistaking the certainty. She was trapped in Keystone Village.

One of the tears she'd been fighting escaped and traced a path down her cheek. Maybe she was trapped *for now*, but she would find a way home. Whatever it took. Whatever the cost. She would find a way to stop the jumping. And if the town ever stopped within a few years of her time, she would return home.

"What if—what happens if the town hops to the location of an already existing town? Or a city? I mean, have you ever jumped into the middle of New York City?"

"Thankfully, it doesn't seem to work that way, or we'd be spliced apart, objects trying to occupy the same space-time as each other. Keystone only works or hops into more rural areas."

"What about sewer, water, infrastructure? Building supplies?" Thoughts tumbled around her brain, numb and half-formed.

His arm dropped, and the warmth and comfort it had provided left. "Look, I know this is a lot to take in. I've been there. The best thing you can do is go sleep on it. You'll feel better in the morning, I promise. I'll stop by and answer more questions then. You need time to digest this. Just know, what you're feeling, all those questions, we've all had them. We've all been through this."

He paused as if considering his next words. "You may not want to hear this right now, Ella, but Keystone Village really is a great place once you give it a chance."

"You mean a great place *besides* the jumping through time and people dropping dead in the middle of a restaurant?" Her eyes fell. "Sorry, that was insensitive."

He shot her a tired smile. "I understand."

Ella swiped the back of her hand over her damp cheek and climbed to her feet. This was too much to process, and already, her brain was shutting down.

They shuffled down Main Street together until they stood outside of the inn. She glanced at her watch. It was nearing ten o'clock at night.

"What do you do about the time changes?"

"Mostly, we ignore them and continue following universal time. But if it seems to be a twelve-hour difference between Keystone's time and wherever we are and we're there longer than three days, we'll adapt. If not, it starts messing with people's circadian rhythms and psyches."

Ella nodded, only taking in half of what he said. Her hand curled around the door handle, and she shuffled inside.

Cinnamon lingered in the air, and a dying fire popped in the hearth of the study. She supposed there wouldn't be much need of the fire now that they were in a desert.

As she slid the door shut, Will said, "Oh, and Ella? Welcome to Keystone Village."

Ella spent the night tossing and turning, never falling into a deep, restful sleep. When she wasn't awake staring at the ceiling, she was plagued by nightmares. In one, a sand dune swallowed her mother while her father watched, telling her it wouldn't have happened if she'd just listened to them.

Around five in the morning, she finally gave up on sleep. She slipped on jeans and a t-shirt, splashed cold water on her face in the bathroom, then padded downstairs in search of coffee in the twilight morning. A chill crept through the mansion, so she slipped on her polar fleece jacket from the entryway.

The house was silent and the kitchen empty. After searching for a few minutes, she located the percolator and turned on the stove.

Now, she understood the wind farm she'd seen her first night here. The traveling town would be unable to hook up with an electrical grid, needing to generate its own power.

While she waited for the water to boil, she sat at the table, looking out at the lake. Most of the snow had melted to patches. From her vantage point, she couldn't see the dunes. She could almost pretend that she was still in Oregon, waiting for her car to be fixed.

Ella shook her head. When she didn't show up for work, her boss would call her parents. Then, there'd be frantic phone calls, search parties, and tears. But they wouldn't find a trace. The snow bank she'd crashed in was probably snowed in by now. It would be like she vanished.

Her heart ached for her family and her best friend just as much as it did for herself. Sure, she had issues with her parents and they gave her a hard time about her future, but she knew this would devastate them.

Ella cleared her throat and rubbed her tired eyes. Perhaps Will was working on the problem, but she was going to search for an answer too. She was going to find out what was causing the jumps, then she would use it to go home again.

There was always an answer, always a solution to every problem. She would get back to them. And until then, she'd search for the positives because that's what she needed in order to keep going.

And really, in the grand scheme of things, was it *that*

bad being stuck in a town capable of time travel?

The pot started to bubble on the stove, filling the kitchen with the aroma of mornings and late night study sessions. There was a rustle at her feet, and she looked down to see Fluffy weaving a pattern between her legs.

"Hey, bud. How did you get in here?" She hefted the ginormous animal onto her lap. He was so heavy that his paws dug divots into her skin. Wincing, she scratched him behind the ears. He began kneading, purring loud enough to drown out the percolator.

A golden morning shone on Twin Hills, tinging the white-capped mounds with fire. Ella held Fluffy while she poured a cup of coffee then settled back into her chair. It creaked and sighed, matching her mood. Her fourth day in Keystone.

Her previous annoyance at the sheriff and Jimmy for trying to hustle her out turned to gratitude. They weren't being jerks; they'd been trying to save her.

She took a long swig from her cup. Since she would be staying in Keystone for the indefinite future, she needed to get both a job and to find a place to live. Perhaps she could keep renting her room, but that still left her with the problem of cash flow. Specifically, a lack of it now that she couldn't access her bank account.

If there was anything her lean college years and watching movies had taught her, it was that there were two ways to solve money woes: get a job or rob a bank. Since she hadn't located the bank yet, stealing money was out. She'd ask Rose if she knew of anyone looking to hire.

Fluffy sat up and butted her chin, nearly sloshing her hot coffee over both of them.

"Yeah, I know. I should quit freaking out." He swished his tail in response, his purring revving up.

Ella poured a second cup of coffee then went in search

of the elusive conservatory. It turned out not to be so elusive and made her question her observational skills upon her first time in the library.

Inside, the expansive space took her breath away. From what she could see, glass panels stretched from the ground up and partially over the ceiling, but most of the view was obstructed by leaves, vines, and branches.

The air was moist and smelled of dirt and flowers and endless summers. Ella filled her lungs with strawberries and green beans, with gardenias and jasmine.

She followed a narrow path, brushing aside the reaching branches of an overgrown rhododendron in full pink bloom. Near the glass wall, two potted star jasmines climbed an arching trellis.

Beneath the trellis, she found a café table and two metal chairs. She set her mug down and slipped back into the library in search of a book. Overhead, footsteps and creaking floorboards announced the house's occupants were beginning to stir.

Her gaze flickered over the dated spines, her breath hitching when she found some gardening books. A particular title caught her attention, and she pulled it out. *If Plants Could Kill: One Hundred and One Toxic Plants.*

Ella chewed her lower lip. Poison. The idea had been rolling around in her mind since she began to doubt Kay's death was due to an allergic reaction. It seemed the next obvious explanation.

But if it was poison, would it be natural or something manufactured?

Fluffy butted her leg then sat his generous backside on the hardwood floor, staring up at her with his green, hazel-flecked eyes.

"What do you think?" She showed him the book. He mewed and swished his tail. "Yeah, me too."

After settling into her chair in the conservatory, Ella cracked open the book and sipped her coffee. Starting with the first page, she skimmed, pausing to read a paragraph here or there when some of the symptoms matched Kayline's.

Pulling out her cell phone, she opened her notepad app and started a list, taking pictures of any possible offending plant. A half hour later, she'd found three other plants, all with side effects matching what had happened to the waitress.

Ella snapped the book shut and stared at one of the jasmine's blooms. If Kay's death was the result of poison, some household product might be just as likely. This was such a small, narrow place to start.

And now that she had a list of suspicious plants, what next? Wander all of Keystone to see if any match?

Her eyes roved the walls of green all around her. The inn was closest in proximity to the diner. Maybe the conservatory was the first place to start searching.

Nearby, Fluffy rolled in a swath of sunshine.

"What do you think?" she asked the pile of fur. "Want to be Watson to my Sherlock?"

His ears twitched—the only indication that he'd heard her.

"Fine, fine. You can be Sherlock." That earned a tail swish.

The faint clatter of dishes brought Ella back from her mostly one-sided conversation. Her stomach rolled with hunger, protesting for not having eaten yet.

Ella shoved her phone into her back pocket and grabbed her empty coffee cup, praying to God there wouldn't be lime flavored trout leftovers for breakfast.

CHAPTER 11

"ELLA!" ROSE'S SOFT curls bounced as she bounded across the kitchen and squeezed Ella. "You stayed!"

Ella returned the hug. "Not exactly by choice."

"I'm sorry. I know it's hard. We've all been there." Her lower lip jutted out slightly. "But I'm glad you're here."

Jimmy lounged at the kitchen table, his arm draped across the back of his chair. The usual mask of apprehension he wore each time he saw her was gone. "I'm sorry you're stuck with us." He grinned and lifted his coffee cup. "But Keystone's a great place once you give it a chance."

Across the kitchen, Rose's ruby lips thinned into a tight line as she poured a steaming cup of coffee from the percolator.

"Anyway, we're glad to have you here. And I'm sorry if I seemed inhospitable before."

"No worries. I understand now." Ella picked the seat next to him and dug into a pile of scrambled eggs and slices of ham as thick as her arm. As she chewed, her gaze wandered from the kitchen decor to the two innkeepers. Now, the antiques, the dated outfits, all made sense. "So, if you don't mind my asking, where are you two from?"

Jimmy opened his arms. "We're from Keystone. Born and raised."

"Okay, *when* are you two from?" Ella scrunched her face up and tried to think of a better way to phrase the question that didn't sound like a butchering of the English language.

"Colorado, 1951," Jimmy responded. "We'd just bought the inn right before the first jump. I felt awful for our poor guests. One moved out into her own house, the other left at a flash similar to his own time, and one stayed here. That's how we gained Mr. Kellerman."

"What about Crazy Flo?"

Rose placed a cup of coffee in front of Ella. "She came to live here after her last husband died."

"Sorry to hear that."

"Don't be," Jimmy said. "The old bag's probably the one that did him in."

"Oh, Jimmy." Rose gave his shoulder a playful slap.

Ella buttered a slice of homemade bread, eyeing Jimmy. She wasn't sure if he was serious or not. She shifted the conversation to another burning question. "How do you know where or when the town jumps to?"

"We don't," Jimmy explained. "Not unless a volunteer risks crossing the boundary to explore, then reports back."

Rose sipped her coffee. "Or unless an outsider wanders through Keystone. Like you."

Ella nodded. "Like me. Lucky me." She suddenly surged with hope. "Wait, how do you know that we're not in my time *right now*? Maybe we're in the same year but in the Gobi desert or something."

Jimmy gave her a sympathetic look. "There are a

couple people living here from the late twentieth century. They use their technology to connect to any sat-lights in orbit—if there are any."

"Satellites?"

"Yeah, that. Anyway, they would've spread the word by now. Since we haven't heard anything, chances are we're in a pre-technological age."

"So, I've been dying to ask…" Rose leaned forward. "…what's the future like?"

Ella swirled more cream into her coffee. "The future?"

"Well, sure. The time period you're from is the future for us. We've had a couple of newer residents from the twentieth century tell us how different things are." Rose's eyes grew to the size of their breakfast plates. "That there are phones that fit in your pocket without cords, and you can dial from anywhere."

Ella smiled. "Depends on the carrier." She waved her hand at their blank expressions. "Doesn't matter. It's not just the ability to contact someone from most any place, but the wealth of information at our fingertips is astounding."

Ell pulled her cell phone out of her pocket. "Most of our collective knowledge is available on here, so we're not just tapping into one person's expertise, but many. There's a wealth of information on here, more than a person could ever have time to read. Don't know the best recipe for zucchini bread? Look it up. Not sure how to change the oil in your car? Watch a—video. It's all right here."

She waved the device in front of their confused faces. "Of course, it works best when I have a connection to the internet."

What followed was a ten minute, rather painful and clumsy explanation of the internet.

"But where is it kept?" Jimmy asked for the third time.

"And what's it look like?"

Ella let out a slow breath that tossed a lock of hair away from her face. "It's not really a thing but many things."

She realized she'd have to go more into depth about computers and servers and networking and the cloud. She poured a generous third cup of coffee, no longer having energy for the conversation. "It's-It's… magic!" She made jazz hands to emphasize her point. "No?"

Neither seemed to buy the magic explanation, but neither belabored the point. Or they were just as tired with the topic as she was.

After that, they chatted about various Keystone residents. It began to dawn on Ella that she'd been given a rare opportunity her colleagues would be jealous of, a chance to meet peoples from different time periods and different lands, a chance to brush up on a rusty language or learn a new one—maybe even an ancient language.

While Ella stood at the sink, washing dishes, she approached the subject of renting her room from them for an indefinite period of time.

Rose grabbed a sopping plate from Ella and began to dry it. "Of course! We'd be happy to have you here."

"I'm not sure when I'll be able to pay you." Ella frowned again at the thought of her anemic savings account sitting in Oregon in another era. She was poorer than a freshman in college. Again.

"Don't worry about it for now." Rose grabbed another wet plate. "We like to help those new to the town get on their feet."

Suds climbed Ella's arms and sloshed onto her sweatshirt, but she ignored the growing dampness. It was hard to believe people she had met only a few days before were so willing to help. Trust and leaning on others for support were two of her biggest weaknesses.

"Okay, but I insist on helping out around here until I find work. Do you know anyone looking to hire?"

"Not sure, but I'll keep my ears open. Jimmy?"

"Don't know anyone off the top of my head. Maybe Gladys down at the greenhouse?"

The washcloth in Ella's hand paused mid-swipe of a fork. "Keystone has a greenhouse?"

"Have to," Jimmy said, leaning against the island counter. "We need a reliable, main source of food. Since our weather is so erratic, most of our crops are indoors. Without the greenhouses, we'd be up a creek."

Ella lapsed into silence, her hands working over bacon grease as she turned an idea over in her mind. When she finished with the dishes, she got directions to the greenhouses from Rose.

"It's a bit of a walk."

"Oh, I don't mind. I could use the exercise."

"It's a couple of miles one way."

Ella shrugged. "Sounds like a good walk." Truth was, she could use the time to sort out her thoughts.

A coy smile played at Rose's lips. "I'm sure you could get a ride from a certain handsome inventor."

Ella smoothed an invisible wrinkle from her damp sweatshirt. "I don't know who you're referring to."

After changing into yoga pants, a sports bra, and a tank top, Ella strapped her phone into her armband and secured it around her bicep. Not only did it have a robust library of her favorite songs, but it also had her list of poisonous plants which she planned to access once she reached the greenhouses.

Outside, a warm, dry breeze played across her face as she stepped onto Main Street. She turned right—which she considered north even though the sun was in the wrong place.

It was still before nine o'clock, but she could already tell it was going to be a warm day. The sudden change in climate would definitely be something she'd have to adjust to.

Ella clipped along at a brisk pace to warm her muscles. She passed Lou's broken down sedan and sent it a withering glare that should've turned it to dust. Maybe on her way back, she'd pay Lou a special visit—the kind full of heated words and empty threats.

When she reached the library, she broke into a jog until she passed the sheriff's office and kept up the languid pace. She wasn't sure how he'd take the news that she was in Keystone to stay, but she guessed it wouldn't be the same as Rose's reaction.

As storefronts turned to houses, a side street broke off from Main Street and curved around the lake, narrower and with a trail for a sidewalk. Ella made note of it with the intention of circling the lake in the near future, but for now, she stuck to the main road.

She hugged the shoulder as the road brushed the base of Twin Hills and disappeared over a gradual incline.

Halfway up the slope, sweat rolled down her back and her forehead. Her breath came ragged, and she had yet to hit her second wind. Either Keystone was now at a higher elevation than she was acclimated to, or she was really out of shape. She leaned towards the latter.

When it felt like her lungs would burst, she slowed her pace that barely qualified as a jog to a walk, muttering under her breath about her decision not to catch a ride to the greenhouses.

The exercise wouldn't be as necessary if she just laid off Wink's food. Of course, if any more meals consisted of gelatin molds, she wouldn't have to worry about an expanding waistline.

The rumble of a car sounded behind her. She turned in time to see a classic marine blue Chevy pickup straddle a pothole, swerving her way. Ella edged further onto the shoulder to give the driver more room, but the engine whined down as the vehicle slowed to a crawl beside her.

"Want a lift?" a familiar, deep voice asked.

Ella ducked out of the sun to peer through the open passenger-side window. Will drummed his fingers on the steering wheel and smiled.

"Rose didn't call you, did she?"

He stopped drumming. "Maybe."

Ella withheld a sigh and tugged open the door, thanking him. As she was settling in, Will pulled away from the side of the road.

"Sal says it's going to be a hot one," he said by way of hedging a conversation.

"Sal?" Ella recalled one of the storefront's painted windows with the same name. "The barber?"

"Yeah. He's sort of our unofficial weatherman, too."

"A regular renaissance man." The vinyl seats stuck to Ella's skin, and she rolled down the window. "Nice car."

"Thanks."

"It'd be nicer if it had air conditioning."

"Do all dames in the future complain so much?"

Ella fought a smile. "Dames? Okay, old man."

He chuckled. "I guess they don't say that where you're from."

"Not unless you want to get punched."

He glanced sideways at her as if he couldn't determine whether she was kidding. "They were still testing cooling systems in vehicles back in my day. Do all your cars have them?"

She nodded. "The ones worth having do."

The car crested the hill. Large oak and fir trees lined the way. The previous snowfall had caused the leaves of the oaks to shrivel, but they still provided shade against a hot desert sun.

Overnight, Ella had gone from snow and pumpkin spice lattes to the scent of sun heating dirt and oven roads. The wind whipped through the pickup's open window, pulling loose strands from her ponytail.

Will interrupted the silence. "Any particular reason you're wanting to go to the greenhouses?"

"Call it curiosity."

His eyes flitted from the road to her face, searching.

"If this is going to be my home for a little while, I should probably learn where everything is." The reasoning for her motive was mostly true.

Will's knuckles tightened over the steering wheel, and he fixed his gaze ahead.

"What? You don't agree?" She rotated to face him, trying not to stare at his strong jaw and lips.

"No, I do. It's just, you said, 'a little while.'"

"Yeah, so?"

"It sounds like you aren't going to stay."

She held back a snort, not wanting to sound cruel. "I'm not though. Not if I can help it."

"Do you want to know the probability of landing close to your time period again? It's slim. I can give you the exact calculation if you like. And if you were to factor in location, as well, it's next to impossible."

"I'll settle for close," she said softly. She'd taken enough math classes to understand the variables involved, to know the probability was remote. The chances were slim to none she'd ever return home by sitting and waiting through each flash or time jump.

Which was why she didn't plan on waiting.

Will sighed. "Look, Ella. I'm not trying to discourage you or dash your hopes. But I've seen it before. The first jump for a person's always the worst.

"In the years that followed the town's first jump, people searched for answers to why this was happening, held out hope that if they could just figure out the *how*, they could get back to their own time. But with each flash, no answer came, and hope died.

"In Keystone, there are two choices: either accept your fate and find some semblance of happiness living here or go crazy. Most of us chose the former because we had to to survive. But some chose the latter. They just couldn't take it. They grew depressed and made rash decisions. There were a lot of suicides around that time. A lot of people going missing, wandering out of town and getting stuck wherever we were." His voice dropped. "It was a dark time for Keystone."

The road dropped. The roofs of several large structures stood in sharp contrast to the sandy backdrop. Ella was momentarily distracted by the sight that would've made a nursery green with envy before shifting her gaze to Will.

His face was a storm of emotions, his jaw flexing as he battled them. She could tell the memories of the early years still haunted him, but there was something else. The way his voice broke as he spoke, the far-off look in his eyes, suggested something more personal.

"I'm sorry, Will."

He dipped his head in acknowledgment and lapsed into silence the rest of the cruise down the hill. Ella tried to count the many greenhouses but lost sight of them as they came eye level with the structures.

The car rolled to a stop in an expansive, half-full gravel parking lot. Ella reached for the warm handle and thanked him for the ride.

"Oh, no. You're not getting rid of me that easily." His quick grin chased away the shadows that had been there a moment before.

"You want to go with me?" Her mind warred with her emotions. The thought that she'd be spending more time with him made her stomach flutter, but it also made it harder for her to get the information she sought.

"Unless you don't want me to?" His hand, like hers, also froze on the door handle.

Her mouth suddenly felt dry, and she found she could do little more than nod and squeak—which she quickly covered with a cough.

As she climbed out of the car, Ella had to remind herself she was spending time with a man from her grandfather's time and the ex-boyfriend of a murder victim. While she thought Will innocent in Kay's death, when it came to men, she'd learned she was usually more wrong than right.

CHAPTER 12

THEY WANDERED FROM greenhouse to greenhouse. Despite the fans and open doors at both ends, the desert sun heated the humid air inside worse than a sauna.

Ella was in the middle of inspecting what she hoped was a blueberry bush when Will's voice filled her ear.

"You want to tell me why you're really here?"

She jumped, not realizing he'd been standing a breath behind her. Ella put space between them, and her stomach tightened. "What do you mean?"

His eyes pierced hers. "I mean, I've been watching you —"

"Creepy."

"We've been here nearly an hour. That's more than just a curious resident wanting to learn about the town. And you've been inspecting the plants like a horticulturist."

"Maybe I'm interested in becoming one."

"Is that why you keep checking that gadget of yours at the same time?"

Ella glanced at the cell phone in her hand, opened to

her notes on poisonous plants.

"You're searching for something," he said. "If you tell me what it is, I can help. Otherwise, we'll be here all day." He looked up, his eyes roaming the walls. "And you know how many more buildings we have to get through."

Ella bit her lip. After a drawn-out pause of consideration, she gave in. "Okay, I had this thought. I know it's crazy, but what if Kayline was poisoned by a plant?" She waited expectantly for his reaction.

His eyebrows lowered in thought. "That's not crazy. But how? Are you thinking she ingested it? And what plant?"

"I don't know." She shook her head in frustration and put her phone between them so he could see too. As she showed him the suspicious plants, complete with pictures and descriptions, she explained, "These are the ones that would result in the same symptoms we saw."

The inventor's eyes widened, a hunger burning in them. He ripped the device from her hand and turned it over and over. "This is amazing. One of the twentieth century guys who got stuck here let me play with his cellophane once before the battery died."

"Cellphone," she corrected, but if Will had heard her, he didn't acknowledge it.

He mashed his finger on the screen, pressing it like a button. The keyboard popped up, making his eyes grow even larger, then he squinted.

"So small," he muttered.

As he inspected the exterior, his thumb depressed the power button, and the screen went dark.

"Oh, no. I broke it."

Ella pressed her lips together to keep from laughing and showed him how he'd just powered down the screen. She stepped closer, their shoulders brushing, as she showed him how to use the smartphone.

"I'm looking for any of these." She pointed at the images she'd taken. She reached for the phone, but Will maneuvered it out of reach.

"We could just ask Mrs. Faraday. She's one of the horticulturists who runs this place," he said absently.

He held the phone at arm's length and tipped it from side to side as he tried to scroll up the screen. He jabbed his finger at the screen.

"It's not a button. You don't press it. Just touch—"

"Yeah, I got it." He shooed her hand away and accidentally opened the phone's settings. "Uh, what do I do?"

She managed to retrieve the phone, internally compared him to her parents, and pulled up the note she'd had opened. "It takes getting used to—"

He swiped the device out of her hands. "Got it."

Ella rolled her eyes and continued to search the aisle. Tomato plants climbed cages on her right, while grapes vined on her left. "We can't ask this Mrs. Faraday, anyway."

"Why not?" Will trailed several paces behind her, eyes on the screen, slowing with each step. Ella paused for him to catch up.

"What would she think if we were asking her about poisonous plants and word got out that Kay died from poisoning?"

"But it's after the fact."

"Will Sheriff Chapman see it that way?"

"Good point." The flashlight on her phone flicked on. "Oops. Hey, that's nifty." He pointed it up at her, blinding her with the small light.

Ella grabbed the device away again. "I'll give this back *after* we've found any of these plants." She froze, closed her eyes, and murmured curses. "I just sounded like my mother."

"Okay, I'm sorry. I'll help."

They spent another hour exploring, covering five more greenhouses. Ella's eyes burned with overstimulation by the time they'd finished, and she couldn't hide her disappointment.

They hadn't located a single plant from her list. There were still at least a dozen more structures, but she was tired and hungry and cranky. Clearly, her hunch had been wrong.

"Maybe we missed one," Will suggested when they stepped outside.

Ella shielded her eyes and swiped away the sweat that had become a permanent fixture on her forehead. "Or maybe I'm wrong."

"Or maybe it's just not here. Why would the greenhouse keep a poisonous plant, anyway?"

She shrugged, her spirits buoying a little. "Good point."

Her running shoes crunched over the gravel as they headed back to his car. "Too bad we can't get a look at the coroner's report. Any chance you can ask Pauline more about the autopsy?"

"We're not *that* close. She's pretty tight-lipped about things unless she's been drinking. Then again, who isn't? It's one reason I don't drink." A few yards from the car, he said, "Hey, Barton, catch." He tossed his keys at her.

Ella caught them and arched an eyebrow. "You're going to let me drive?"

"Only if I can see that phone of yours again."

Ella pulled the pickup out of the gravel parking lot and onto the road, relishing the gentle breeze created through the open window. She couldn't believe there'd been snow on the roads just yesterday. Several standing puddles of water dotted the shoulder and fields, the only sign of the recent accumulation.

After a minute of listening to Will muttering, "astonishing" and "amazing," Ella decided now would be a good time to broach a sensitive subject.

"Can I ask you something?"

"Shoot."

"You and Kay, what were you arguing about at the diner?"

He looked up from her phone for the first time since they'd left, his face darkening. "Her house had been broken into a few nights before. I was worried about her. Told her she should stay with me until Sheriff Chapman caught whoever was responsible."

Her house had been broken into? Ella turned over this new bit of information and stored it away.

"She told me she appreciated the thought, but she wasn't my concern anymore," he continued, his voice tinged with bitterness. "I told her that we didn't have to be a couple for me to be concerned for her well-being."

They reached the town, and Ella let her foot off the gas. "Was anything taken?"

"Not that she could tell. But they tore the place up pretty good."

She didn't respond immediately as she wondered if there was a connection between Kay's death and the break-in. After a while, she asked, "Did Kay have anything of value that would get her killed?"

He shook his head.

"Seems too much of a coincidence."

"I agree. That's why I've been pushing Chapman to investigate the break-in. Maybe they're related. Maybe someone saw something."

"And he's not investigating it?"

Will sighed. "He's got his hands full. And he comes from the nineteenth century. He doesn't really *investigate*."

She jerked her head around, almost taking the steering wheel with it. "He's from the nineteenth century?"

"Around 1850s if I remember right. Six Shooter too."

Ella gaped at the inventor a moment before tearing her attention back to the road. The last thing she needed was another car accident.

"Suddenly the cowboy outfits make sense." She'd always been fascinated by the American frontier time period. More accurately, her father had had a passion for it, and by proxy, Ella did too.

She nudged the car into an empty spot along Main Street, directly in front of the inn.

"Although, Jesse seems to have adapted better to the town than the sheriff. Sartorially speaking." She recalled his sweatshirt clashing with his cowboy hat and spurs.

"So, you've met Six then, have you?"

Was it her imagination or did his voice sound strained?

"We met my second day here." *Right before Kay died*, she added internally.

"He's dangerous, Ella. Be careful around him." His hands worked around the brim of his fedora sitting in his lap.

"Yeah, I got that impression. And I will."

They slipped out, and he came around to the driver's side.

She thanked him for the ride then dangled his keys in the air. When he reached for them, she pulled them back, holding her other hand out, palm up.

He shot her a dashing smile that would put a Crest commercial to shame. "Heh, slipped my mind." Reluctantly, he deposited her phone in her outstretched hand.

"Uh-huh." She handed him the keys.

As he pulled away from the curb, she waved then dashed up the steps of the stoop to escape the heat. However, inside the inn proved to be a letdown as she found it only a few degrees cooler than melting, but still an improvement from outside.

Back in her room, she plugged her phone in to charge, grateful that the town had an alternative, independent source of energy. At least being off the grid hadn't put them back in the dark ages. Her brain perked up, wondering if they'd actually visited the dark ages.

Kicking off her shoes, she flopped onto the bed, torn between eating a late lunch and napping. Maybe this whole not having a job thing wasn't so bad.

Ella winced, realizing she'd left the greenhouses without checking to see if Mrs. Faraday was hiring. Groaning, she rolled off of the comfortable mattress and headed downstairs.

First, she'd eat, then she'd look for work. Her thoughts wandered from potential jobs to her family. That topic quickly became too painful, so she found herself ruminating over Will instead.

She shook her head as if to shake him from her thoughts. Surely he was this friendly to all the newcomers. But part of her hoped he wasn't, that his behavior towards her was unique.

Grandma's Kitchen was still closed, so she opted to make a sandwich back in the inn's kitchen. What started as a sandwich quickly became half the contents of the crisper sticking out between two pieces of homemade bread.

She piled the food on a plate and meandered her way to the inn's library, hoping Rose wouldn't mind her eating in the room.

She searched for Fluffy but didn't see the large Maine Coon anywhere. After looking over the bookshelves, she swallowed the last bite of ham and cheese and other stuff, then she slipped into the conservatory again.

The intoxicating fragrance of gardenias, jasmine, and earth greeted her. She picked her way through the overgrown jungle to the café table and planted herself on a chair. Overhead, brave clematis vines clung to a thin seam of metal where panels of glass met, creating a ceiling of glass, vines, and flowers.

She drank in a long breath. Then, a frown formed as a thought occurred to her.

Ella jumped from the table and inspected the nearest cluster of plants, eyeing the different leaves. She darted to the next and the next, again and again, until she'd covered nearly every square inch of the twenty by thirty-foot sunroom. By the time she reached the back corner, she was breathing easier with the relief of being wrong.

Ella pulled aside the spindly branch of a Chinese maple, and a familiar leaf caught her eye. She wrenched her hand away as if it had burned her.

"No," she whispered. The word repeated from her lips over and over like a prayer.

Ella darted from the conservatory and sprinted through the library and up the stairs. Inside her room, she tugged her phone from its charging cord and dashed back to the conservatory. Swiping through her pictures, she found the one she was looking for.

Holding the phone side-by-side with the plant, she blinked at the white clusters of flowers and oval, toothed leaves. Jewelweed. She'd found a poisonous plant in Keystone that matched Kay's symptoms.

"*Puedo ayudarle?*"

Ella froze, her heart leaping to her throat. Slowly, she turned on her heel to find a woman with dark hair and olive skin staring at her. The knees of her pants were darkened as if they'd grown from dirt, and she wore pink gardening gloves.

The woman asked again if she could help Ella.

"*No, gracias.*" Ella started to walk away, then stopped. "Actually yeah. This plant—*¿Qué es esta planta?*"

Part of Ella hoped she'd misidentified it because the presence of it in the inn complicated things a great deal.

"*No lo sé.*"

"Who picked out the plants? *¿Quién...?*"

"Mrs. Murray."

A knot formed in Ella's stomach. Rose had chosen to have jewelweed in the inn. Why?

Ella shook the dark thoughts away, not wanting to think her new friend capable of murder. Stretching out her hand, she introduced herself.

"Angelica," the lady replied in turn, pumping Ella's arm with a firm handshake.

Ella abandoned Angelica and the conservatory for her room and a nicer change of clothes. Her mind swirled with doubt about what she'd just found.

She had to be wrong. But what if she wasn't? She knew she should tell the sheriff. If Pauline had a specific plant to test the poison against, maybe she could compare it to Kay's blood work.

At least that's how Ella assumed it worked. She was as knowledgeable about the coroner's job as a marathon of *Crossing Jordan* and *CSI* could make a person.

But the thought of bringing this information to Chapman made her hesitate. If she was right, Rose and anyone else with access to the plant would fall under suspicion of murder, including herself—someone who also so happened to be there at the time of Kay's death.

Additionally, Ella would be jeopardizing her lodgings. Because what innkeeper wouldn't want a boarder who'd suspected them of murder, she thought sarcastically.

Ella tipped her head from side to side as if weighing scales. Between finding Kay's killer and a roof over her head, clearly, it was no contest. She was selfish but not *that* selfish.

Still… there had to be a reasonable explanation for the plant being there. And before going to Chapman, she should be damn sure about what she said.

With that decision made, she focused on changing her outfit. Her limited supply of clothing didn't provide many options.

Nothing screamed, "Please hire me." Not unless it was a yoga studio. And something about Keystone made her think the only downward dog the town had seen was from an actual dog taking a dump on someone's lawn.

In the end, she settled on her nicest pair of jeans and a top with capped sleeves. To spruce up the ensemble, she added earrings, a touch of blush, and mascara—which promptly smeared over her eyelids, making her look like a washed-up rock star. After fussing with her eyes for several minutes, she gave up and decided to just go with the new look.

With a newfound confidence that only looking like a hot mess could provide, Ella slipped out of her room to find a more disturbing image than the one she'd just seen in the mirror.

Flo stood in the hallway, waving an awkward device around that looked part-microwave, part-metal detector. Ella watched her a moment, turning aside slightly and covering her midsection in case the device gave off any kind of radiation. She'd always been on the fence about having children, but she liked the idea of having the option.

"Is that safe?" she asked. Flo looked up, and that's when Ella noticed the tinfoil covering her beehive like a fat lightning rod. "Oh my gosh."

Flo squinted at her behind her coke-bottle glasses. "Who did your makeup? A clown?"

"Catch any reception with that headpiece?"

Flo smirked at her.

Ella pointed a finger at the device. "What's that for, anyway?"

"Ghost finder."

"Oh. Sure." They stood in awkward silence a moment, the machine whirring. Ella rocked on her heels. "Welp, carry on, then."

"I planned on it." Flo turned the ray-of-death towards the end of the hall.

It screeched then wound up in pitch until Ella could no longer hear it. She hugged her hands over her uterus tighter and made a beeline for the stairs.

Outside, she turned left down Main Street, which she still considered south despite the location of the sun. After passing the diner, she strolled until she hit the first open door.

What she'd thought was a bait and tackle store turned out to be a small market and produce establishment called, "Stewart's."

Barrels of apples and pears stood near the door, and she could see a shelf full of fresh bread, flour, sugar, and other staples she wouldn't know the first thing to do with. Along one wall was a small refrigerated section stocked full of milk, butter, and eggs. The rest of the store was filled with odds and ends, some packaged, most not.

Overall, she was surprised and pleased with the

selection. If she squinted a good deal, she could almost mistake the little market for a Whole Foods Market. She just needed to see a couple of guys in ponytails to complete the image. However, the jars of homemade animal fat kind of threw her.

A single customer stood in line, wearing fur despite the heat and some sort of sword at his hip. Ella watched him out of the corner of her eye, trying to figure out what century he was from. When he left, sword swinging by his side, she introduced herself to the clerk who turned out to be the owner of the market—his name, aptly, Stewart.

He was sweet, welcomed her to the village, but unfortunately wasn't looking to hire. Ella left, slightly disappointed, and moved on to the next place.

One by one, door after door, she tried each business. No one was hiring. With each shake of their heads, her spirits deflated. She had expected it to be hard but had thought there'd be *something*, even if it was part-time cleaning.

Ella reached the end of the road—literally. With a sigh, she turned towards the park and followed the gentle slope of the lush grass to the lake. Her shoes made sucking sounds in the mud as she walked along the water's edge until the park met the encroaching forest.

Here, the narrow road around the lake began or ended, depending on your point of view. Quint cabins and cottages dotted the lane.

She opted to keep to the soggy grass and moved away from the water, towards the forest. Tall pines towered overhead, mixing with oak and maple. Judging by the height of them, the forest was old, creating a canopy of leaves and needles over a dim undergrowth.

Slowly, she became aware of a soft, tinkling sound like loose change in a pocket. Her ears pricked, tuning into it.

Just as she turned her head towards the source, something moved behind a tree. Ella froze and stared at the spot. Her hand rose to her head as a shield against the sun's glare. Someone wearing a button-down shirt, vest, and cowboy hat strode along a narrow path cutting deep into the trees. *Six.*

CHAPTER 13

THERE WAS SOMETHING strange about seeing the cowboy strolling through the forest, like she expected to see him in a saloon or rounding up cattle instead. He didn't exactly strike Ella as the hiking type.

Crouching low, she slipped just inside the tree line, watching until his tan shirt became a dot. She lingered next to an elm, battling between the temptation to follow him to see what he was up to and the echo of Will's warning that Six was dangerous.

Just as the tan dot melted into the shadows, Ella made up her mind. She stalked over the worn muddy path, cringing as her once-white canvas shoes sank an inch into the drying muck.

The emerald canopy overhead provided a welcome shade against the blistering sun. Ella quickened her pace until Six came into view again.

A twig snapped under her, and she froze. Several yards ahead, the cowboy turned. Ella sucked in a breath and slid back a few inches until an ivy-covered trunk obstructed her view.

A trickle of sweat broke from her hairline and fell down her face. Her ears strained, listening for any movement from the man.

This was a bad idea.

Finally, she heard the jangle and rustling as his footsteps resumed, moving away from her. Ella hissed out a slow breath and wondered not for the first time if she should turn back.

However, something about the outlaw's slinking movements and paranoid glances told her he was up to no good. And if there was one thing Ella was good at, it was sticking her nose into other people's business.

After several minutes of creeping through the forest, the gradual incline of the path leveled out, a fact her now-blistered feet were grateful for.

She'd lost sight of Six several paces back, causing the anxiety that had been building in her gut to slither up her spine.

There was a break in the trees ahead. Ella crouched low and kept to the shadows as she approached.

A small breeze carried through the branches and leaves, and a powerful smell akin to solvents hit her nostrils. She put one careful toe in front of the other and stopped beside a large ponderosa pine at the edge of the path. The rough bark bit into her palms as she peered around the side.

The path led to a small clearing. Six stood in the center in front of a labyrinth of tubes that snaked from a copper contraption to a tall, thin container to something resembling an enlarged pressure cooker. Several wooden barrels dotted the area.

It looked like either a redneck's mad scientist laboratory or a still. Ella had watched enough TV to hedge her bet it was the latter. The pungent odor permeating the air also made more sense now.

At the base of a large cylinder, a fire burned. The cowboy stoked it, and she heard a faint hiss of something bubbling inside. Then he moved to a spigot and poured a clear liquid into a jar. His nose hovered over the glass, his nostrils flaring as he sniffed the contents. Even from several yards back, the smell alone was enough to curl her hair.

With all the secrecy, there was no way he had a permit for what she saw. Whatever his reasoning for making it, she had her answer about what he was doing in the middle of the woods.

Ella sidled away, towards the path, intending to creep back the way she'd come. She went to lift her right foot only to discover it wouldn't budge.

Her heart hammered against her chest. She tore her attention from Six long enough to see what the problem was. While spying on him, unbeknownst to her, her shoes had sunk another couple of inches in the mud, creating a strong suction.

Ella set her jaw and tried to move her foot again, this time getting her hands involved. The mud made a suckling sound she found disconcerting as it finally relinquished its hold on her tennis shoe.

She hadn't expected her foot to be freed so suddenly, and the momentum sent her flying back. Her arms wheeled through the air like the world's worst gymnast, but rather than help her find balance, the movement only served to ensure she fell harder.

The shriek of a wild animal rent the air, and she realized as she landed spread-eagle in a bed of ferns that the noise had come from her. The ferns themselves made for a soft landing, save for the hidden branch jammed into her hip.

Pain radiated across her side. Ella lay there a moment, inwardly groaning and cursing every tree, fern, and speck of dirt in the forest, and she probably would've remained in the plant for all eternity were it not for the approaching jingle of Six's spurs.

Rolling over, she staggered into a runner's stance and did her best Usain Bolt impression. Two steps later, she surrendered to the pain and settled on a rapid hobble.

"Where do you think you're goin'?"

A strong arm wrapped around her waist and yanked her back. Before she could put up much of a struggle, Six had already dragged her back into the clearing. He spun her around with rough hands and squeezed her arms in an iron grip.

Ella blinked at his sneering face then did her best to feign surprise. "Jesse? Oh, hey. Fancy seeing you here. I was just out for a stroll through—"

"Nice try."

A long, awkward pause followed, mostly filled with him leering at her and her staring over his shoulder at nothing in particular.

"Anyway, good talk. Nice running into you and whatnot. I should probably head back now." She wiggled to free herself from his hands, but it was like trying to wrestle out of concrete after it had already set.

He laughed, the noise grating like a barking dog. A startled bird squawked and took off nearby.

"You're not going anywhere. I know you saw it."

"Saw what?"

"My still."

Ella blinked innocently. "What still?" He sneered. Her eyes drifted over his other shoulder. "Oh, *that* still."

Her surprise turned genuine when his hands slipped

from her arms. He walked a slow circle around her like a lion stalking its prey.

Ella weighed the probability of success if she ran, the throbbing in her hip against his long, lean legs. The odds were not in her favor.

"So, you decided to stay, huh? Good. Another pretty face around here. Hell, maybe the only one. 'Cept Jimmy's girl ain't half bad." He cocked his head to the side. "But what am I going to do with you now? That's the question."

"Look, I really don't care what's going on here." She waved a hand over the setup that certainly violated several health codes on top of breaking the law. Probably. "It's none of my business."

She actually did care and would go to the sheriff first thing, but there was no sense in telling the outlaw that.

"That so?" He walked around her again, his eyes narrowing to slits and full of dark thoughts. Pulling out a rolled cigarette, he lit it and took a long drag, his inky eyes never leaving her.

She blew the smoke out of her face, trying to come up with a distraction. "So, what is it? Moonshine?"

"My means of making a livin' here. It ain't like I can just walk into Lou's shop and ask for a job, now, can I?"

Apparently, work was scarce for even long-time residents. "Why not start a brewery in town, you know, *legally*?"

He barked out a laugh, ending in sour, bitter notes. "You're still new, so let me educate you. The only businesses allowed in Keystone are what the town council deems worthy. Without their blessin', you're as worthless as a bullet without a gun."

"And they'd never approve you having your own still?"

"Now you're catchin' on."

Ella took a beat to gather her thoughts, wondering how she could end this conversation. "Okay, fair enough. I get why you've set up shop out here. Who am I to stand in the way of an entrepreneur?"

She took a step back. He mirrored it. "Anyway, best of luck and all that."

She slid back again, and he slid forward again. "You're secret's safe with me. I won't breathe a word of it."

He puffed out a cloud of smoke, a wild grin spread across his leathered skin. "No. You won't." Reaching down to the holster on his hip, he pulled out his six shooter. "Cause you can't breathe a word if you got no breath."

Ella's heart leaped to her throat. She held her hands up. "Jesse, please."

"That ain't my name."

"*Six*, please, don't do this."

"Sorry, darlin'. It ain't personal. To be honest, I was warmin' to you."

Ella took a step back, followed by another, then her back met a tree trunk. She was trapped. Her hands trembled, and she struggled to get her brain to cooperate and come up with a plan.

Now, she understood Kay's facial expression in the diner window when Ella had first met Jesse.

Right before she was murdered.

Despite the gravity of her situation, Ella couldn't help but glance back at the still and wonder.

She swallowed. "Did Kayline find your still?"

"She was nosy just like you."

"Is that why you killed her?" Ella whispered.

His face twitched. "I didn't kill her. I needed her."

Ella frowned. "Wait. What? You weren't in love with

her, were you?"

"Not me, no." His lips twisted sadistically. "She had eyes for a married man. That Jimmy fellow. Saw them stalking off into the woods together." He waved the gun in a wide arc off to her left.

In a random moment of clarity that defied her current predicament, Ella recalled Kay's shoes had tree sap on them which more than likely came from the forest.

Six pulled back the hammer on his revolver. A click broke through the still forest.

"J—Six, you're not a killer."

"You're wrong, darlin'. I am."

The rolled cigarette dangled from his lips, fouling the air with tobacco. He was so close, she could see the stains on his fingers, the mother-of-pearl buttons on his tan shirt, the top one missing.

Ella stared down the barrel of his gun. Her heart thrummed a wild beat in her ears, and her legs felt like Rose's lime gelatin mold.

This couldn't be it. She couldn't die in the middle of a forest in some God-forsaken, unknown location, her family never finding out what happened to her.

No. She would not let some outlaw with a gun decide her fate.

A burning anger for justice gave her focus and flooded her system with adrenaline. Her last breath would not be one trembling in fear. She would die fighting.

As he closed one eye and centered her in his sights, Ella made her move. She shifted her weight to her left leg and kicked hard into his stomach with her right. He grunted, and his hand twitched on the trigger.

Ella thrust the gun away as the muzzle flashed. A crack split the air like thunder, and the bark on the tree behind her exploded. She couldn't hear anything over the ringing in her ears.

As Six swung the gun back over her chest, Ella kicked again, this time connecting her shoe between his thighs.

The cowboy swore and doubled over.

Ella wrenched the gun from his grip and threw it into the woods. He screamed at her.

Her adrenaline kicked up a notch, and for good measure, she swung her fist around, connecting it with his jaw. His head flipped to the side, then his body followed, twirling through the air and landing in the mud like a drunken ballerina.

Ella had either just gotten really lucky or Six wasn't used to his victims fighting back. Either way, she wasn't sticking around to find out what happened when he recovered.

Leaping over his sprawled body, Ella sprinted down the hill. Her legs felt like rubber, and her hip complained with every other step. She stumbled over a rock and landed in the mud.

Scrambling to her feet, she continued fleeing, no longer able to swallow her fear. Tears streamed down her face. Her lungs felt like they would burst.

It wasn't until the shadows waned and light poured in through a break in the trees that she slowed.

Ella burst out into the light of the hot sun, running straight into something tall wearing a blue, button-down shirt.

"Ella?" Will put both hands on her shoulders and put her at arm's length. "What's wrong? What happened?"

She didn't know why Will was there, nor did she care at the moment. The words struggled out of her tight throat and between gasps of air. "Jesse... woods... gun..."

Will's eyes widened to full attention, and his head swiveled, looking for Six. He stepped around her, staying close. The scent of sandalwood and machine grease replaced Jesse's stale cigarettes, and she didn't mind.

Back at the sheriff's office, Ella sat on one side of Sheriff Chapman's desk, a far improvement over her old cell a few feet away. Will sat beside her, his eyes fixed on Sheriff Chapman's pencil as it traveled over a pad of paper.

Ella bounced her leg at his sluggish pace. She leaned forward, didn't find it any more comfortable, so she leaned back again.

"Okay," the sheriff said, finally looking up, "that everything?"

Ella nodded.

"Are you going to arrest him?" Will leaned forward in his chair, his muscles taut like a caged animal about to spring.

The sheriff picked his black derby hat up off the desk, shaping the brim between his hands. "Oh, he'll be brought in, all right. And if I find his still, I'll lock him up."

Ella gaped at the sheriff. "I'm glad your priorities are in order. So what about attempted manslaughter?"

He studied her. "Yeah, I reckon I can charge him with that too."

Ella furrowed her brows and glanced sideways at Will.

"The sheriff's still getting used to how the law works in the twentieth century," he explained.

"Actually, it's the twenty-first century for me," she said helpfully. At the look Chapman shot her, she shriveled back in her seat. "Just saying."

"Speaking of," the sheriff drawled, "I thought I told you to leave town." His tone was void of the anger or annoyance she'd expected.

"I tried. Believe me. That mechanic of yours—" she bit the inside of her cheek to stop from saying words she'd regret later. Not for the first time did she silently curse Lou.

"Well, it looks like we're stuck with you. Can't say as I'm happy to have another citizen to protect in my town—especially one that's got a penchant for trouble." He dipped his chin slightly, so his icy gaze looked down the crook of his nose at her.

Ella couldn't help but squirm, feeling like she was in the principal's office again for putting a fly in Jennifer Sloan's sandwich. To be fair, Jennifer had punched her in the stomach during recess.

Ella shifted the topic away from herself. "I was wondering, do you know what poison killed Kay?"

"Who said she was poisoned?" He let out a sigh. "This town and people's loose lips." He rubbed a weathered hand over his face, the first fracture in his facade she'd seen. "Not yet. Pauline's having trouble identifying it, but even if she'd found something, I wouldn't tell you."

Ella nodded. She hadn't really expected him to tell her. The sheriff may be from the nineteenth century, but he struck her as someone who played his cards close to his vest.

Chewing her lip, she debated whether to say anything about the jewelweed. If she told him and was wrong, she'd hurt Jimmy and Rose.

She decided to wait. If Pauline still couldn't identify it within the next day or two, she'd float the idea out to the sheriff and tell him about the plant in the conservatory.

"Is that everything?" Ella scooted to the edge of her chair, anxious to leave.

Chapman stood, his lanky frame unfolding to well over six feet, as he slipped his hat on. "That's all."

Will followed Ella to the door. Outside, he scuffed his shoes down the sidewalk beside her. "You just gave him everything he's always wanted."

"What? Chapman?"

"Yeah. He's been dying to book Six with more than just menacing, vandalism, and reckless endangerment. You handed the outlaw over to him on a silver platter."

"Jesse brought it upon himself. I can't help the actions he's chosen."

"No, you can't." Will lapsed into silence.

Ella felt both sorry for the inventor and a little guilty. She'd been so wrapped up in her own problems, she'd forgotten he had recently lost someone close to him.

"Do you miss her?"

"Kay? All the time." He sighed, shoving his hands in his pockets. "I wasn't in love with her anymore, but we remained close. When the romance fell away, our friendship remained. I miss that."

It took a few steps of silence for Ella to work up the courage to ask the next question. "What happened between you two? Never mind. You don't have to tell me. It's not my business."

"No, that's fine. I like talking to you. It feels… effortless. Like it was with her."

Ella smiled but felt conflicted by the compliment.

"It's simple, really. She wanted to leave Keystone. I wanted to stay."

"She wanted to leave the village?"

He nodded. "We'd talked about it for a while. At first, it was just a casual conversation, but then she brought it up more frequently until it became something we argued about constantly. Anytime the town flashed into a beautiful location with rolling green hills or snowcapped mountains, she'd get the itch again to run."

"I'm sorry."

"Me too. I'm sorry she didn't do it."

Ella stopped. "What do you mean?"

Will nudged a pebble with the toe of his shoe and seemed to search the ground for the right way to phrase his words. "Kay didn't want to leave Keystone because of some bright future she was running towards. She was running *from* something. And as much as I loved her, I couldn't abandon my work here—not at the time, anyway. See, I thought I could solve the time jumps, thought I could stop them. And I didn't want to leave all the citizens stranded. But I never blamed Kay for wanting to leave. I understood her reasoning. Heck, I *wanted* her to leave, because then I knew she'd be safe."

Ella's hand twitched at her side. She wanted to reach out and comfort him, but she shoved it into her jean's pocket instead. "Safe from what?"

Will stared past her at some distant memory. He didn't answer, but rather, shook his head. "Doesn't matter anymore."

Ella didn't push the issue, but that didn't keep her from wondering. What had Kay been so afraid of that she needed to leave?

They resumed their stroll back to the inn. "So, how close did you get to figuring out these time jumps?"

"Not close at all, I'm afraid."

The flame of hope that had been kindling in Ella's heart flickered out. "But you're still trying, right?"

"Not anymore. What's the point when you keep hitting a dead end?"

It was hard to miss the bitterness in his voice. The inventor, along with most of the residents she'd met, seemed to be resigned to their fate. How long had it taken them to go from heartache to desperation to accepting this new way of life? Was this disappointing acceptance of fate what she had to look forward to?

Ahead, she spotted the inn's front garden.

"I'm really glad I ran into you," she said, "literally. What were you doing near the forest, anyway?"

"Visiting the professor. He lives on Twin Hills, and I took the scenic route. I'm glad I did."

"Does this professor have a name?"

Will smiled. "He does, but it hasn't been used in years. Everyone calls him, 'the professor.' He doesn't get out much, and he doesn't really have any friends. Everyone thinks he's crazy."

"Is he?"

Will considered the question. "A little. But he's also brilliant."

"Ah, the ol' crazy and brilliant combo."

"You know people like that?"

"No."

He opened his mouth to say something then appeared to change his mind. "Anyway, I think geniuses have to be a little crazy, like their minds can't process as much as they do, so it wears on their gray matter." They slowed at the wrought-iron fence. "Maybe you'll get to meet him tonight."

Ella frowned. "What's tonight?"

"Town hall meeting. There's a lot to discuss in Keystone, a lot of moving parts, so we meet bi-weekly. Sometimes, the professor shows up—mostly when I drag him down from the hill."

Ella tucked a loose strand of hair behind her ear. The thought of going to an event with so many people after such an emotionally exhausting day didn't appeal to her. On the other hand, it was a great opportunity to observe the locals in their natural habitat. She'd be Jane Goodall, and they'd be...

Ella shook her head, abandoning the analogy. "Do the

Murrays usually go?"

"Usually."

The meeting would also give her a chance to watch Jimmy. If anything untoward had been happening between him and Kay, he hadn't seemed that broken up about her death. No more than Rose or Kay's other friends. Ella suspected Six had lied about their involvement. Although, she wasn't sure what his motivation in doing so would be.

Across the street, the man Ella had seen earlier in the store with the thick fur draped over his bare shoulders walked by and nodded in Will's direction.

"So, I'll see you tonight?" Will asked her.

"Yeah, I think you will. Are we not going to talk about the walking bear over there?"

"Leif? What about him?"

"It's like a hundred degrees. Why the fur?"

"It's Sunday," he said as if that explained everything.

"Yeah, that's what I was going to say." Ella waved bye and approached the stoop, muttering, "This town's weird."

"You say something?" Will called.

"See you tonight."

CHAPTER 14

ELLA WILED AWAY the few hours until the town hall meeting by swiping through photos on her phone from Thanksgiving. A pang of homesickness she hadn't felt since leaving for college ached in her chest.

With a sigh, she tossed her phone across the bed. The photos only cemented her resolve to figure out a way to stop the town from traveling, or rather, control it so they could all return to their respective eras.

She hadn't realized she'd drifted off to sleep, nestled in a trough atop the satin comforter, until someone knocked on her door.

"Ella?" Rose's sweet voice drifted through the mahogany door. "Are you going to the town meeting?"

Ella shot out of bed and banged her knee on the nightstand in the process.

"Yeah! Be right out!" She hopped on one leg like a pirate, massaging her injured kneecap, right over an old bruise in the same location. She was nothing if not consistent.

Ella looked down at her mud-splattered clothes. She'd planned on changing out of her "interview" attire before the all-important town hall meeting. Without time to rummage through her clothing selection, she settled on the nicest t-shirt she had left in her backpack and her last pair of clean jeans.

Scrambling over to the mirror, she fought a couple of unruly curls that refused to do anything other than reach for the ceiling, then she snatched her lip gloss.

Her unskilled application of eyeliner had gone from a 1980s televangelist to full-blown raccoon. She did her best to swipe and confine the circles to within the vicinity of her eyes before sprinting for the door. She hoped she looked more put together than the hot mess she felt.

Flo bumped into her in the hallway and whooped up a storm. "Looks like you got into a fight with a boxer."

She leaned in close to Ella, her magnified eyes opening until she looked like a giant fly. Her wrinkled hand reached for Ella's face.

Ella swatted her away. "I didn't get into a fight."

"You sure?"

"Pretty sure."

"Don't sound sure."

"I think I'd know if I got into a fight."

"What flight? Never been on an airplane."

Ella's eyes narrowed in confusion. "What are you on?"

"Don't mind her," Rose called from the bottom of the stairs. "She needs hearing aids."

"I hear fine," Crazy Flo snapped. As she passed Ella, she winked and gave a wicked grin. "You've no idea the things people say when they think you can't hear so good."

"Or when they think you're nuttier than a bag of trail mix."

Flo shrugged and clung to the banister as she descended the stairs. Halfway down, her voice creaked out, muttering to herself, "This girl's a keeper."

When Ella joined them in the entrance hall, Jimmy gave Ella, Rose, and Flo a smile that revealed gleaming white teeth.

"Looks like I get the pleasure of escorting three ladies this evening."

"Two ladies and Sugar Ray here," Flo jerked her head in Ella's direction.

Ella looked at Jimmy. "I don't think the crypt keeper qualifies as a lady."

"All my husbands seemed to think I was woman enough."

Jimmy crooked his elbows out, and Rose slipped her arm through one.

"Let's go before she recounts the tales of her wedding nights," he said. A shudder rippled through him. "I still get nightmares hearing about that one."

Flo snorted and scooted out the door. "You're just jealous that you weren't husband number five."

"Six," Jimmy called out to her hunched back.

Flo didn't respond, but Ella spotted her ticking off her fingers, silently counting.

As they strolled north on Main Street, Ella filled Rose in on what happened in the forest, while Flo and Jimmy listened on. It turned out that word had already spread to the innkeeper about the incident.

"I heard sheriff brought Six in for questioning about an hour ago," Jimmy said. "He put up quite a fight. They had some shootout on the edge of town."

Ella lifted her eyebrows, surprised she hadn't heard the commotion and equally surprised at the casual way Jimmy floated the information out as if a shootout was a regular occurrence in Keystone.

At some point, they had all passed Crazy Flo, who now huffed a few yards behind them despite the short walk. Between gasps of air, her voice floated up, "Six is in the slammer again? Now where am I supposed to get my whiskey?"

Rose gasped and glared over her shoulder at the elder woman. "Flo!"

Ella looked back. Flo was now fanning herself.

"Good Lord. I'm having my own private summer back here."

Ella grimaced. "That was an image I didn't need." She dabbed away beads of sweat and tried not to think about what it was doing to her makeup. If she didn't show up at the meeting looking like the Joker, it'd be a miracle.

Overhead, the sun was just starting to crawl towards Twin Hills. Ella wondered if Keystone Village had jumped to the southern hemisphere. If she'd paid more attention in astronomy—and had the proper equipment and several more IQ points—she'd probably be able to guess the location and date.

A welcome breeze replaced some of the heat rising from the sidewalk, and Ella reveled in its relief.

Swarms of people buzzed down the sidewalks on both sides, more than Ella thought the little town held. They shouted greetings at each other across the river of pavement separating them. Laughter floated on the breeze, mixing with the aroma of gardenias from the hanging basket in front of the library.

As she passed the sheriff's office, her gaze darted to the window. The scarlet sky reflected off the window, and she was unable to penetrate its glare.

But she knew who was inside. She could still smell his tobacco, could still see the barrel of his revolver pointed at her. His words crawled over her skin.

"*It ain't personal.*"

The town hall was one of the last buildings on the left side of the street and wasn't so much of a hall as it was a church.

Ella tipped her head. Actually, it was *exactly* a church, complete with white siding and steeple.

"You gonna stare at it all day or go inside?"

A sharp finger dug into her back.

Ella hadn't realized she'd been barring Flo's entrance into the building. She took her time shuffling through the door, earning a glare from the curmudgeonly lady.

Beyond the foyer, the church looked more grange hall or turn-of-the-century schoolhouse than sanctuary. The air buzzed with moving bodies and conversation, an electric hiss of whispers and excitement. Ella wondered if the noise was standard for a town hall meeting or if it was due to Kay's murder.

"I think that cotton candy on your head's crooked," Ella said as Flo passed.

To her surprise, the older woman flipped her the bird, but the gesture didn't go amiss by Wink who strolled through the entrance at the same moment. She gave a good whack to the backside of Flo's head, causing the tumbleweed of hair to bounce.

Ella hid a smile. She was definitely starting to like this town.

"Watch it. I spent an hour on this." Flo dabbed at her hairdo as they filed into the building.

"Why? Who're you trying to impress?"

"None of your business," Flo bit out, but Ella noticed her eyes dart across the sanctuary. Apparently, the movement was also noticed by Wink.

"Oh, no you don't. He's at least twenty years your

junior."

Flo mumbled something under her breath about Wink always ruining her fun as she scanned the rest of the crowd. Her eyes settled back on Wink.

"What's going on with this here?" Her veiny hand gestured to Wink's pink tracksuit, the color reminiscent of cough medicine Ella was forced to drink as a child.

"What? I look dynamite." She turned sharply towards Ella. "Do they still say that in your time?"

Ella was too taken aback by the abysmal attire and Chester—who she just noticed rode shotgun on Wink's shoulder in a matching tracksuit—to answer immediately. "Um, maybe? I don't really hear it that often."

"Oh, what do they say then?"

"Hot, I guess. Maybe pretty. Depends on who you're talking to."

Wink blinked at her. "Hot?"

"Yeah, as in, 'Damn, nice outfit. You look hot.'" A passerby glared at Ella, and she guessed it had something to do with either her swearing in a church or her KISS makeup.

Flo took out a handkerchief and dabbed away sweat on her upper lip. "But she is hot. I can see the pit stains on her blouse."

Wink rolled her eyes. "It's nothing compared to that bib of sweat between your bosoms."

"At least I got bosoms."

"Hush, you two," Rose interjected. "We're in public. Just pick an aisle and sit down."

"Thank you," Ella whispered. She had no interest in hearing more about anyone's bosoms. In a louder voice, she added, "Wink, I think you and Chester look adorable. It's like looking at a set of twins."

Grandma Wink made a grandiose curtsy before

leading them down the main aisle.

"They do look a lot alike," Flo said, her hand moving to her beehive again as she followed Wink. "Both small, hairy, and won't shut their yaps."

"Okay," Jimmy said, "save it until after the meeting."

"That's what happens when you're best friends with someone since the second grade," Rose said in a low voice.

Ella looked back at the innkeeper, mouthing, *They're the same age?*

Maybe it was Flo's indeterminate multiple marriages and booze-addled skin or Wink's electric-colored hair, but the two appeared to be a decade apart in age.

Rose nodded. "Honestly, I feel like their mother half the time. Who needs kids when I have them?"

Behind his wife, Jimmy's eyes roamed the sanctuary. Ella didn't have time to wonder who he was searching for because her attention was drawn to the center of the room. Wink and Flo had picked a row on the left, near the front. They stood arguing about who got the chair nearest the center aisle. Meanwhile, more chairs began to fill up around them.

"For crying out loud," Jimmy said, pushing past both of them and flopping down into an empty seat.

"I need to be closest to an exit," Flo said, ignoring him. She made a huffing noise.

"Why? So you can empty that ancient bladder of yours?" Wink steadied Chester on her shoulder.

"No! You know I need to be near an exit in case there's an emergency."

"There's not going to *be* an emergency."

"You said that, then there was that tornado, remember?"

"One time."

"And that herd of buffalo—"

"Two times. Move over. I need the leg room. You know my arthritis gets bad in this weather."

The volume in the room had lowered considerably, and Ella became very aware that they were now attracting attention.

"Both of you," Rose hissed, "sit down."

She elbowed past them and settled next to Jimmy. Ella attempted to squeeze by as Rose had, but Flo picked that moment to put her hands on her hips, adding to her already ample width.

"You know what? You can have it, Pearl. I actually see someone else I'd rather sit by." She gave a Cheshire grin and flutter of her lashes to some far-off, unwitting victim. She moved to leave, then paused. "You with me, Ella?"

Ella coughed to give herself time to formulate a response. When none came to mind, she held up her hand and continued to hack like a smoker.

"You okay?"

Before Ella could stop her, Flo slapped her back in a way Ella was sure shook a lung loose. The third hit sent her sprawling headfirst into a middle-aged woman in a bonnet. Ella rasped out an apology and batted Flo away before the old woman could render any more "aid."

Wink settled into her victory chair, a look of triumph on her face. "Oh no you don't. El is new and doesn't need your colorful interpretations of our town whispered in her ear the entire time. I don't want her thinking Keystone's Satan's armpit."

"I would never," Flo huffed. She situated her glasses on her nose and stalked towards her new seat and unsuspecting prey.

"Do we need to go warn someone?" Ella asked, her eyes still following Flo.

"No. Most single gentlemen between twenty and ninety know to steer clear of that storm." Wink patted the empty seat between her and Rose.

Ella climbed and tripped her way over the older woman and finally got to sit down. The cool cushion of the chair was a welcome relief from the stuffy air.

"So, you two have been friends a long time?"

"Fifty-three years. She grows on you—like a rash you can't shake." Wink sighed and glanced across the main aisle at Flo. "She wasn't always like this, you know."

"Oh? What happened."

"Time." Wink situated Chester on her lap then produced a couple of nuts from a pocket in her tracksuit. "Time's a funny thing. I call it the Great Judge. Some people age like a wine, becoming better with time. Others spoil and become bitter. Rotten. It's up to us to decide which we want. Life throws all this stuff our way, and we decide to make castles or landfills."

"So, how is it a judge?"

"Has someone harmed you or wronged you in some way and gotten away with it?"

Six sprang to mind, but Ella felt confident he wouldn't get away with trying to kill her. Or at least, she hoped he wouldn't.

She nodded.

"I guarantee you that they pay in their own way. Time is an equalizer."

Ella churned Grandma Wink's words over in her mind then stole a glance over at Crazy Flo, wondering what had made her that way. Was she paying penance for a wrongdoing?

Ella didn't believe the woman's gruff, sandpaper facade for a second. Still, in her experience, people tended to develop prickly behavior as a defense mechanism. Or maybe Flo had just decided she didn't give a crap about social niceties.

The room stilled by several decibels, and there was no more time to dwell on the fellow boarder and ghost hound. The small, quaint church was filled to the brim, nearly every seat taken, with a handful of residents forced to stand along the walls.

Ella craned her neck as she scanned the crowd, looking for familiar faces—one in particular. Her gaze kept snagging on random people who looked like they'd stepped straight out of a television set. Most of the folks wore clothing similar to Rose and Jimmy.

However, a few stood out with their cutlasses or kilts or loincloths—especially the loincloths. Surely they'd been offered more appropriate attire? Although, given the dramatic change in weather, the narrow strip of leather appealed to her at the moment.

She finally spotted Will across the aisle and back a row, sitting next to a man in unkempt clothes with white hair that looked like a tornado had been used on it in lieu of a comb. Ella guessed she was looking at the professor.

His eyes darted back and forth, his movement furtive, not with shiftiness but a severe lack of comfort in his environment.

"Who're you looking at?" Wink's voice sounded in her ear.

Ella jumped. "No one." And here she thought she'd been subtle. She was going to have to work on her spy skills.

Wink's eyes followed where Ella's had been. Slowly, a smile crept over her face, her eyes twinkling.

"Uh-huh." Then the smile faded. "I wonder why he's not sitting with us. He's usually over here."

As if he could feel their gaze, the inventor turned his

head, locking eyes with Ella. He smiled and dipped his chin in greeting, but his expression was tense. He snapped his head back to the front of the room.

Ella frowned. Had she done something? Was he not sitting in his usual spot because of her? She recounted their last conversation and retraced her actions.

Unless he took issue with her napping, she hadn't done anything wrong. She inwardly shrugged it off as having nothing to do with her.

A short man with a round midsection and a bowler cap approached the lectern at the front of the church. He turned to face the audience, his skin glistening in the stifling heat. Behind him, seven people took seats on a raised platform behind folding tables.

Ella squirmed, suddenly feeling like she was on trial.

"That's the council," Wink whispered in her ear. "And that," she nodded at the man, "is Mayor Bradford."

Ella focused on the man fussing with his hat, the name rattling around in her brain until it clicked into place.

"Wait—Bradford. As in, Kayline Bradford?"

CHAPTER 15

BEFORE WINK COULD confirm that the man at the front was related to Kayline, the mayor cleared his throat and tapped the microphone. It hummed through speakers strategically placed around the sanctuary.

"Good evening, everyone. Thank you, all, for coming. Before we begin, I'd just like to personally thank everyone for their kind words over the last few days." He slipped his hat off, worrying the brim in his hands. "As you all may have heard, my precious daughter, my June bug, has passed on."

He squeezed his eyes shut, pausing, and placed his hand over his heart. There was something theatrical about the movement, Ella thought.

"And to confirm the rumor that you all have no doubt heard, yes, Sheriff Chapman does believe her death intentional. Now, I will not be commenting further on this tragedy, and I'd ask that you respect my privacy during this difficult time. A memorial service is planned for Sunday at eleven o'clock. Everyone is invited. My Kay loved this town, and she would've wanted the doors open to all."

He cleared his throat and replaced the bowler hat on his head. "And now, Councilman Sal will begin by reviewing the minutes from last week."

A man rose from the table and read from a weathered legal pad. Meanwhile, Mayor Bradford strode over and seated himself with the rest of the council. The entire time he'd been speaking, Ella's skin had tingled with dislike more and more. It wasn't until his chair squeaked under his weight that she realized why she'd reacted that way.

When he'd mentioned Kay, his expression fell with sorrow, but his eyes were dry, glittering with delight at all the faces staring back at him. Maybe he was someone who preferred to mourn privately or maybe he was still in shock.

Regardless, he clearly loved the attention. Even now, he leaned back in his chair, chest puffed out, face glowing with eagerness.

The meeting clipped by at a rapid pace. Ella was interested, despite the discussion topics being about which crops should be planted next in the surrounding fields, how much wheat they had stored up in the silos, and discussing the town's power supply shortage.

The meeting took a tense turn when a councilwoman suggested they start implementing brownouts. Once the dust had settled and brandished swords and bows had been confiscated, it became rather dull by comparison.

After most new business had been discussed, the mayor stepped up to the pulpit-turned-lectern again. "I just wanted to say that thanks to our rather reliable star charts and a brave volunteer who ventured over the border, we now know that we're in Southern Africa in 1740. Jack had to hike a couple of miles out, but he ran into a traveling caravan."

A wave of mixed reactions rippled through the room. The mayor held up his hand for silence, his barreled shoulders arching back.

"I just thought everyone would want to know. Any more new business?"

"This is where these usually get good," Grandma Wink said under her breath.

"And here I thought that man throwing a hatchet at Sal was exciting."

"Nah, happens more often than you think at these meetings."

"Wh-should I be worried? Do I need to arm myself?"

Wink waved her hand in dismissal. "You'll be fine. And don't let Flo overhear you talking about armaments. I think she has the largest arsenal in town, no matter how much the sheriff or I confiscate from her. I swear that woman could take over a small country."

"Where's she getting it all?"

"Your guess is as good as mine." Wink shrugged, unworried about her best friend being her own private militia.

Ella glanced over at Crazy Flo whose arm now draped across the back of the man next to her. She made a mental note to never get on the woman's bad side. Also, she needed to talk to her about potential self-defense given her encounter with Six and the alarming amount of weapons she'd seen tonight.

She turned her attention back to the meeting. A middle-aged man with tattered overalls and a thick layer of grime covering his weathered skin walked up to the mic. "I'd like to lodge a formal complaint against Rodney Gunderson. My apple trees got a bug moving through 'em, and he put it there."

In the audience, an old man with gnarled joints and a stooped back climbed to his feet. "Did not, you crazy ol' coot! Why would I do that? *How* would I do that?"

"Don't know. But ya did."

"Why would I loose a pest that could destroy my trees too? Huh? You batty ol' loon."

"Then why's my trees the only ones dying?" The farmer with the overalls turned a violent shade of red. "This is a warnin' with all these witnesses here, if I see you on my property, I'll shoot ya."

The two traded shouted insults. When Rodney tried to climb out of his row to get at the other man, the mayor rolled to his feet from the council table. Even without a microphone, his voice boomed over the hall.

"Gentlemen, please!" He swayed on his heels, his arms crossed with a bored expression. "Now, Carl. You're lucky the sheriff's not here to hear your threats. I'm getting tired of saying this tonight, but there'll be no shooting anyone.

"Rodney, stay off his property. I'm far more interested in our produce dying off. Maybe Mrs. Faraday can go have a look?" His eyes searched the crowd before a woman shouted an affirmative response.

"Good. Let's move on."

Grandma Wink leaned back in disappointment and muttered something about how boring the evening had been.

The rest of the meeting went without further incidence. Judging by the room full of dead expressions, Wink wasn't the only one who seemed let down by the uneventful final minutes.

Ella felt like she'd just watched a soap opera, only with a crazier cast and half of them armed. When she thought about it, it actually made sense in a town full of people from all walks of life and different eras. There was bound to be friction. If this was normal for Keystone, then Six was a run-of-the-mill citizen. It also made Kay's murderer a lot harder to catch.

As the meeting drew to a close, Mayor Bradford faced the mic again. "I'd just like to say one last thing before we eat..."

Ella sat up, her head swiveling. She hadn't noticed any food.

"...welcome our newest citizen, Ella Barton."

Ella froze, all of the air leaving her lungs. The mayor motioned for her to stand. She shook her head and sank deeper into her chair. Now would be a really good time for a tornado to hit.

The mayor's hand wouldn't stop flapping for her to get up, and Wink's elbow wouldn't stop digging into Ella's side.

Resigned to her fate, Ella took a deep breath and stood. Heat bloomed across her cheeks as she felt every pair of eyes on her. So, she did the only thing an embarrassed, sane person would do. She dipped in what started as a curtsey but quickly became a half-bow, resulting in a hybrid move that belonged on a Lord of the Dance stage more than at a meeting hall.

Wink choked on her spit. "What was that?"

"Shut up," Ella whispered. She was ready for the earth to open up and swallow her whole.

"Please, everyone," the mayor said, "make her feel welcomed."

A polite applause surrounded Ella. She was sure she'd heard more clapping at a eulogy, but she did hear a few catcalls. So, there was that.

"Where're you from, Ella?"

"Oregon."

The mayor nodded knowingly. "From our last jump,

yes? You were, what, a couple decades into the twenty-first century?"

"Almost, yeah."

The air hummed with murmurs, and she felt the crowd's interest pique. She would've preferred the golf clapping over this.

"Well, isn't that something?" The mayor's mouth curled up. "The furthest year we have yet. I'm sure there's a lot we could learn from you. I'm glad you decided to join us."

Despite it not being her choice to *join* them, Ella was grateful to be in Keystone. She was even more grateful when she dropped back into her chair.

Grandma Wink patted Ella's knee. "Forgot to warn you about that."

Ella eyed her skeptically. "Sure. I guess it wasn't that painful. I survived with my dignity intact."

"Really? After that weird bow thing you did?"

Ella squeezed her eyes shut and muttered a profanity. "Hey, it's a salutation of respect where I'm from."

Now it was Wink's turn to look dubious. Ella didn't break. After a long pause, the older woman said, "Really?"

"Yep."

"Will you teach me it?"

Ella's mouth twitched, but she kept her composure. "Absolutely. I should probably teach Flo, too. Wouldn't want her to miss out on all the fun."

"Oh, good idea." Wink's hair bobbed with enthusiasm as she bounced in her seat.

Ella was just turning over ideas on how to expand the botched curtsey-bow-hybrid when Pauline caught her eye. The coroner and town doctor sat near the front and to the side.

Ella's mind shifted gears abruptly to the mystery of Kay's death. If there was anyone in that room that had answers about how she died, it was Pauline. If Ella learned that Kay hadn't died from jewelweed, then there was no need to mention her suspicion to the sheriff.

CHAPTER 16

WITH THE TOWN hall meeting over, the crowd shuffled to their feet and set about the ear-splitting task of rearranging the chairs to accommodate fold-up tables. In minutes, the sanctuary had been converted into a large dining hall.

Townspeople disappeared out the front and side doors, coming back with armfuls of platters, warming dishes, and slow cookers. Soon, food covered a line of tables along the north wall into one of the longest buffets Ella had ever seen. All the while, she stood back and watched the practiced frenzy with awe.

She glanced over at her quarry only to realize she'd lost Pauline in the fray. Ella teetered onto her tiptoes, scanning the bobbing sea of faces.

"Looking for Will?"

Ella jumped. "Geez, you need to wear a bell."

Wink stood at Ella's elbow. On her shoulder, Chester alternated between gnawing on a slice of apple and using his hind leg to scratch his ear.

"And no, actually. I was looking for someone else."

Rose joined them a moment later, a shortbread cookie between her fingers. "I'm really glad it wasn't my turn to bring food. Carol brought a gelatin mold. I can never compete with that woman."

Ella's eyes darted over to Wink who looked away and coughed. When Wink had regained her composure, she asked Ella, "So, who were you looking for?"

"Oh," Rose said, "Will's over there with the professor."

"She's not looking for Will."

"Then who's she looking for?"

"Okay, you two. I was looking for Pauline."

"Pauline?" Wink's face scrunched up.

Rose popped the last of her cookie into her mouth and brushed crumbs from her hands. "I think I saw her by the punch, waiting for Paul to show up with his flask and give it that extra kick." Her eyes lit up as if a thought occurred to her. She shooed Ella away, saying, "You go find her, dear. Wink and I need to talk about something." She winked conspiratorially.

Ella began to maneuver away when Rose called out to her.

"Oh, Ella. You're not seeing anyone, are you?"

"You mean in the few days since getting stranded here? No. No, I'm not."

"Oh. Right." Rose's face melted into a smile that gave Ella pause.

"Wait. Why?"

Rose ignored her and pulled Wink by the elbow, speaking in low tones and giggles.

"Why, Rose?" Ella asked louder.

The two women slipped through the crowd. Ella considered following them to put an end to whatever they were scheming but decided to hunt down Pauline instead.

Kay's death was a greater priority than her love life.

She sighed and moved towards the buffet tables, sure she'd see the fallout of her decision soon enough.

After several minutes of weaving through the crowd and smiling politely at all the comments welcoming her, she spotted the doctor coming through a side door, a warming dish cradled in her arms and a stack of cloth napkins teetering on top. Ella made a beeline for her.

She was only a few yards away when a tall figure stepped into her path. Will dipped his chin in greeting. His hair looked naked without his fedora. It swooped over his forehead in a deep side-part, sharpening his handsome features.

"Ella, I wanted to introduce you to the professor."

The older gentleman that Ella had seen sitting next to him earlier stuck his hand out. She shook it with a firm grip, and they exchanged pleasantries.

There was something wild and dark in the professor's brown eyes, like a deep sadness that came from tragedy. Deep lines ran down the center of his brows, giving him the expression of constant concern and deep thought.

He bent towards her with interest. "Twenty-first century, huh?"

"Yes, sir."

"Do you have flying cars, yet?"

Ella laughed. "No. But they were working on self-driving ones."

His eyes widened. "Really?" He scrutinized her, making her feel like a specimen under a microscope.

"How would that work?" Will asked.

"You know, I didn't read up too much on it, but I think it used a lot of sensors and cameras around the vehicle, processed by a central computer that controls steering, gas, and brakes and such."

"Interesting."

"Fascinating."

Both the professor and Will said at the same time.

"So, what are you a professor of?" She glanced over their shoulders, watching Pauline find a table.

"Theoretical physics."

Her eyes darted back to the older gentleman. "Really? Does that mean you can figure out why the town's jumping around?"

Will slipped behind the professor and shook his head at her. The professor's mouth turned down in a deep frown.

"No." He turned back towards Will. "I'm tired. I'm going home."

"But sir, you haven't eaten yet."

"I'll eat at home." With that, the professor shoved his hands in his pockets, ducked his head, and headed for the front doors.

"Oops," Ella said.

"Not your fault. He's just sensitive about the topic, that's all."

Ella felt foolish. The man had probably tried to solve the problem for ten years. She could only imagine how frustrated he must feel.

Her heart sank. If he couldn't solve the problem, what chance was there that she could?

She realized she'd been staring absently at Pauline while Will stood in awkward silence. A considerable dent had been made in Pauline's plate of food, meaning that any opportunity for conversation was dwindling.

"Anyway, it was good seeing you." Ella patted Will's arm, her eyes glued to the coroner.

"Wait, where are you going?"

"Uh, to get some food."

"Mind if I join you?"

Ella blinked. Of course, she didn't mind, but she was on a mission. "Sure."

As they passed Wink, Flo, Rose, and Jimmy's table, Rose gave Ella a thumb's up, Grandma Wink whistled, and Flo rolled her eyes. Ella shook her head and pretended they didn't exist.

While they moved through the food line, she kept eyes on Pauline, who now only had a small mound of potato salad left on her plate.

Ella tried to hurry by invading the personal space of the older gentleman in front of her, hoping he would take a hint. Her plan backfired as he seemed to appreciate the close proximity and took up winking at her.

"You alright there?" Will asked behind her.

"Yeah, why?"

"Because you just put corn on your mashed potatoes."

Ella looked at her plate, the mix of foods looking like a Thanksgiving table turned over. "I know. That's how we eat it where I'm from."

"But it's not, is it?"

"No. But it *could* be."

"What's that mean?"

"I have no idea. But do you realize what a gift it is to be the only one from the furthest point in the future? I can mess up all I want, and no one'll know any different. They'll just think that's how it is in the twenty-first century."

"Solid plan."

"I think so."

"Can't possibly go wrong."

Ella stopped short and considered this. Maybe it wasn't the best scapegoat, after all.

As they grabbed their cloth napkins, he asked, "So,

who do you keep looking at? Anyone I should be jealous of?"

"What?" Ella fumbled with her napkin before dropping it. She considered telling him that's how they preferred napkins where she was from—on the ground—but didn't think he'd fall for it. "No. I was looking at Pauline."

"Oh?" His voice dipped in disappointment.

"Not that. I just thought, maybe we should go join her, you know? She looks lonely."

His eyes reflected the fading sun pouring in through the windows. "You mean, here's your chance to see what she knows about Kay's death?"

"And who said you were just a pretty face?"

He looked confused. "Who said that? Flo? Did Flo call me stupid? Sounds like that ol' batty woman—"

"Will, I was joking. It's just an expression where—"

"Don't tell me they say that where you're from." He straightened his shoulders. "Anyway, I'd be happy to help you pump her for information. I want to find out what happened just as much as you do—if not more."

Ella nodded, feeling foolish for the second time in less than an hour. Of course, he did. Kay had meant something to him. "Lead the way, then."

Working their way around the other tables, they settled into chairs across from the doctor. Pauline looked up from her now empty dish, drinking heavily from her punch.

"Evening, Pauline." Will tore open a roll and slathered it in butter. "Can I get you something? Rodney's letting everyone sample his latest batch of hard cider."

Pauline's glassy eyes widened, and Ella noticed that a couple of rivulets of grease were still on her chin from her meal.

"Nah, probably shouldn't. Gotta head back and do some more work." Her head bobbed before she took another deep drink from her "punch."

"Come on. Just one round." Will scraped his chair back and stood. Leaning over, he whispered in Ella's ear, his warm breath tingling over her skin. "Get some giggle water in her, and she'll tell you her life story."

Ella opened her mouth to inform him that Pauline was already managing it on her own, but he'd already wandered off.

"Heh," she said under her breath, "giggle water."

"How's that?" Pauline's voice carried over the din, and she tipped forward.

"Oh, nothing." Ella picked up her fork and excavated a chunk of potato that had chosen to fraternize with her fruit salad.

She figured she'd warm Pauline with casual conversation about the weather and would pry her for information when Will got back. This, however, proved difficult as Pauline seemed more interested in the bottom of her cup than the sand currently blowing through town.

Will returned quickly, saving Ella from having to drum up another dry topic. Three glasses full of amber liquid sloshed in his large hands as he set them on the table.

Ella picked the nearest one and noticed it was chipped. He insisted on trading her, and they argued before she acquiesced.

"We're limited on our dishes and utensils around here," he explained. "You get used to drinking around the broken stuff."

"What about wood from the forest? Can you make cups and plates from some of the wood?"

"They're trying, but it's not ideal stuff for carving."

"Be nice if a truck with a shipment of dishes got stuck

here," Pauline chimed in.

"Like a Walmart semi," Ella said.

A wistful expression came over Pauline. "Ah, Walmart."

Will blinked at both of them. "What's a Walmart?"

Ella sipped her cider, grimaced, and set it aside. "A one-stop shopping haven with affordable prices and questionable quality."

"Oh, we have one of those."

Pauline snorted into her cider. "Trust me. It's different."

Ella fell silent. It was finally starting to sink in just how different she was from most of them. She also realized that if the coroner knew of the superstore, then she was a transplant just like Ella.

Pauline slammed down the empty mug of cider Will had just given her and swiped a sleeve across her face. Ella marveled at the woman's ability to drink, wondering if she wasn't part frat boy. Will casually scooted his untouched cup in Pauline's direction.

The doctor's hand moved from the empty mug to the full one like the smooth hand of a surgeon. By the time Ella had finished her food, Pauline was well into the third and final cup, giggling at anything Will said.

Will glanced sideways at Ella, and his chin dipped in a subtle nod. Across the table, Pauline swayed and tried her best to cover a belch. She reached back to the jacket draped over her chair, into the coat of many pockets, and retrieved a handkerchief and a bag of what looked to be homemade mints.

Pauline concentrated on getting the mint to her mouth, missed, then tried again. "So, I said, 'Get the goat's milk!'"

Ella laughed, unsure if the punchline was for a joke the woman had told several minutes ago or a conversation

Ella had tuned out.

Leaning in, Ella dropped her voice. "Speaking of your work—"

"That wasn't from work."

"—I heard Kay was poisoned. That true?"

Pauline's mouth drooped, and she struggled to focus on Ella. "Can't say."

"Can't say because you don't know?" Will said.

"Can't say... 'cause it's a going on... investigation."

"Ongoing investigation?" Ella helped.

"That's what I said," Pauline said indignantly before draining the last of her cider.

Ella tried not to be disappointed. She hadn't expected it to be easy to pry information from the doctor, but she'd hoped for *something*.

Shooting Will a pointed look, she tipped her head towards Pauline, hoping he could get further. The coroner seemed soft on him. If anyone could pry answers from her, it'd be him.

Will pressed a smile across his face, his white teeth on display. "Thanks for being so professional about it. I'm glad to know Kay's in such good hands." He reached over and patted Pauline's hand. "It's just—" his voice broke "—Kay meant something to me. I don't like not knowing what happened to her. I watched her die, Pauline. And it's something that'll haunt me the rest of my life."

Ella felt a pain in her chest. The memory haunted her too. She could only imagine how hard it was for him.

Teetering on her chair, Pauline stared at him, her eyes shifting in and out of focus. Finally, she patted him on the cheek. "I like you, you know that, Will? So cute. Such a shame it didn't work out between the two of you."

She tried to stuff the handkerchief back into her jacket, missed several pockets, but managed to stuff it into her sleeve.

"Thing is, we're having a hard time identifying the poison. It's not showing up in the blood work. 'Course, it's probably because we lack the equipment. Keystone is a far cry from where I did my residency, let me tell you."

"Do you know how she was poisoned?" Ella asked.

Pauline narrowed her eyes at Ella as if she'd forgotten she was there. "How would I know? Look, I'm just a general pract-pract... I'm just a doctor. Not a medical examiner."

"Did you look at the stomach contents?"

"Oh, that. 'Course I did."

Ella looked at Will for help.

"What did you find?" he asked.

Pauline's expression softened. "Some partially digested hamburger and fries. Milk protein, which meant she probably drank a shake three to four hours before her meal. Did find traces of something I couldn't identify, though."

"Really? What was it?" Ella said before she could stop herself. "Right, silly question. You just said you couldn't identify it. Was this unknown substance or whatever in the food itself?"

Pauline shook her head. "Can't be certain without testing the source of the meal she ate, and that's long gone. It was in higher concentrations in the liquid contents, but only a trace of it in the partially digested food."

"Meaning it most likely didn't come from the fries or burger." Ella bit her cheek to stop herself from saying more.

"Not that I can tell. Look, I don't know what they have where you're from, but for toxicology, I only have half the chromatography equipment I need and a homemade centrifuge thanks to Will here. That's it. Don't even have a blood gas analyzer. Everything has to be done the old-fashioned way."

Will's brows puckered. "So, really, we don't know what killed her?"

"That's what I said. We know what *didn't*. It's not rat poison, not strychnine, not any cleaning substances or pesticides. I've ruled them all out."

Her words had begun slurring, and Ella feared she was only good for a couple more questions. Beside her, Will stared at his empty plate, emotion swirling behind his eyes. It was Ella's turn at bat again.

"What about that rash on her arms? Could it have something to do with the poison?"

"The rash? You mean her poison oak rash?"

"So, it really was caused by poison oak?" Ella tried to keep the disappointment out of her voice.

"Yep." Pauline blinked slowly over glossy eyes. "I should probably head home."

She managed to get one arm through a jacket sleeve. When she tried to scoot her chair back, it caught on a floorboard.

In slow motion, the coroner tipped back and went down like a bowling pin. Limbs and jacket splayed out over the ground. A marble rolled across the floor from one pocket, a few strawberries from another.

Nearby, a voice yelled, "Timber!"

"There goes my snack for the walk home," Pauline mumbled, struggling to a sitting position.

Will and Ella dropped on either side of the doctor to help her up. They were just gathering her elbows when a blur of fur and pink tracksuit hit Pauline like a cannonball square in the chest.

Chaos broke out. Pauline screamed and flailed,

jumping to her feet. She clawed at Chester.

Wink appeared, shouting at the squirrel who was now headfirst inside the pocket of strawberries, bushy tail waving through the air.

Pauline's frantic wails kicked up a notch when she realized the rodent was attached to her. She swatted and turned a circle.

"Get this thing off me!"

She twirled, causing Chester's tail to flare out around her like a fluffy tutu. Wink grabbed for the rodent, but her hand clutched air after each pass.

"Grab a cookie," Wink yelled at Ella and Will.

Without waiting for an explanation, Ella sprinted for the dessert table, searching for a cookie. Wink hadn't said what kind to grab. Assuming that it was for Chester and not Wink having a sudden sugar craving, Ella grabbed a peanut butter cookie and raced back to the fray.

A small crowd had gathered around the dancing doctor and varmint, probably more for the spectacle than actually to help. A little boy clapped and pointed at the "woman with the tail."

Ella shoved the cookie at Wink. The older woman held it above her head and hollered, "Chester, cookie!"

He must've stopped squirming because Pauline's jig became less frantic and more of a waltz. Two gray ears emerged followed by beady eyes and a twitching nose.

The crowd held a collective breath.

Wink dangled the cookie in the air, calling the squirrel's name. Chester's nose worked double-time. A moment later, he scrambled out and flew through the air at the treat.

Grandma Wink snatched him up and cradled him. An enthusiastic applause broke out—with more gusto than the welcome Ella had received—and the diner owner gave a tired smile before disappearing through the throng of people.

Beside Ella, Pauline swayed, her eyes wide in shock. Ella feared a light change in air pressure would knock the doctor over.

She and Will steadied the coroner and insisted on walking her home, especially after Ella found out Pauline lived across the lake in one of the wooden cottages that looked a gingerbread house.

Outside, the air was fresh, the temperature dropping rapidly, going from sauna to tolerable. The walk went smoothly, with Pauline trying to take a swim in the lake only twice.

Once at the cottage, they deposited her on her couch, covered her in a quilt, then made their way back to the walking trail around the lake.

The sun dipped behind the distant dunes, shooting rays across a blood-red sky. Ella always loved this time of day, when the world around her turned to gold and magic.

"Kind of a waste of cider," Will said.

She glanced at him, noting the edges in his features had softened since the beginning of the meeting. He was back to his charming self. Whatever had been bothering him had vanished.

"Oh, I don't know. We learned what didn't kill Kay, and I learned how many glasses of alcohol it takes to get information from Pauline." Unfortunately, it seemed the jewelweed was still in the running for the possible murder weapon. "So, as far as town hall meetings go, was that your standard fare?"

"More or less. Every once in a while, we'll get one that's like watching paint dry. Other times, they'll end in death threats or fights.

"Once, we had a meeting that seemed to go well enough until the refreshment portion. Then, Mable Gray called Susanne Smith something colorful, and one thing led to another, and it turned into the largest food fight I've ever seen. It took weeks to clean all the whipped cream and pie from the walls and ceiling."

"What a waste of pie."

"The mayor canceled the next two meetings until people could agree to be more civil." He chuckled to himself. "So, yes, tonight's meeting was pretty standard and tame by comparison."

Ella tried to picture such a food fight and found herself wishing for a repeat in the future. It seemed her new home would never be dull, and she would not lack for entertainment—which was good considering there wasn't television or internet.

They walked in a comfortable silence. Ahead, water lapped at the docks. A few old boats bumped against the pylons, bobbing over the dancing jewels of sunset glistening on the lake. Maybe she could find someone that owned one and borrow it for a day full of fishing and reading.

"Are you going to the memorial tomorrow?" Will asked.

"Yeah, I am." She didn't bother asking if he was as she scratched an itch on her arm.

By the time they made it back to Main Street, the street lamps were on, chasing away growing shadows. When they passed the sheriff's office, Ella noticed the lights were still on. Without the glare of the sun, she was able to see inside.

Six stood in his cell, arms threaded between the bars, staring out the window. Ella barely had time to process the sight and look away before he saw her.

They locked eyes.

His lips twisted into a sadistic grin. He leaned into the bars, his eyes wild like a predator.

Ella and Will were nearly past the window when the outlaw raised a tobacco-stained hand, made a gun shape with it, and pointed it at her.

The hair on the back of her neck stood up, and before she could react, he slipped out of sight, the image burned into her eyes.

"Ella, you okay?" Will asked.

She nodded, not trusting her voice. *It doesn't matter,* she told herself, *he can't touch you now.*

But as the inn came into sight, she was certain of two things: she'd have a hard time falling asleep tonight, and she was no longer confident Six hadn't killed Kay.

CHAPTER 17

SINCE ELLA DIDN'T have any clothes appropriate for a memorial service, she thought she would visit the shop down the street and see if she couldn't find something black and somber close to her size. It also needed to cost under twenty dollars since that was all the cash she had left on her. Her hopes weren't high that she'd find anything, but at the very least, she'd get to see more of the town.

After downing two cups of coffee to fight her restless night, she marched down the sidewalk with determined steps. Already, the concrete was warming underfoot, promising to be another blistering day.

Instinctively, her eyes darted down the street towards the sheriff's office three blocks away. It was just a blurry dot, but she shivered as if Jesse was there, staring at her.

A clanging sound drew her gaze, and she found that she'd stopped across from L Street. She could see the door for Lou's auto shop open, the raucous noise coming from inside.

Ella's hands curled into fists. She adjusted course and tore across the street, nearly getting hit by a horse-drawn wagon. She did a double-take at the strange transportation before churning her heels across the pavement.

When she reached Lou's, the sound of an electric drill broke over the quiet morning. Ella homed in on the noise. Two legs stuck out under an old Buick. She grabbed the dodgy mechanic's boots and yanked, rolling him out from under the vehicle.

"Hey—"

"Lou, bet you hoped you'd never see me again?"

He squinted up at her. "E-Emma?"

She bent low, swallowing the space between them. "Ella. E-L-L-A. You traded me a lemon."

"Pardon?" The toothpick nestled in the corner of his mouth worked overtime, decoding the word.

"That piece of junk you traded me didn't make it two blocks. And now I'm *stuck* here. Because of you."

Until the words spilled out of her mouth, she hadn't realized how much bitterness stewed inside of her towards the mechanic. Her fingernails dug into her palms so hard she was sure they'd puncture skin.

He held up his hands, his eyes darting around, clearly uncomfortable being on the ground with her towering over him. "That ain't my fault, though. That car worked fine. Honest."

"You're going to give me my Jeep back."

"What? No—"

"Yes," she hissed. "And you can have that clunker back. It's still parked in front of the inn, baking in the sun and taking up space."

"That ain't a fair trade."

Ella's eyes widened, a fire burning in her. "What?!"

Lou scrambled out from under her and staggered to his feet. "I just mean—"

"Where's my car?"

Fear crept into his eyes. Finally, he pointed a meaty finger at a cabinet against the wall. As she marched over to it, he said, "You coulda left at any time, you know. You were *warned* to leave the moment you got here, yeah?"

She didn't respond as she ripped open the cabinet door. Dozens of keys dangled on hooks inside. Her eyes raked over brass and silver colors, searching for hers.

"It ain't my fault you ignored advice and waited to leave."

She didn't want to hear anymore, didn't want to admit he was partially right. She *had* dragged her feet acquiring different transportation.

Spotting her set of keys, she snatched them up and spun. "But if that hunk of metal you call a car *hadn't* broken down, I would've been out of here."

His shoulders sank in defeat. "Look, doll, I really am sorry."

She knew it would take time for her anger towards him to fizzle out, would take time before she could look at him without wanting to deck him.

She dangled the key in his face, her eyebrows raised.

He jerked his head. "It's out back."

"Is it fixed?"

His right eye twitched. "Yeah, it's fixed. Nearly good as new."

"Good. I'll leave the keys for the sedan on the seat."

Without another word, she strode out of the shop and to the fenced-in lot behind. Once inside her SUV, she inhaled the deep, familiar scent and patted the steering wheel. It felt like a small piece of home had returned to her.

Her car purred to life. As she rolled out of the gravel lot, she caught Lou watching her from the shop. She resisted the urge to spin her tires and kick gravel at him, instead, doing the adult thing of muttering curses at him under her breath.

She glanced in her mirrors at the man. His face had fallen, and she almost felt sorry for being mean. Almost.

Ella slipped into the same church used for the town hall meeting the night before. She sat near the back, self-conscious about her attire. She'd been unable to find anything suitable and was forced to borrow one of Rose's dresses. It was rather elegant for a memorial and far too nice compared to the usual garb Ella wore, making her feel like she was going to a cocktail party.

On the bright side, she'd managed to apply eyeliner with a light hand, but that hadn't stopped Flo from inspecting her and calling her a "painted woman." The comment was ironic coming from a woman whose face looked like an entire Clinique counter.

The sanctuary was packed with mourners. Up front, above a garden of floral arrangements, a large banner draped over the stage with Kayline's name painted in black cursive lettering.

Today, Ella sat between Wink and Flo, separating the two women who'd bickered the entire walk over. What had started as an argument about Frank Sinatra somehow turned into a fashion critique over Wink's outfit (a lime-green dress). Wink insisted that Kay would've liked it.

Beside Ella, Flo continued to grumble about the dress. "She looks like a salad."

"Nonsense," Wink said. "I look cold."

It took Ella a moment to parse out her meaning. "Do you mean hot?"

"Poop," Flo said a little too loudly. "You're the color of newborn baby poop."

Several heads turned. Grandma Wink's cheeks reddened. "Don't mind her. She drank a little too much 'shine on the way over." She made a drinking motion with her hand.

Ella gave Wink's outfit another appraisal. "If poop comes out of any living creature that color, then you have a problem."

"Why must you two always have the most irreverent discussions in church?" Rose asked in a low voice on the other side of Wink. She pointed a finger at Ella. "And don't you go joining in. I don't need three of you."

"I can't help how the good Lord made me." Flo slipped her hand into her purse, retrieved a handkerchief, and proceeded to blow loudly, adding a honking noise partway through.

Ella grimaced as Flo slipped the snot rag back into her purse then did a double take when she caught the metal gleam of a flask.

Ella shook her head and scanned the crowd. The mayor sat in the front row, dabbing at his eyes. Opposite him and a few rows up from Ella, the back of Will's wavy rich brown hair stood out. The professor sat on Will's right and a woman whose face Ella couldn't see sat on his left.

Ella leaned forward, trying to get a better look at the mystery woman. Before she could ask Wink who she was, the memorial service began, and Ella settled into her seat but kept glancing at the back of the woman's honey blonde hair.

During the service, Grandma Wink, along with two other ladies, got up and sang one of Kay's favorite songs, which turned out to be a Boyz II Men ballad that had no business being sung under a church roof. Steamy lyrics aside, their voices blended and harmonized, filling the hall with beautiful notes.

As Wink walked back to her seat, her bright green dress stood out like the sun, burning retinas and glowing with its own radiation. A couple of mourners shook their heads, and the rustle of whispers followed in her wake. Wink stuck her chin out as she took her seat, her back ramrod straight.

When the church's pastor got up to speak about how important it was to treasure every moment, Ella took the opportunity to steal a glance at Jimmy. He gripped Rose's hand, his eyes glued forward. Ella searched his features for a trace of emotion, something to indicate if he felt Kay's loss deeper than a friend, but the man was as stoic as a statue.

She checked periodically as the service wore on, always using her hand to sweep back a curl and hide her wandering gaze. Finally, when Mayor Bradford lamented over the future robbed from him and that he'd never get to walk his June bug down the aisle or meet his grandchildren, Jimmy's facade cracked. His jaw twitched, and he closed his eyes.

Rose leaned into him, squeezed his hand, and whispered in his ear. He nodded then affected a blank expression once more.

Ella looked away, her mind churning. It could be nothing. It could be the reaction of losing a friend. Then again, his reaction gave credence to her suspicion.

Even though she'd only met the innkeeper five days prior, he didn't strike her as the cheating type. Still, she'd been surprised by unfaithful men before. It was rarely the ones she suspected, and sometimes the ones she didn't.

Ella briefly entertained the notion that the innkeeper had been having an affair with Kayline to see if the puzzle pieces fit. It explained the clandestine meeting in the woods between him and Kay—assuming Six was telling the truth about spotting them together.

What if that wasn't the only time they had met up in that spot? What if Kay had arrived early one day, waiting for Jimmy, and stumbled onto Six's secret still much like Ella had? It seemed plausible that the unpredictable outlaw could have killed Kay in a fit of rage. But if he had, why not just use his revolver?

To cover his tracks, she thought.

Surely, a bullet in a body would put Six at the top of the suspect list. So, if he had poisoned Kay to throw suspicion off him, then where had he gotten the jewelweed, supposing that was what killed her? And did he still have it?

On the other hand, the jewelweed grew right under Jimmy's roof. What if Kay had tried to break things off or threatened to tell someone about the affair?

Ella's stomach tightened with a new thought. What if Rose had found out about the affair?

It was a lot of supposition on ground as unsteady as Rose's gelatin mold. Six had a strong motive coupled with the appropriate temperament, which made him her best suspect, followed by Jimmy, then Rose. Both innkeepers had access to the jewelweed, whereas Six... well, she couldn't be sure without seeing his place.

As the service drew to a close, Ella decided she needed to rule one of them out. She needed to check out Six's house.

There was a great shuffling of suits and dresses as everyone filtered out of the church, shaking hands below somber expressions, a great exodus of black—save for Wink.

Climbing to her feet, Ella trailed behind Flo and Wink,

dodging her head to get a better look at the woman accompanying Will. Finally, the crowd parted enough for her to make out the woman's face, and Ella's shoulders slumped. She was beautiful, with soft features and sweeping blonde curls.

Ella stared so hard, she didn't see that the aisle of mourners bottlenecked at the door, and she smacked into Wink's lime-colored back. Chester dug his claws in for dear life, causing Wink to let out a startled cry. Both squirrel and woman chittered at Ella.

Ella apologized and returned the rodent's glare. After Wink turned back around, Rose sidled up to Ella's elbow.

"You alright?"

"Yeah, fine." Ella resisted the urge to see if the inventor had noticed the commotion. "Who is that woman with Will?"

Rose's ruby lips twitched as she fought a smile. "Oh, that's Jenny. She owns the salon across from the inn."

Ella remembered passing the Jenny's Salon while job hunting but hadn't gone inside. She figured no one in their right mind would let her near a pair of scissors.

"She's pretty. You know, if you're into nice hair, a symmetrical face, long legs…"

"They're not that close," Rose explained as they stepped out into the dry, afternoon heat. It hit Ella like a furnace blast.

"Back when he first got stuck here, before he met Kay, he went through what we all went through: denial, depression, and such. Jenny helped him adjust. Wagging tongues claim they dated, but he denies they ever did. Says they've always just been friends. She's not his type, anyway."

"He has a type?"

This time, the smile broke free. "I don't know about

physically, but let's just say that Jenny's... high maintenance. And she's as friendly and sweet as a cactus." Rose's cheeks flushed. "Oh, dear. I didn't just say that, did I? Well, I suppose there's no shame in telling the truth. But you didn't hear it from me."

"Hear what?" Ella caught the innkeeper's eye and winked.

After a few moments, Rose abandoned Ella to gossip with Wink and Flo about someone's hat. The three waltzed a few steps ahead of Ella in rapt conversation, setting the pace at a gentle roll over the sidewalk that might get them home before midnight, maybe sunset if they picked up their feet a little.

As curious as she was about the offending headpiece that had her friends in a tizzy, Ella hung back until she fell into step beside Jimmy. She searched for a conversation opening, one that would land near Kayline, and decided on a simple approach.

"Sorry for your loss."

He started at her voice. "Oh, thanks."

"Were you two close?"

Jimmy looked from his polished black leather Oxford shoes to the three women in front of them. "About as close as anyone else, I suppose. In a small town like this, you get to know everyone a bit."

Ella scratched her arm, searching for more questions. This was one of the few times she'd seen him alone, and she didn't want to lose the opportunity to dig for answers.

"Jimmy? Can I ask you something?"

"Just did." He chuckled at his own joke.

"Okay, Dad."

He shot her a confused look.

"You know, dad joke?" When his eyebrows didn't budge, she said, "Doesn't matter." She took a breath. "My question is, what was Kay afraid of?"

Will had said Kay was scared of something. Maybe it had been her secret with Jimmy.

The laugh lines around the innkeeper's eyes melted away. "What do you mean?"

"I'd heard that she was scared of something, wanted to leave Keystone because of it."

His features hardened. "You shouldn't believe everything you hear."

"No, I—"

They'd arrived in front of the inn. Without another word, Jimmy squeezed past the trio of women and marched under the iron archway. He leaped the stoop in one bound, shoved the front door in, and disappeared inside.

Ella wasn't sure what she'd said to set him off, but she was now certain that Kay had been scared of something or some*one*, and it may have gotten her killed.

After lunch, Ella sat in the backyard with Grandma Wink under an old oak tree, enjoying good company, the dry heat, and drowning in her own sweat.

Keystone Inn towered at their back, providing little by way of shade as the sun reached its zenith. The lawn sloped gradually until it met the lakeside trail.

Ella listened to the water lapping at the shore, sipping lemonade and wishing she'd packed a swimsuit for Thanksgiving with her parents. Overhead, the leaves of the oak tree provided a modicum of relief from heat.

Ella traced her finger through the condensation on her glass before setting the cup down, then she stretched out on her lawn chair the best she could, matching Fluffy's prone body beside her. It was hard to believe that only a couple days prior she'd been trudging through snow banks up to her knees.

"So, what do you think of our little town?" Wink asked.

"It's beautiful. And full of crazy people."

"Present company excepted?"

"Nope," Ella teased. "But honestly, once you get past the whole never-see-your-family-or-friends thing, Keystone's pretty great." A breeze whispered through the leaves and played across Ella's skin.

The tranquility broke with the sound of Wink slapping a fly. "I love it here. It's a great way to travel the world. 'Course it's too risky crossing the boundary line to explore, but I do get to see a lot from my house."

"Oh yeah, you live on Twin Hills. I bet you have a great view."

"I do indeed. You should stop by sometime and see it."

"I would love that." Ella's eyelids began to droop.

"Why don't you come over for dinner tonight? Say, six o'clock?"

Remembering Grandma Wink's moist banana bread and how it had melted over her tongue set Ella's mouth watering. If Wink's cooking skills were half as good as her baking, Ella would be crazy not to accept.

The diner owner slapped at another insect. The movement made Ella's right forearm crawl. She scratched it.

"Whatcha you got there?" Wink leaned over, wrapping her bony fingers around Ella's wrist. She whistled.

"What?" Ella followed her gaze to her own skin.

Red splotches covered her from wrist to elbow. She straightened in her chair, pulling the sleeves of her t-shirt higher.

"What is this?" Now that she noticed the rash, it felt like her whole body crawled with invisible ants.

"Just some poison oak. Must've gotten it when you went on your little escapade into the woods. There're loads of it there." When she caught the horrified expression on Ella's face, she smiled. "Don't worry, dear. It's nothing a little jewelweed won't clear up."

Ella froze. "What? What did you say?"

Wink laughed, the melodious sound bringing Chester down from his branch. "It's just a poison oak rash, dear."

"No, not that. Jewelweed?"

"Yeah. Some of the residents grow it. It helps with rashes and other skin ailments. Since we can't exactly run to the local drugstore, we have to look at alternative treatments and medicines."

"But isn't jewelweed poisonous?"

"Only if you eat it, for heaven's sake. For a rash, you just mash it up and slather it on your skin."

Ella sank back into her chair, her mind racing. "So, most residents grow this plant?"

Wiggling her fingers at Chester, Wink said, "I wouldn't say most. But a handful. Most know to stay out of the forest or know what poison oak looks like enough to avoid it."

"Who grows jewelweed?"

"Let's see, I think Rose might have some in the conservatory."

"Who else?"

Grandma Wink's hand paused from playing with Chester, and she peered at Ella. "Oh, I don't know. But why not just get some leaves from the conservatory? Rose wouldn't mind."

Ella chewed her lip. "I wasn't asking because of the rash. Kay was poisoned."

A weighted silence followed, and she allowed Wink to process the news about her employee and to come to the same conclusion Ella had.

Taking a slow breath, Wink's hand dropped to her lap, causing the squirrel to wander in search of his playmate. "I see. You know this for a fact?"

"Yeah. Pauline doesn't know by what yet."

"Hmm, I see," Wink repeated. "Even if it was jewelweed, anyone has access to the conservatory. The inn's open to the town. Have you noticed anyone hanging around there lately who shouldn't be?"

"No. No one besides the usual."

Wink's chest deflated, and she looked tired. "Well, as I said, other people grow it."

"Yeah, but that could at least narrow down the suspects, couldn't it? Does Six grow it?"

"Not sure. It's possible." Her mouth turned down as she swept back a strand of runaway blue hair. "You think Six might've had something to do with her death?"

Ella nodded.

"But why?"

Ella rubbed her hand over her lemonade glass, working out how much to tell Wink. It wasn't that she suspected the diner owner, but she didn't know Wink well enough yet to know if she could keep a secret or not.

Wink seemed to pick up on her hesitation and put Ella out of her misery. "That's okay. You don't have to tell me. Besides, I'm sure Pauline will figure it out."

Ella wasn't so certain. At the potluck, Pauline had said Kay's stomach contents only had trace amounts of the poison. Meaning that if the plant was what had killed Kay, it would have had to have been ground to a fine pulp and already absorbed, otherwise Pauline would've found plant fibers.

Ella needed to look at the jewelweed in the conservatory again. If some leaves were missing, maybe that would help narrow down which plant had been used.

"I have to go."

"Investigate a murder?"

Ella downed the last of her lemonade and searched the older woman's face. "You going to tell me not to?"

"Not at all. Sheriff Chapman's got his hands full enough, what with Six tearing up the town and that Viking throwing his ax at anything that moves."

"There's a Viking in Keystone?"

"Point is, don't let Chapman know what you're up to. He's a decent man, and he's the hand of law in Keystone. But he comes from a different time. Truth be told, I'm not sure he knows how to investigate a murder like this."

Ella felt both relieved and grateful for the support.

"Also," Wink continued, "don't go having fun without me. I've already lost one friend. I don't want to lose another. And I'm getting bored. There's only so much trouble Flo and I can get into."

Ella squeezed the older woman's shoulder. "I'll keep that in mind."

She rushed over the lawn, her bare toes tangling in the thick grass before she reached the terrace. Inside the conservatory, Ella breathed in its earthy aroma, then she homed in on the jewelweed.

Bending low, she pulled aside the plant's stems. The wispy white flowers shook with indignity at being handled.

Near the back, she spotted what she was looking for but hoped to not see. Several stems had been severed.

Ella's chest tightened as she realized the implication. She knew it wasn't catching either Jimmy or Rose red-handed. Knew it could've been anyone. It was even possible that Six had sneaked inside and clipped the leaves. It was also possible that the leaves had been used for medicinal purposes as a topical like Wink had explained.

She also knew it wasn't definitive that the plant had killed Kay. But what she did know was that it was time to present this information to the sheriff.

"*Hola nuevamente.*"

Ella jumped and whirled around. Angelica stood in the doorway, a pair of gardening gloves and clippers in her hands.

Ella let out a breath, grabbing her chest. "Angelica, you scared me. Is everyone in this town part cat?"

"*Disculpe*, you need help?"

"No, *estoy bien*." Ella jutted out her arms, revealing the offending red splotches creeping up her skin then pointed at the plant. "I just came for some of this."

"Ah, *sí*." Angelica clipped some leaves off for Ella and dropped them into her palm. Then, she motioned how to mash up the leaves, clicking off instructions in rapid Spanish. Thankfully, Ella understood most of it.

Ella thanked her then began to walk away before she stopped. "Angelica? Who else clipped this plant?"

The gardener furrowed her brows in confusion. Ella pointed at the naked spot where other leaves should've been. "*¿Quién tomó estas hojas?*"

"Ah. Señora Murray."

CHAPTER 18

A BEAD OF sweat rolled down Ella's back. The sun had carved its path across the sky and turned the day into late afternoon, causing the heat to radiate off the sidewalk like the inside of an oven.

She teetered outside the sheriff's office, debating on whether or not to barge in. There had been no doubt on the walk over, but once she'd peeked through the window and saw Six pacing his cell, the doubts crept in.

The thought of seeing the outlaw again caused more sweat to break out, prickling her forehead—or maybe it was just the heat. The rash on her arms worked overtime in making her miserable, and she resisted the urge to scratch her skin raw. She wished she'd taken the time to make up the jewelweed paste before leaving the inn.

Ella rolled her shoulders back and took a deep breath. So what if Six was inside? He was behind bars, and she wasn't. Was she really going to pass up the opportunity to rub it in his face?

The old hinges on the door creaked as she walked in.

Inside, the temperature wasn't much lower and had the added benefit of smelling like a high school boys' locker room.

"Miss Barton," Sheriff Chapman drawled from his desk. He shoved some papers around before tipping back in his chair and looking at her. "Help you?"

She rubbed her arms absently before she caught herself and stopped. She hadn't looked over at the cells yet, but she could feel Six's cold eyes on her and could smell his tobacco and woodsy scent.

"Um, yeah. I may have information that could help your investigation."

"Which one?"

"Kay."

The sheriff shifted his body so that his whole lanky frame faced her, giving her his undivided attention. With a leathered hand, he tipped the brim of his hat up. "Go on."

The sweat had now collected at the small of Ella's back, and she was sure she'd have an attractive dark spot on her shirt.

"Can we talk in private?" Her eyes darted over to the cells. Jesse's arms draped through the bars. He, too, was giving her his undivided attention.

Ella glared and before she could stop herself said, "How's that cage treating you?"

"Why don't you come closer and find out?"

She flipped him off.

Sheriff Chapman cleared his throat. "Let's step outside. I could use some fresh air, anyway. Something's fouling this place up." He glanced pointedly at Six.

As he walked towards the door, he said over his shoulder, "Don't go anywhere, now." His mustache twitched in a surprising show of humor.

Maybe he wasn't so bad, Ella thought. Old-school in his methods, but she was beginning to warm to him.

They stepped out onto the sidewalk, and he led her to the library's overhang where they could find a reprieve from the sun.

"Whatcha want to tell me?"

As she searched for the words to begin, her gaze wandered from the badge pinned to his vest to his holstered revolver, different from Six's, with ivory grips.

"I found some jewelweed in the inn's conservatory," she blurted out then winced at how ridiculous she sounded now that she heard it aloud. "There are several clippings missing. I noticed it when I went to get some for myself." She showed him her poison oak rash.

"Ain't nothing special about that." His gaze drifted across the road, seeming to grow bored with the conversation. "Lots of folks use it for skin ailments."

"Well, Kay had a poison oak rash, remember?"

He squared his face on her again, and his chest heaved with a big, impatient breath. "Miss Barton, I'm failing to see what this has to do with anything."

"What if the jewelweed is what poisoned her?"

"She would've had to ingest it."

"Okay. So, maybe someone smashed it up and put it in her food or drink."

"Or maybe Kay took the jewelweed that's missing from the inn and used it on her rash."

"Maybe. But it's at least worth looking into, right? And Rose was the one that took the clippings."

He tipped his head, seeming to consider this.

Ella chewed her lip, wondering how best to broach the next bit of information. She didn't want to throw Jimmy under the bus, so subtly was key.

"Did you know Jimmy was having an affair with

Kay?"

Sheriff Chapman's eyes snapped back to her. "Where d'you hear that?"

"Six."

"And you believed him?"

"Well, maybe. Yeah."

The sheriff continued to study her, searching her thoughts.

"Look," Ella said, "I've only been here a few days, but even I know Six has fewer scruples than I have hairs on my chin."

His eyebrows rose a fraction of an inch.

"Which is to say, none," she added, feeling that point hadn't been clear.

"Hmm."

"What was my point? Oh yeah. Point is, he said he saw the two of them sneaking off into the woods. He had no reason to lie about it. I can usually tell when people are lying. I'm a pretty good judge of character."

"Aren't you friends with Wink and Flo?"

"I stand corrected. *Usually*, I'm a good judge of character." Ella rocked back and forth on her feet. The conversation wasn't going as smoothly as she'd hoped. "Also, Kay had tree sap on her shoes the day she died, remember?"

His eyebrows crawled higher still.

"Then again, that could've been because Kay found Six's still…"

"What?"

"I didn't tell you that?"

"No."

"Really? Huh, I thought for sure I had."

He let out an exasperated sigh. "No, you failed to mention it."

Ella clicked tongue against her teeth. "Well, that's awkward. My bad."

The sheriff stood quietly for a while as his fingers continued to work over his mustache. She could almost see the cogs turning in his head. Jimmy and Kay were having an affair. Jimmy's wife cut the jewelweed. But Kay had found Six's still.

"It's all just a bunch of jawing, though. Just gossip and speculation. I need evidence," he said, more to himself than to her. He looked back at the small department building. "But I'll be having another chat with that barker back there about more than just his illegal, backwoods operation. And it won't be a friendly one."

Ella wasn't sure what a *barker* was but knew it was a barb against Jesse, in which case, she liked the term. "Don't forget, he also tried to kill me."

"Miss Barton, I appreciate you bringing all this to my attention. But in case you forget, this is my investigation. I know you're new, so I'll give you leeway. But from here on out, stay out of this. Focus on settling in and leave murderers to me."

He brushed the brim of his hat and strolled back to his office. Ella watched the door close with a *bang*.

After glancing at her watch, she headed back to the inn. She worked her hair into a high bun and instantly felt ten degrees cooler. She blew a loose strand away from her face and admired the disaster in the mirror.

"Maybe I should go see this Jenny," she muttered at her reflection. It had been a while since she'd had her hair cut. A new town, a new hairdo might help turn her situation into a fresh start.

If she were being honest, she hadn't left much behind in Oregon. A string of lousy boyfriends—none too serious —and a rocky relationship with her parents. They'd go through spells of getting along, followed by blowouts and not speaking for months. They'd just so happen to be going through a good bout during Thanksgiving.

Still, the idea of seeing none of them again or not being able to continue her research reignited the flame that she would return someday. She had to. She wasn't ready to say goodbye to that life forever.

Sighing, Ella gave up on her hair and pushed away from the mirror. She still had forty-five minutes before dinner with Wink. She figured it would take twenty minutes to reach the top of Twin Hills—a good part of it uphill. She was tempted to drive there but wanted the exercise since she planned on indulging at Wink's.

One thing was certain, she didn't want to be around the inn in case Sheriff Chapman stopped by to see the plant in the conservatory or to question the Murrays. Guilt was gnawing a hole through her stomach enough as it was.

Ella reconsidered and decided to leave for Wink's early, not only to avoid a possibly uncomfortable situation, but also to help Wink if she needed it.

She departed the inn and hiked up Main Street. Despite the heat radiating from the concrete, she wondered if she shouldn't have changed out of her shorts before leaving. Once the sun dipped behind the hills, the cool, evening air would blow over the lake, and the temperature would drop. It was going to be a chilly walk home.

When Ella reached the edge of town, the sidewalk became a gravel shoulder, and she pressed on, past the point Will had picked her up on her way to the greenhouses. Everything appeared different at this pace, and she noticed scenery she'd overlooked while going thirty in Will's pickup.

Just before the road began to climb, large fields stretched out on her left for several acres before running into a massive orchard that nearly swallowed the dunes on the horizon.

A white fence ran the perimeter of the nearest field, and a dairy sat in the center. Several hundred cattle—both Holsteins and Jersey—roamed around, their jaws working back and forth as they chewed their cud.

Soon, the unpleasant odor of manure filled her nostrils, and she took care to breathe through her mouth until she passed the field.

A large white house sat near the road, and Ella assumed the owner of the dairy lived there. Splashes of color lined the abode in flower beds full of Gerbera daisies, geraniums, and something that reminded her of a white sea anemone.

She noticed that part of the white fencing around the yard was missing, replaced with four by six-inch boards of grayed wood. The repair appeared recent.

The steep hike up Twin Hills was as exhausting as she'd anticipated. The dirt road meandered up the hill in a corkscrew pattern that had her huffing and puffing within minutes. As she neared the top, she was convinced that not only had she burned off the calories from all the sweets she'd consumed since arriving in Keystone, but from her Thanksgiving meal and maybe even all the Halloween candy she'd bought to "give out to the children" but ended up gorging on herself.

Wink's house rested at the very top of the left hill, a blurry speck of blue glimpsed between evergreens. Ella paused by another house, taller than it was wide, complete with stamp-sized yard, to catch her breath for the tenth time.

While she swallowed air, the professor popped out

onto the porch, the screen door slamming shut behind him. He looked in Ella's direction, and she waved, unsure if he was actually looking at her or not. With an abrupt turn, he bolted back into his house.

Ella dropped her hand and hollered to the empty air, "Good to see you too, professor!"

Will wasn't kidding about the man's social skills. Some people just liked their privacy. Of course, it stood to reason that anyone who lived on a hill, away from a small town, preferred more privacy than most.

Which left Ella wondering why Wink lived at the top. The older woman seemed to relish other's company, so it seemed odd she would live apart from them.

But Ella had learned people were not always what they appeared to be. Sometimes, a person would project themselves opposite of the flaw they sought to cover up. People insecure about their height wore taller shoes or someone who had grown up poor might hoard money and put on a wealthy front. Whatever the compensation, it could be traced back to an insecurity.

Wiping beads of sweat from her forehead, she collapsed onto Wink's porch steps, looking with longing at the door. A moment later, a shadowy figure stood on the other side of the screen. Wink shoved the door open.

"My goodness, you okay?"

"Fine. Hill," Ella gasped and pointed at the offending landscape as if Wink weren't aware that she lived on a hill that seemed more mountain with each stab of pain in Ella's side.

"My stars, child. You need more exercise."

"You need to move to a new house."

Wink disappeared and came back with a glass of water, ice tinkling against the sides. Ella sucked down the cool liquid.

"You do that hike every day?"

Grandma Wink shrugged. "Most days. Sometimes I drive if we're in a snowy climate or the weather's too hot."

"We're in a freaking desert."

"I know. I drove."

Ella made loud, pointed slurping noises with the last sips of water and handed the empty glass back to Wink. Now that she didn't feel like a potential heart attack victim, she climbed to her feet and admired the view.

The vista stole her words away. Keystone Village was an oasis in a vast desert. A sharp line of green grass and cream colored sand marked the town's boundary of what jumped through space-time and what stayed behind.

She let out a low whistle. "You can see everything from up here."

"I know." Pride was evident in Wink's voice. "I've seen the ancient pyramids from my window, hiked Greenland's glaciers, wandered the ruins of Angkor Wat, swam the Mediterranean, and walked the Great Wall of China. I've seen it all, and I've never stopped being in awe of it."

A deep ache grew in Ella's chest. A wanderlust she'd long ignored began to awaken. If she remained long enough in Keystone, what wonders might she see?

Ella traced the demarcation between town and desert with her gaze, rotating a full three hundred and sixty degrees. She stopped. There was something strange about the delineation.

Shielding her face from the sun, she studied the landscape again and realized what it was with a jolt. It was so apparent, she wondered how she'd missed it before.

"Wink, you ever notice how the town's border forms a

perfect circle?"

"Strange, huh? One of the many mysteries about Keystone."

There was something else nagging in the back of Ella's mind, something she couldn't put her finger on.

After appreciating the view until they could no longer tolerate the heat, Ella followed the older woman inside. The house was bright, an old colonial style painted in vivid, vibrant colors that matched the owner's personality. Light poured in from many windows, washing over knickknacks and comfy chairs.

The smell wafting in from the kitchen was heavenly and promised to make up for all the calories she'd just burned hiking up the hill. A ray of golden light fell on Wink's couch, and Ella felt she could curl up and nap for hours. The whole place was cozy, made for peace and warm memories.

In the kitchen, Wink directed Ella to a cupboard full of dishes. Ella set the dining room table then helped bring in several trays of food. By the fifth platter, she began to wonder if they weren't having a Thanksgiving meal.

"Are you expecting more company?"

A coy smile played at Wink's lips. "I may have invited a guest. Speaking of, we need another place setting."

Ella narrowed her eyes. "Who?"

Wink ducked back into the kitchen.

"Who did you invite, Wink?" Ella had a sneaking suspicion she knew who it was and glanced at her reflection a couple of times to be sure she didn't have perspiration rings anywhere on her clothing.

However, when Wink returned cradling a bowl of creamy mashed potatoes and chives, Ella quickly forgot about their mystery guest.

While they ate, Grandma Wink regaled Ella with tales

of travel from all the different locations the town had flashed to and of the various animals and people who had passed through the village.

"I know it's hard being so rude, but really, we're doing them a favor," she explained. "We don't want them getting stuck here."

Ella understood that now.

"I saw your hang glider outside. Do you fly often?"

"When the wind's right."

Ella tore open a homemade biscuit that both flaked and felt like butter in her hands. "The wind would never be right for me. You couldn't pay me to hang from one of those."

"Oh?" Wink's eyes glinted.

"That wasn't a challenge."

"Sure, dear."

"No, really. You'd have to drug me."

"Okay."

Ella eyed her new friend over her glass of tea and sipped slowly. Then, she glanced at the amber liquid in her cup and made a mental note to be suspicious of any food or beverage Wink offered her in the future.

She set the glass aside and opted for a thick fillet of lemon dill rainbow trout. "Do you worry about landing outside the town limits?"

"It's only happened a couple of times, and thankfully, I was able to foot it back quickly."

Digging into her trout, Ella changed the subject to Wink's diner.

"Sheriff says I can open back up tomorrow morning," Wink said.

"That's great." Ella looked over the expanse of food. "And not just because I'll have another place to eat besides raiding Rose's fridge every day."

Wink's smile faltered as she slathered butter and honey onto her biscuit. "It just won't be the same without my Kayline there. And I'm not sure Horatio and I can run the place by ourselves. You'd be surprised at how busy we get in such a small town. Most folks get tired of prepping and cooking at home. And secretly, it's the best spot to gather a bit of gossip."

She took a bite and continued. "As it is, I'm going to have to be there all day now. Might have to close a few hours early just to give myself a break."

Ella's hand paused in front of her mouth, a fork ladened with fish hovering in the air. "Maybe I can help out until you find someone. I worked as a waitress, and by 'worked' I mean I broke dishes and scraped gum off tables for a year between high school and college." After that ringing endorsement, she felt the need to add, "I'd be an extra set of hands."

"You make it sound so enticing," Wink said. Ella knew she was being sarcastic, but what she couldn't tell was whether or not Wink was considering the offer.

"Hard to resist, I know." She waited with bated breath.

"Well, why on earth didn't I think of that?" Wink dropped her biscuit as she stared at Ella. "I'm looking for help, and you're looking for work. It's perfect." She beamed across the Caprese salad. "You're hot."

"Nope. Only works to describe appearances."

Wink's face fell. "Oh dear. I told my butcher the way he cut my steaks was hot. No wonder he was confused."

Ella choked on a bite of biscuit. "Actually, that works. But..." She shook her head. "Know what? Doesn't matter."

If Wink kept insisting on using the word, Ella would explain the more nuanced meaning to it later.

"Maybe I should work at the diner on a trial basis,

first. I don't want you to feel obligated to keep me if I'm not working out. It's been years since my short stint serving tables. On an unrelated note, is there an acceptable number of dishes I can break before you fire me?"

"I'm sure you'll be perfect."

The screen door squealed open then slapped shut. "Perfect for what?" someone asked.

Ella recognized Will's smooth, deep voice without turning around. She shot daggers at Wink, who opened her eyes innocently before she beckoned the inventor to the table.

Slipping into the chair across from Ella, he glanced back and forth between their expressions, and his ears turned pink. "Wink didn't tell you I was joining you, did she?"

"Nope." Ella kept her eyes fixated on Wink, who became far too intrigued with searching for a bone in her rainbow trout.

"Will comes over for dinner a couple times a week. It's not unusual. It ain't right for a person to not get three square meals a day." She grabbed his plate without asking and shoveled a mountain of mashed potatoes onto it.

"I eat fine," he protested, but when she set the plate in front of him, he dug in with gusto. Soon, gravy ran down his chin and flakes of biscuit sprinkled over his shirt like dandruff.

Ella gaped at him. "You sure you get enough to eat at home?"

He blinked then looked down at the mess he'd created. After swallowing a rather large bite, he dabbed at his mouth with a cloth napkin and cleared his throat.

"I just get so focused on my work sometimes I forget to take a break." He shot Wink a look before returning his blue eyes back to Ella. "I didn't get a chance to talk to you at the memorial."

Because you were distracted by a pretty blonde. The moment she thought that, her cheeks flushed. What did she care?

"I appreciate you coming to the service."

Ella nodded, her mouth too full of string beans to respond properly.

"Ella's going to be working in the diner," Wink said.

"That so?"

When Ella finally managed to swallow the vegetable, she said, "I think she'll regret having me the moment the fire engine shows up." She paused. "Wait, do we have a fire department?"

"Sure, if you count Old Smokey." Wink slapped another piece of trout onto Ella's plate.

"Is that a person, place, or thing?"

"A truck," Will said. "And it's gone."

"What? It is?" Wink asked. "What happened?"

"Caught on fire a few months back, ironically."

"And I missed it? Where was I?" Wink snapped her fingers. "Must've been when Flo and I were in the slammer." She looked back at Ella. "I guess we don't have a fire department then. Just some volunteers and their garden hoses."

"Good to know. I'll carry an extinguisher around with me." Ella eyed her plate, feeling her pants grow tighter each minute. Just when she was starting to glimpse the bottom, Wink would pile more on. "Where's Chester, by the way?"

The older woman motioned towards the back porch. "Out making eyes with another squirrel. He's got a girlfriend."

Ella was tempted to ask more questions but let the matter drop, fearing Wink would give details about

Chester's love life that would make Ella want to set her ears on fire. And since there wasn't a fire department to put out the blaze, Chester's date was best left to the imagination.

After they'd finished eating, they began clearing the table. Wink set their dirty plates in the sink and attacked them with suds from handmade soap, talking over her shoulder as she did.

"I forgot to ask you, Ella, but what did you find out about the jewelweed?"

Ella's mouth went dry. Should she tell them about the leaves missing from the conservatory? They were both close with the Murrays and would probably be offended that she suspected anything untoward about them or that she'd told the sheriff about the plant.

"What about jewelweed?" Will asked.

"Oh, Ella had this theory that maybe that's what killed Kay."

"Really?" He rummaged through a cupboard in search of a lid, his back to Ella, but there was no mistaking the frown in his voice. "But it's only poisonous if you ingest it. And Pauline would've found bits of the leaf in her stomach."

"How do you know Pauline *didn't* find that in Kay's stomach?" Grandma Wink asked, sloshing soapy water all over the counter.

Ella and Will exchanged a glance, and she answered for him.

"Because we asked."

"And she was just nice enough to tell you out of the goodness of her heart?"

"Yep."

Wink lowered her eyebrows. "Hmm, doesn't sound like Pauline."

"What can I say? I think she's got a thing for Will."

"Hey—"

"She is sweet on him," Wink conceded.

Will set the dish containing the one leftover fish fillet in the fridge and grumbled about not liking where the conversation was going. "If you want me, I'll be in the other room, reading."

"Oh no you don't." Wink grabbed him by the ear and redirected him back to the counter, leaving a trail of suds in her wake. "You enjoyed that food, didn't you? Want more of it in the future? You ate, same as we did. You'll clean the same as we do. Just cause your plumbing's a bit different—" she glanced at his nether regions "—don't excuse you."

Ella applauded then handed him the plate of biscuits.

After the kitchen looked less like a tornado had come through, they settled into the family room. Ella had been right about the couch. It swallowed her like a cloud, and her eyes began to droop.

They popped back open when the couch dipped as Will settled in beside her, pulling an old album from under the coffee table.

"Have you seen this?"

"No, what is it?"

The spine made a cracking noise as he opened it up. "Clippings of the town newspaper over the years."

Ella stared at the yellowed paper behind the clear sheet protector. "Keystone has a newspaper?"

"Well, *newspaper* is being generous, but yeah. It's only a couple pages and comes out on Sundays."

Leaning over, she brushed her finger over the words *Keystone Corner*. The article was dated from 1920 and was about the local store burning down. She wanted to point out that the blaze probably could've been avoided if there had been a fire department but didn't think it helpful to point out after the fact.

"Wow." Her eyes scanned the article then drifted up to Wink. "Why do you collect these?"

"I only collect the ones of big events. I'm the town historian. I catalog all of the major goings-on over the years."

"There are big events in Keystone?" Ella held up her hands. "Only kidding. But seriously, this is pretty cool."

Wink's eyes lit up. "Kids today are still saying, 'cool'?"

"First of all, thank you for thinking I'm remotely in the vicinity of being young enough to be called 'kid,' and secondly, always."

Ella turned back to the clippings, to the snippets of history, and marveled at the woman across from her, with her blue hair, eclectic fashion, and questionable taste in pets.

Will flipped through the thick pages, searching for a section. "Here. This is after the first flash."

He shifted the album in his lap so Ella could see better, but she still had to lean in to read the tiny print. The clipping was dated August 23, 1951, and the headline read, "Where are We?"

"That was two days after the jump. I'll never forget it," Wink said. "I was getting ready to hang glide, staring over the valley, when a blinding light shot out of the earth and engulfed the town like a bubble. I couldn't see for several minutes after that. And when the afterimage was gone, it was night, and there was a bright city on the horizon."

"Chicago," Will mumbled.

Ella remembered what he'd said, about his home and time being the first jump. "And that's when you found Keystone?"

He nodded, his fingers pressing against the article as if trying to erase a memory. Ella could feel the town's horror dripping from the page. She was about to immerse herself in the clipping when he abruptly flipped the page.

He leafed through the rest, giving her just enough time to glimpse headlines. At one point, he paused again, his fingers caressing the photo of a profile piece on the latest people to be stranded in Keystone—or "arrivals" as the writer more appropriately termed them. Ella guessed "poor saps" wouldn't do much to boost morale.

At the time of the clipping, the town had jumped to 1990s Michigan. Ella had been starting grade school during that time, but she hadn't escaped the crimped hair bundled in a scrunchy phase unscathed. Her class photos were a series of awkward perms, bangs reaching towards the heavens, and stirrup pants.

But the twenty-something woman in the clipping had escaped the fad. She also looked familiar. She wore a sly smile, but there was some haunting secret in her eyes.

"Kayline," Will said.

Ella's mouth fell open, and she turned the album for a better look. In the picture, Kay stood with three other people. The caption underneath read, "Two families out camping get stranded in Keystone." Behind Kay stood a squat man with more hair and a slimmer waist than his present-day self, but there was no mistaking Mayor Bradford.

He scowled at the camera. One hand rested on Kay's shoulder, the fingers forming divots in her ivory skin.

Ella finally understood the wild look in Kay's eyes as fear. Kay had been afraid of her father.

CHAPTER 19

WILL GAVE ELLA a ride back to the inn. The front desk was usually empty, so she was surprised to see someone standing behind it. She was even more surprised that it wasn't Jimmy or Rose.

"Edwin?"

The other boarder who'd been stooped over the counter stood abruptly. "Hello. Welcome to the Keystone Inn. Would you like a room?"

"I live here now, Edwin. We met over breakfast a couple of days ago."

"Oh, right. Gemma."

"Ella."

Edward rubbed a hand over his textured skin, his expression flickering with memory. "Right, right."

"How come you're up front here? Where's Jimmy or Rose?"

"Jail."

"What?!"

"Well, not jail, per se. But the sheriff came by and

hauled them in for questioning. Jimmy asked me to man the desk for him." Edwin pushed thick glasses up his nose, the kind her grandfather used to wear, before puffing out his chest. "And that's what I intend to do. Man my post until he returns."

Ella's stomach felt like she'd swallowed a circus and any moment she'd see the dinner she'd just eaten. "Both of them? He took both of them in?"

"Yes, ma'am."

Ella gripped the cherry wood desk. He was just questioning them, she told herself. Nothing to worry about. The sheriff was just doing his job, and she'd anticipated this outcome might be a possibility. It didn't mean they were arrested or even guilty.

She kept reassuring herself silently all the way upstairs. Still, it didn't help her sleep any better.

The next morning, Ella rubbed the sleep from her eyes as she stumbled into the kitchen. The blue light of dusk stretched through the windows and across the floor. She fumbled for the light switch then choked back a gasp. A disheveled figure sat at the table, their head in their hands.

"Hello?" She snatched the nearest object—a banana—and crept forward.

Four feet from the intruder, she recognized Jimmy's thinning brown hair. His eyes were open, staring at the surface of the table in abject dejection.

"Jimmy, you scared the poop out of me. I was about to seriously hurt you." She tossed the banana on the table then laid her hand on his shoulder. "Jimmy?"

Startling, he blinked blood-shot eyes at her from above thick stubble.

"You okay?"

He started to nod then shook his head. "He kept her."

An icy feeling crept up Ella's spine. "Rose? Sheriff Chapman kept her?"

"He thinks she killed Kay. Says she has motive because Kay and I were having an affair." The mask fell away, and his expression stormed with rage. "An affair, can you believe it? The utter thought is ridiculous. Why would I? Rose is my life."

Guilt stabbed Ella's heart, a knife twisting deep.

"Where on earth would the sheriff get an idea like that?" Jimmy whispered. His eyes glistened when he looked at her.

Ella sank onto the chair beside him. "Yeah, why would he think that? That's insane." She stared at the banana. "But, uh, you two were seen secretly meeting in the woods together."

The innkeeper turned his palms up towards the ceiling. "That doesn't mean we were having an affair. For crying out loud, you can't do anything in this town without the gossip mill spreading lies." He scraped his slender fingers down the stubble on his cheek. "I was helping her out, that's all."

"Kay? Helping her out with what?"

His chest deflated in a deep sigh, taking some of his anger with it, and he stared out the window. The first kiss of morning stretched golden light across the lake.

"Her father? Were you helping her deal with her father?" Ella guessed.

He dipped his chin in a small nod. His eyes became vacant windows, and she knew she wouldn't get anything more out of him.

"I'm really sorry, Jimmy. Sheriff Chapman will get to the truth, you'll see. Rose will be free."

He remained as still as a statue. She sat with him for a

while longer before attempting to make them a breakfast of scrambled eggs sans shells and burnt toast. Unsure of how else to help, she plied him with the charcoaled toast and managed to coax a bite from him before she slipped out of the kitchen, coffee cup in hand, to get ready for her first day of work at the diner.

She felt fortunate to live next door to her new job. Getting to sleep in was a luxury she was growing fond of.

At the top of the stairs, the wood plank flooring creaked underfoot, filling the quiet inn with groans as her thoughts turned to Jimmy again. A new wave of guilt mixed with nausea from her barely edible breakfast churned her stomach.

This was all her fault.

However, a small part of her wondered if the sheriff knew more than she did. Maybe he'd uncovered more information. He wouldn't keep Rose unless he'd had good reason to, would he?

She had to make this right. Rose was locked up because of her. Maybe she didn't know who killed Kay, but between Jesse and Rose, her money was on Six being the murderer.

She paused outside her door. A horrible idea was forming in her mind. The sheriff had warned her to stop investigating, but that was before Rose was locked up because of her. And she wouldn't be *investigating* per se.

Ella changed direction to another door, a replica of her own just across the way. Her knuckles tapped a light rhythm on the wood. The boards creaked especially loud in this spot.

Ella prepared to rap her knuckles again when the door tore open. A death ray apparatus burst through the opening followed by wild waves of hair.

She jumped back, holding her hands up, and wishing

she had a banana on hand to defend herself with.

Crazy Flo let out a string of curses that would make a pirate blush. "It's just you."

"Who the hell did you think I was?" Ella clutched her chest. Between Flo and Jimmy, it'd be a miracle if she lived to see her first shift at the diner.

"A ghost."

"A ghost? Do you normally get ghosts knocking on your door?" Flo didn't respond. Ella motioned to the weapon still pointed at her. "You mind?"

Flo lowered it, and Ella eyed the triangular-shaped barrel and duct tape. "Does that thing shoot a projectile of any kind?"

"No, 'course not. That'd go right through an apparition."

"Of course." Ella put her fingers to her neck, taking her pulse while surveying Flo's appearance. "Sorry, did I wake you?"

"No."

"So, that's the normal state of your hair?"

"Looks better than that nest you got there." Flo started to close the door, but Ella barricaded her foot in the closing gap.

"Wait, I've got a quick question."

"Well, out with it. Don't dawdle."

"Do you know where Six lives?"

"'Course I do."

Ella took a slow, patient breath. "Okay… *can* you tell me where?"

"Why you wanna know? That man's trouble. Best to steer clear." She started to close the gap in the door again, and with it, Ella's chance to prove Rose innocent.

"Wait! I appreciate the concern. Really, it's touching coming from—" She stopped when Flo's nostrils flared.

"Anyway, Six's in jail. How much trouble could he pose? I just want to know where he lives, that's all."

Flo's beady eyes took Ella in from head to toe, then she shrugged. "Whatever. He lives on the rock flats. There's a small cabin there."

"Thank you. And the rock flats would be…?"

Flo let out an exasperated sigh, and part of her hurricane of hair flopped forward. "Head like you're goin' to the greenhouses, but instead of turnin' right to Twin Hills, turn left. There's a large orchard on one side of the road and Twin Springs on the other. That's where our drinkin' water comes from, by the way. They didn't want to drill a deeper pipe, but I told the council we needed to if we wanted enough to supply the town's needs. It was just a trickle before I—"

"Thanks, Flo. And the cabin's past the spring?"

"What? Oh, yeah. Just up the road. Can't miss it. If you're planning on going there though, I'd wait 'til dark."

"Why?"

"Because this town has eyes everywhere. If any nosey body sees you goin' to his place, they'll think you're in cahoots with that scoundrel. Or worse, it might get back to Six that you were on his property. My advice? Stay away."

She slammed the door before Ella could say anything more. It cracked open a second later. "But if you're hellbent on trespassing, do it right and take Wink and I with you." She slammed the door again.

Ella shook her head as she quickly got ready for work. Everyone in Keystone was full of advice, only half of it with a kernel of wisdom she intended to heed. And the other half, well, if she lived her life in constant fear, she'd never get out and do anything.

She decided that after work, she'd check out Six's place. She didn't know what she thought she would find, but she hoped there'd be *something* there to take the heat off Rose and put it back on the outlaw.

After changing into jeans and a black t-shirt, she strolled through the entrance hall with five minutes to spare. Rushing to the front door, Ella's foot caught on something soft. A howl broke the morning peace as she fell.

Fortunately, her left elbow broke the brunt of her fall. White, hot pain shot up her arm. Massaging it, Ella rolled over to glare at whatever she'd tripped on. Fluffy stood several feet away with his back arched and his eyes the size of Twin Hills.

All the anger in her dissipated as she cooed apologies and crawled forward. He stared at her, betrayed, before finally acquiescing and slinking towards her. After another couple of minutes of coaxing, she was able to pet out her apology. Sighing, she climbed to her feet, now certain she'd be late.

As she bolted out the front door, Fluffy slipped past her then followed her the half-block to the diner.

The bell above the front door tinkled merrily as Ella walked in. Before she could stop him, Fluffy hurdled over her feet in a blur of brown fluff.

Ella gave chase as best she could without drawing attention. He skittered around the checkered vinyl floor and ducked under the cover of an empty booth.

As she inched towards the booth, Fluffy hissed. A lone customer sat at the lunch counter, sipping coffee. He turned at the noise.

Ella flitted her hand in what she hoped was a casual greeting. "Good morning, Mayor."

"Miss Barton."

He turned back around to Wink who stood on the other side of the counter, cleaning the soda fountain. To make matters worse, Fluffy's nemesis Chester gnawed on a piece of donut a few feet away, unaware of the cat.

Ella glanced at the clock. A minute late. She mouthed an apology to Wink then looked pointedly from the hissing table beside her to the mayor and Chester.

Wink picked up on the hint. Leaning her elbows onto the counter, she said to the mayor, "I ever tell you the time I glided into a tree?"

Mayor Bradford sipped at his coffee while Wink enraptured him with her harrowing escape from a tall cedar tree. While Wink's mouth did the heavy lifting, her fingers broke off a chunk of donut and dropped it onto the floor, behind the counter, forcing Chester to have to flit over to it.

With both politician and pet distracted, Ella dropped onto the floor beside the booth. Kneeling, she reached into the shadows and felt a fluffy paw swipe at her.

"Please don't do this. Not on my first day."

Fluffy responded by rolling over.

Wink laughed a little louder than was necessary at something Mayor Bradford said. Ella glanced over her shoulder, making eye contact with the older woman. Wink's eyebrows rose a fraction of an inch. Ella shook her head and shifted to reveal the feline under the table.

Just as the mayor began to spin on his stool, Wink grabbed the pot of coffee again. "More sludge, Earl?"

While Wink poured, Ella dived under the table. Hands met fur, and she gripped the cat and pulled. Twisting, Fluffy sank his claws into her forearm. Ella ground her teeth and managed not to scream or let go. She pulled both herself and the fur ball out from under the table, but not before hitting her head.

Once extricated, she tried to console the Maine Coon. "Sorry, buddy. I'll make it up to you."

Turning her back slightly to the counter, Ella managed to get Fluffy out the front door without the mayor or Chester seeing. The moment his paws hit pavement, the cat cried at her and stuck his tail in the air.

Sighing, she pulled the door shut again. It wouldn't surprise her if she found something special on her bed later as a form of payback. She had a lot of making up to do.

The mayor turned as the door jingled, confusion on his face at her second entrance in less than five minutes.

"There was a bug," she explained.

He shrugged and mumbled something about "newcomers" before rolling his generous body back to face Wink again.

Ella slid behind the mayor and shot Wink a thumbs-up. The tension in the diner owner's face eased.

Ella joined her behind the counter, accidentally mashing donut crumbs as she went. Chester paused mid-chew and chittered at her for ruining the morsels as more crumbs fell into the bib of his green overalls.

"I'm not stealing your donut, you nutter," she muttered. "And I just saved your life. You owe me."

After a few minutes of listening to the mayor drone on about the responsibilities beset him, the trouble he's having with council members, and what to do about another dead cow on his hands, Ella draped herself over the counter and fought the urge to snooze. Mercifully, Wink told her to get acquainted with the cook and the kitchen, giving her an excuse to leave.

As Ella picked a careful, donut-free path towards the kitchen, her gaze snagged on where Kay had collapsed and died. She shivered at the memory, glanced back at Mayor Bradford, and stepped over the spot.

She swung the kitchen door in. The room appeared to

be an addition built onto the old railcar about a decade after the fact. It gleamed under candescent lightbulbs and smelled of cleaning supplies.

Horatio stood behind a large island, slicing a knife through purple onions. She recognized the cook from the day Kay died, but they'd never officially met.

When he looked up, she could see the same emotion in his eyes that she felt. They reminded each other of that gruesome day.

Ella cleared her throat awkwardly then introduced herself. She held out her hand then retracted it when she remembered that one of his held a knife and the other was covered in onion slices.

"Yeah, I was at the town meeting when the mayor introduced you." Horatio spoke with an accent—Italian if she had to guess. He broke the tension with a laugh. "He sure knows how to welcome a person."

"Is 'welcome' the right word?"

"Embarrass?"

"I was going to say 'humiliate and make me wish I'd never come here', but sure, we'll go with 'embarrass'."

The air filled again with the *chop-chop* of his knife, and Ella's eyes began to water.

"We're sure glad to have the help. I wasn't sure how we'd get by without..." He let the sentence die. His lips pressed together, and the chops of his knife bit into the cutting board.

Ella picked at an apron hanging against the wall but didn't take it off its hook. "It's just a trial until we're sure I can hack it."

"You'll be fine."

People seemed to have far more confidence in her than she did or severely underestimated her ability to screw up an order.

"Sure, so long as no one asks me to cook anything."

He laughed. "That bad, huh?"

"Let's just say I once microwaved a burrito that caught on fire."

His eyebrows knitted with confusion. "What's a microwave?"

"God's gift to humanity. And a college student's means of survival." She then proceeded to describe the appliance but stopped when he started asking *how* the food heated up so quickly.

Grandma Wink swept through the door and caught the last bit of their conversation. "Oh, I read about those. Saw an ad for one, but that was shortly before our first jump. Those things are expensive. Wish we had one here." She looked over the kitchen wistfully.

After telling them how affordable the invention was in her time, Ella apologized for being late and for Fluffy.

Wink dismissed the apology. "Happens all the time. That cat is constantly hunting my poor Chester—" She stopped and took in Ella's outfit. "You're not changed yet."

Ella looked down at her pants then at the apron still hanging on the wall. "What's wrong with my jeans?"

A drawer squealed as Wink opened it and produced a pink gingham print waitress uniform. "With a town all over time, people need a place that feels like home. For most of us non-transplants, it's the era of burned coffee and poodle skirts."

Ella accepted the uniform, grateful she didn't have to wear a poodle skirt.

After changing in the small restroom, she became Wink's shadow, greeting customers as they walked in and watching how the owner took food orders.

Ever the linguist, Ella used the back of an order pad to

keep a running vocabulary list of all the diner lingo. It wasn't just "eggs on toast," but "chickens on a raft" and so on.

Five hours later, after the lunch rush, Ella had a moment to catch her breath and rest her tired "dogs" as Wink would call them.

Leaning against the kitchen counter, she guzzled a glass of water and mopped at her forehead. The smell of freshly baked bread permeated the room while Horatio stood over the island, sharpening his knives.

They made idle chitchat about his wife and kid until the kitchen door whooshed open, and Wink swept in. Wisps of flour floated from her apron like clouds.

She squeezed Ella into her bony side for a hug. "It's so nice having you here, dear."

"It's nice being here."

"And not a single fire yet."

"Give it time. Oh, and sorry about the dish. And the pickles." Ella winced, remembering the tangy smell as she'd mopped up the mess.

The front door jingled. Wink peered through the pass-through window where Horatio usually placed plates of food.

"Ella, would you mind? I need to run some errands, and I have an appointment with Jenny." Her veiny hand brushed her blue bob, leaving a flour residue behind.

"Of course." Ella pulled out her order pad.

"Oh, and can you pull the bread out in about ten minutes?"

"Yeah, or Horatio could—"

"Nonsense, dear. You'll be fine. I gotta run."

Ella made note of the time on the kitchen clock before going to greet the newcomer. After putting the ticket on the pass-through, she glanced at the clock over the milkshake machine, filled the customer's glass of water, and rushed to the restroom. When she returned, Horatio placed a large basket of fries and trout salad with dill lemon dressing in the pass-through.

"Order up!"

She carried the pile of steaming food over to the lunch counter.

Horatio poked his head through the pass-through. "Hey, I'm stepping out back for a smoke. Need anything else?"

"No, we're good." She shot him a smile before glancing at the clock again.

After she heard the back door close, Ella lounged behind the lunch counter next to the soda fountain, sipping coffee and eyeing the display of donuts.

The smell of baking bread wafted in from the kitchen and filled the diner. She pulled the mouth-watering aroma into her lungs, paused, and sniffed. She straightened and sniffed again, her mouth turning down at the corners. Another scent rode along with the bread.

Ella burst into the kitchen and tore open the oven door so hard it nearly broke off its hinges. A dark brown lump sat in the loaf pan.

"No, no, no!" She started to reach for it then realized the error in doing so.

Frantically searching for potholders, she settled on Horatio's stained towel. After sliding out the pan, she dropped it on top of the stove with a clatter.

Ella grabbed at the roots of her hair. How could this happen? She looked over at the clock on the kitchen wall. It had been twenty-four minutes since Wink left! The bread had been in the oven fourteen minutes too long. But how?

Ducking back into the diner, she peered up at the

clock. The hands were frozen in the same position since the last time she'd checked. On closer inspection, she realized that the smaller hand was three hours off.

Ella squeezed her eyes shut and silently chided herself for such a careless mistake. She'd been so focused on the minute hand. Hopefully, Wink didn't have her heart set on freshly baked bread. Maybe she could turn the rocky loaf into croutons or stuffing.

Or a boat anchor.

Back in the kitchen, she turned the oven off and slumped against the counter just as Horatio stepped in through the back door.

He whistled. "It's gonna be another hot one."

"That clock in the diner doesn't work."

"Sì, It's been out for months. The town's battery supply is low. Need more rechargeable ones, I guess. Most people have switched back to the—what do you call it? Windups? The council's been talking about sending a couple of volunteers to make a supply run next time we're near a town." His eyes snagged on the bread, his mouth forming a tight "O."

When Grandma Wink returned a couple hours later, Ella broke the news gently, explaining how the mistake happened. The older woman laughed, her freshly styled hair brushing over her collarbone like a blue waterfall.

"Oh, honey. I've burned tons of loaves before. Don't worry about it. It's not your fault. I should probably just take that clock down. Only reason I haven't so far is 'cause it bugs Flo so much." She poked the rock-hard bread, her chuckles turning into peals of laughter.

"Couldn't you smell it?"

"Well, yeah. After it started burning."

Wink wiped her eyes. "I could use a new doorstop. Or paperweight."

"Glad I could help, then."

The afternoon wore on, with another rush of customers trying to beat the heat with soda floats and shakes. Ella darted about, doing her best not to spill anything, while Wink ran the register.

By the time the steady stream became a trickle, Ella's shift had finished. She dragged her feet over to the coffee maker and poured a stale cup of mud. Then she settled into the same booth Will had sat in the day they'd met.

Overall, her first day had been a success—burnt bread notwithstanding. Most of the people she'd met had been friendly, welcoming her to Keystone, with only a few giving her the stink eye.

One had grunted and growled, but she was pretty sure he was a Neanderthal. Either that or a really hairy person with abnormal facial features and an aversion to clothing.

She stretched her tired feet across the booth to the other seat and released an audible sigh. A warm slice of fresh banana bread sat in front of her, the butter making a small lake in the center.

She'd just popped the first gooey bite into her mouth when the front door burst in with such force it knocked a picture off the wall.

"William Whitehall, what on earth?!" Wink scrambled around the counter, throwing the cleaning towel she'd been working back and forth over the surface across her shoulder.

Ella craned her head around. Will's pale face scanned the diner, ignoring Wink. The moment he spotted Ella, he made a beeline for her. "Did you hear?"

"What?" she said around a mouthful of banana bread. She swallowed the barely chewed morsel, the glob catching in her throat.

"Chapman released Six."

CHAPTER 20

"WHAT?" ELLA STARED at the handsome inventor, trying to process what he'd just said.

Wink shoved a basket of fries in front of a customer and joined them. "Chapman let Six go? After what he did to Ella?"

"Yes. That badge said all he could charge him with was the illegal still."

Ella gaped at him. "But he was going to kill me."

"*We* know that. And I'm sure Chapman believes us, but he didn't have any evidence to prove it."

"Alright, but what about Kay? He had the motive to kill her."

Will deflated, and he seemed to shrink in stature. He pulled off the fedora he was wearing and ran his hands through his hair. "Six has an alibi for the hours leading up to Kay's death. The sheriff had locked him up for something else."

"But I saw him in front of the diner that day."

"Yeah, but Chapman had just released him. He came

straight here from the sheriff's office. Pauline found nothing in the diner to account for poisoning."

Wink motioned them to keep their voices down in case the two patrons at the counter grew curious ears. "Meaning…"

Ella picked at her banana bread, no longer hungry. "Meaning Kay was poisoned before coming to work. Meaning Six is covered for the murder."

"Well, one thing's for sure," Wink said, placing her hands on her hips, her pink uniform swaying. "You're not going anywhere alone. You've got a target on your back, and Six has a bullet with your name on it."

"Agreed," Will said.

Ella opened her mouth to argue, thinking about her plans to poke around the outlaw's homestead. But now that he was out of the holding cell, she'd have to come up with a new plan.

"Sorry, El. I just thought you should know."

A new feeling besides panic fluttered in the pit of her stomach at the nickname he'd just given her. "Thank's for the heads up."

He touched the brim of his hat. "I have to go. Chapman gave me permission to go to Kay's place and pack up some of her belongings."

"How come her father isn't doing it?"

Will exchanged a glance with Wink before he explained, "Doesn't want any of her things."

Ella's mouth puckered as if she'd just sucked a lemon. She couldn't imagine the pain a parent experienced going through the belongings of their only, recently deceased child.

On the other hand, it seemed strange that the mayor didn't want *any* of it. Will's expression said he didn't look forward to the task either.

"I'll come with you," she offered.

Wink stood aside and slightly behind Will, so he couldn't see her. She nodded enthusiastically behind his back. Ella ignored her.

"I'd love the company, thanks."

He held the front door open and waited while Ella slid out of the booth, her uniform tugging at an awkward angle. "Mind if I change first?"

"Of course."

While Ella walked into the kitchen, her blue-haired friend stepped on her heels. "Great thinking, dear. Let him get to know you better."

"Wink, I'm going for moral support."

"Sure, sure. And I'm a vampire who's able to come out during the day."

Ella feigned surprise. "You are? But you hide it so well."

"You know, if you wanted to run home and change first…"

"And your skin. That explains why it's so pale."

"Okay, okay." Wink held her hands up in surrender. "Nothing more about Will. You done?"

Ella grabbed one of the cloves of garlic beside the soup pot. With her other hand, she covered her neck and backed into the bathroom to change.

Ella hopped up a meandering path of stepping stones that led to a small cottage overlooking the lake. The heart of Keystone Village sat along the shoreline across the way, sprawled out and sleeping in the heat of the day.

A wall of pine and spruce trees towered behind the house. The trail entrance into the woods she'd followed Six down sat a half-mile away on her right. No wonder Kay and Jimmy met there. It was both near her house and private.

Ella's shoes slapped over the stones as she made for the cute red door, but Will veered off around the side of the structure.

"She was renting the studio upstairs."

Ella followed him around the corner to a set of stairs. What she had neglected to tell Wink earlier was a secondary reason for accompanying the inventor. It gave her a good excuse to poke around Kay's apartment.

It had been broken into just before her death, and Ella found it hard to believe the two tragedies were unrelated. If there was anything inside that could throw suspicion off Rose, Ella would find it.

At the top of the stairs, Will slid a key from his pocket and turned it in the doorknob. The door creaked open into a quaint studio, complete with a kitchen nook just big enough to turn around in. Windows on either side overlooked the forest and the lake.

Ordinarily, the space was probably cozy. However, as it stood, the twin bed sat shoved against a corner at an odd angle, the rug flipped over, and papers littered the floor. In that sense, it reminded Ella of her own apartment in Oregon, only she didn't have the excuse of a recent break-in.

She stood in the doorway, surveying the damage while Will picked a careful path around the room. His face was clouded with emotion.

"The break-in happened a day before her murder, right?" Ella's fingers brushed over a deep scratch in the doorjamb. The corresponding location on the door wasn't any better.

"Yeah," Will said softly, his voice heavy.

"She didn't clean any of it up?"

His hands curled into fists, and she feared she'd

pushed too hard. Finally, he shook his head.

"She probably left it for Chapman to investigate. She came home after her shift at the diner, saw the place, then ran downstairs to call the sheriff."

"Did Chapman come by?"

"Said he did." Will sighed, picking up a picture frame of a black-and-white photo. In it, he and Kay sat on a grassy knoll, the lake in the background. Their heads touched in intimacy as they smiled up at the camera.

"Fingerprints?"

"The sheriff got prints, but nothing but friends and family."

No fingerprints? Someone knew what they were doing.

"I don't see anything here that could've gotten her killed," Will said and let out a frustrated sigh. "Maybe the two incidences aren't as connected as we'd thought."

Ella's foot crunched on glass next to the bed. Kay's nightstand lay sprawled on the ground, a shattered picture frame beside it. Another photo of Kay and Will stared up at Ella, and her heart broke anew for the man.

"Hey, Will?" He looked up from a pile of books. "I'm sorry again for your loss."

He pressed his mouth into a grim line and nodded. Unsure of what else to say, she gave him space to brood in silence. He'd found an empty milk crate in the lone closet and used it to begin collecting Kay's belongings.

Standing by a window, Ella watched a fisherman cast out onto the lake. A gentle breeze danced through the open windows, fluttering the curtains, bringing the scent of the forest and song of birds.

Kay's studio, though small, was the kind of refuge people dreamed of, filled with long, lazy days of reading, listening to classical music, watching the forest grow, and drinking in life. It was filled with silence that was more than just the absence of sound, but the lull of a Sunday afternoon when the sun poked out from a cloud. It was the birth of spring. The patter of rain on a roof. The roll of a distant thunderstorm. It was solitude and reflection.

It was peace.

And it was a special kind of horror that would make Ella want to leave such a place. But Kay had met that darkness. She had wanted to flee Keystone.

Ella let the gauzy curtain fall back into place. Turning, she spotted an old television set in the corner. It was the size of a mini fridge, with curved glass and knobs across the front.

Ella gaped at it like she'd just won the lottery. "You have televisions here?"

Will followed her gaze. "Remnants of Keystone before the flash. They're useless unless we're in a time that transmits analog signals the receiver is able to pick up."

"Not useless if you have a DVD player," she said under her breath. Judging by the looks of the monstrosity, the picture probably wasn't in color, let alone capable of hooking up to anything digital.

"That set was left by the previous renter." Will returned to packing the crate.

Ella wandered into the kitchenette. Compared to the rest of the place, it seemed unscathed. Only a few cupboard doors stood ajar.

She took her time shutting them before moving to the refrigerator. A grocery list in flowery cursive was still fastened to the front, and the door stood open, cold air spilling over her skin.

Ella widened the gap to check for any contents that could spoil. She didn't want the landlord to have to deal with a foul-smelling fridge—something she'd learned after an unfortunate power outage while vacationing in California for a week. Her apartment had never smelled the same after that.

The refrigerator was mostly bare except for some eggs, bread, and milk. Ella grabbed the glass bottle and poured the contents into the sink. On the whole, it didn't smell too bad; she'd certainly smelled far worse—a thought that made her sad.

While Ella rinsed out the bottle, the light from the kitchen window hit the painted logo of Bradford Farms on the front. Ella froze.

Kayline Bradford.

Dripping water across the counter, she turned off the faucet and tilted the glass towards the rectangle of sun pouring in.

"Will? Did Kayline own a dairy?"

His eyes darkened from above Kay's extensive vinyl record collection. "It's the mayor's dairy. It's up Main Street, just out of town. We passed it on the way to the greenhouses."

Ella nodded, remembering the fields of cows, the pungent smell of excrement, and the adjacent manicured yard and house. "They didn't have a great relationship, did they?"

"No, they did not."

"Did he know she was unhappy here?"

His green-blue eyes had shifted to the color of a stormy sea. "She was only unhappy here *because* of him. And yes, he knew. They fought a lot about it. He did everything he could to keep her here. The compromise was letting her move out and get this place."

Ella's grip on the bottle tightened. *Let* her get her own place? The woman was an adult, for crying out loud.

Her fingers brushed the fading lines of the logo,

turning over the information. The more Ella learned about the mayor, the more she didn't like him.

Had the mayor really done *everything* to keep Kay in Keystone?

As she wiped her hands over her jeans, something flickered in the sunlight on the floor. Ella knelt and picked up the object, turning it over in her palm. It was a button with a mother-of-pearl finish.

Her mouth went dry. She'd seen this button before. On a tan shirt in the woods when a gun was pointed at her.

Ella stared at the milky-colored clue, considering the implication: Jesse had been in Kay's apartment.

But the sheriff should've found his prints. Unless… unless the outlaw was smart enough to wear gloves.

Regardless, the small object wasn't much, but maybe it was enough to divert suspicion away from Rose and back to Six.

Ella rose to her feet, her shoulders slouching. Or maybe it was a coincidence, and the button came from one of Kay's blouses.

There was only one way to find out. Ella already felt strange rummaging through Kay's stuff, but the feeling she was intruding amped up when she pulled open the closet door. She tried to think of an excuse to tell Will.

"What's going to happen to all her clothes?"

"They'll go back to the clothing pool. Why? You want 'em?"

Ella swept her hands over the spartan collection of attire, considering her own sparse wardrobe of jeans and t-shirts, but it didn't sit right with her, wearing a dead woman's clothes.

"No. I'm not sure they'd fit."

They lapsed into silence again while Ella gently lay Kay's wardrobe on her bed, searching for buttons that matched the one tucked into her pocket.

The process didn't take more than a minute, nearly everything she pulled out had a Nike logo on it, sans buttons, yielding nothing. She pulled out the last item, a button-less dress, and laid it down, frowning.

Something about the closet seemed amiss. There were still nearly two dozen empty hangers in it—far more than one kept for spares.

Her eyes raked over the small apartment, but she didn't spot any clothes she'd overlooked. There was nothing in the hamper, and even the dresser drawers were lacking.

It was possible that Kay never acquired much by way of clothing after arriving in Keystone, but something in Ella's gut told her the woman had to own more than two dresses, two pairs of jeans, and a few t-shirts.

"Will, after the break-in, did Kay stay somewhere else?"

He shook his head and gathered up a stack of important looking manilla folders, unique by a massive pink stain that marred the bottom left side of every one. It looked like half a bottle of nail polish had spilled its guts over them.

"So, is this the normal size of her wardrobe?" She swept a hand over the clothes covering the bed.

He looked up from stacking the folders into the crate, and a crease formed between his brows. "No, actually. Is that all you found?"

She nodded. Was the intruder a clothes thief?

She puzzled again over the lack of fingerprints. It didn't seem like Six's style to be careful.

She stood in the center of the room, weighing her options. If she brought the button to the sheriff's attention, he'd question the outlaw again but wouldn't have anything more to hold him on. And if word got around to Six that she'd been the one to tip off Chapman, it'd give him even more reason to come after her.

No. She would need to find the evidence herself. The outlaw was in this apartment, searching for something. If he'd found whatever it was he'd been looking for, then it was most likely at his cabin. If she found it, she could connect him with Kayline.

She revisited the idea of poking around his place that night but with the now added danger of the cowboy being on the loose. What she needed was a distraction, something to keep him occupied long enough for her to investigate.

A heavy, broken sigh escaped Will as he stacked the last photo frame into the crate. The pile teetered, threatening to spill.

She considered telling him about the button but wasn't certain how he'd react. Patting the evidence in her pocket, she felt it best to keep it to herself—for now.

CHAPTER 21

ELLA WAITED IMPATIENTLY back at the inn for the sun to dip behind the sand dunes. As she changed clothes in the sauna that was her room, she wondered if the town ever jumped somewhere with a beach nearby.

She surveyed her outfit in the mirror. The only dark clothing she'd brought to Keystone were her calf-length yoga pants and black running shirt.

She sighed at the exposed patches of skin. At least she had her dark hair going for her. Briefly, she'd entertained the thought of borrowing one of the winter jackets hanging on the coat tree downstairs, but she decided she'd rather chance the patches of skin being spotted than die from heat exhaustion.

Before leaving, she grabbed her snow gloves from her open suitcase and slipped them on. No sense in leaving fingerprints.

When the shadows stretched and covered the town, Ella crept out of the inn, passing her Jeep along the way. She'd have to foot it; the vehicle was unique in a town of mostly antique cars, some buggies, a few horses, and even a chariot. If she drove the SUV up the road, she may as well post a bright, neon sign that flashed, *Ella's car.*

Her foot had just stepped off the curb at the end of the block when a rustle sounded from the bushes outside of the conservatory. Ella dived for cover behind a parked car. She held her breath and listened for several painful seconds. When she didn't hear anything, she poked her head up, expecting to see Six lurking nearby.

Two shadows emerged, both in dark clothing, shoving each other and tripping out of the rhododendrons. By the way they moved, Ella thought they were two drunks until they stepped closer to the lamplight.

Ella let out a heavy breath and stood. "You two nearly made me wet my pants."

"Told you we looked scary," Flo said to Wink.

"What are you doing here? Isn't it past your bedtime?" Ella redirected the last question to Flo who stuck out her tongue.

"We're going with you," Wink said. "You're going to Six's, right?"

Ella swallowed. "Maybe." She knew she shouldn't have gotten directions from Flo. "But you can't come. It's too dangerous."

"Dangerous?" Wink scoffed. "Honey, we've been painting this town red since before you were in diapers... actually since before your parents were in diapers."

Flo huffed and patted a dubiously shaped bulge under her jacket. "Oh, I got us covered."

Ella narrowed her eyes. "What's under there?"

"Nothing," Flo said at the same time Wink said, "A gun."

Ella's mouth dropped open. "You're *armed?*"

Flo's eyes widened, and for a moment, she seemed like

a sweet, innocent grandma. Until she opened her mouth. "You don't want to go anywhere near Six's without firepower."

Wink clicked her tongue and looked up and down the street. "We're a bit conspicuous standing here, chatting. Maybe we should get a move on?"

"That's why we're wearing black," Flo said.

"It only helps camouflage if you're not standing *under* a street lamp."

Ella closed her eyes and pinched the bridge of her nose before taking in their outfits. At least they'd given thought to their nighttime, skulking attire. "Wink, what is that? Is that a cape?"

Lifting her chin, the diner owner grabbed a swath of knitted yarn and threw it over her shoulder like a movie star. "It's a *shawl*, and it's the only top I own that's black." She clapped her hand like she was herding school children. "Now let's get going. I need to get back to Chester. He doesn't like being left alone."

Flo leaned close to Ella, put her hand to her mouth, and whispered loud enough for the whole block to hear. "She's got an unhealthy attachment to that fleabag. Know what I mean?"

Ella crossed her arms, rocking back and forth. "Fine, fine. You two can come along… *if* you can keep up."

With that, she dashed across the pavement, zigged down a side street, then zagged onto J Street, running parallel with Main.

Glancing back over her shoulder, she couldn't see the old broads anywhere. She felt a tinge of guilt but told herself it was for their own good.

Ella decided to keep to J Street. It didn't run the length of town like Main did, but there was less of a chance of being spotted on the sleepy road.

She continued her stalk up the sidewalk, keeping to the shadows like the invisible badass she was.

She began an internal monologue.

I am darkness. I am the night. A superhero—

"Evening, ma'am."

Ella straightened as she passed an older gentleman. "Good evening, sir. Nice night for a walk, no?" She hid her gloved hands under her armpits until he was several paces past her.

She melted into the shadows again. Just as she reached the end, where the only option was to turn back onto Main Street, she heard a steady hissing sound and realized it was someone wheezing.

A few yards away at the corner, hovering over the sidewalk, Flo bent over her knees, her large sides moving in and out. Wink stood over her, patting her back and muttering half-hearted encouragements like, "I told you, you need to exercise more."

Flo cursed at her between bites of air. Meanwhile, Ella avoided the nearest street lamp so the duo wouldn't spot her and stole across someone's lawn on tiptoes. She'd nearly made it past them when Wink said, "See? I told you we'd beat her. It's simple geometry."

Ella stopped, straightened, and her hands fell to her sides. "Son of a—can everyone see me?"

"Pretty much," Wink said.

"Helen Keller can see you," Flo said. Some color had returned to her cheeks, but a white, frothy substance had formed at the corner of her mouth.

"Whatever. Let's get going." Ella glanced over at Flo. "You going to be okay?"

"You don't need to worry about me." She patted her side to emphasize her point.

"All the armament in the world isn't going to help you

from having a stroke," Ella said.

She eyed the suspicious lump with a growing wariness. She wasn't a handgun expert, but even she could tell it was large and abnormally shaped.

They walked in silence down Main Street and quickly left Keystone proper behind. The sidewalk ended, as did the street lamps, and the darkness seemed absolute. With little illumination by way of moonlight, Ella used the flashlight app on her smartphone to keep them from tripping.

While they trekked, Wink began asking questions about why Ella was so sure Six was guilty. After several minutes of her prodding, Ella broke down and told them about what Six had said, about Kay finding his still, about the break-in at Kay's apartment, and about the button she'd found there.

While Wink had heard some of what transpired in the woods, she hadn't heard the details. All the while, Flo remained silent, but Ella suspected this had more to do with the strange whistling sound that accompanied every heavy breath than an actual disinterest.

Soon, Wink indicated that they were nearing the cutoff. Using her phone-turned-flashlight, Ella located the dirt road to Six's cabin.

The narrow lane shot out perpendicular from the main road and contained the orchard on one side. As their feet left the busted pavement, dust and the scent of apples filled Ella's nostrils.

With the sun gone, the temperature dropped rapidly. A chill crept over her skin, and she now wished she'd grabbed that winter coat after all.

After ten minutes, they passed an outcropping of trees and a wooden sign marking Twin Springs. The cluster of evergreens, oaks, and willows surrounding the spring stopped abruptly, and a vast, empty field stretched before them until it met the dunes on the horizon, blotting out the stars.

Ahead, a black rectangle marred the barren landscape. Dull light poured from the windows of Six's cabin.

Ella's stomach tightened into a ball of nerves. She shut off her light in case he looked out and spotted its movement, and she plunged them into near darkness.

"He's home," Wink said.

"Very observant," Flo said. "We suspected as much." As she spoke, the older woman's hand caressed the lump in her side.

Shaking her head, Ella redirected their course to the rundown barn next to the cabin. "My plan was to draw him out and away from the house."

She crept forward on the balls of her feet, tripping on clumps of sod, and being generally stealthy as she led them over to the sagging outbuilding. But she was a ninja compared to the Golden Girls behind her, hissing at each other like cats.

"Ow, Wink, that's my foot."

"Well, don't step in front of me."

"Then don't move so slow."

Ella motioned for them to keep quiet. "You want to be a little louder? I don't think they can hear you up in the ISS."

"What's the ISS?" Flo asked.

"International Space Station."

Flo stopped in her tracks, causing Wink to plow into her. "There's a space station?" Her voice carried across the still night like a foghorn.

Ella whipped her head towards the cabin and froze. Her breath stopped, and she was pretty sure her heart did too.

After several tense seconds, when it seemed Six hadn't heard them, Ella released the air from her lungs and glared at Flo.

One of the doors on the dilapidated barn hung at an angle she was sure wasn't intentional—unless the builder had suddenly gone cross-eyed. In which case, it looked just fine.

She slipped into the inky blackness inside and nearly choked on the pungent odor of manure and hay. Flo and Wink joined her, and both began to gag.

Air slipped through wide cracks between the slats that made up the wall but did little to alleviate the God-awful smell.

Ella had been in barns before, been around livestock before, but this took that marked scent to a whole new level.

Six had clearly thought maintaining stalls was a mere suggestion. Either that or an elephant lived there. She felt sorry for any animal living in this excuse for a barn.

But that was about to change.

A soft neigh came from a stall five yards away. Her plan had worked so well with the sheriff's horse, she figured, why reinvent the wheel?

She motioned for the others to keep quiet before fumbling with the latch. Once freed, she tugged open the stall door.

The horse—a beautiful buckskin—reared its head and backed into the depths of the stall. His hooves made sucking noises as they sank in several inches of mud and manure.

Ella held out her hand, trying to coax the majestic beast forward. Her initial plan rested on the assuredness that the animal would make a break for freedom—it hinged on this fact.

"Come on," she whispered.

The horse whinnied loudly.

"He's not moving," Flo said helpfully.

"Hadn't noticed." Ella squinted towards the back of the stall. "Why don't you go in and give him a little encouragement.

"Oh no. You're not getting me anywhere near its rear. My grandfather got kicked in the face. Never saw straight after that."

"Wink?"

The diner owner made a grand gesture to her outfit, emphasizing her footwear.

Ella did a double take. "Why on earth are you wearing heels? You walked all the way here in those?"

"They were the only black shoes I had."

Ella silently counted to five then inched forward herself. Her running shoes squashed two inches into the muck.

Pulling her shirt up over her nose, she extended a hand and crept towards the horse's backside. She was no horse expert, but she knew enough to not stand directly behind it.

She approached what she was calling the backside-side and tapped the soft surface as she had with Chapman's Appaloosa. The animal didn't so much as flick its tail.

She poked it, this time receiving a snort.

"Growing old here," Flo said from the other, more appealing end of the horse.

"You're already there," Wink retorted.

Ella grew bolder and nudged it. When that failed, she pushed, but the beast may as well have been a wall. "Anyone know how to move a horse?"

"Sure," Wink said. "Flo, get some hay."

"Why do I have to get it?"

"Fine," Wink said with an exasperated sigh. "I'll get it."

Ella heard Wink trip around in the dark, moving deeper into the barn. When she didn't immediately return, Flo took to humming show tunes as off-key as possible. After Ella asked her to keep her voice down so Six didn't overhear, she took to pestering Ella about the ISS.

"They probably built it so they could have a meeting place for the aliens, you know, out of the prying eyes of the public."

"Yes. That *must* be why." Ella shifted her weight from foot to foot. She could no longer smell the manure underfoot, which she found disconcerting.

Wink's voice cut through the darkness. "Couldn't find any hay."

"What? Seriously?" Ella stared at the animal in front of her—mostly its backside because she hadn't moved.

"Just give it a good tap on its hindquarters," Flo suggested. "It's what they do in the movies."

"You mean its backside-side? I already tried that."

"Hindquarters," Flo repeated, drawing out the word like she was talking to a six-year-old.

Ella eyed the *hindquarters* skeptically and muttered, "I like my word better."

After much deliberating, she stepped sideways, closer to its tail and gave the horse's flank a generous pat.

She'd expected it to react, make some sort of vocalization, and trot out of the stall like a perfectly good horse. What she hadn't expected was for it to whinny like it'd been shot, kick its back legs out through the side of the barn, and retreat further back, all while knocking Ella over.

She landed with a nice *splat* in a soft pile of excrement and let out a scream that came out a gurgle due to her mouth being inches from the manure.

"Ella!" Wink's silhouette appeared at the stall door. "Are you alright?"

It took Ella a few shuddering breaths to be able to find her voice. "No. But I'm not hurt."

She bit her lip to keep her mouth closed. She could *taste* the manure. Taste it. Her gag reflex kicked in, and she was grateful no one could see her.

"Are you throwing up?" Flo asked.

"What? No." Ella wiped her mouth.

Wink's voice was urgent. "Come on! There's no way Six didn't hear that."

Ella started. In her manure-filled horror, she'd forgotten about the outlaw.

Her heartbeat drummed in her ears as she did her best Michael Phelps impression and swam for safety. What started out as progress deteriorated when she slipped, limbs flailing, and made a perfectly formed poop angel.

Somewhere outside, a screen door slapped open then closed. Through the slats, Ella saw a shadow pass over the windows of the cabin.

"I think he's coming," she rasped as she rolled onto the dry ground at Flo's feet, fighting the urge to kiss the excrement-free ground.

Wink had stationed herself near a hole in the boards. "I don't think so. He's walking around his house."

"We should go." Ella made a move for the door, but Wink stopped her. If they went out the front, Six would see them. They had to find another exit.

"Let him find us." Flo ripped open her jacket and pulled out something long and dark.

Ella stopped mid-search for an exit. "Oh my God. Is that—is that a Tommy Gun? You brought a Tommy Gun?!" She tried to keep her voice down but with each passing moment, it became more shrill.

"Wink said, 'bring a gun,' so I bought a gun." Flo struggled to keep the gun aloft with her soft arms. "What's got your panties in a twist?"

"Wh-what? *You* do. *You've* got my panties in a twist with your freaking bazooka!"

"It's not a bazooka." She seemed far too disappointed by this fact. "It's just like the one Bonnie and Clyde had."

"It didn't work out so well for them," Wink pointed out from her post.

"Yes," Ella said, "yes, thank you, Wink. It didn't work out well for them at all." Her voice had risen a whole octave now.

She glanced over at Wink while her hands went back to groping along the wall, finding nothing but ropes and sharp pointy things. "Why aren't you more upset by this? I feel like you should be more upset."

"Used to it, I guess. Just be grateful she didn't bring her howitzer."

Ella's mouth worked back and forth like a fish sucking air, and she rounded on the large outline wielding a deadly weapon. "You—you have a howitzer? Like the heavy artillery militaries use? The ones that look like cannons?"

Flo's chest inflated, but before she could answer, Wink said, "We've got bigger fish to fry. He's coming this way. Hurry!"

Since there was nowhere to run, they scrambled for a place to hide. Just as they leaped into an adjacent stall, the barn door squealed open.

Ella tensed and held her breath. The jangle of spurs broke the silence followed by Six's throaty drawl.

"Who's there?"

CHAPTER 22

SIX STOOD IN the doorway, a black shape against freckles of stars. "Anybody there? Come on out. Ain't gonna hurt you much. Just put a couple of holes in you."

The click of his revolver bit the air.

Ella's whole body went rigid. On one side of her, Wink tensed, while on the other, Flo's hand was searching for the trigger on her own weapon.

Ella reached over and covered the woman's veiny hand. It wasn't that she didn't want her shooting at Six. It was that the gun was currently backward, the barrel pointing behind them.

Six's spurs jangled like loose change with each step, marching a rhythm that matched Ella's heart, beat for beat.

Should they make a run for it? There was only one of him and three of them—two of which were handicapped by either footwear or an alarming lack of fitness. So, his chances of shooting them were still high.

She looked over at Wink, trying to pierce the darkness

with her silent question. Wink's head dipped in a nod.

With slow, silent movements, Ella situated into a crouch, her legs coiled with tension, ready to sprint.

She pulled in a breath. The outlaw was only five yards away.

Meanwhile, her hands moved over their surroundings, searching for anything that could be used as a weapon—besides the Tommy Gun on her left.

Three yards.

Her hands found neither a sharp nor a blunt object, but what they did find was hay. Lots and lots of hay.

One yard.

The clink of his boots stopped.

Ella froze. She could hear Six breathing.

Any moment, he would peek over the stall door and spot them. If they moved now, they had the element of surprise. Also, she was concerned that if she waited, Flo would take matters into her own hands.

Ella gritted her teeth and flung herself at the stall door.

Two things happened simultaneously.

As the door hit Six with the force of a hurricane, the buckskin startled and finally bolted out of its stall, colliding with the cowboy a second after the door did.

Six became a heap on the ground, the horse towering over him.

"Whoa, Duke. Easy. How d'you get out?"

But Duke, the horse, would hear none of it. He reared again then vaulted over the outlaw and made a mad dash for freedom. Duke's hooves thundered over the ground as he fled, carrying on like a bat out of hell.

Six scrambled to his feet and chased after the horse, yelling obscenities. The barn grew oddly still.

Wink picked dirt off her shawl. "Well, that worked out well."

Ella looked over and blinked. Flo's gun hung limply at her side, her shoulders drooping. "I didn't get to use my gun."

"Gee, that's too bad." Ella patted her on her back. "Maybe we can do some target practice with it later." *A lot* of target practice.

Flo's back straightened, and her beehive swung back and forth like a dog wagging its tail.

"Well?" Wink said, moving towards the stall door. "What are we waiting for? Let's get to snooping."

"What?" Ella said. "Are you serious? That was too close of a call."

"That? That was nothing. And circumstances haven't changed. Rose is still a suspect, isn't she?"

"I guess so." Ella kicked the ground and moved towards the door, her shoes shuffling over the soft surface of straw.

"Hay," Flo said loudly.

Ella gave her a once-over, growing more uncertain of the woman's frame of mind. "Hey, yourself."

"No, idiot. Hay." Her hand swept over the ground then to the corner of the stall, a few feet from where they'd been hiding. Ella turned on her phone's light and directed the beam over stacks and stacks of hay.

"Well, that's useful." She turned off the light, sighed, and headed for the barn door.

The two women trailed behind her.

"Didn't you check that stall?" Flo asked Wink. "It was literally across from us."

"I did. But if you hadn't noticed, it's dark."

"Not too dark to see a mountain of hay. I saw it."

Ella shushed them as they stepped outside, unsure of Six's current location. Hopefully, Duke had lured him far, far away. Across the border would be helpful. The night air sent goosebumps up her arms as she strained to hear either man or horse.

It took a great deal of effort to get her two accomplices to be quiet long enough, but finally, Ella heard a faint whinny followed by shouts from somewhere deep in the apple trees.

With the coast clear, they stole towards the cabin at last. Ella pressed her back against the smooth logs. Her ears pricked at the smallest of sounds.

Something crashed into a bush. Ella whipped her head around. Bending low, Flo fished out her gun.

"Oops." As the older woman grasped the weapon, she lingered, her nostrils working as she sniffed the air. "Poop."

Wink let out a disgusted noise. "What?"

"I smell poop."

"We just came from a barn," Wink replied.

Ella moved away from Flo. "I don't smell anything."

"It literally smells like we're standing in horse sh—"

"Well, we're not," Wink snapped. "Honestly, I think you've lost it sometimes."

"How can you not smell that? I can practically *see* it, it's so strong."

While the two bickered over the source of the smell and whether or not they should burn their clothes after this, Ella stood on tiptoes at Six's window.

She had expected to see a dilapidated, trashed-out interior, full of dust and clutter, but was surprised to find the living quarters clean and sparse. The lodging consisted of a single room with a mattress for a bed, a table and chair, and a blackened fireplace. A couple of candles burned on the table, giving the weak illumination they'd seen from the lane.

A small lean-to was attached at the north side of the

cabin. Judging by the many holes in the structure and the smell wafting out, her guess was it had to be an outhouse. She made a point of blaming it on the source of the smell.

Looking over the interior, Ella wondered what their next move could be. If there was any evidence connecting Six to the break-in, it wasn't observable from her perch outside.

"We could go in," Wink suggested.

"Then we'd be breaking and entering."

Flo's face lit up. "So?"

Ella opened her mouth then stopped, considering it. They *were* already trespassing.

She glanced back inside the cabin, her eyes catching on the table shoved against the opposite wall. "Maybe we won't have to. Follow me."

Without waiting for a response, Ella traipsed around to the backside of the cabin, her two friends tripping their way after her.

Unlike the windows on the front of the cabin, this one was higher, but it was also perfectly positioned over the table.

"I need a boost," she said.

Both women stared at her.

"Why you?" Flo's lower lip jutted out. "I want to see. It's my turn."

"If we hoist you up," Wink said, "we'd be in back braces for weeks."

Flo gave Wink the bird.

Ella feared Six would be back soon and pleaded with them. After a little more deliberation and name-calling, they relented.

Weaving their fingers together, their hands became a base that Ella could step on.

"Higher," she whispered.

Wink groaned, and Flo made a squealing noise that wasn't unlike a balloon slowly deflating as they lifted Ella higher. As she rose unsteadily, Ella was forced to use both sets of hair as holds to steady herself.

On closer inspection, "furniture" would be too generous of a word to describe the pile of sticks joined by straps of leather that made up the table and chair directly beneath her now.

"Jesus, Mary, and Joseph," Flo hissed, "why do you smell like a sewer?"

Ella ignored her and dug her manure-covered sneaker in to get higher. This resulted in Flo's hands sagging and her complaining about the stench kicking up a notch.

Papers and manilla folders littered the scratched surface of the table. Ella pressed her nose to the glass, her breath fogging up the surface.

Familiar, elegant cursive writing filled the smattering of papers. It tickled her brain, but she couldn't place where she'd seen the penmanship before.

On closer inspection, the leafs of loose paper weren't letters like she'd thought. They were formatted more like journal entries, or a log of some kind, with dates posted in the margins.

Ella turned her attention to the folders to see if she could read the tabs. That's when she caught the pink nail polish stain pooled in the bottom left corner of nearly every one.

She let out a small gasp. She'd done it, she'd found the missing link between Six and the break-in.

"What?" Flo's hands gave out, and Ella toppled over, landing on Wink.

The diner owner flailed about like she was covered in bees. "Get off! You're getting poop all over me!"

Ella rolled off, pouring apologies out of her mouth in

an endless stream, ending with, "It's Flo's fault."

"Is not! I can't help it if you weigh too much."

Wink struggled to her feet. "She's half your size! And maybe if you used those arms to lift more than ice cream, you could've held her up!"

"Sh!" Ella broke in. "Do you hear something?"

They stood still, straining their ears. It wasn't what they heard, but what they *didn't* hear. Six's shouts—which had up until now been a constant accompaniment to the crickets—had gone silent.

"We need to get out of here." She turned to find Flo had already deserted them. "I see how it is."

Wink pushed Ella into a jog. Within a minute, they'd caught up with the old coot.

Ella took the lead, glancing over her shoulder. It was too dark to see much, but Flo's Darth Vader breaths assured her she was still there, although the distance between them was growing greater by the second.

"Wink?" Ella called, trying to keep her voice down.

"I'm here. I can't run in these shoes."

"So take them off." Ella paused so Wink could kick off her heels, telling Flo to keep going.

Her hands on her hips, Ella stared out into the orchard, trying to pierce the veil of darkness and branches. A moment later, she heard the sound of hooves pounding over the ground off to their right followed by Six's verbal commands for Duke to run faster.

Ella wrenched Wink's elbow forward, and they broke into a run.

"Flo!" Ella said when they came astride of her. "He's coming!"

"Hide in the trees!" Wink ordered.

With surprisingly strong hands, Wink shoved them towards the orchard. They each took a tree and ducked behind them.

Ella pressed her body against the bark and listened for Duke over the sound of Flo's wheezing. She couldn't tell which direction Six was headed.

"I think he's moving away," Wink whispered.

Ella nodded then remembered they couldn't make out the movement in the dark. "Let's wait it out another minute, then get going."

They stood quietly, listening and waiting. Ella scratched at her poison oak rash, wishing she'd applied more of the homemade remedy.

A tree over, Flo sighed for the fifth time. "Can we go yet?"

"Hey, Flo, remember that time you were too winded to talk? Happened, like, a couple minutes ago?" Ella said. "Remember that? I miss that. That was a good time."

Before Ella could hear whatever great comeback the crazy woman had, Wink said, "I think it's safe. Let's get out of here."

There was a rustle of twigs and leaves as they emerged from their cover.

Ella set the pace to a brisk walk. "So, what are the chances Six knows it was us?"

"I'd say pretty high," Wink responded.

"Yeah, but he didn't see us."

"Still high."

Flo elbowed Ella out of the lead, forcing her to walk "downwind" from them.

When they passed Twin Springs, Ella felt safe enough to turn her flashlight app on. The small light illuminated her ruined clothes and a rather disheveled looking Wink.

What surprised Ella the most was that Flo's hair appeared to still be intact. She couldn't be certain, but if she had to guess, the woman used one part glue, one part cement for her beehive.

She watched her struggle with the Tommy Gun. "Flo, I'm no firearms expert, but I'm pretty sure, you're not supposed to have your finger on the trig—"

The rest of Ella's words were cut off by the rapid succession of gunfire. The end of the barrel lit up like a Christmas tree.

Even if Flo had been ready for the gun to fire, Ella wasn't sure she had enough muscle to control it.

Flo's one-handed trigger pull sent the submachine gun firing in an arc. She toppled backward in slow motion, the weapon firing all the way down like it was glued to her hand.

When Flo's curvy backside hit the dirt, it wrenched the gun loose. A sudden silence took over, but Ella barely noticed over the ringing in her ears.

Nobody moved. Flo's chest pumped up and down, her arms and legs spread akimbo. Even the crickets were silent.

Ella cleared her throat. "You think Six heard that?"

Wink didn't bother responding. She grabbed a handful of Flo's clothes and dragged her a foot before Flo found her footing and stood. They took off sprinting.

Ella scooped the antique gun up and ran. As if they had one mind, all three jumped into the orchard and kept running.

She ducked through row after row, hoping the shortcut would get them to Main Street faster, as well as provide the necessary cover needed to outrun Six.

More than once, she stumbled over clumps of dirt or tree roots. She had thought it dark at the rock flats, but even the faint starlight was swallowed by the orchard.

It wasn't until she spotted the warm glow of the street lamps that she realized she'd lost sight of her friends.

Her shoes squished and pounded onto the sidewalk. Ella collapsed under the nearest light, gulping for air, and waited for the other two to emerge.

Shortly after, Wink rolled out of the branches, breathing heavily. Ella patted the grass beside her.

Sweat beaded down her forehead. She swiped it with her glove, then realized she'd just spread manure and mud over her skin.

They waited ten minutes before they climbed to their feet and began pacing the tree line. Another five minutes elapsed before Flo crawled out of a row, hunched over, her lungs making a concerning whistling sound.

Without a word, Wink pulled one of Flo's arms over her shoulder while Ella grabbed the other. Together, they dragged their feet down the sidewalk, the Tommy Gun swinging beside Ella.

CHAPTER 23

ELLA SLEPT IN the next morning. When she awoke, she rolled onto her back, took stock of her sore muscles, and stared at the ceiling.

Despite it being well after midnight when she and Flo had stumbled up the stairs, Ella had gone straight to the bathroom and taken the longest bath in the history of baths. Up until now, she hadn't minded that the old bathroom didn't have a shower, but last night had proved to be a chore, digging out manure from every nook and cranny.

She let out a long-suffering sigh. It was Saturday, and, mercifully, Wink had told her she could take a later shift.

This was her seventh day in Keystone Village. So many events had been packed into the week that it felt like she'd lived in the town for months. The inn was already beginning to feel like home. Heck, she'd even experienced two different seasons in the span of a few days.

Her thoughts drifted to what she'd seen at Jesse's the night before. What was in those folders that was so important? Those scraps of journal papers were Kay's. Had she mentioned Six's still? But why not just burn them if there was something incriminating? Also, there was still the issue of Kay's missing clothes.

Ella felt like she was putting a mental puzzle together but the pieces didn't all fit. She was missing something.

She'd hoped to find something that took the spotlight off Rose and put it back onto Jesse. The folders and papers did that, but now there was the problem of how to tell the sheriff without explaining how she knew.

Ella slipped into her running clothes for the comfort and the fabric's amazing ability to wick away sweat rather than for any ambitious plans to go for a run. She'd had her fill the previous night. Besides, her running shoes were currently outside on the stoop in their poop-covered glory, baking in the sun.

In the kitchen, after she'd rubbed the late night from her eyes and poured a cup of coffee, she picked apart one of Wink's gooey apple cinnamon rolls.

She had just poured cream into her second cup when she noticed Jimmy outside the picture window. He sat under the towering oak tree, staring at the glassy lake, his shoulders slumped.

Pain pierced her heart, and she felt the sudden urge to unburden her conscience. She took a couple of steps towards the back door then stopped. He had a right to know she was the reason his wife was in jail, yet, she couldn't gather the courage to face him.

"I'll fix this," she whispered.

Slowly, she turned on her heel, laced up her less-than-white canvas shoes, and walked out the front door. She mentally added cleaning shoes to her list of things to do as she stepped onto the sidewalk. She didn't feel like running, but a long walk would loosen her muscles and clear her head.

The desert sun had long since crested Twin Hills, and she could tell it was going to be an especially hot one. As her feet found a rhythm, she strolled through the heart of the town, passing the library and the sheriff's office. She tried not to think about Rose huddled in her cell inside.

She needed to figure out a way to tell the sheriff about Kay's files in Six's cabin. If she could think of a reason to get him to search the place, he'd come across them himself.

Already, Ella's lungs burned. She chose to believe the desert was at a higher elevation than she was used to and the lack of oxygen was why she gasped for air and not because she had put on weight.

Veering off the sidewalk, Ella followed the trail circling the lake. A couple of fishermen on the docks waved at her as she passed. Beneath them, water lapped at the pylons, and she listened to the steady sound fade as she passed.

A quarter of the way around the lake, the serenity was interrupted by loud, angry voices. Ella slowed her steps, homing in on the cacophony. Two male voices came from one of the small cottages, booming and overlapping each other, one of them sounding familiar.

"They're dead because of you!"

"I didn't do nothing!"

Ella's shoes stuttered to a stop. Who was dead?

"I pay you to fertilize my fields, not kill my livestock," the familiar voice said.

"I used the same stuff I've always used! It's safe, I tell you."

The first voice swore then said, "I'm not paying you."

"You have to! My family and I will starve if you don't!"

"Not my problem."

Footsteps sounded, and the screen door on the cottage burst out. Ella jolted and resumed her walk, hoping she succeeded in making it look like a late morning stroll and that she hadn't just been eavesdropping.

When she felt enough time had passed to be nonchalant, she looked back in time to see a flash of a gray suit before the bushes lining the bend in the trail hid the person from view.

Ella pumped her legs as she resumed her trek around the lake, all the while playing the conversation on a loop in her head.

Back at the inn, she chugged down a glass of water then changed into her last pair of clean clothes. Her fingers brushed over a sweater, the one piece of clothing she'd packed that wasn't a t-shirt, sweatshirt, or running gear. She'd have to ask where people shopped in the village.

She remembered seeing a sewing machine in one of the rooms downstairs, and her stomach tightened. If the residents *made* their own clothes, she was out of luck. If her attempt at sewing a dress was anything like her one and only attempt at making a pillowcase, then she suspected it would come out with an extra sleeve and an unintentional a-line... much like the pillowcase had.

Since Rose was in the slammer, Ella's choices for wardrobe advice on where to shop were limited to Crazy Flo or Grandma Wink. She shivered. Maybe she'd wait for Rose.

When finished changing, she tossed dirty clothes atop the Mt. Everest-sized pile in the corner. If she put off doing laundry any longer, the patrons at the diner would complain about the stench.

Speaking of stench, she thought, looking over at a bag in the corner that held her clothes from last night. She didn't have much experience with manure—virtually none—so she wasn't certain how well it washed out.

Since the town had a finite supply of clothing, Ella decided to try to salvage the outfit. She left her pants and shirt soaking in the bathtub, the task taking twice as long with one hand since the other was occupied plugging her nose.

When Ella stepped out into the hall, she noticed Flo's door was cracked, a single eye peering out.

"Flo," Ella said by way of greeting.

Flo spoke through the crack. "That was fun last night."

"You have a very messed up idea of fun."

"I want my gun back."

Ella hesitated, wondering if the town was safer with the woman down one less weapon. "Under my bed."

She left Flo to her lurking and headed downstairs. After grabbing a couple of soft chocolate-chip cookies from the cookie jar, she settled into a chaise in the library.

Warm sunshine poured through the windows, melting the chocolate chips and blanketing her. After she'd licked her fingers clean, she began to nod off.

An hour later, Ella descended the grand staircase, gingham dress swooshing from side to side like a bell with each step. She'd managed to smear on some mascara and lip gloss, as well as gather her hair into a high knot. She felt pretty put together. Not Rose put together, but presentable.

In Grandma's Kitchen, a couple of lone customers sat at the lunch counter and a family with two small children occupied the corner booth.

Ella found Wink in the kitchen, elbows-deep in suds, scrubbing dishes.

"Don't you have a dish washer? I mean, not a

dishwasher, but like a person to do that?"

Wink's lips puckered with effort. "I do. But I like to take a turn now and then. Keeps me young."

Ella eyed the woman with blue hair up and down. If she started behaving any younger, the years might peel right off. Actually, maybe that wasn't a bad idea, and she should have a turn.

"Did I see you walking around the lake earlier?" Horatio asked from the fryer. A burger patty sizzled on the grill next to him.

"Yeah. Hey, do you know who lives in that green cottage over there." She pointed in the general direction of the place. "It's got a large lilac bush in the yard and a picket fence."

"If it's the one I'm thinking of, that's Tom's place." Wink let the dish fall in the sink. "That's as good as I'm going to get it."

"I'll take a turn." Ella elbowed her out of the way then attacked the caked-on cheese with a scouring pad.

"I thought that was the Millers' place." Horatio waved a spatula at Wink, sending drops of grease spraying over them.

"No. The Millers' house is that gaudy purple. Why anyone would paint their house that color—"

"But they got a picket fence."

"So does half the town. Do the Millers have a lilac bush in their front yard?"

The cook's face scrunched up. "I am not sure what a lilac bush looks like."

Wink rolled her eyes as she scooted out of the kitchen to check on the customers. After she left, the door swung back and forth on its hinges several times.

Ella asked, "So, who's Tom?"

The spatula scraped the grill, and the sizzle of the

burger filled the air.

"Farmer."

"A farmer who's got a cottage by the lake?"

"Well, he was a farmer from his time. He's a—what's it called? Transplant? He's like us. Wasn't any farmland available for him here, so he took what he could. I think he's hoping one of the families will leave, and he can buy some property."

Ella churned the words over in her mind as she laid a plate next to him then set to work prepping the fixings for a Belly Buster. "What's he do?"

"Oh, he still helps out where he can. Either on the Bradford dairy or the ranch south of town."

"Keystone has a South?"

The cook laughed. "Good point. For us, Main Street runs north and south."

Ella nodded. It was similar to how she'd orientated the town. "So, Twin Hills is northeast then?"

"Yep."

"Except when the sun sets behind it."

"Yeah, it gets confusing. But you'll get used to it."

Ella appreciated the confidence, however misplaced it might be. "So, this Tom, does he fertilize the fields around Bradford Farms?"

Horatio shrugged, slapping a patty down on the bun. "Probably. I don't really know."

His hands worked like a machine. She'd barely blinked, and the burger sat before her, dripping with blue cheese and crisp strips of bacon.

He handed it to her. "Why're you so curious about him, anyhow?" His face lit up, and he wiggled his thick eyebrows. "He's married. But I got another friend who's single and would suit you. About twenty years older, but who can be picky in this town?"

Ella grimaced. "I'll keep that in mind. Your buns are burning."

Horatio looked over his shoulder, yelped, and frantically freed the buns from the toaster. She whisked out of the kitchen before he tried to fix her up on a date.

Another customer had set up at the counter, and Ella was surprised to see it was the mayor. His suit jacket spilled over the sides of the swivel seat. He leaned forward on his elbows, tie bathing in his coffee, as he talked animatedly with Wink.

Ella kept one eye on them as she placed the Belly Buster in front of the man in the corner booth. Wink's typical smile didn't reach her eyes, and her body language conveyed that she had better things to do besides listening to him drone on.

After refilling the family's cups of waters, Ella wandered over to the counter to see if Wink needed rescued.

"Ah, Ella. Nice to see you again."

Mayor Bradford's hand shot out and pumped hers in a hearty, sweaty shake—most of the enthusiasm on his part. The moment he released his grip, she discreetly wiped her hand over her skirt.

"You going to the potluck tomorrow?"

She shot Wink a confused look. "I thought the town hall meetings were every other week?"

"Oh, they are," he answered for the older woman. "But we have a potluck the other Sundays."

"So, a potluck every Sunday?"

The Mayor's face scrunched up, and he looked to Wink for help.

"Ella," Wink said, "that wasn't a potluck after the meeting."

"Then what do you call that spread? Looked like a

freaking buffet to me."

Wink shrugged. "That was just some post-meeting refreshments."

Ella wasn't certain she'd put glazed ham and homemade ice cream in the refreshments category, but who was she to judge?

"Well," she said, "if there's food, then I'm there."

The mayor beamed. "You're in for a real treat. When I got to this town, you should've seen it. Everything was so disorganized. New people were getting stranded here all the time, and no one knew about it."

Ella nodded politely, wondering what this had to do with the potluck.

"So, I decided to do something about it. Every two weeks, the townspeople gather to socialize, get to know each other better, and learn the new faces. It's worked out better than I could've hoped." He leaned in, a greasy smile spreading over his face. "Our people have been united ever since. Now, I don't think I deserve all the credit, mind you, but if it weren't for our meetings and the potluck—"

"The potlucks have been going on long before you arrived in town, Earl." Wink's usually sweet tone had a bite to it.

"True. But they weren't *consistent*. And there was still chaos—"

"Because we were just trying to figure out how to survive. There was no electricity. No food. If it weren't for Twin Springs, we would've had to boil lake water."

Mayor Bradford leaned back so far on his stool, Ella feared he'd fall over. His eyes darted back and forth as he searched for a response.

A customer approached the cash register, putting an end to the discussion. Ella eavesdropped for a moment as he tried to settle his bill with a dozen eggs as payment.

"Can I get you anything, sir?" she offered the mayor.

"Sure. Be a dear and top off my coffee, will you?"

Ella's hackles raised at him calling her *dear*, but she gave him a pass since he was from a different era.

After obliging, she refilled the cream and sugar tray in front of him. Despite the facade, she knew he had to be hurting. His only child had been killed the week before.

Ella tried to make small talk as she wiped up the mess of spilled sugar she'd just made.

"I got to see Kay's place yesterday. It's really cute."

"Why were you at her place?"

The rag in Ella's hand froze halfway across the counter. "Will wanted to pick up a few things there. He'd said you were fine with it."

He blinked before taking a long slurp from his coffee. "Right, right. That place was a dirty hole in the wall. She didn't belong there."

Ella stared at him. "I didn't see the studio before the break-in, but I thought it looked pretty clean. And cute. There's a great view of the forest—"

"What break-in?"

Her insides turned cold. He didn't know? Of course, Kay wouldn't have told him. They hadn't been close. But Ella figured in such a small town, everyone would've known about it.

"Break-in? Did I say 'break-in'? I meant, 'Taken'." As if that was somehow better.

Quickly, she screwed the metal lid back on the sugar, misaligning the threading. She'd fix it later.

"That still doesn't make sense."

"Hmm? Doesn't it? I'm sure it does."

She took a step back to make a hasty retreat, but Mayor Bradford's clammy hand shot out and curled around her forearm.

His genial demeanor slipped away. "What break-in?" His words turned stoney, grating her ears and filling her with fear. So, this was the man whom Kayline had known.

"I don't know anything. Just that her house was broken into." She wasn't trying to protect Six so much as protect Kay's privacy.

Something shifted behind his eyes, and the unctuous smile returned as he released her. "I see. I'll have to pay Sheriff Chapman a visit then. See what he can tell me."

He got up from his stool, situated his tie, and turned to leave without paying. He paused.

"Word of advice: you may want to keep out of other people's affairs. Small town like this, no one likes a busybody, and there's still a killer on the loose."

The door jangled pleasantly as he stepped out onto the blistering sidewalk. Despite the wave of heat blasting through the open doorway, a chill crept up Ella's spine.

CHAPTER 24

By the time Ella turned the sign for Grandma's Kitchen to "closed," she'd made a plan. She couldn't tell the sheriff about Six's possession of Kay's journal and folders without revealing she'd trespassed on his property.

She could, perhaps, show him the button she'd found in Kay's apartment, the one tying the outlaw to the break-in, but it wasn't a very convincing piece of evidence. What she needed was something more solid. She needed Six to admit to it.

Deciding to take advantage of her era's technology—and watching too many episodes of crime TV—she'd come up with an idea. It wasn't her best, but definitely in the top five. Above straightening her hair but below dumping her last boyfriend.

Ella found Wink in the kitchen, her arms dusted in flour, lasagna noodles scattered about like a deck of cards. The diner owner's brows were furrowed, and she muttered under her breath.

"You okay, Wink?"

"Fine, fine." The older woman's blue hair slid forward, her eyes trained on the knife in her hands. Her lips moved fervently, muttering, "She isn't beating me again. I don't care what she says."

Ella backed through the swinging door on tiptoes, calling out, "Okay. I'll just be heading out now. Night and good luck with… whatever this is." If Wink had heard, she didn't respond.

After changing back into her least fragrant clothes, Ella scooped up her phone from the dresser and left the inn. Outside, a lone cloud drifted across a pink sunset.

She swallowed the doubts rising in her chest and marched down Main Street, going over her plan. Her phone had nearly a full charge, and her voice recording app was open. All she had to do was press the big red symbol, and it would begin recording. Of course, Six would probably put a bullet between her eyes on sight, so getting the details right really didn't matter.

She'd gone two blocks when screams and a hail of gunfire pulled her from her thoughts. She spun around. Her first thought was to look for Flo and her Tommy Gun.

A handful of people fled L Street, screaming and dispersing. In the chaos, a bicyclist slammed into a bush, popped up, and rabbited away.

A moment later, Six and Duke burst onto Main Street. The outlaw's arm flailed back, pointing his six-shooter behind him. The air exploded with more gunfire.

All around, passersby dived for cover. Ella scrambled for the first thing she could find: a rust-covered, neglected post office drop box.

Nearby, Will's friend Jenny ducked behind a blue Oldsmobile, her expression frozen in terror.

"Not again," she cried.

Again?

"What's happening?" Ella called over, but her words were drowned out by several more shots. The brick in the library behind her exploded, spraying red shrapnel over the sidewalk.

Jenny made eye contact with Ella before bolting from her cover, leaving Ella alone.

"Really?" Ella shrieked.

She shrunk further behind the drop box, wondering if she could make it to the line of parked cars. Back on the street, the thunder of hooves reached a crescendo, and Ella peeked around the side of her cover.

Sheriff Chapman rode his Appaloosa horse, gun drawn. "Stop right there, Six!"

By way of response, Six loosed another volley of rounds. He dismounted from Duke and dodged for the line of parked cars—right in front of Ella.

He slid over the hood of a jalopy, *Dukes of Hazzard* style, and crouched behind the wheel well five feet from Ella. He spilled the spent shells from his revolver all over the sidewalk.

"Where d'you go, Six?" Chapman's voice sang from some place down the street. "You can't hide from me. I got you this time."

Six pulled more ammo from his cartridge belt and scrambled to load his gun. He hadn't spotted Ella yet. His attention elsewhere, she could end this before someone got hurt.

After sucking in air, she sprang from her hiding spot and leaped the distance to him, arms out for a tackle.

He moved, and she landed next to him in a heap.

"Howdy, Ella." His tone was as casual as if talking about the weather. And then he did talk about the weather. "Nice day, huh?"

"Sure, if you like skin-melting temperatures," she

gasped, clutching a rib.

His cavalier attitude over the fact that she'd just tried to tackle him got under her skin. He clearly didn't see her as a threat.

She rolled onto her knees, brushing gravel from her palms. "Jesse, what're you doing?"

"Name's Six, darlin'. And what's it look like I'm doing?"

"Like you're trying to get yourself killed."

"That sorry excuse for a badge has messed with me for the last time. The jig is up. It ends today. They'll be buryin' one of us six feet under, and it ain't gonna be me." The gun now loaded, he slammed the cylinder home. "Say, you wouldn't happen to have been on my property last night, were ya?" The muzzle pointed lazily in her direction.

"Nope. Definitely not. I don't even know where you live."

Chapman's voice broke through the air, closer this time. "I know you're here, Six. Save me some time, will you? Surrender now, and I might not kill you."

Ella rolled onto the balls of her feet, thinking of how best to get the sheriff's attention without Six putting a bullet in her. The outlaw seemed to read her thoughts, and the barrel of the gun drifted in her direction again.

"Don't even think about it."

"You know, before I arrived in Keystone, I'd never had a gun pointed at me. Can you believe it? Not a single one." She let out a dramatic sigh. "Now, hardly a day goes by I don't."

As she situated herself to a more comfortable position, it occurred to her that she had been on her way to Six's to talk to him, and now, here he was. Maybe she could still get what she wanted while keeping him distracted at the same time so the sheriff could do his job.

"You want me to stay quiet so the sheriff doesn't find you? Then I need something from you in return." It took nearly every bit of grit she had to meet his gaze. It was getting to be dusk, and his coal eyes were almost lost in the shadows of his cowboy hat. "Why did you break into Kay's place?"

A crease formed across his forehead. "How d'you know?"

"Just tell me, and I won't scream for Chapman."

He continued to glare, but a different emotion flickered across his features. "Maybe you ain't so yellow after all."

"Thank you. That's very kind of you to say. Now, why were you there?"

"I was looking for something." He paused to listen, inclining his head in the direction of Chapman's spurs singing through the air only ten yards away.

Ella was running out of time. "What were you looking for?"

"A folder."

"What was in the folder?"

"Needed dirt on the mayor. See, he's the one on the council that won't approve my still. So, I figured, if I get dirt on him, then…"

"Then you could use it to blackmail him?"

"Somethin' like that."

Ella processed the information. "Did you find anything?"

He chuckled. "Sure did. But I ain't tellin' you. What good's a secret if everyone knows?"

She couldn't argue with him on that point. "How come Chapman didn't find your prints anywhere in Kay's?"

"Don't they have gloves where you're from? I mostly wear 'em for riding, but they come in handy when I go places I don't want others to know about."

Before Ella could school him about DNA, Chapman stepped out from behind the jalopy and cocked the hammer back on his gun.

"Come out with your hands up. Not you, Ella."

"Oh. No, right. Of course, you didn't mean me." She dropped her hands into her lap.

Six's finger quivered near his trigger.

Chapman raised his weapon higher. "I wouldn't."

Sneering, Six tossed his revolver aside.

"Come on. Back to jail." The sheriff shoved Six in front of him, one hand holding the gun to his back, the other clutching Six's sweatshirt, and marched him down the sidewalk.

Ella watched their retreating backs. Just when she thought she was getting used to this town, it revealed a new facet of crazy.

"Crazy Village, that's what it should be called," she muttered as she stretched her legs and tried to pump the adrenaline from her cramped muscles. It felt like she had ten cups of coffee coursing through her. It'd be a miracle if she could sleep tonight. But at least she'd gotten the information she wanted before Six was carted off.

Ella slapped her forehead then fished her phone out of her pocket. She'd been so focused on not dying that she hadn't pressed record.

She ground her teeth. Maybe it wasn't for nothing. She could tell the sheriff what Six had confessed, and he could finally have the right to search the cowboy's cabin.

As she trudged back to the inn, her thoughts turned to the stolen papers and folders. What secrets lay within?

She couldn't imagine collecting dirt on her own father, which made her shudder to think what the mayor could have done to drive Kay to that point.

Back at the inn, Ella dragged her feet up the stairs, taking extra care to step over Fluffy, as exhaustion set in. It had been a long twenty-four hours. Between work, snooping around Six's place, and the wild West shootout, she felt she could sleep for days.

As she stopped in front of her door, her right shoe stepped on a folded piece of paper. Her name was scrawled in lazy letters on the front.

Who would write her a note? Her heart fluttered at the thought that maybe it was Will's handwriting.

She flipped on the light in her room and clicked the door shut. Sinking to her soft mattress, she unfolded the scrap of paper.

There was only one sentence:

Stop poking around, or you'll be stranded in the desert forever.

CHAPTER 25

ELLA SIPPED HER coffee in the cool morning breeze. The large oak leaves overhead whispered as she watched the ripples in the lake lap over the rocks.

Try as she might, she couldn't forget the note she'd found at her door the previous night. Someone knew she was snooping around. But who? Had Six suspected she'd sneaked onto his property and written it before the shootout?

Her mind drifted back to Kay's notes on her father. With Six secured behind bars, maybe she could chance a second peek through his window to see if she could read them. Or maybe…

She swallowed the smooth roast, leaning forward. Will and Kay had been close, even after their breakup. Maybe she'd confided in him about the dirt she was collecting on her father. He had alluded to the fact they didn't have a good relationship, but maybe he knew more than he let on. Chances were good he'd be at the potluck that evening, but Ella didn't want to wait until then.

She hurried through the rest of her coffee before going upstairs to get ready for the day. Her pile of dirty laundry taunted her from the corner of her room. It was next on the list of things to do after visiting Will.

As she closed her door behind her, she realized she didn't know where Will lived. She teetered at the top of the grand staircase, weighing her options.

She could ask Crazy Flo, but she worried that conversation would devolve quickly. Rose was still locked up, and Wink lived too far away. She considered taking her car to Twin Hills but thought it ridiculous to drive out there unannounced, just to ask where someone else lived.

She wished she knew the local phone numbers so she could make a call on the landline.

A loud crash echoed downstairs from the direction of one of the hallways. Flo's raspy voice spilled profanities that made Ella want to wash out her ears.

Scrambling down the steps, Ella hooked a hard right down the hall and glanced through each doorway she passed. Finally, she swung open the kitchen door and gasped.

"Flo! What happened?"

"That damn cat, that's what happened!"

As she spoke, the cloud of fur that was Fluffy blurred past Ella's feet before the door had a chance to swing shut.

Ella's hand covered her mouth, her eyes taking in the carnage. Glass shards glistened from all over the waxed linoleum floor. However, what drew her attention, and what she found more disconcerting, was the smears of red.

"Is—is that blood?"

"Don't be silly. Tomato paste."

"Oh." As if that explained everything.

Her gaze finally tore away from the destruction on the

floor to the counters. Measuring cups, mixing bowls, and spatulas littered the top. What little surface was visible was covered in what Ella approximated to be an entire bag of flour.

"Did Fluffy do that, too?" She pointed at the blizzard.

"Huh?" Flo followed her gaze. "Oh. No, I did that. It's part of my process."

"It looks like an entire season of *Chopped* in here."

"I don't know what that means."

For the first time since Rose had been arrested, Ella hoped the innkeeper didn't come home soon.

She cleared her throat and tried to avert her gaze from the kitchen fray—which left her staring at the ceiling.

"What are you making, anyway?"

"Making my famous lasagna for the potluck. It's always the first thing gone, and everybody raves about it."

"Oh, Wink's making lasagna too."

Flo's voice turned to a growl. "I know. Mine's better."

The old woman bent and began gathering the largest chunks of glass. After a few deep breaths, Ella looked down, groaned, then helped.

"I see. Well, one could never have too much lasagna, as my grandma would say. Actually, no. That's a lie. She never said that. But still... lasagna." Ella patted her stomach.

Flo sniffed as she dumped the glass into the trash. "She thinks hers is so great. Then why does she always have leftovers, hmm?"

Ella gave a small, noncommittal shrug, not wanting to get in the middle of a feud over a pasta dish. "I'm sure they're both great."

She gathered what food she could with the dishrag while Flo rooted a mop out from the closet. As they cleaned, Ella asked if bullets flying down Main Street was a semi-regular occurrence.

Flo shook her head. "Nah, only happens once every couple of months, maybe."

"Every couple of months?! What—why?"

"Dunno. Just how it's always been since they showed up."

Ella sputtered then shook her head. She was going to have to come up with a bulletproof vest of some kind.

She rinsed the rag out in the sink, and the water turned cherry red. As nonchalant as she could, she said, "Oh, I was wondering if you could give me directions to Will's place? I wanted to ask him something about Kay."

Flo's face lit up. "More investigating? That's great 'cause I've been wanting to try out my Colt—"

"No. No investigating. Where do you get these weapons, anyway?"

The older woman's glasses slid down her nose as she turned away. "No place."

"So, Will?"

"Couple blocks away. Over on J Street. Used to live by the lake, but he needed a bigger workshop. That's where you'll find him; not in his house. Just follow the noise."

After much chiding about Ella cleaning "wrong," she told her the house number along with a description then kicked her out.

Ella was happy to oblige, told Flo not to burn the manor down, then let the kitchen door swing shut behind her.

J Street looked different in the daylight, without her slinking along the bushes, trying to shake Wink and Flo. Houses lined both sides of the street, the lots growing larger the further "south" she went.

Where the road ended in the distance, the wind

turbines she'd seen when she first stumbled into town rotated in a lazy breeze. Beyond the houses on her right, fields full of either wheat or grazing cattle and sheep stretched all the way to the distant demarcation of dunes.

Ella found the house number Flo had given her on a painted sign attached to a white picket fence. The two-story house was... unexpected.

Its soft yellow paint and white trim glowed in the morning light. Large hydrangeas grew next to a wraparound porch. Between the bursts of flowers, English ivy crept up the sides of the abode.

Ella stood under the shade of a tall maple tree, admiring the house. It was the kind of place she dreamed of owning one day. Cozy and safe. Full of dozens of summers with iced tea and gardening and cold winters of curling up by the fireplace.

A prick of jealousy at Will's good fortune distracted her momentarily from hearing the *whir* of machinery coming from around the side of the house. Ella remembered Flo saying that he'd probably be in his shop and headed towards the noise.

The lawn swallowed her shoes as she wandered around the side, and she wondered how long it would take to turn brown if they remained in the desert.

A squat, metal structure that looked more overgrown shed than shop sat in the back. Ella rapped her knuckles on the heavy door and pressed her ear to its surface.

"Hello? Will?"

She wasn't sure he could hear her over his metal grinder, so she slipped inside. She waited for her eyes to adjust to the yellow bulbs and dim light streaming from the one, grimy window. When they had, her jaw dropped.

The place was filled to the brim with tools, hardware, trinkets, gadgets, and many other things she couldn't identify. But there was an organized chaos to it. It was like being in the laboratory or workshop of a mad scientist, parts Dr. Frankenstein, mechanic, and Martha Stewart rolled into one.

She wove around three busted TV sets and ducked under coils of power cords hanging from one of the rafters.

Will leaned over a workbench, a soldering tool in hand. Light flashed in staccato bursts like she was at a dance club. Ella placed her hand on his shoulder, causing him to jump and whirl around.

"Just me, Will."

"Ella?" He turned off the soldering iron, and the faint buzz that had been coming from it cut off.

"Sorry, I knocked a few times, but…" Her voice trailed off as she turned a slow circle. "This place is amazing."

"It's a mess, but thank you."

"What're you working on?"

"Short distance, two-way radios."

"Oh, like walkie-talkies?"

His face clicked with recognition. "Yes… yes. It was after my time, but I remember hearing that's what they called them. Anyway, some of these farmers don't have access to the landlines, and we don't have the parts to hook up more lines."

"That's a great idea."

"Thanks. They're a long way off from finished. These smaller transceivers are proving to be problematic, especially since I'm salvaging the parts from other things."

"Like MacGyver. All you need is duct tape."

"I don't see how tape would help."

"No, it's—doesn't matter."

He seemed relieved to drop the subject. "So, what

brings you by?"

Ella sank onto the stool next to him. It rocked a little, so she was forced to lean into the workbench. "I—are those scones?" She indicated the plate full of fluffy white cranberry scones across from her.

"Yeah. Wink stopped by earlier to thank me for fixing her sink."

After dragging the plate closer, he offered her one. She grabbed two. The first bite broke off and melted in her mouth.

"I'm surprised she left the kitchen. She was working so hard on that lasagna of hers last night I thought I'd have to send for help."

"Yeah, she and Flo have a bitter rivalry over who makes the better one. We've all agreed not to step in so we can keep reaping the benefits."

"But what if it gets more serious?"

"Oh, it's been serious the last few months. Back in March, Flo poured laxative all over Wink's dish. Nobody knew until the first bout of incontinence hit."

Ella choked on a bite of scone. "What? And you guys still let them do this?"

"Sort of. That's why the town bylaws were amended. They can only bring their lasagnas once every two months. Their names are in it and everything. Keeps the bathroom issues to a minimum." His expression became haunted, and he shifted on his stool, leaving little doubt that he was one of the unfortunate ones who'd partaken in Wink's dish.

"Those two fight like cats and dogs."

"I think their friendship just goes back so far they forgot what made them friends in the first place."

"Like a married couple." Ella took another bite of scone, thinking about her parents. And her grandparents.

And most of her married friends.

Will frowned. "It doesn't have to be that way."

"Doesn't it? Do you know any happy couple?"

"Jimmy and Rose."

"But they're still in love. Everything's still new and fresh, makes the love easier. No, I mean, do you know a married couple that's been together longer than, say… thirty years who don't peck at each other like hens?"

"Every couple argues. That doesn't mean there's no love in the marriage."

"True. But there comes a point when that's all they do, tear each other apart. They get so sick of each other, so familiar, that the love fizzles out. But they're too codependent they can't conceive of a life apart, so their relationship becomes this toxic, suffocating quagmire built on bitterness. It happens in every marriage." She took a breath.

"My God. You don't really think that, do you?" Will searched her face.

Ella bit her lip as she felt tears prick the back of her eyes. Did she? "I don't *want* to. But that's all I've ever seen and experienced. I want to believe that it can be better, that a couple can argue and have their rough patches and still love each after fifty years. But time makes all things grow dull."

He was quiet a long time before he finally said, "I feel sorry for you, El."

His words stung and hit a part of her heart she hadn't felt in a long time. She placed her half-eaten, forgotten scone back on the plate and stood, putting more space between them.

"Sorry, I didn't come for the heart-to-heart or the pity. I actually wanted to ask you something."

He didn't say anything but his face was open, waiting,

so she plunged ahead.

"Did you know Kayline was gathering dirt on her father?"

Will's eyebrows reached for his hairline. "What?"

Ella relayed everything Six had said.

"I had no idea. I wonder why she didn't tell me." He stared past her at some distant point. "It doesn't surprise me, though."

"What would she have found?"

He let out a deep breath. "Honestly? She wouldn't ever tell me. She alluded to her father having done something unforgivable, something unspeakable, but she wouldn't ever say what. I got the impression her tight lips were due more to trauma than anything else.

"But I do know the reason the two of them were on the road that day they arrived in Keystone was because they were on the lam."

"Really? From what?"

He shook his head. "She would never say. Why did Six tell you all this, anyhow?"

Ella picked at an invisible spot on her pants. "I may have threatened to reveal his hiding spot to the sheriff if he didn't." She told him about the shootout.

"Ella, that was foolish. He just tried to kill you."

"I know, I know."

"You sneaked into his cabin. What if he'd found you?"

"Technically, I didn't go inside."

He shot her a withering glare.

"Right. Not the point." She held up her hands. "Look, there's more I have to tell you. I'm sorry I waited. I just didn't want you involved until I had evidence to back up my suspicions."

"Why do I get the feeling I'm not going to like this?" He crossed his arms. "Go on."

"Six is the one who broke into Kay's."

CHAPTER 26

WILL STARED AT her. "He broke into Kay's? Are you sure?"

"Yes. He all but admitted it."

Will's jaw twitched. Without warning, he slammed his hand down on the workbench. "That rummy! That sap! Good for nothing dewdropper!"

"Language, Will." She feigned a gasp. "I'm just kidding. I have no idea what you just said."

"And he did it just to get those documents?"

"Looks like it."

He slouched on his stool, most of the fire dying in his eyes. "Well, you should've told me you were going to his place."

"So you could stop me?"

"Well, that. And if I failed—"

"You would have."

"—I would've gone with you."

"Really?" She tilted her head, seeing him in a different light.

"Really. I'm on your side, Ella. Why does that surprise

you? What happened to you to make you distrust people so much?"

Something pinched in her chest. She pressed her lips together, collected herself, and stood. Their whole conversation that morning had gotten too personal, too fast.

"Look, I just thought you should know what's going on." She backed towards the door. "I'm sorry I didn't tell you sooner. Next time I do something stupid, I'll invite you along."

"See that you do." His mouth twitched, and for a moment, she thought he might smile. But the moment passed, and the levity in his eyes faded.

"Thanks for the scone," she said then slipped out the door.

Her stomach twisted into knots the entire walk back home. Why had she said all of those things about marriage? Where had that even come from?

Sure, the topic had come up in past relationships, but it'd never gotten to the point where she needed to pick out bouquets. It wasn't that she didn't want the whole marriage, kids, white picket fence, but she wanted so much more. They just kept getting shoved down her list of priorities.

Or maybe today's verbal diarrhea with Will had been her way of telling herself how she really felt about marriage. Her view of marriage was so jaded, maybe unconsciously she didn't want it after all. She didn't want it because she saw the monster it would become, full of bitterness and regret. How could she want that?

After she got back to the inn, Ella decided to go for a short run to clear her head. It was 11:15, and the temperature was already flirting with ninety-five degrees. But the trail around the lake would be cooler.

As she passed through the park, she spotted Wink walking Chester on a leash—or rather, Chester jumping around spastically while Wink tried to keep up. Ella wondered what was with the harness and sudden reining in of the animal.

She waved at both as she passed. Chester scrambled up a tree, pulling his leash taught.

"Need help?" Ella called.

Wink shook her head, too distracted to give a proper response. With hands planted on her bony hips, she gave the squirrel a tongue lashing that could still be heard even after Ella rounded the park.

Back in her room, she peeled off the sweaty clothes and tossed them onto the mountain in the corner. The time had come.

With a heavy heart, she stuffed the pile into her suitcase turned laundry basket and lugged it down to the basement. During one of her first days there, Rose had given her a quick tour, pointing out the different doorways. Ella couldn't remember what all of them were for, but the one for the basement stuck out by way of creepiness and cobwebs hanging just inside the darkened staircase.

Old boards protested with each step on the stairs. The smell of mothballs and moisture clung heavy to the air. Before reaching the bottom, she had ducked half a dozen cobwebs, ninja swiping two that had been eye-level.

As she stepped onto the cold concrete subfloor, her hopes that the rest of the room would be an improvement over the stairs came crashing down.

A couple of bulbs hummed with electricity overhead—their wan light unable to pierce the shadowy corners. The expansive room looked like something out of a low budget horror movie. Any moment now, someone with a chainsaw was going to jump out from the shadows.

She set to work sorting and dumping her clothes into the washing machine, all the while, keeping one eye on her surroundings. The concrete walls muffled any noise, and the silence felt like a force pushing on her ears.

After starting her load, the ancient washing machine wobbled, mercifully breaking the silence. Finished, she half ran to the bottom step. The staircase was one of those open ones, and she could see piles of clutter behind it.

In the shadows, under the third step, a white t-shirt with a black Nike logo poked out of a suitcase.

Ella paused, quirking her head to the side. In a town quite literally from the past, the item seemed out of place, not impossible, but definitely unusual.

Retracing her steps, she edged into the darkness behind the stairs and dragged the heavy luggage over the concrete floor.

After pulling out the shirt, she held it aloft under one of the incandescent bulbs. It was just a plain t-shirt, nothing special.

Ella frowned. *Why is it here, though?*

Before last week, she would've thought nothing about stored clothing in a basement, but in Keystone, a town where clothing was in high demand, it seemed odd not to at least give it away. Odder still was imagining either Jimmy or Rose wearing it. Her mind tried to conjure up the image but came up blank.

Ella bit her lip, her pulse soaring. There was, however, a closet rife with this brand.

Her breath quickened as she unzipped the suitcase the rest of the way.

"No," she whispered.

It was filled with Kay's missing clothes. Jeans, sweaters, and even a swimsuit. Ella rooted around gently to see if there was anything non-wardrobe related deeper inside.

Her hand hit something hard in the folds of a sweatshirt. Peeling back the layers, she pulled out a picture frame of Will smiling adoringly at Kay.

Ella didn't know how long she stared absently at the photo, her mind racing with the implications of finding the suitcase in the basement. Eventually, she replaced the frame, zipped the luggage up, and shoved it back to its spot under the stairs.

Her breath came in spurts as she took the stairs two at a time. She just wanted to get out of there. On the last step, she tripped and spilled into the hallway. Pain shot up her shin, but she ignored it as she sprinted down the hall.

Back in the safety of her room, she shut the door and slid to the floor.

What was Kay's suitcase doing in the basement? Had she put it there or did Jimmy or Rose? She reached for any other explanation, intentionally ignoring the obvious.

It was there because she was going to run away with Jimmy. Had he gotten cold feet? Had Rose found out? With each passing second, Ella was growing less and less confident that Six was the murderer and more certain one of the innkeepers was responsible. The problem was, which one?

CHAPTER 27

ELLA PACED THE wooden floor of her bedroom. She needed to figure out her next move.

With a deep breath, she made the decision to tell Sheriff Chapman everything she knew. But first, she needed a cool, quick bath to wash away the sweat from her run and the cobwebs from the basement of horrors.

The water was a salve for her frayed nerves. By the time she stepped onto the fluffy bathmat, Ella felt fresh and smelled miles better than before.

She debated whether to go back to the basement to retrieve her wet clothes but in the end decided her visit to the sheriff's office was more important. The decision wasn't, in any way, influenced by her fear of the creepy basement.

Ella dragged her shoes down the sidewalk, dreading her conversation with Chapman. Ahead, the silhouette of a cat moved under the jalopy she'd used as cover during the Tombstone Shootout, as she was now calling it. She was pretty sure this car had sprouted from the ground, and the town grew around it. If anyone ever moved it, it was sure to have roots going deeper than any tree in Keystone.

Crouching next to the vehicle, Ella reached a hand under and scratched Fluffy under his chin. Between his paws was a dead mouse. She retracted her hand as if bitten by a snake, and her face scrunched up.

"Hmm, I see now why you didn't eat your breakfast. You were saving room for this. Very smart, very smart."

Ella had seen his empty bowl in the kitchen and filled it with the homemade, raw mixture from the fridge when she'd made her coffee. She wasn't sure who typically fed him—Jimmy or Rose—so it was possible that he was already getting second helpings.

Her eyes flitted to the massive belly currently splayed on the pavement. Actually, it was *very* possible.

He rolled over, his generous body rolling with him.

"Maybe you should go on a diet."

His ears twitched, apparently not fond of the idea.

"Ella, dear." Grandma Wink's shadow fell over them.

Ella stood and greeted her friend.

Chester sat on Wink's shoulder, his nose sniffing the air. Fluffy suddenly appeared at Ella's feet, curling around her legs, his eyes fixed on the squirrel.

Wink shielded her eyes from the sun. "I saw you running earlier, crazy lady. It's too hot for that. It's too hot for anything. I can't wait until we flash somewhere cooler."

"The arctic sounds nice."

"Hmm, not as fun as you'd think."

Ella opened her mouth to ask more then changed her mind. "How's the lasagna coming?"

Wink's eyes hooded over. "It's my best one yet. Flo's going to eat crow tonight."

"You're such a good friend."

"Good friends push each other to produce their best."

"And compete... and call each other names... and pour laxative on each other's food..."

"That too."

Wink then enlisted Ella's help to serve hors d'oeuvres she'd prepared, instructing her to arrive at the potluck fifteen minutes early.

"I'm assuming the dress code to this soiree is casual, right?" Ella looked down at her worn but now clean tennis shoes and faded shirt.

"'Course. We're all family here—" Wink's lips puckered slightly as she took in Ella's outfit. "Unless we're talking about your current attire. Then, I'd suggest changing."

"Everyone's a critic." Ella tugged at the hem of her shorts. "I'd love to, but all my clothes are dirty. Also, I didn't bring anything nice to begin with because, you know, I planned on returning home."

"Well, why didn't you say so? I've got lots of things you can have that I've outgrown." Her veiny hand smoothed over her hip.

"Outgrown? What, were they your baby clothes?" Images of herself in a fuchsia tracksuit flooded Ella's mind. "I appreciate the offer, but I don't think any of your stuff would fit me."

"Nonsense. Come along."

"It's just, I've got so much to do. Bills to pay..."

"No you don't."

"...and Fluffy needs fed."

"He's eating right now."

Sure enough, the feline had gone back to gnawing on his treat, causing Ella's stomach to churn.

Wink dragged her by the elbow to a blue Cadillac.

"Help! I'm being kidnapped!"

"Hush. People'll report you for disturbing the peace."

"Good to know if I ever get abducted." Ella looked around the interior of the car. At least they wouldn't be trudging up the steep hill to Wink's place on foot. "Nice car, by the way. Hey, I have a question for you, how does everyone drive around? Do you have an endless supply of gasoline?"

"Don't be silly. We don't drive around that much. We mostly walk, bicycle, or ride horses."

"Okay. But still, there's got to be a finite supply of fuel. When did you last fill this baby up?"

"Few days ago." Wink glanced down at her dash. "Will retrofitted a lot of the tanks to take some bio-something sludge."

Chester chittered angrily from the backseat.

"You're in his spot."

"That's too bad," Ella said without the slightest hint of remorse. "Hey, what's with the harness?"

"Oh, he's just gotten into wandering off while we're in town. He knocked over Sal's bird feeder. He threatened to shoot my Chester if I didn't restrain him somehow. We're just doing this until things cool down a bit. Or until Chester learns how to behave." She shot a dark look at the rodent in the rearview mirror.

"He said he'd shoot him just for knocking over a bird feeder?"

Wink was slow to respond. "Well, maybe it had more to do with Chester wandering into his shop and attacking a customer."

"He attacked a customer?"

"It was Lenny Holstein. You ever see Lenny? Hair like a squirrel nest."

Ella choked on a laugh. "Chester attacked his head

because he thought it was a nest?"

"That's my working theory."

"That's hilarious." She looked back at the squirrel with a renewed appreciation.

"Sal didn't think so."

They lapsed into a comfortable silence. The rest of the way to Wink's, Ella considered telling her friend about the suitcase of clothes she'd found in the basement, but every time she opened her mouth, she couldn't think of the words to start.

All too soon, the gravel crunched under the car as they pulled into Wink's driveway. Ella took a deep breath and steeled herself for what was to come.

"Wow." Ella couldn't think of anything else to say, so she said it again. "Wow."

They stood in Wink's bedroom. An antique bed with an ornate headboard sat shoved in the corner, like an afterthought, crowded by a nightstand and armoire.

Fabric of every shade of the rainbow vomited out of Wink's closet, spilling into the room. It looked as if adding a single sweater would cause the wardrobe to burst.

"Nearly all of this was before the first flash. So, some of it's getting a bit frayed around the edges. There's more in the spare bedroom."

"Wow," Ella repeated a third time. She whistled. "I'm sorry, did you say there's more?"

Wink nodded.

"Wow."

"You keep saying that."

"Because this... this is just... you could clothe a small country."

Ella ran her fingers along the hangers, surprised to see a few elegant dresses in the vein of Rose's taste.

"I've put the newer stuff here." Wink pointed at the far end.

Ella spied too many velour tracksuits in bold colors. One even had the word "Juicy" on the buttocks. It was obvious that this was the side Wink tended to pick from.

"About seven years back, we flashed into the... 1990s wasn't it? When we picked up the Bradfords and Pauline. Anyway, it was some place south, like Texas, and a large truck passed through with a shipment of goods. The driver was heading to a department store. Pulled over to get gas. While he was paying, Six broke in and took a few boxes. Before anyone knew it, the guy left."

Ella wasn't surprised. "How did anyone find out?"

"Oh, the next time Chapman arrested him, he found the stash. Got the story from him, eventually. Wouldn't you know it? The thief actually stole something useful to the town for a change."

Ella looked over the *newer* outfits with a different perspective.

An hour later, she was up to her chin in cocktail dresses, blouses, sweaters, and pants. Wink kept insisting she take more, piling tracksuits into Ella's arms which Ella promptly returned to their slot in the closet. Where they really belonged was in a bonfire with a gallon of gasoline dumped on top, but she refrained from sharing this opinion aloud.

She was lucky the clothes she'd picked out fit. They were a bit snug in places, but overall, they looked halfway decent on her.

"If it keeps you from wearing those tight pants—"

"They're my running leggings." Ella held up the pile in her arms. "We'll call it an extended loan."

After thanking her friend profusely, she asked if she could get a ride back into town. The thought of hiking in the heat with her burden didn't appeal to her at all.

"I'm sure Will would give you a ride."

Balancing the bundle of clothes with a knee, Ella freed up a hand to swipe hair away from her face. "No, that's okay."

"Why not? He's just at the professor's."

"He is? How do you know?"

"Didn't you notice his pickup in the driveway as we passed?"

So much for being observant.

"I'll call over there, now."

"No, Wink, really—"

But Wink had already retreated down the hallway. With a sigh, Ella trudged into the living room and hefted her new wardrobe onto the couch. After her morning visit with the inventor, she was less than thrilled to see him again.

Five minutes later, a knock came at the door.

"Your ride's here," Wink called from the kitchen.

The smell of lasagna wafted into the living room. Ella shot a traitorous look in Wink's direction before yelling goodbye.

After gathering her bundle of clothes, she stepped onto the porch, nearly bowling Will over.

"Sorry," she muttered.

They walked to his pickup in silence. Ella wasn't mad at him, but she also didn't know where they stood after their morning chat.

The vehicle wound down the hill. She searched for a way to break the ice.

"Thanks for the ride," she said, finally, as they reached the outskirts of Keystone.

"My pleasure." Judging by his tone, he seemed relieved to be talking.

As they passed the sheriff's station, she leaned forward. "Can you pull over here? I need to see Chapman about something. I'll walk the rest of the way."

"Sure." His voiced edged with disappointment as he nosed the blue pickup next to the sidewalk.

Ella unbuckled and hugged the clothes against her. As she reached for the door handle, she paused. "Will? I'm sorry about this morning. It wasn't until then that I realized I'm having a harder time adjusting than I thought."

"I understand. If you ever want to talk, Ella, I'm here for you."

She smiled and dipped her chin in acknowledgment. "Thank you. I just might take you up on that offer."

"And I'm sorry too. I overreacted because—because I don't want to lose any more friends."

"You won't. I'm being careful. See?" She nodded at the station. "I'm going to tell Chapman everything."

She slipped out of the car and waited for him to drive off, the purr of the motor fading, before she struggled for the door.

Inside, Ella scanned the musty room for the sheriff.

A soft, feminine voice spoke. "He's not here."

Rose unfolded from her cot and approached the bars. Her lips were pale, naked of their trademark lipstick. She looked tired and broken.

Ella shuffled her feet, and she struggled to look the innkeeper in the eye. Part of her still carried guilt about Rose being there, but another part of her remembered the jewelweed and the suitcase of stolen clothes.

"Rose." Ella approached, leaving a gap between them.

A mound of blankets in the cell next door stirred. Six's dark hair stuck out from one of the folds.

"He's asleep," Rose said.

Ella let out a breath, feeling her shoulders relax.

"Do you know where the sheriff went?"

The innkeeper's eyebrows rose. "Why? Going to accuse someone else of murder?" Her sweet voice took the bite out of the accusation, but it still stung.

"Rose, I didn't—I didn't know he'd arrest you. I thought he'd ask a couple of questions, get to the bottom of it, and let you go."

"So you think I'm innocent?" When Ella didn't respond, she said, "I see."

Rose sauntered back to her cot and flopped on top. Her grimy dress no longer swayed with each step but hung limply around her legs.

Ella began to second-guess her suspicions. This woman had been nothing but kind and warm, had taken her in and given her shelter.

"Can I ask you something?" Ella dropped the clothes from Wink onto the sheriff's desk.

"Go on."

Ella's eyes flitted to Six before she leaned into the bars. "Why did you cut that jewelweed?"

Rose let out an exasperated sigh. "To give to Kay, of course. She had a poison oak rash. I cut the leaves and gave them to her. What she did with them after that, I have no idea. But I'll tell you one thing: it's a foolish person who would stick stuff in their bodies without knowing what it did. And Kay was no fool."

Ella nodded and decided to reveal one of her cards. "Then why is there a suitcase with her clothes in your basement?"

"What?" Rose's back stiffened. Her shocked expression appeared genuine.

She slid off the cot and shuffled closer. This time, Ella didn't back away.

"What are you talking about?"

Ella hesitated a breath then spilled about the evidence in the inn's basement.

Deep creases formed in the innkeeper's forehead, and her hand hovered near her mouth in silent horror. "You mean, they really were having an affair?" She shook her head. "No, my Jimmy would never do such a thing."

"Why else would her getaway bag be in your inn?"

Rose chewed her lip and paced. When she spoke, her voice was small. "Because they were going to run away together. It's the only explanation that fits."

She seemed to shrink before Ella's eyes. A fat tear rolled down Rose's cheek, and her lips quivered. Despite everything, Ella's heart hurt for her. She reached out and curled her hand around Rose's.

"I'm so sorry."

Rose sobbed silently.

Ella comforted her the best she could through the bars, all the while, the gears in her head turning. If Jimmy and Kay were going to run away together, what would his motive be for killing her?

She couldn't think of one which put him back in the "maybe" category of suspects. Which left Rose and Six.

The innkeeper seemed genuinely shocked by the affair, taking away her motive. Unless she was the world's greatest actress, she was also innocent.

If neither innkeeper was the killer, that left Six. Her gaze wandered to the sleeping lump one cell over.

"Rose, it's really important I find the sheriff."

Rose's sobs softened to sniffles, and she dabbed her eyes. "All he said was he had to go out and that he'd be gone for several hours."

Several hours?

"Ella, I need to be alone, if you don't mind."

"Of course." Ella backed away. "I'm sorry again, Rose. For everything."

Rose wiped her sleeve across her face. "I know."

Ella trudged back to the inn, her heart as heavy as the clothes in her arms. She'd ruined a couple. Her doubts about marriage was an infection she'd allowed to color her suspicions. Was she so set on the idea of a *happy* marriage that she'd sabotaged a healthy one?

It didn't matter that her suspicions had proven right, or that Jimmy was responsible by his actions. She had definitely had a hand in making the situation worse.

Maybe when this was all over, and the killer was behind bars, she could mend her frayed friendships, try to repair the damage she'd caused.

CHAPTER 28

ELLA TWIRLED ONCE, watching the sundress flare out in the mirror. She felt overdressed for the occasion, but her typical jeans and t-shirt were currently having a spa day in the washing machine. At least she'd fit in better with the local color now.

Despite the outfit coming from someone twenty-five years her senior, it had style. The zipper pulled at the seams near her mid-section—something she could blame on Wink's banana bread—but, overall, it fit nicely.

She managed to detangle her hair and pin it back with a barrette, then she added a touch of lip gloss.

Her bare feet stepped across the hardwood floor, and she realized she'd forgotten to borrow shoes. The least sneaker-type shoe she had were a pair of flip-flops she'd packed to pad around her parents' house.

They would have to do. At least they were encrusted with cheap jewels. And if Flo gave her a hard time about them, she had several comebacks just sitting in the chamber about the woman's beehive.

On Main Street, Keystone residents were already marching towards the white steepled church. Despite the doors and windows being open, the sanctuary felt stuffy. A warm breeze pushed through but did little to abate the heat.

Across the room, Wink flitted behind one of the long, serving tables that had been set up. Two large glass dishes of homemade lasagna sat on trivets.

Flo hovered over Wink's, sniffing at the pasta, and making a face.

"You put too much oregano in."

"Did not."

"I can smell it from here."

"You're batty. Now, are you going to zip your trap and help or what?"

Ella cleared her throat. "Ta-da!"

Both women looked at her and said, "What?"

"I'm here."

"We see that," Flo said.

"*Early*. I'm here early."

"You want a trophy or something?"

"Actually—"

"Ella, you look wonderful." Wink corralled her to a spot further down the table, pointing at small pieces of toast she'd baked about the size of a cracker. Immediately, Ella popped one in her mouth, then made it her last after seeing the look on Wink's face.

The older woman slowly and deliberately placed a thick slice of smoked gouda on top, followed by a chunk of pear, and finally topped the creation with a drizzle of pineapple salsa.

Ella found the combination of ingredients strange until she popped the one she'd just assembled in her mouth when Wink wasn't looking.

"Oh my gosh," she hummed around the food. She wiped her mouth as Wink turned back her way.

"So, you think you can assemble the rest so I can go make the punch?"

Ella nodded. Even this, she'd have a hard time screwing up. "Did all of these ingredients come from Keystone?"

"Of course. The cheese is from Bradford Farms. The pears are from the greenhouses. And a local resident makes the pineapple salsa."

"Gotcha. So, hypothetical question, how many of these hors d'oeuvres can I eat before you get mad? Ballpark a number. Ten? Twenty?"

"None. You eat none."

"None. Got it." Ella winked at her.

"No, really. You don't eat any."

"Sure, sure. Don't eat any. Got it." She shot Wink finger guns.

Wink narrowed her eyes. "So help me, Ella, if I find fewer than fifty on a platter, you will be cleaning Chester's poop for a month."

She left Ella with that horrible prospect and marched off, yelling at Sal for putting his homemade macaroni and cheese too close to her lasagna.

"Bit harsh." Ella looked sideways at Flo. "Now I get why you two are friends."

Ella worked on assembling the pieces on what may have been a serving platter but looked an awful lot like a used hubcap. Once she got into a steady rhythm, she had the "platter" filled in ten minutes, just as the sanctuary-turned-hall overflowed with people.

Ella wiped her hands and surveyed the crowd, doing her best car salesman impression and pointing out her creations to anyone who passed. Further down the line of serving tables, she spied a suspicious looking red gelatin that shook as a result of all the foot traffic.

She grimaced, remembering the trout lime mold Rose had made. It was a happy memory, tinged with the regret of current circumstances. So much had changed in a week.

Mayor Bradford waltzed up to the lectern, and the din fell to a whisper. He leaned forward, seeming to relish the control, and said two words: "Let's eat."

The room broke into chaos. It was as if he'd announced the last donut on earth was theirs for the taking.

A tsunami of townspeople rolled towards the table. Someone jumped over a chair. A little boy kicked another boy, gladiator style.

"Incoming!" Flo yelled. She yanked Ella aside in time before she got body-checked by a man in a kilt.

Ella's mouth fell open as the flow jostled her further and further from the table.

"What are you doing?" Wink hollered at her. "Grab a plate and get in here before all the good food's gone!"

This was insanity. She seriously considered skipping a meal.

A woman in front of her was already sporting a goose egg on her cheek. All things considered, Ella was rather attached to her own face the way it was.

Then, a squat man with a box-shaped head started piling up the hors d'oeuvres she'd just made.

"Oh no, you don't." Sticking out her sharp elbows, Ella shoved him aside using a wrestling move she'd seen on TV that everybody tried to convince her was fake.

He coughed, giving her enough time to snatch the platter. She ran down the line, made it to two other trays, and piled the contents on top. She didn't even bother seeing what the last one was. Just grabbed.

"Ella! Catch!" Wink tossed her a roll.

A few feet away, Flo did a fake sneeze on the remnants of the potato salad. A few groans and "gross" comments later, she beamed at Ella as she slopped it all up for herself.

Once Ella's platter was piled high and the perimeter of the tables became too thick with bodies, she stepped out of the fray. Within a few minutes, it was as if someone had rung a bell and all the fighters retreated to their corners.

Smears and crumbs were all that remained of the potluck, except for some less appetizing dishes, which were mostly still intact. Ella noticed very little of the vegetable tray had been touched.

She wandered until she found Wink, Flo, and Will sitting at a table with an elderly couple. When Will spotted Ella, he smiled and pulled out a chair for her.

"Thanks." Her cheeks flushed, and she avoided looking at Wink.

"Which lasagna did you get?" Flo asked before Ella's bottom had even touched the seat.

"I think I got yours. I couldn't get to Wink's. Some ten-year-old girl was guarding it, and she looked pretty mean."

"That's Sally. You made the right call."

"So, that blood bath's normal?"

"What? Did someone get hurt? I missed it." Flo's face fell.

"Not that I saw."

"Oh. Then, that was pretty tame."

Ella looked to Wink and Will for confirmation, then swore under her breath. Next time, she'd come armed with a helmet and elbow pads. Maybe boxing gloves, too.

Wink shoveled a portion of her lasagna onto Ella's plate.

Flo's eyes gleamed. "Well? Which do you prefer?"

"She literally just put it on my plate. You just watched her do it." Ella's fork poised over the untouched food to prove her point.

The Bobbsey Twins continued their staring contest. Ella looked to Will for help.

He held his hands up. "You're on your own."

"Traitor." She cleared her throat. "I guess I'll be eating lasagna now, but only because I want to. It has nothing to do with you two annoying me."

Ella cut through one with the side of her fork. Cheese and marinara sauce gushed out. She slipped the bite into her mouth, the flavors melding together, and she let out a sigh.

"That's amazing."

"Which one?" Flo jumped from her seat and leaned so far over the table her blouse took a swim in her salad dressing.

"Um…" Ella had already lost track of whose slice she'd tasted.

Wink fished Flo's top from her food. "Flo, you got ranch on your—"

"Ha! She tasted mine. Did you see that? She preferred *mine*."

"Give it a rest. She hasn't tried mine yet."

"Oh. Right. Carry on then."

Ella stared at Flo like she'd grown two heads. After forcing Flo back a few inches, Ella took a bite of Wink's entrée. The flavor kicked up a notch more than Flo's, but the cheese was creamier.

"Huh. I like both."

Flo dropped into her seat, her mouth sputtering. "You can't like both."

"What can I say? I do." Ella made a grandiose sweep of her hand over the lasagnas and raised her voice as if directing a play. "These two pasta dishes are the best—nay, the *greatest*—slices of Italian cuisine I've ever—"

"Take it down a notch," Will muttered. "They bought it."

"Oh." The two women had already tuned her out and were bickering in low tones. Ella let out a heavy sigh. "Too bad. I was really winding up to something. Did you see my hand wave?"

"I saw your hand wave."

"I could be a magician. Or Vanna White."

"Whatever you do, don't pick a favorite."

"Magician?"

"No. Lasagna. If you do, then they'll stop making them."

"Good point." After devouring one of the lasagnas—she didn't know which one—she bit into a homemade brownie.

Blonde hair and the scent of strawberries swirled through the air as Jenny sat down on the other side of Will. Ella's veins turned to ice, but she shot Jenny her best chocolate-ladened smile, anyway.

Jenny flipped her hair over her shoulder. "Ugh. I didn't see anything low fat over there."

"Pretty sure this brownie's low fat." Ella held it up.

"Hey, I know you. You were there during Jesse's shootout with the sheriff."

"Yep." *Right before you ditched me.* "I'm Ella."

"Jenny."

Ella extended her brownie-covered hand but was disappointed when Jenny noticed and refused to shake.

The conversation drifted while they ate, mostly to people Ella hadn't met yet. Growing bored, she watched the elderly couple across the table.

The woman dabbed at a bit of whip cream on the

man's cheek. A few minutes later, when she came back complaining that all of her favorite chocolate chip cookies were gone, he dug his out under a mound of mashed potatoes and gave it to her, resulting in an affectionate peck on the cheek.

Ella smiled to herself then looked away, feeling like she was intruding.

Will dipped his head close to hers. "Frank and Grace."

She hadn't realized he'd been watching her watch them.

"Hey, creeper," she said. He ignored her comment.

"Been married forty years. *Happily* married, I might add."

Ella's gaze turned back to the couple eating in comfortable silence. When they looked at each other, their eyes still sparked with a deep love and passion she rarely saw. She looked back at Will.

"Did you plan that?"

"Them kissing? No." He winked at her. "But I may have invited them to sit here knowing how they behave around each other."

Watching them, Ella's chest tightened, and a small lump formed in her throat. So, it *was* possible.

"Thanks," she whispered.

Jenny clued in to their conversation and called over to Frank and Grace, "You two are so adorable." She had to repeat the comment three times before they heard her.

Ella left them to get a second helping of homemade ice cream. As she drizzled a generous amount of caramel and fruit on top, the side door burst open, and a glowing sunset washed over her, blinding her.

One of the last voices Ella wanted to hear yelled her name.

"Ella Barton!"

Her heart stuttered, and she dropped the serving spoon back into the ice cream.

Jimmy marched towards her. "We need to talk."

CHAPTER 29

"Oh hey, Jimmy," Ella said, laying the enthusiasm on thick. "Come here often?" She cracked a smile. "No? What about the ice cream? Have you tried it yet? I was just about to, but then I thought, 'Ella, you should probably watch what you eat.' So, that's what I'm doing…"

While she rambled on, she took a step back, and her eyes raked the crowded sanctuary in search of an exit. The nearest one currently had a frothing, red-faced innkeeper filling it.

She raised her chin. He wouldn't dare hurt her with all these people around.

His eyes bore through hers as he stalked around the serving table.

She let out a hollow laugh. "You know, I'm just going to—" She turned and leaped into the crowd.

If she could just get back to her table, then she'd be safe. Chances were good, Flo was packing.

But doubt niggled the back of her brain. They were all Jimmy's friends. They didn't know he possibly murdered

Kay, and Ella didn't have time to explain why he was guilty.

In front of her, two men—one with a farmer's tan and the other in tailcoats who looked like he'd stepped out of a Dickens novel—parted. Jimmy stood there, waiting for her.

She skidded to a stop. She didn't know how he'd managed it, but he'd cut her off from her only refuge.

His eyes were wild above heavy bags and shadows. He took a lumbering step towards her.

Instinct kicked in, and she ran. Her brain told her to stay, search for Will and Wink, but her legs had their own idea: to get as far away from Jimmy as possible.

She bolted through the open front doors. The sound of her flip-flops slapping against her heels echoed over the empty street. They made running a challenge, and she almost bit concrete twice.

In hindsight, she wished she'd just committed the fashion faux pas and worn sneakers with her dress. She kicked the footwear off, deciding it was safer running barefoot.

Ella pumped her legs as hard as she could down Main Street. Ahead, she spotted the shadowy gap of an alley.

"Ella! Stop!" Jimmy's heavy footfalls pounded behind her.

"Sure thing, Jimmy!"

She ducked down the alley—the same one where she'd met Six—and sprinted the length of it until it spilled out in front of the lake.

"Why are you running? I just want to talk!"

Sure you do.

His long legs swallowed the distance, and he was nearly upon her. Ella lunged around a maple tree, nearly clotheslining on a low-hanging branch.

"Ella!"

He let out a frustrated growl as his lithe body hit her back like a freight train. They tumbled into the grass, limbs tangling as he tried to pin her down.

She attempted another move she'd seen on TV and collided her forehead with his. She let out a hiss between her teeth. "Ow! Oh, that hurts. Oh that really, really hurts."

She clutched at her skull, and Jimmy stared at her in bewilderment, his forehead barely red.

"That's *nothing* like on TV. Is my head cracked open? It feels cracked open." She checked for blood. Her heartbeat pulsed at the injury site which she was sure wasn't a good sign.

"Enough!" He fastened her arms down and sat on her legs.

"Let me go!"

"We have to talk!"

"Let me go or I'll scream." She twisted against his grip.

He moved so less of his body was on her, and she was able to pull in a full breath. "Better?"

"Fan-freaking-tastic. Now, will you let me go?"

"No." Anger flashed over his ruddy face, making him appear his age for the first time. "I just had an interesting conversation with Six. He said he saw you talking with the sheriff not too long before Rose got arrested. Said you pulled him outside to discuss something important. That true?"

Ella squirmed and pulled at his steel grip. "You really trust anything that outlaw says?"

Jimmy narrowed his eyes. "Just answer the question."

Before this morning, she would've spilled her guts to him, the guilt weighing so heavily on her. But now, now she knew the truth.

"Why? So you can kill me like you did Kay?" She tensed, waiting for him to hit her. Her heart thumped so loudly she was sure he could hear it.

"What did you say?" Jimmy tilted his head back, his eyes cold.

No. Not cold.

She searched his face. He was desperate. Hurt. Angry.

"Why would you think I killed her?"

"Because she changed her mind. She wouldn't run away with you."

His eyes widened. "Seriously? That's what you think?"

"I found her suitcase in the basement."

The innkeeper stared open-mouthed at her for what felt like an uncomfortable amount of time. Then, he shook his head, and his grip eased but didn't release her.

"We weren't having an affair. How many times do I have to tell people that? We weren't going to run away together. *She* planned on leaving. Alone. I was helping her. *As a friend.*"

Ella studied him. He was telling the truth.

She released the tension in her body and stopped struggling. Rose was innocent. Jimmy was innocent. That left Six.

"Ella, what did you say to Chapman?"

She looked away, the guilt feeling like a weight on her chest. "I'm sorry, Jimmy. All I did was repeat what Six had said: that he saw you and Kay meeting up in the woods."

"That can't be all. What aren't you telling me?"

Ella closed her eyes, took a breath, and opened them. No more lies.

"I may have mentioned that Rose had recently clipped the jewelweed in the conservatory. If ingested, its symptoms are similar to what Kay experienced."

His jaw clenched and unclenched. He raised a fist. Ella

squeezed her eyes shut and turned her head. But the strike never came.

She peeled one lid open at a time. The storm in his face subsided. He released her and rocked back onto his heels.

She scrambled out from under him, keeping him in her sights.

His hand ran through his disheveled hair. "You have your sights set on the wrong people, Ella. None of us killed her. I'd hoped you would be a better judge of character. I was wrong."

"Can you blame me? How well can any of us really know someone?"

His eyes snapped to hers. "I'm not a killer. And I know Rose. She's no killer either. I feel sorry for you that you've never trusted anyone that deeply."

His words were venom and pierced her heart, echoing Will's from earlier.

"I don't want your pity." Ella jumped to her feet. "You all view each other with rose-colored glasses. Someone in this town killed that poor woman, but you all refuse to believe it."

Pain flashed across his face, and she wished she could bite back the bitter words. She was a better person than this. Her conversation with Will had revealed something toxic inside of her that she clearly needed to work on.

She stared at the ground. "Jimmy, I'm sorry—"

"Ella, we've all been there. Transitioning here isn't easy. Let us help you. You don't have to go it alone. We choose to be around each other despite our flaws because the alternative's worse."

"Being alone doesn't mean you're lonely," she countered. "I'm not lonely."

"No. But not having faith in others is."

Ella backed away, too emotionally exhausted to

continue the conversation.

Without another word, she turned her back on him and trudged up the bank. When she reached the top, she stopped and faced him again. "Why was she leaving?"

"Pardon?"

"Why was Kay leaving? Was it because of her father?"

Jimmy pressed his lips together and slowly nodded. "I guess there's no use keeping it secret anymore. He was not kind to her. Not a good father. He beat her for years and controlled every aspect of her life. He's not a good person."

Ella stood in stunned silence. Emotions competed for priority, mostly sadness and anger.

"The saddest part of it? She was planning on leaving that night."

"What?" Ella turned his words over. "Did Mayor Bradford find out?"

He shrugged.

"Did you tell Chapman any of this?"

He sighed and ran his fingers through his hair again. "I'd promised Kay—swore to her—I'd never tell a soul."

What if Kay's father had found out she was leaving that night?

Something clicked deep inside her mind, a memory of a familiar voice she couldn't place. The voice. He was the voice she'd overheard by the lake.

Ella smacked her forehead. "How could I have been so stupid? He did it."

"Who? The mayor?"

But she wasn't listening. The conversation she'd heard, the shouting about his cows dying. But that would mean...

She rubbed her fingers over her temples. She'd hiked by the dairy and farmhouse but hadn't noticed any jewelweed. Of course, she hadn't been looking for it.

"I gotta go." Ella dashed up the bank the rest of the way.

"Where're you going?" Jimmy yelled after her as she crested it.

Ella waved her hand dismissively, not wanting to stop and explain her theory. She'd already wasted too much time looking at the wrong suspects. As it was, the plant was probably already destroyed.

She raced down Main Street, her bare feet hitting the pavement and sharp rocks. Periodically, her hands drifted down to the hem of her dress to keep from flashing anyone.

Conversation and laughter floated through the open doorways of the church as she passed. Shadows grew over the sidewalk in the fading light like hands telling her to slow down and think through what she was doing. But Ella ignored them.

He did it. Mayor Bradford had killed his own daughter, and this time, she was certain.

CHAPTER 30

MANURE AND HAY wafted on the breeze as gold and red bands of light stretched across the sky.

By the time she reached the dairy and adjacent farmhouse, Ella was walking half bent over her knees, gasping for air. Her feet felt like they'd walked over glass.

Clutching a stitch in her side, she pulled herself together. The fence around the yard stretched the perimeter like a white skeleton—except in the spot where the repair had been made.

Ella studied it with piqued interest this time. The new boards stood in sharp, dark brown contrast to the rest of the enclosure.

That's how they got in.

After wiping her damp forehead, Ella hobbled over to the flower bed bordering the old farmhouse. She didn't see any jewelweed, so she slowly walked the entire bed, scanning the foliage, until she'd arrived back in her original spot. No jewelweed.

Ella shook her head, hands on her hips. She had been

so certain. It all made sense. It was possible he'd ripped the plant out afterward, but she hadn't found any disturbed soil.

She was missing something. Squeezing her eyes closed, she went over her theory again.

A thought hit her. Plunging her hand into the pocket of her sundress, she retrieved her cell phone. Despite not being able to make calls or access the internet with it, she found herself carrying it out of habit, as well as comfort.

Ella swiped through the notes she'd taken several days prior. For each hand-colored drawing or photo of a poisonous plant, she scanned the flower bed.

On the third swipe, she landed on one that looked familiar. In front of her, directly under a window, were clusters of small white flowers amidst leaves, unique in that if she squinted the flowers were reminiscent of puffy clouds.

She pulled in a sharp breath and held the colorful drawing up to the live plant. It was a perfect match.

Excitement rolled through her, immediately followed by a wave of fear.

She zoomed in on the paragraph of information regarding the poisonous plant.

Ageratina altissima, also known as *White Snakeroot*:
   ...poisonous to humans. Symptoms include: weakness, nausea, severe vomiting, tremors, delirium, and death.

Ella swore under her breath. She'd done it. She'd found the plant responsible for killing Kay.

Behind her, footsteps whispered over the grass. She shot up as a two-by-four swung at her. Her hands were halfway to her head when the board connected with the right side of her skull.

She stumbled back and tried to face her attacker, but the ground tilted underfoot. The corners of her vision dimmed, then all faded to black as she felt herself falling into an abyss.

Ella's bed shook. Her first frantic thought was that it was an earthquake. She shot out of bed, only to hit her head on something metal.

A splitting headache radiated from a different spot. When she attempted to reach up and touch it, she discovered her hands wouldn't work properly, like they were glued together.

She blinked away the fuzziness and confusion. Images flooded back. The white snakeroot. The two-by-four coming at her.

She sucked in a lungful of stuffy air that smelled faintly of grease and something she didn't want to know the source of.

Her "bed" was still shaking. On her left, light seeped in through a seam. She waited for her eyes to adjust.

"Oh, crap."

She was in the trunk of a moving car. Panic spread through every nerve ending.

Ella screamed and pounded her fists against the trunk, discovering her wrists were bound together with rope.

Despite her hysterical cries, she knew it was of no use. She could scream as loud as a fog horn, but no one would hear her. The entire town was at the potluck, enjoying lasagna and homemade ice cream like she should be doing.

Ella gasped and swallowed. Her head pounded like a steel drum. Gingerly, she reached for the knot on her scalp and winced.

Think, Ella.

This was almost worse than Six pointing a gun at her or that time she'd leaned over a candle and accidentally set her hair on fire.

Her situation was bad, granted, but she'd been through worse—which really said something about her life decisions if being knocked out, kidnapped, and locked in the trunk of a car wasn't her worst day.

Where was he taking her?

She sucked in a ragged breath and wondered how much oxygen she had left. Squinting in the dark, she searched her surroundings.

She remembered some cars had safety release cables in case people got stuck in the trunks, but that was in newer vehicles. In a town from the past, who knew how ancient this car was?

Her fingers probed all around but found nothing except rusted metal and moldy carpet liner. At least she'd found the source of the smell. She was beginning to fear it was her.

In the absence of a release cable, the taillights were her next best option or at least that's what she remembered from a news segment on television.

"And who said TV was useless?" she muttered to herself as she maneuvered her body.

Her building headache had now bloomed into a jackhammer in the side of her skull. Gritting her teeth against the pain, she groped around for the taillights, found one, then kicked it hard using her bare heel. Not only did it not crack, but her heel had a *buzzing* feel to it.

Again and again, she kicked until she heard a *crack* split the glass. Bearing down, she gave it one last donkey kick. Her bare foot broke through the glass, and the shards ripped through her skin.

She hissed but shoved aside the pain as she twisted to

peer out the small opening. Fresh air whipped at her face.

Outside, the sun had dipped below the horizon, but there was still enough light by which to see.

Now what?

Her stomach lurched into her spine, and the dust cloud trailing behind the car began to dissipate as the vehicle rolled to a stop.

A cold sweat broke out across her forehead. The driver-side door opened, and one side of the car rose as someone heavy got out. This was her chance.

Ella scrambled onto her back, her feet towards the latch. Just as the trunk popped open, she kicked with her bloodied foot.

But her abductor had been expecting it. He dodged his head to the side.

"Oh, Ella." Mayor Bradford sounded as disappointed as if she'd just spilled his favorite drink. "Why couldn't you just mind your own business?"

"I've been asking myself that same question."

"I noticed Jimmy chase you out of the potluck. He certainly knows how to make a scene. When he came running back, whispering something to Will, I knew you'd figured it out. You're just too clever for your own good." He sighed then motioned her out with his thick fingers. "Well, come on. Haven't got all day."

"No, you know, I'm good. This is actually quite cozy in here. I was—"

"Out." He snaked his fingers around her arms and yanked with surprising strength.

"Where are we?"

"Come see."

Ella reluctantly followed him around the side of his car and faced the direction of Keystone. Twin Hills stood sentry behind the greenhouses' plexiglass roofs. He'd driven her past all of it, further north than she'd ever been in the traveling town.

His hand clamped around her elbow, and he whirled her around. The road stretched before them a few yards before ending abruptly in sand. Endless dunes stretched to the horizon.

He had taken her to the boundary line.

"See that? It's the end of the road for you." He barked out a laugh, doubling over. When he'd collected himself, he gasped, "Pretty clever, eh? I didn't plan that."

"You're a regular Bob Hope."

He wiped a tear from the corner of his eye. "We're at the border."

"I noticed. Thanks for playing tour guide. I appreciate it, but I really should get back to the potluck. Those cookies aren't going to feed themselves." She tilted her head. "Wait, no. That's not right. That sounds like I want to *feed* the cookies—"

"Enough!"

Ella winced slightly then did her best to mask the quiver in her voice. "Okay, I'll play. Why have you brought me here?"

"Why do you think?" His gaze lifted from her to the dunes. "We're due for another flash."

"I thought you couldn't predict them?"

His face turned purple with a building annoyance. "Here's what's going to happen. I'm going to put you back in that trunk, put the car in drive, and place a brick on the gas pedal. It's going to roll forward, taking you over the line. I imagine you'll crash, oh... there." He jutted a finger at the trough of the nearest dune. "Then you'll probably bake in the car and die within a day or so—"

Ella slammed her foot onto his shoe. The move did little damage but succeeded in distracting him. He growled in pain and released his grip on her.

She ran towards town, her hands still awkwardly bound in front of her. Two yards later, his feet crunched over gravel right behind her.

He caught a handful of her hair and ripped it back. Pain tingled over her scalp, adding to her splitting headache, and stars traced her vision.

He wrapped a thick arm around her waist and dragged her back to the car.

"Valiant effort, my dear."

"Can't blame a girl for trying," she wheezed.

"I'm afraid you're not going to escape death today. Now, where was I? Oh yeah. How long you last will be up to you. I'm going to ask you some questions, and if you tell me everything, I'll throw you in the back seat. However, if you lie to me or hold anything back, I'll throw you in the trunk. Deal?"

Maybe he wore a suit and tie, but he was no different from Six, a wolf hiding in plain sight.

A hot tear threatened to escape. "You're a monster."

"Mm." He glanced at his watch.

Suddenly, everything about the man in front of her disgusted her. The crescents of sweat under his arms. The way his pale, clammy skin pulled taught over rolls of fat. Even the smell of mothballs and cedar turned her stomach.

She swallowed the bile at the back of her throat and spat, "How could you kill her? Your own daughter?"

His eyes widened a fraction as if he'd never considered the question. "Because she was going to leave."

"Other people have left."

"Yes. But who would want to live in a town where the mayor couldn't get his own daughter to stay? We were supposed to be a family."

"Then, why not leave with her?"

"Why would I want to? I run everything here. This is *my* town."

She didn't buy it. "She was going to expose you before she left, wasn't she? My God, the dirt she must've had on you…"

He bent so close she could see the spittle on his lips. "You have no idea."

She recoiled until she ran into the car. "I heard you at Tom's. You poisoned the cows to test—"

"I didn't kill them. They're the ones that gave me the inspiration, actually. They broke into the yard. Ate the snakeroot and died."

His words churned in her head. "The milk?"

He clapped as if she'd just performed a trick.

"But why accuse Tom of killing them in the first place?"

"To throw you off. I was already there, squaring my bill when I saw you running. I knew you were poking your nose where it didn't belong."

Ella's cheeks burned at being duped so easily.

It dawned on her that he might actually succeed in killing her. A hot lump formed in her throat at the prospect of not seeing her friends again, at not ever getting the chance to return home.

"You know why the town jumps, don't you?"

He laughed. "I'm glad you think so much of me. I know nothing about it, except that it's great. I wouldn't change it even if I could."

"But all of these people separated from their families…"

"I'm done answering your questions." He pulled a handkerchief out of his suit jacket and dabbed at the sweat glistening over his pate. "Now, you answer mine.

Who broke into Kay's, and what did they take?"

"I don't know." The response came too fast, and she knew he didn't believe her.

Without warning, he slapped her across the face. She saw stars again and bit her tongue to keep from crying out.

"Who?"

"His name's Casper. Real friendly ghost—"

He slapped her again. Her face began to grow numb, and she ground her teeth, glaring at him. If her hands weren't bound, she would've pummeled his face into ground beef by now.

He repeated the question.

Ella pressed her lips together. If she told him the truth, he'd just kill Six. She had no love for the outlaw, but nobody deserved to die at the hands of this monster.

She couldn't do that to another human being. If she was going to die today, then let it be saving someone else.

Raising her chin, Ella glared at him, making it clear she'd say nothing more.

"How very disappointing."

He picked her up. She screamed and kicked the air as he tossed her into the trunk. Her coffin.

"If you'll excuse me, I have a long walk back. Enjoy the ride."

CHAPTER 31

THE TRUNK LID slammed shut, and darkness engulfed her. A moment later, the engine roared to life.

She was rolled into the back as the car lurched and crawled forward, then she heard the driver-side door slam shut followed by the crunch of gravel as Mayor Bradford walked away.

Ella thrashed at her metal cage, screaming until her voice turned raw.

Gradually, the car slowed, crested a dune, then picked up speed. It was not unlike being on a roller coaster—only without the fun.

With no means of escape, Ella orientated her body to brace for impact. It came a second later, rattling her teeth and jarring her bones.

She blinked away more tears that threatened to flow. Crying would not save her.

"Well, it can't get any worse," she said aloud.

The car jolted and settled, sinking several inches in the soft sand.

"I stand corrected."

Time behaved strangely, slowing then speeding up again. She had no idea how long she was in there, but sweat poured down her face and each breath was a struggle, despite the broken taillight.

The pain in her head had dulled and now felt like a stake driving slowly into it, which wasn't really an improvement so much as a lateral move. All the while, the temperature inside continued to climb.

Putting her mouth to the broken glass, she screamed for help. Her hope that someone would hear her sank after each unanswered shout. A sob escaped her, and she rolled onto her back.

This was it. She'd never stop the time flashes, never see her parents again, never find out who won the latest season of *The Voice* or whatever iteration of singing competition Hollywood producers would come up with.

"They're all just a bunch of *American Idol* wannabe shows, anyway," she rasped aloud to console herself then realized those would be her dying words.

She shrugged inwardly. She was okay with that.

"Ella!"

Shifting her ear near the busted glass, she stilled and listened to the delusion playing out in her head that sounded so much like Will.

"Ella!"

She rolled her head in time to see the inventor slide down the dune. After blinking a few times and ensuring herself that she was, in fact, seeing him, she shouted for him to hurry.

It wasn't just the heat and lack of oxygen that concerned her, but the haunting words that they were due for another flash. She didn't want both of them stranded in the desert.

Will scrambled out of sight around the side of the vehicle. It shifted, and she feared it would keel over onto its side. A second later, she heard the jangle of keys as he unlocked the trunk.

A wave of cool, oxygenated air swept over her. He helped her crawl out, and together, they collapsed back onto the dune.

"When you slid down the sand, you looked just like Indiana Jones."

"Who?"

"I may have a concussion." She rolled over and flung her wrists over his head for a hug. "Thank you."

Embarrassed, she untangled herself and tugged at the ropes digging into her skin. There wasn't time to undo them.

"We have to hurry," he said, getting up. "It's not safe to be outside the boundary."

He helped her stand, and they clawed up the dune. Overhead, stars began to pierce the veil of the oncoming night as the last of dusk touched the landscape.

They jogged towards the demarcation in the sand and gravel. Sand stuck to Ella's blood-covered foot.

"It was Mayor Bradford," she panted.

"Yeah, I figured that's where you went based on what Jimmy said."

"Did you pass him on the road? The mayor? He was walking back towards town."

"No. He must've ducked into the forest when he heard my car."

The moment they crossed the boundary, she let out a breath. They were safe.

"That's right, Will. I did run into the forest." Mayor Bradford stepped out from behind a tall pine.

Ella choked back a scream. For a large man, he was

stealthy.

"I'd hoped that luck would be on my side, and you'd both be stranded. But it appears—once again—that I'm going to have to intervene."

He lunged at Will, and they toppled onto the boarder, onto the sand and gravel line, in a tangle of fisticuffs. The mayor's weight proved to be an advantage, and he kept Will pinned to the ground.

The inventor's fist connected with Mayor Bradford's face in a right hook that'd make Muhammed Ali proud.

Ella jumped onto the mayor's back and tried getting him to move by choking him, but it was like trying to move a house. He threw her off, and she rolled onto the ground.

She frantically combed the area for anything she could use as a weapon. Nearby, Will let out gurgling noises as the mayor wrapped his hands around the inventor's throat.

Ella shot her leg out in one of her donkey kicks. Her foot landed in the mayor's side, sinking a couple of inches before springing back.

Not only did the move not help Will, it actually made the mayor's grip tighten even more. Like a predator, he'd latched onto his prey.

Will's skin was turning an unsettling shade of purple. Ella's hands groped the ground, scraping over rocks and needles before feeling a sturdy branch a few feet long. A perfect nature-made bat if there ever was one.

As she was picking up the weapon, a glow burst all around them, permeating the air as if a light switch had been flipped. Ella looked up.

Keystone Village was under a giant dome of crackling electricity. The starry, dusky sky warped like a magnifying glass, turning shades of turquoise and purple. She stood memorized by the scene.

"Ella—" Will's gasp from the ground brought her back.

The tussling had taken the two men over the boundary line. The crackling dome of light bisected the mayor and Will, their legs in Keystone, their torsos and heads in the desert.

"No!" she screamed.

She leaped towards them as she swung the branch, her muscles remembering her high school softball days.

With a loud crack, the wood connected with Mayor Bradford's head. She followed the move with a hard kick between his legs. He slumped against Will, whimpering.

She brought her bloodied foot up and shoved his haunches with all the energy she had left. He tumbled over Will, head-first into the sand, stirring once then growing still.

Will's eyes were closed. Ella dropped the branch and called his name, but he was unresponsive.

The crackling light of the dome was nearly blinding now, brighter than the brightest, sun-filled day, forcing her eyes into slits.

Frantic, she gripped his feet and pulled. Her bare heels scraped over the gravel for purchase. Inch by inch, she scooted him closer until only his head was over the line.

Then the world turned white.

CHAPTER 32

ELLA GAPED AT the tall trees and vines of a jungle. In the spot where the mayor had been a second before, a massive fern danced under the steady patter of raindrops. Going from the arid desert, the high humidity took her breath away.

"Is it over?" Will rubbed the water from his face and sat up.

"Oh good. You're awake. Could've used that a few seconds sooner, but whatever. How do you feel?"

He touched his throat. "Like I almost died."

"I know the feeling. Thanks for coming to get me, by the way." She didn't want to think about what would've happened if he'd arrived a few minutes later.

She propped him up and helped him stagger to his feet. The air was alive with the songs of hundreds of birds, the buzz of insects, and what she would swear were monkeys swinging and jumping between branches.

"Looks like we're in a tropical rainforest," she said. "But what year?"

"That's always the question." His eyes strayed to the fern. "He's gone?"

She nodded.

"Good."

She stared at the spot too. She'd given him the death sentence he'd chosen for her. It was poetic, yet it dragged on her soul.

"You did what you had to, Ella."

She didn't say anything but let the steady raindrops wash away her guilt. They lingered near the new terrain for some time, getting soaked and listening to the patter of rain on the canopy above.

Ella broke the spell and held her wrists up. "You wouldn't happen to have a pocketknife on you, would you?" Her skin around the rope had been rubbed raw.

The inventor tugged at the bindings with the patient hands of someone used to intricate, methodical work. Once she was freed, they trekked up the road towards town, their clothes now soaked to the skin.

As they crested the slope, Keystone came into view in the bright light of a new day. Keystone's tall evergreen forest was swallowed by the backdrop of dense jungle.

At the south end of town, a rainbow appeared over the fields, reminding Ella that filth could be washed away.

She sucked in a slow, cleansing breath. It was still Sunday. The start of a new week. A new beginning.

It took several days to unravel the mystery of Kay's death. After getting a thorough checkup by Pauline, Ella stayed at the sheriff's office through what was, for the village, Sunday night.

Sheriff Chapman grilled her for hours, extracting every detail, including how she knew Six had broken into Kay's apartment.

He promised not to reveal to the outlaw how he'd come upon the information, as well as promising not to throw her in jail for trespassing and hindering a police investigation if she promised to stay out of trouble in the future. She readily agreed.

Pauline took samples of the white snakeroot and was able to identify it as the poison that had killed Kay. Now that they knew what to look for, Chapman and Pauline were able to get enough of a sample from the Bradford Farms milk container that had been in Kay's fridge that Ella had foolishly poured out and was able to match it to the white snakeroot.

After Ella's recount of events, Chapman came to the conclusion that when Mayor Bradford's cows had broken through the fence, they ate the poisonous plant, then died shortly thereafter.

It was anyone's guess as to what happened next, but Chapman's theory was that it gave the mayor a solution to his problem and that he intentionally let one of his cows eat the snakeroot, milked it, then gave that bottle to his daughter.

Ella also relinquished the note she'd found outside her door that warned her to stop snooping. Chapman was able to identify and match it to the mayor's handwriting.

With most of the loose ends tied up, he retrieved Kay's stolen documents from Six's cabin and charged him with breaking and entering on top of a litany of other charges. Ella learned that Keystone's justice system didn't have the infrastructure to incarcerate criminals for long and that the cowboy would be let out after a short stint in the slammer. She let the sheriff know exactly what she thought about this and only stopped yelling when he threatened to put her in a cell with Six.

By Wednesday, the whirlwind of an investigation was

finally drawing to a close, and Ella could get home for some much-needed rest. She had practically lived at Chapman's office the past three days.

Maybe it was the time change, but she couldn't remember the last meal she'd had or the last time she saw her bed. With the investigation finally closed, she crashed onto her mattress at 6:00 PM on Wednesday. She rolled out of bed Thursday morning to the smell of freshly brewed coffee and pancakes—a scent that hadn't filled the inn since Rose's arrest.

Fluffy stretched out on Ella's bed like a throw pillow. After rubbing his belly until she couldn't resist the call of caffeine any longer, she went downstairs.

In the kitchen, Rose sat at the table, impeccable as ever, a fork waiting in her hand. Carefully, Jimmy set a tower of pancakes in front of her. "Welcome home, love." He pecked her cheek.

Ella teetered in the doorway, unsure if she should intrude. Eventually, the prospect of coffee and the sizzle of bacon on the stove won out. Armed with coffee and a plate of crispy bacon, she settled at the head of the table across from Jimmy, and the room fell silent.

She shifted in her chair, wishing either Flo or Edwin would join them. The awkward quiet stretched, broken only by the sound of her chewing and the rattle of Rose's knife resting on her plate.

At some point, Fluffy sat at her feet, staring at her with luminous eyes. After slipping him scraps of bacon, she scratched his chin.

Across from her, Jimmy unfolded the latest addition of *Keystone Corner*. He rattled it pointedly until Ella looked up. The entire front page was taken by a picture of Mayor Bradford's smarmy face.

She swallowed a particularly sharp bite that scratched

her throat on the way down and looked away.

Despite coming out once a week, the paper had put out a special edition, detailing Kay's murder and the mayor's scandalous backstory—or so she'd heard from Wink. Ella had yet to read it.

She kicked back the rest of her coffee like it was beer and cleared her throat. "Alright, I can't take this. I just want to say *again*, how truly sorry I am. I never should've thought either of you killed Kay. And honestly, I didn't at first. But when the evidence—you know what? I don't have to justify my actions. They were reasonable conclusions about people I'd just met. Nevertheless, I do feel terrible.

"You two were nothing but kind and took in a stranger." Her eyes dropped to the bottom of her empty cup. "I just want you to know, I'm looking for my own place. Once I get my first wages from the diner, I'll move out. I was even thinking about Kay's studio, but... it feels weird." She pressed her lips together, realizing she'd been rambling.

Rose exchanged a look with her husband then reached across the table. Her eyes scrunched with a smile behind her cat-eye glasses. "Ella, it's okay. We forgive you. No hard feelings."

"Really," Jimmy said. He rested the paper on the table. "I probably would've done the same thing."

"And if you want to move out," Rose said, "that's up to you. But I'd like to see you stay. It's been nice having another guest here, even if she was the reason I was in jail." She laughed. "I'm just playing. But really, please stay."

Ella looked back and forth between them. They had truly forgiven her.

"Thank you."

She searched for more words to express the depths of gratitude she felt, but nothing was adequate. She couldn't believe there were really people in the world who were so quick to forgive.

Unwittingly, she'd stumbled into a town full of loving, caring residents, even if some of them were nuttier than a bag of trail mix.

After pouring another cup of coffee, Ella said, "So, can I ask a serious question?"

Rose's mouth turned down, and she glanced sideways at Jimmy. "Of course."

"Are all those pancakes for you?"

Rose cracked a smile and forked over three fluffy pancakes which Ella promptly doused in syrup. She pointed a drenched fork at the paper in Jimmy's hands. "I heard there are some salacious details about the mayor in there."

"My heavens, yes. I read it earlier." Rose leaned in. "Did you know he was on the lam?"

"I did hear that. What was he running from?"

It was Jimmy's turn to answer. "Apparently, he knocked his wife around one too many times, and it left her brain dead—"

Ella swore then slapped her hand over her mouth, apologizing.

"When the police came to investigate," Jimmy continued, "he ran, taking Kayline with him. Keystone turned out to be the perfect getaway."

Ella lapsed into silence. The taste of the pancakes dulled as she thought about Kay's life. That poor young woman had had such a rough start and was searching for a break from her prison, fleeing the shadow that was her father.

But the darkness had caught her and swallowed her

whole. At least in death, she was finally free.

Out over the lake, mist floated in from the rainforest, settling over the dark water like a fog. It gave the illusion of a crisp fall morning, except she knew better.

"Got any big plans today?" Rose asked.

Ella shook away the melancholy. "Actually, I convinced Will to go on a run with me."

Jimmy looked up from the paper. "William Whitehall said he'd go on a run with you?"

"Yep. I'm thinking of making sweatbands out of some rags and convincing him that that's what we wear in the future, make up something about the aerodynamics of it."

"Well, I'll be. What's this town coming to?"

Fluffy curled around Jimmy's leg, startling the innkeeper. He bent to pet him, but the feline hissed and batted his hand away.

"Glad to see some things never change," he muttered.

Out in the park, a speck of bright neon pink that could only be Wink was attempting to climb a tree. Even though she couldn't see him, Ella knew the reason was Chester related.

She smiled. For the unforeseeable future, this village was now her home. This was her new family.

Maybe she struggled to open up, struggled to trust people, but it was something she could work on. She could change because that's what Keystone Village was: new beginnings.

Hello, friends!

Thank you for reading my book! It would help me greatly if you left a review on Amazon and Goodreads. I truly appreciate each one, and it helps my series gain visibility.

Want to keep informed of the going-ons in the town between books? Subscribe to *Keystone Corner*! You'll get the latest gossip, along with other fun tidbits, such as: deleted scenes, recipes, and information about upcoming releases.

www.subscribepage.com/amidiane.

You can also follow me on BookBub or Facebook (search for @AmiDianeAuthor). Stop by and say hello. We can chat about cats, food, and coffee. I'm on Facebook all the time. I mean a lot. Too much, if I'm being honest.

Happy reading!

Ami Diane

TRAVELING TOWN MYSTERIES

#1 Pancakes and Poison

#2 The Body in the Boat

#3 Christmas Corpse

#4 Phantoms and Phonographs

#5 Perils and Plunder

#6 Ghastly Glitch

#7 Campfire Catastrophe

PET POTIONS MYSTERIES

#1 Potent Potions

#2 Ghostly Garlic

#3 Brutal Brew